Scand...

"A touching love story.

"Romance with the spa[...] lar debut from a major n[...] —Anna Campbell

"A charming romance brimming with emotion and humor. The sensual intimacy between Sebastian and Gemma mellows like a fine wine within the friendship forged long before their first kiss. Christine Wells makes the Regency as fresh and real as her characters, and I expect it won't be long before she's a favorite on every romance reader's bookshelf." —Kathryn Smith

"Witty, emotionally intense, and romantic—Ms. Wells beguiles us in this stellar debut. Put this writer's name on your list of authors to watch." —Sophia Nash

"A brilliantly seductive love story that belongs on every keeper shelf . . . sizzling with sensuality." —Kathryn Caskie

"A lovely story of best friends discovering there could be more, *Scandal's Daughter* charms and delights with humour, wit, and intelligence. An enchanting debut [that] engages all the senses and leaves a smile on your face and warmth in your heart." —*The (Brisbane) Courier-Mail*

"A wonderful debut. With both humor and heat, Christine Wells has crafted a compelling story of two wounded people—a sensitive rake and an independent miss—struggling to find love and meaning in their lives." —Sally MacKenzie, *USA Today* bestselling author

PRAISE FOR

Scoundrel's Daughter

"..." —Mary Balogh

"...sparkle of vintage champagne. A stel-... new talent." —Anne Campbell

Scandal's Daughter

CHRISTINE WELLS

BERKLEY SENSATION, NEW YORK

THE BERKLEY PUBLISHING GROUP
Published by the Penguin Group
Penguin Group (USA) Inc.
375 Hudson Street, New York, New York 10014, USA
Penguin Group (Canada), 90 Eglinton Avenue East, Suite 700, Toronto, Ontario M4P 2Y3, Canada
(a division of Pearson Penguin Canada Inc.)
Penguin Books Ltd., 80 Strand, London WC2R 0RL, England
Penguin Group Ireland, 25 St. Stephen's Green, Dublin 2, Ireland (a division of Penguin Books Ltd.)
Penguin Group (Australia), 250 Camberwell Road, Camberwell, Victoria 3124, Australia
(a division of Pearson Australia Group Pty. Ltd.)
Penguin Books India Pvt. Ltd., 11 Community Centre, Panchsheel Park, New Delhi—110 017, India
Penguin Group (NZ), 67 Apollo Drive, Rosedale, North Shore 0745, Auckland, New Zealand
(a division of Pearson New Zealand Ltd.)
Penguin Books (South Africa) (Pty.) Ltd., 24 Sturdee Avenue, Rosebank, Johannesburg 2196,
South Africa

Penguin Books Ltd., Registered Offices: 80 Strand, London WC2R 0RL, England

This is a work of fiction. Names, characters, places, and incidents either are the product of the author's imagination or are used fictitiously, and any resemblance to actual persons, living or dead, business establishments, events, or locales is entirely coincidental. The publisher does not have any control over and does not assume any responsibility for author or third-party websites or their content.

SCANDAL'S DAUGHTER

A Berkley Sensation Book / published by arrangement with the author

PRINTING HISTORY
Berkley Sensation mass-market edition / September 2007

Copyright © 2007 by Christine Diehm.
Interior text design by Kristin del Rosario.

All rights reserved.
No part of this book may be reproduced, scanned, or distributed in any printed or electronic form without permission. Please do not participate in or encourage piracy of copyrighted materials in violation of the author's rights. Purchase only authorized editions.
For information, address: The Berkley Publishing Group,
a division of Penguin Group (USA) Inc.,
375 Hudson Street, New York, New York 10014.

ISBN: 978-0-425-21832-7

BERKLEY® SENSATION
Berkley Sensation Books are published by The Berkley Publishing Group,
a division of Penguin Group (USA) Inc.,
375 Hudson Street, New York, New York 10014.
BERKLEY SENSATION is a trademark of Penguin Group (USA) Inc.
The "B" design is a trademark belonging to Penguin Group (USA) Inc.

PRINTED IN THE UNITED STATES OF AMERICA

10 9 8 7 6 5 4 3 2 1

If you purchased this book without a cover, you should be aware that this book is stolen property. It was reported as "unsold and destroyed" to the publisher, and neither the author nor the publisher has received any payment for this "stripped book."

For Jamie,
who never doubted this day would come

Many thanks to my agent, Jessica Faust, my editor, Leis Pederson, and everyone at Berkley Publishing who helped this book reach the shelves; to my parents, Cheryl and Ian, for their incomparable support; and to my writer friends for their advice and encouragement: Denise Rossetti, Anna Campbell, Anne Gracie, and all at the Historical Fiction Critique Group.

One

SEBASTIAN Laidley, sixth Earl of Carleton, paused on his drawing room threshold and surveyed the aftermath of last night's orgy. Whoever revived the fashion for these vulgar affairs should be shot.

Half-clad bodies sprawled over Chippendale chairs and gilt satin sofas. More bodies littered the floor. Wine from overturned bottles bled into the Aubusson carpet among mashed clumps of birthday cake and glittering shards of crystal. His prized bronze Venus sported a curly brimmed beaver hat, tilted at a jaunty angle, and a corset dangled by its strings from the chandelier.

Someone groaned. High-pitched giggles and rustling skirts sounded from behind a Chinese screen.

A naked nymph lay curled on the pianoforte, blinking like a newborn kitten at the late-morning sunlight. When she saw him, her eyes widened. She sat up and thrust out her breasts with a crooked, come-hither smile.

Sebastian ignored her. His gaze lifted to the frescoed ceiling, a celestial expanse filled with stormy-faced angels scowling at the debauched tableau below. He imagined his dead father's spirit floating with the seraphim, smiting these sinners with the force of his icy glare.

The image did not amuse him as it should.

He took a deep breath and almost reeled from the smell: a musky, pungent stench overlaid with sweat and red wine, like a low-class brothel. Unable to contain a fastidious shudder, Sebastian turned on his heel and strode along the corridor in search of Romney. He was the only one of Sebastian's house guests who had declined to attend the previous evening's revelry, and thus, the only one likely to be awake at this hour.

Sebastian found his friend with Mortimer in the breakfast room, wolfing down a sirloin with obvious relish. Romney preferred staying with Sebastian when he was in town rather than staying in a hotel, or worse, rattling around in that tomb of a place in Brooke Street his father had bequeathed to him.

"The trouble with orgies," Mortimer was saying, "is that one always wants what the next fellow has."

"The trouble with orgies is they're so deuced uncomfortable." Sebastian nodded a greeting to his friends and crossed to the sideboard.

Romney snorted. "Lord, yes! I've seen less complicated contortions by the India Rubber Man at the Bartholomew Fair." He squinted into the depths of his empty tankard and reached for the ale jar. "But all that's behind me, now I'm to be a married man."

"I'm overjoyed to hear it, since you're wedding my sister." Sebastian checked under the domed cover of a silver chafing dish and wondered if his uneasy innards might tolerate devilled kidneys. "I'd hate to be obliged to grind that pretty face of yours beneath the heel of my boot. You are a guest in my house, after all."

Deciding against the kidneys in favour of York ham and fried mushrooms, he joined his friends at the table.

Romney shook his shaggy auburn head. "I'm not afraid of anything you can do, Carleton. It's that sister of yours who terrifies the living daylights out of me."

"Under the cat's paw already, Romney?" Mortimer chortled and slapped the table with a plump hand as if he'd made a witty joke. "Where were you last night?"

Romney grunted. "In bed."

"Bed, eh? Curled up with a tasty bit of muslin?" Mortimer winked at Sebastian.

Shooting Mortimer a scathing look, Romney said, "Not at all. I was reading, if you must know."

"Oh?" Sebastian's lips quivered. *"Reading?"* The vision of his rakehell friend sitting primly in bed with his nose in a book while an orgy raged below struck his mind's eye.

Mortimer burst into a rich guffaw.

Ignoring him, Romney turned to Sebastian. "Did you enjoy your birthday, old man? Sorry I couldn't attend last night but I have morals, now, d'ye see."

Mortimer, who had masterminded the evening's celebrations, looked up from his plate, his pale eyes alight with hope. Like a puppy who had dropped a bone on the hearth rug, unsure if he'd won his master's approval.

Sebastian hesitated. If the truth be known, the affair had turned his stomach. He'd no taste for public fornication, but his friends had surprised him with a troupe of Madame du Pont's finest whores and a frosted pink birthday cake in the shape of naked breasts. How could he refuse? He'd always been partial to breasts.

But he hadn't stayed. He'd drunk a lot and kissed a willing wench or two for form's sake, then slipped away once everyone was too intoxicated or otherwise occupied to notice. At least, he hoped no one noticed. His reputation as London's wildest young rake was becoming difficult to maintain.

He sipped his coffee. "The evening was . . . memorable."

That seemed to satisfy Mortimer. Romney, on the other hand, regarded him shrewdly. He waved his beef-laden fork in Sebastian's direction. "If you wish to know what I think—"

"I don't give a toss what you think."

"—it's that you should get married, too. Do you the world of good."

Why did the newly converted always turn around and preach? With a sigh of infinite patience, Sebastian ticked off points on his fingers. "I have wealth, I have position, I have an heir dangling somewhere on the family tree. I have a beautiful mistress I'm not obliged to live with, who does not enact a Cheltenham tragedy if I neglect her for a week or a month. As long as I hand over an expensive bauble now and then and pay her gaming debts and dressmaker's bills, she couldn't give a tinker's damn if I hold an orgy in my house every night." He selected a roll from the basket in front of him and broke it apart. "What could I possibly want with a wife?"

Romney grinned. "Oh, nothing, old fellow. You have it all."

That smug smile gave Sebastian the sudden urge to stab his future brother-in-law with the butter knife, but Yelland came in, bearing a silver salver.

"My lord, a letter for you arrived by messenger from Ware."

"Ware?" Sebastian straightened, snatched the letter, and ripped open the seal with hands that were not quite steady. Urgency always meant bad news, and his godfather was no longer at the peak of health.

The looping script confirmed his fears. A leaden weight settled in his gut. He blinked, tossing the letter onto the table.

"Tell the messenger I'll be there as soon as I can."

"Something wrong?" Romney half rose as Sebastian pushed away from his place.

"It's Sir Hugo, my godfather. He's ill. Dying." The last word stuck in his throat. He couldn't believe it. Not Hugo. "I must go."

He stood and turned to his butler. "Have the chaise brought around immediately. Tell my man to pack enough clothes for an extended stay."

"Very good, my lord. And the, er, persons in the drawing room?"

Sebastian indicated Mortimer with a jerk of his head. "Mr. Mortimer will get rid of them after breakfast."

"And what message shall I give your steward, my lord? He arrived last night with some pressing matters to discuss about the estate. He says his business cannot wait."

Scowling, Sebastian strode to the door. "Tell him to go to the devil."

SUMMER sunlight flooded the library, illuminating swirling dust motes and flashing off gilt letters on tooled leather books. But despite the bright warmth of the day, the long windows remained obstinately closed against the slightest draft and a fire crackled in the grate.

For an instant, Sebastian wondered if the stifling heat had made him delirious.

"I beg your pardon?"

"You heard," grunted his godfather. "I said I want you to marry Gemma."

Sir Hugo Mainwaring cradled an illicit glass of burgundy in his gnarled, arthritic fingers and hitched the rug on his knees higher. "Damned leech says I'm like to cock up my toes any minute. Well, I won't, mind you, I've got a few months in me yet, but I want that granddaughter of mine settled before I die. And I want you to marry her."

The old gentleman took a long draft of wine, contemplated his glass for a moment, then drained it and thrust it out for a refill.

Sebastian took the glass and crossed to the drinks tray. Tilting the decanter, he watched the ruby liquid tumble and cursed under his breath.

Caught in parson's mousetrap at last.

If the old gentleman were not dying before his eyes, he could have laughed. Eight years eluding the snares set by determined matchmaking mamas and their equally tenacious daughters; eight years styling himself as the kind of man no virtuous lady dared be seen alone with, lest his wicked reputation taint her purity; eight years of hedonistic, reckless, extravagant living, only to be caught by this wizened, dying old gentleman commanding him to marry . . .

Gemma.

Sebastian nearly snorted out loud. She'd be mad as fire if she found out. It was almost worth agreeing, if only to see the look on her face.

But no, he couldn't do it. Not even for that satisfaction; not even to grant an old man's dying wish.

"I doubt I am husband material, sir." He handed Hugo the glass and sat down. "And even if I were, Gemma and I have not set eyes on each other for years. What makes you think she would have me?"

Hugo gave a grim smile. "She'd have you. I'd see to that. And as for not being husband material, that's bilgewater. Have to get married some time, don't you? Why not now?"

Because I would rather be staked out naked in the woods, covered in honey, waiting for the ants to nibble at my nether regions, thought Sebastian.

He settled for a more diplomatic response. "You are forgetting I have three male cousins, sir. I need not marry for the sake of an heir."

"Poppycock," growled Hugo. "Your father would have committed bloody murder before he let one of those whey-faced poltroons inherit. Your trouble is you are still thinking like a younger son. No sense of what is due to your position and your name."

Sebastian stretched his legs out before him and contemplated the golden tassels on his black Hessian boots. An all-too-keen sense of his responsibilities had caused him to flee them so expeditiously, but he kept that reflection to himself.

"Hugo, I regret to disoblige you after all you have done for me over the years—"

"Aye!" The old man's frail hand slapped his knee. "Sponsored you at White's, didn't I? Took you sparring with Jackson. Damme, took you to your first whorehouse, so I did! And this is the thanks I get."

Sebastian grimaced. He'd been thinking, rather, of his godfather providing a welcome second home for him on school holidays, but the old gentleman was correct on those worldlier counts as well.

Hugo's hand balled into a fist, as if to haul tight on the reins of his temper. His breath came in gasps. "I'm offering you a sound bargain, Sebastian. Gemma's a good girl. Substantial heiress, impeccable bloodlines. Do your father proud."

Sebastian bared his teeth in a smile. "Ah, but you see, it is a rule of mine never to do anything that would have made my father proud."

Catching Hugo's startled glance, he shook off the threatening darkness. "You don't know what you're asking. Were it anything else, I should be yours to command, but marriage? Sir, I could not do it."

The old gentleman raised his glass to quivering, corrugated lips and sipped. Half-curtained by drooping folds of skin, his eyes glittered as he set down the glass with a snap. "I seem to recall a time when you were not so averse to the prospect of marriage. I seem to recall a certain yallerhaired doxy in the village . . ."

Heat stole along Sebastian's cheekbones. This time, it had nothing to do with the fire. Was he actually blushing? What was it about Hugo, about this place, that always reduced him to schoolboy status? "I was a stripling at the time, young and foolish. And lamentably lacking in discrimination."

"Luscious little thing," said Hugo. "You always did have a good eye for a woman, I'll say that for you, but she scarcely would have done for your countess." The wicked dark eyes snapped at him over steepled fingers. "Proposed marriage, didn't you?"

"I believe I did."

Hugo nodded. "And before the old earl could get wind of the whole sorry business, fly into one of his rages and cut you off without a penny, I bought the little harpy off." He frowned, picking up his glass. "What was her name again?"

"Caroline." After all these years, the name still tasted bitter on his tongue. "As to that, sir, I am in your debt—"

"Then you can repay me by doing as I ask!" roared Hugo, erupting into fits of painful coughing.

Burgundy slopped and splashed over his trembling white hand and dripped to the Turkey carpet. Sebastian leaned forward to remove the wineglass, poured a tumbler of water, and guided it to the old gentleman's lips. Hugo gulped and spluttered and turned purple.

He did not look well. Sebastian sent the bell pealing for a servant, called for Hugo's valet to be fetched at once, and did his best to make the old gentleman comfortable in the meantime.

While Hugo clenched his jaw and suffered his valet's attentions, Sebastian stood by the window and stared out at the undulating country of the Downs.

If what Hugo said was true, Gemma would be quite alone in the world when the old gentleman went to his dubious reward. Of course, there was the girl's mother, but one could not set any store by that woman. Gemma would have to marry someone, and soon.

But that someone would not be him.

The devil of it was, he recognised the justice of Hugo's claim on him only too well. From the time he was six until Andy's needless travesty of a death made him heir to their father's title and estate, Sebastian had not been invited home more than seven times, often not even for Christmas. He'd spent most of his school holidays at Ware, and Hugo and Gemma had been the closest thing to real family he'd ever known.

But marriage? He'd be damned before he'd bow to his father's wishes. The old earl had made plans for him to step into his brother's shoes before poor Andy was even cold in his grave. Chief among those plans was Sebastian's immediate marriage, closely followed by the begetting of an heir to ensure the title never deviated from the old earl's line.

The revulsion and hatred Sebastian had felt then for his father, for such ruthless, cold ambition, returned now in a sickening wave. A thick band of desperation tightened around his chest. His mind raced, trying to think of some way out.

Suddenly, an idea struck him; a form of compromise that, in effect, would leave him free.

He waited until Hugo's temper had been stretched to snapping point by the little valet's fussing. Quietly he intervened to dismiss the man.

As soon as the door closed behind the valet, Hugo ground out an oath and fell back in his chair, gasping.

Sebastian gave him a few moments to recover. He watched his godfather fight for breath, driving to its outer limits a constitution ravaged by fast-and-furious living, and thought, *One of these days, that could be me.*

A log in the fireplace cracked and fell, showering sparks over the hearth rug. He moved to the hearth and rolled the firewood back into place with the toe of his boot. Finally, he sat opposite Hugo in a wingback chair and flicked open the lid of his snuffbox.

"If I agree to this scheme of yours—" Sebastian took a delicate pinch, ignoring the old gentleman's sudden alertness "—there must be conditions attached."

He paused, wondering how best to phrase them.

"Well, go on. I'm listening."

Sebastian tapped the snuffbox shut with his thumbnail. "First, you must let me take Gemma to my mother to do the Season. Second, I will offer for her only if she is not betrothed to some other gentleman before the Season's close. And third, this arrangement is between you and me. Gemma does not hear of it."

"Season's months away. I can't wait that long, I tell you! I must see her settled before I go."

Sebastian sucked a breath through his teeth with a hiss. Did Hugo mistrust his word? Were it any other man, he would call him to account for that. He was tempted to reject the whole business, but the pain and fatigue that shadowed the old man's face made him pause, and the weight of Hugo's past kindnesses and present frailty pressed upon him. He must find a solution to his godfather's dilemma. He owed him that much.

He fingered his lip and stared into the flames. Perhaps there was another way. His mother would scarcely thank him for it, but . . .

"My sister, Fanny, is to be married in a month or two. I might contrive a series of festivities leading to the event. If I can persuade Gemma to stay at Laidley for the duration, I have no doubt she will attach some poor—ahem—I mean, some fortunate fellow before long. If she is not betrothed by the end of, let us say, three months, then I will pay my addresses."

Satisfaction gleamed in Hugo's black eyes, even as he winced at some inner pain. "Done!"

A papery-skinned hand mottled with liver spots sought Sebastian's. He returned its weak clasp, his smile affectionate and a touch rueful. "I'd make the devil of a husband, sir. I wish I knew what game you think you are playing."

This surprised a snort out of the old gentleman, but he did not answer. Hugo gazed at some fixed point before him, the muscles of his jaw twitching, the hands that had once punished a younger Sebastian in the boxing ring now skeletal and curled rigid, like the talons of a hawk.

Abruptly, he said, "I'll thank you not to say a word to Gemma about the state of my health. She thinks it's the gout, no worse than usual, and I'll have no one tell her different. She'd not consent to leave me if she knew I was about to fall off the twig."

Hugo sank back into his chair, as if striking this bargain had taxed his strength. Closing his eyes, he murmured, "You'd best go and find the chit and tell her she's for Laidley. I'll wager she'll be glad to hear it."

Sebastian gave a crack of laughter. "She'll be in transports, no doubt."

❧

A T the top of a rise, Gemma Maitland reined in and gazed down on Mainwaring Hall. She breathed in the sweet scent of hay and harvest and felt the familiar, fierce surge of love and pride rush through her veins.

Nestled in a shallow hollow like a nugget of gold in a cupped hand, it was a noble house for a country squire, built of honey-coloured Ham Hill stone. Gemma shaded her eyes against the lowering sun that gilded the landscape, glanced off mullioned windows, and shimmered on the lake with fire.

The fire entered her blood, tempering her resolve to fight, to regain control over this land that was like her own flesh and bone. Ware did not need a land agent with fancy, modern ideas who knew nothing of the estate's heart or its people. No one could care for Ware as she did. She would show her grandfather that truth, or kill herself trying.

"Gemma? Did you hear what I said?"

She glanced over and saw her companion's mouth turned down at the corners. Though strapping and solid astride his chestnut gelding, John Talbot reminded her of a sulky child denied a parent's attention.

She bit back a smile. "Oh, John, I do beg your pardon, I was daydreaming. Whenever I come up here, I cannot help feeling very grand and lord-of-the-manor-ish. Ridiculous, is it not? How frightfully rude of me. What were you saying?"

John squared his big shoulders and settled his fidgeting horse. "I wondered whether you might journey to London when the harvest is over. I must visit town on some business and had thought to look in at a few entertainments there."

Gemma shook her head, urging Tealeaf to a brisk trot. "No, I never go to London. There is too much to do here."

That was perfectly true, but it was not the real reason she had never made her come-out. The real reason, however, was none of John Talbot's affair.

John glanced at her. "Cannot Mr. Porter attend to estate matters while you are away? That is why your grandfather employed him, isn't it?"

They approached a steep descent, and Gemma used the excuse of negotiating the difficult terrain to avoid answering him. She slowed Tealeaf to a walk, and preceded John's gelding down the narrow path.

But when the track flattened and widened again, allowing them to ride abreast, he persisted. "I thought it was every young girl's dream to attend town balls and parties."

"Yes, I believe it is, but I am two-and-twenty, almost at my last prayers, you know. I can scarcely be termed a young girl any longer." She threw him a sidelong grin. "And besides, I look a positive fright in white."

John protested at tedious length. Gemma tilted her head to study this prime specimen of ardent male with a kind of detached interest. John excelled at flattery, making up in eloquence what he lacked in originality. But the point was moot. She would not enter Society for all the tea in China.

Gemma waited until he had exhausted his current store of compliments, and smiled. "It grows late. Shall we go?"

With a look of chagrin, he agreed. They wheeled their mounts and set off in silence.

Gemma seldom dwelled upon how different her life might have been had she made her début at seventeen, rather than assuming responsibility for Ware. Burying herself in the country, her mother had scoffed, and in a manner of speaking, she was right. Just like Mama to be so perceptive, while remaining supremely oblivious to the fact that her own scandalous conduct had forced her daughter into rural seclusion in the first place.

Now, Gemma relished her isolation. Far better to be the honorary Squire of Ware than a bored Society matron, or confined to wifely duties at some country estate, the lot of most young ladies of her station.

Of course, most young ladies of her station were not obliged to live with the stigma of being Sybil Maitland's daughter. She wondered where her mother was now. Drawing kohl around her eyes and living with Bedouins like Lady Hester Stanhope, no doubt.

Suddenly, a smudge in the distance resolved into a tall, broad-shouldered gentleman with dark, windswept curls and an air of graceful boredom. She squinted at the figure as it sauntered towards them, then her breath caught.

"Scovy?" She spurred Tealeaf to a canter. Soon, they were flying down the hill.

Pulling up short with a spray of turf, Gemma slipped from the saddle and dropped the mare's reins. She strode towards Sebastian, who continued down the south lawn to meet her.

"Scovy!" She held out her hands. "To what do we owe this pleasure? No, do not tell me. You have dropped ten thousand at Hazard and the bailiffs are hot on your trail."

Sebastian's teeth gleamed as he took her hands in his. "Minx! But I am wounded you do not notice my new consequence. I have come up in the world since I saw you last."

She inspected his expensive dark elegance and chuckled. "Yes, you are fine as fivepence. Indeed, Scovy, I wonder now that I recognized you at all."

There's that damned nickname again, thought Sebastian. How he had hated it when she first bestowed it upon him, her eyes alight with unholy glee. But he did not immediately reply to her teasing, struck by the changes time had wrought in his old playmate.

Gemma wore a drab, ill-fitting, outmoded riding habit and a god-awful nest of braids bunched under her battered hat, an ensemble that would see her maid hung, drawn and quartered, in fashionable circles. But no amount of torture with a hairbrush could dim the darts of flame that sparked in those golden tresses. Swathes of charcoal broadcloth might blur her feminine curves, but they failed to dull the subtle fire in her dusk-blue eyes. Even her creamy skin seemed to bloom and glow with delight. As he looked down at Gemma's upturned face, beaming with pleasure at his arrival, desire stabbed his belly like a thief in the night, stole his breath away.

Take a damper, old boy, he thought, alarmed and a trifle disgusted with himself. There had never been anything like that between them. Clearly, that was how she regarded their friendship, too, or she would not have been so unguarded in her welcome.

The thought gave him pause. He was not certain he liked the notion that the frisson of attraction he had felt for Gemma was one-sided. He was used to making easy conquests of women. He certainly did not wish to add Gemma to the list, but still . . .

Someone cleared his throat and Sebastian realized he had been staring down at Gemma in silence. His gaze flicked past her, and he saw that her companion had dismounted and caught the reins of her mare. The man fairly bristled with pompous indignation. What the devil was wrong with the fellow?

Then Sebastian realised he still held Gemma's hands. This bag-pudding must think he had designs on her.

The devil of mischief roused within.

As Sebastian returned his gaze to Gemma's trusting face, the devil took hold. Before she could guess what he was about, he tightened his grip on her hands and ducked his head to kiss her softly on the lips.

He did not receive the slap he half expected.

Gemma remained very still in the instant his lips clung to hers, and as he lifted his head, he detected a shadow of doubt in her eyes.

Good.

Looking past her shoulder, he saw her companion open-mouthed with outrage.

Ah. Even better.

Recovering with a tiny shake of the head, she tugged her hands from his grasp and said lightly, "Sebastian, I do not believe you know John Talbot. Mr. Talbot bought the property that borders our land to the southeast, and has been kind enough to accompany me on my afternoon rides. John, may I present the Earl of Carleton, an old friend of mine. We used to catch tadpoles together."

Sebastian understood at once. After that kiss, Gemma attempted to colour their connection with the innocence of childhood.

Which was an accurate portrait, but for some reason, he did not wish this Talbot fellow to place any faith in it. Throwing Gemma a quizzical glance, Sebastian moved forward to shake hands.

Talbot's grip was firm. His form was solid, above average

height. His build indicated he would strip to advantage in the boxing ring, and Sebastian wondered idly if it were worth goading the man further. He had not indulged in a decent sparring match for weeks.

Before Sebastian finished his survey, Talbot took the initiative. "I am surprised to hear Lord Carleton is a particular friend of yours, Gemma. I have not heard you speak of him before now."

"Is that so?" returned Sebastian, amused. "Well, perhaps *Miss Maitland*—" he placed a faint, deliberate emphasis on her name "—wished me to remain her guilty secret."

Ignoring Gemma's indignant little choke, he flashed a smile at Talbot and nodded towards the horses, whose reins the gentleman still held. "Take them round to the stables, will you, Turbot? There's a good fellow. Miss Maitland is wanted in the house."

Talbot's pink-and-white complexion did nothing to conceal his emotions. At the calculated snub, his neck and face flushed crimson and he spluttered a wordless protest.

Sebastian raised his brows.

"Nonsense!" Gemma smiled at Talbot with particular radiance. "We shall all go to the stables and then up to the house to dine. You will come, won't you, John?"

Unconsciously, she placed her hand on Sebastian's proffered arm as she spoke. He pressed home his advantage, closing his hand over hers in a clear act of possession.

Which, of course, made Talbot bridle like a matron refused vouchers for Almack's. "No, really, Miss Mait—I mean, really, *Gemma*, I must take my leave."

"Very well," she answered cheerfully, grasping her mare's bridle. "I shall see you tomorrow, sir."

As soon as Talbot rode out of earshot, Gemma rounded on Sebastian. "And you need not look so pleased with yourself! I never heard such insolence."

"Well, I had to get rid of him, because I need to talk to you." He reached for the mare's bridle. "Here. Give me that."

She surrendered the bridle without comment. They walked on, and after a few moments' silence, Sebastian said, "Rather familiar with you after such a short acquaintance, isn't he? Could it be that I hear wedding bells?"

He watched her closely. It would be the answer to his prayers, yet the idea did not sit well with him at all.

"Good God, no!" said Gemma. He grinned at her vehemence, and she primmed her pretty lips. "That is to say, Mr. Talbot is a very amiable man, but we should not suit."

He cocked an eyebrow. "Where did you learn to spout that fustian? Not from Hugo, I'll wager." Horror dawned. "Don't say you have Old Mouldy living with you now."

"If you refer to Great-aunt Matilda, Scovy, then—"

"You know very well whom I mean. In fact, Miss Prunes and Prisms, you gave her that nickname, as I recall."

The corners of Gemma's mouth quivered, but she did not rise to the bait. "Aunt Matilda has made her home with us these four years past."

"Really? As bad as that? No wonder I haven't been near this place for at least that long. I have something of a sixth sense that preserves me from females of her ilk."

"Well, your sixth sense won't do you any good this evening," said Gemma with relish. "You will be obliged to take her in to dinner, you know. No doubt she will read you a lecture on your wicked ways."

"Hmm, you terrify me." He slid Gemma a glance, wondering if she knew how wicked his ways really were.

"She would certainly fall into strong hysterics if she knew you had kissed me like that," she added. "Right in front of John, too! I should think a man of your experience would know better."

Startled, Sebastian halted in his tracks. "Am I to infer you are accustomed to being kissed, Miss Maitland?"

Gemma stopped and stroked the nose of her mare. "I would not say *accustomed*, precisely, but it has been known to happen. Some of them have been . . ."

She trailed off dreamily, then smiled and patted Sebastian on the cheek. "But yours was very nice as well."

Two

⁂

As they reached the stable yard, boots and hooves clicking over the cobbles, Gemma bit her lip to repress a smile.

Oh, she felt so much better now! Even before that warm, light touch of Sebastian's lips to hers, she'd been struggling to regain her footing. When she first saw him— all broad shoulders and masculine energy and vivid dark features—the air around her thinned, leaving her breathless, and something danced a wild beat low in her stomach.

Such a stupid reaction when she had known him all her life, but there it was.

And then that kiss! She clasped her fingers together to stop them stealing to her lips.

Her first real kiss.

Declining the stable hand's offer to take the mare, Sebastian led Tealeaf into her stall. Gemma followed, and watched him remove the saddle and rub the mare's dappled flank with a handful of straw.

She leaned back against the partition, admiring the hard set of his shoulders and the strong grace of his movements as he performed a task most men of his station would leave to a groom.

Gemma's lips twisted in a wry smile. She had not been perfectly honest about her experience of kisses. True, she'd suffered several furtive maulings and a number of blatant attempts at seduction over the years. As the daughter of the notorious Sybil Maitland, she'd grown accustomed to such assaults.

But none of those encounters had stirred her like that light, warm brush of Sebastian's mouth on hers. She was not certain she relished the sensation, and that's why she'd dealt him a setdown. A true lady, of course, would never have mentioned past experience, nor made that teasing comparison. A true lady would not have any experience to compare.

Recalling Sebastian's stunned expression, Gemma chuckled. She was glad she had done it. Now she had placed them on a more even footing, she could relax.

At the sound of her laughter, Sebastian looked up and flashed her a grin—a lightning-quick smile that struck her heart and fizzed right down to her toes.

Gemma swallowed. *Oh, Lord.*

"Why do you look at me like that?" He threw down his handful of straw and picked up a currycomb.

She started. "What? Like what? How do I look?"

"I'm not sure." He cocked his head. "Wary, I think. You needn't worry." He ran the comb through Tealeaf's mane. "I'm not going to kiss you again."

"Oh? Oh! I am not at all concerned on that score." She tried to make her voice sound indifferent, but she had a dreadful suspicion it squeaked. "You only did it to provoke John. I know that."

He stared at her, eyes bright. "Do you?"

"Didn't you?"

Lifting his gaze to the rough-beamed ceiling, he said, "Yes, I suppose I must have."

This was all terribly confusing. Gemma took a deep breath. "What did you wish to speak to me about?"

"What? Oh, yes." Finished with the comb, he patted the mare's flank and relinquished her to the stable hand's care. "Come. I'll tell you on the way back to the house."

⁂

LYING to Gemma proved more difficult than Sebastian had anticipated. He could not fathom why. He lied to women all the time. This lie was for Gemma's ultimate benefit, yet when she smiled at him with such affectionate delight, the words lodged in his throat and refused to be spoken.

They strolled a meandering route back to the house while Gemma chattered about improvements she'd made and plans for the future. At first, he listened with more attentiveness than he showed the steward of his own estate, but her enchanting face distracted him so much, he frequently lost the thread of the conversation. Gemma's body, the way she moved, spoke of such innate, unconscious sensuality, he soon gave up all pretence of paying attention and drank his fill of her instead.

She broke off, seeming to sense his preoccupation. As they climbed the steps to the terrace, she said, "But tell me about yourself. You live mainly in town now, don't you?"

He sighed. "Yes, but you cannot be interested in my frippery existence."

"Of course I am. I often wonder how fashionable gentlemen manage to fill their days."

The slightest quirk of her lips told him she was teasing, up to her old tricks. He gave her a glinting smile. "Our nights are more interesting, I assure you."

She was silent for a moment. "I collect you mean your ladies."

His better self told him to stop right there, but the devil in him wanted to find out how far he could push her till she blushed. "Well, I wouldn't call them *ladies*."

She made a face. "Opera dancers, then."

He spread his hands. "They're so . . . supple, you see."

She stopped and regarded him with her candid blue eyes. "If you are trying to shock me, it won't work. Remember, I've grown up in Hugo's house." She shrugged. "Anyway, I doubt I'd find those tales very entertaining."

"Oh, you might be surprised." His gaze dropped to her mouth. "What about you, Gemma? Have you never fallen in love?"

"No, never. And I fail to see what love has to do with opera dancers." She turned with a swish of skirts and stalked up the last flight of steps.

He grinned and called after her. "All right, lust, then. Have you never—"

"Now this is a glorious prospect!" Her voice was slightly breathless, though that might have been from exertion. She reached the terrace first. Placing her hands on the balustrade, she stared out over the lake.

He chuckled as he caught up with her, but let the subject drop and followed her gaze. She was right. The man-made lake, landscaped by Capability Brown, harmonised perfectly with its surroundings. Even the island with its small Grecian temple seemed to belong in this idyllic slice of Sussex.

But the truly glorious sight was a less cultivated piece of nature. She stood next to him, wearing an expression of mingled joy and pride. Her radiance made him lean closer and voice a spontaneous thought. "It is warm enough to swim in that lake. I might challenge you to a race."

Her face clouded. She stepped away from him. "How long do you stay with us? I trust Mrs. Jenkins has seen to your comfort."

Sebastian wrenched his mind from the sudden vision of Gemma clad in a clinging, wet shift, just as he had seen her years ago when they cavorted innocently together in that lake. With one significant difference, of course. She was a woman now, and if he wasn't mistaken, under that shabby old habit her body was large-breasted, long-legged, and slender—the stuff of men's dreams. Certainly, the stuff of his. And any cavorting they did this time would not be the innocent kind, not if he had anything to say about it.

Reluctantly, he accepted her tacit refusal and made himself focus on the business at hand. "Well, the length of my stay depends on you. I've come to beg a favour."

If she wondered at his gall in approaching her after such a prolonged absence, she gave no indication of it. She tilted her head. "Of course. Anything in my power. You know that, Scovy."

Sebastian grimaced. Didn't that just make it a thousand times harder? He almost told her the truth, and to hell with his bargain with Hugo. But he'd given his word, and besides, he rather thought Hugo was right. Gemma should marry, not waste all that warmth and beauty playing caretaker to an estate that would never be hers. Hugo had always been adamant about leaving Ware to a male relative.

He cleared his throat. "My sister, Fanny, is to wed in three months."

"How lovely!" She smiled and continued to look inquiring.

"I wanted to ask you . . . My mother is not well, but she insists on undertaking all the wedding preparations herself. There will be a house party and a ball to announce the engagement, and then there is the wedding and more relatives to accommodate than I care to think about." He frowned. "Fanny is . . . a trifle difficult, and not the assistance she ought to be." He rubbed his chin. "More of a hindrance, really. And the house needs . . ." *Razing to the ground.* ". . . improvement."

He glanced at Gemma and wondered if he'd convinced her. He was certainly doing a good job of convincing himself. He could almost be grateful to his godfather. He would never have thought of such a perfect solution to his problems without the promise he'd made to Hugo.

"Gemma, would you be willing to leave Ware for a couple of months, come with me to Laidley to help my mother with the preparations?"

She flinched as if he'd slapped her, and gave a quick, firm shake of her head. "No, I could not leave Ware for that long. I am sorry, Scovy, it is out of the question."

It was the answer he'd expected, but her unhesitating refusal disappointed him. "May I ask why?"

"I am needed here."

A remoteness had settled on her face that gave him no clue to her thoughts. Impatiently, he said, "Gemma, even peers of the realm leave their estates while they sit in parliament, or go into the shires to hunt, or do the Season. Hugo has employed an agent. Why can't he look after things when you're away?"

"Ha!" The heel of her hand smacked the balustrade.

Sebastian raised his brows. "You do not think him capable of running the estate in your absence? You mistrust Hugo's judgment, then?"

Her luscious mouth set in a determined line. She braced her hands shoulders'-width apart on the balustrade, scanning the terrain beyond like a general surveying a battlefield. "Hugo is remarkably one-eyed about this subject. I told him we did not need an agent, but he refused to listen." She waved a hand. "Oh, I am sure Mr. Porter has many excellent qualities, but he was not bred at Ware. If I were not here to supervise him, there's no telling what havoc he might wreak."

Sebastian frowned. "Can't Hugo supervise this Porter fellow? I would have thought the old gentleman perfectly sound in that respect."

"Yes, but he cannot be there to see for himself. He cannot ride out to the fields or pay calls in the village, inspect the cottages to make sure they are well maintained, listen to tenants' concerns. I . . ." She swallowed. "Scovy, I love Ware so much, it pains me that after all I have done, Grandpapa hired Mr. Porter behind my back."

Ah, now we are getting somewhere, thought Sebastian. "Do you know, I think you are right."

She lifted her chin and squared her shoulders, spearing him with her gaze. "Of course I am right."

He leaned against the balustrade and inspected his fingernails. "In your shoes, what I would do is leave. Only for a bit. Long enough to show Hugo how the estate will flounder without you. Why don't you do that?"

He slid her a glance. There was an arrested expression in her eye, but she shook her head. "I would never allow our people to suffer for the sake of petty revenge."

"No, no, not revenge, more like a wake-up, that's all. Just to make Hugo appreciate all you have done, all you continue to do." He took her hand and drew her around to face him. "Think what will happen if you *don't* make Hugo see your point of view. Think of the future."

He saw by her stormy eyes that she was thinking of it. The future looked bleak indeed for Gemma. He did not need to spell that out for her. She knew. The determination that drove most females of her class to the Marriage Mart each Season was the same determination that fired her need to control the estate. She was a woman who wished to take charge of her destiny.

Well, a stint at Laidley could not hurt her chances of inheriting Ware. And if a host of eligible gentlemen happened to pay court to her while she was there, she might well exchange her passion for the land for passion of a different nature. Women found it so easy to fall in love.

Looking at her, he wondered why marriage had not entered the equation before. "Tell me, Gemma. Are all the men hereabouts blind?"

She jerked out of her reverie. "I beg your pardon?"

"Or slow-tops like that Turbot fellow, perhaps? Why are you two-and-twenty and still unwed?"

She flushed and stared at her boots. "That is not a very gentlemanly question."

He ducked his head, trying to catch her eye. "This is me, remember? Old Scovy. I was never a gentleman to you."

But she did not answer. She turned and gazed out again, and as the breeze snapped her habit around her legs and the sun teased fiery highlights from her gold hair, those dusk-blue eyes contemplated her domain. Once again, he had lost her to Ware's thrall, and it galled him that she could be oblivious to him when he was so vividly aware of her. He wanted to yank her into his arms and make her forget everything about the damned place, if only for the space of a kiss.

"Will you let me think about it?" She did not look at him as she spoke. "I ought to say no, but I am quite desperate, you see. And I would like to help you if I could."

Sebastian bit back a protest. It was less than he'd hoped for, but undoubtedly more than he deserved. "Of course. I shall stay a few more days and await your answer." On impulse, he took her hand and brushed his lips across her gloved knuckles.

She did not blush or flirt with her eyes as other young ladies would have done. He was not even sure she noticed the small intimacy. Her mind was not on him.

Absently, she withdrew her hand. Then she took one last, long look at that golden panorama, turned her back on it, and led him into the house.

⊗

PINK rose petals drifted in the washbasin, colliding and whirling as Gemma trailed her fingertips through the cool, scented water. She leaned forward to splash her face, and could have sworn the water sizzled on her skin.

She must stop thinking about him.

But his kiss wrapped around her mind, smothering all other thoughts. The light sweep of his lips on her hand before they left the terrace had burned straight through her glove, though she'd tried her best not to react.

What did Sebastian want from her? Or was his purpose what it had always been—mischief, pure and simple?

The man who had kissed her with outrageous assurance that afternoon seemed very different from the youth who spent those carefree summers with her at Ware. Of course he'd changed physically; the gangly limbs had gained strength and power, bringing him admirably into proportion. While he had always carried himself well, despite his angular shape, now his grace appeared natural, less self-conscious.

But the most significant alteration lay in his manner. Once, Sebastian's enthusiasm for life shone from his eyes, from every impetuous movement. Now he seemed . . . contained. Disengaged. Cynical, even. As if life were one big game and he had no wager on the outcome.

Gemma chewed her lip. She would be lying if she did not admit this made him dangerously attractive. For a wild, uncertain moment, she'd ached to respond to his kiss, wanted it to go on and on. Her face flamed. She closed her eyes. Even now, she craved more.

Subduing the mad impulse to tip the basin over her head, she filled her cupped hands with water and held the small pool against her fevered face.

"So he's condescended to visit, has he?" The muffled comment came from the depths of the clothes press.

Gemma gasped, choked, and came up spluttering. She groped for a linen towel to wipe the water from her eyes and answered her maid in what she hoped was a level tone. "Lord Carleton has invited me to Laidley to oversee the arrangements for his sister's wedding."

Dorry drew out Gemma's favourite sapphire-colored silk evening gown and laid it on the bed. "He's got a mama, hasn't he? Why would she hand over the reins to a chit she's never even met?"

Gemma paused in the act of picking rose petals out of her hair. It had seemed reasonable when Sebastian explained it to her. "Lady Carleton insists on making the preparations herself, but her health is not equal to the task. Sebastian thinks if the scheme is presented as a *fait accompli*, she might be persuaded to accept my help." She hesitated. "It will be difficult to refuse."

Dorry shooed Gemma to sit at her dressing table and set to brushing her long, curly tresses. "The master sent for him, did you know that?"

Gemma's head whipped around, jerking taut the coil of hair Dorry held. "Ouch!" She rubbed her scalp. "That doesn't make sense."

"Hold still, Miss Gemma." The maid clicked her tongue and resumed her brushing. "All I know is, he was sent for, he came, and now you're to go back to Laidley with him. Doesn't take much to put two and two together."

Gemma raised her brows. "And make thirteen? What on earth can you be thinking of, Dorry?"

Someone scratched at the door. Gemma pressed a finger to her lips, her gaze fixing Dorry's in the looking glass.

"May I come in?" A long, pinched face with sharp cheekbones and skin like bleached linen peered into the room.

"Of course, Aunt," called Gemma. "Have you heard the news? Sebastian is here."

"Yes, I have seen him just now." Matilda hurried forward to plant a tiny kiss on Gemma's cheek. "Such a fine figure of a man. How he is changed! How truly the gentleman despite all the *dreadful* things one hears about him."

The sapphire silk laid ready on the counterpane distracted her aunt from gossip. "Oh, my dear. Is *that* what you are wearing?"

Gemma blinked. "Why, yes. Is something the matter with it?"

"No, not at all. It is merely . . ."

Avoiding Dorry's eye, Gemma prompted, "Yes?"

"You should wear something more demure for this occasion, Gemma, don't you think? It never does to give the wrong impression, you know, dearest, and after your *wretched* mama . . ." Matilda drifted to the clothes press. "Well, let us just say you must be particularly careful. What about this one?" She took out a gown and held it against herself.

The style was four years out of date, a long-sleeved white muslin gown, made up high at the throat, decorated with knots of ribbon, delicate ruffles at the wrist, and half a dozen frilly flounces. Fresh and virginal as a debutante, the dress looked almost macabre against Matilda's gaunt, withered body.

Gemma supposed it would scarcely appear less ghastly on her. Did Matilda really think a few ells of white muslin could conceal Gemma's background, convince people that her morals were not the same as her mother's? Years of modest, chaste primness, of never giving any man the slightest encouragement to glance in her direction had not achieved that. She could no more rid herself of the taint of her mother's past than she could expel Sybil's blood from her veins.

Suddenly, Gemma realised how tired she was of trying.

Before she could speak, Dorry shot her a warning glance and removed the muslin from Matilda's grasp. "Never you fret, Miss Mainwaring. I'll see to it that Miss Gemma is everything she should be."

Matilda beamed her satisfaction. "Thank you, Dorry. I may always count on you." She gave an airy little wave. "Until dinner, then, my dear."

As the door closed behind Matilda, Gemma glowered at her maid. "I don't believe it. You are in league with her against me."

Dorry shook out the muslin dress and laid it over a

chair. "You know what a ruckus there'll be if you don't. She'll start wailing as how you're a wanton hussy just like your ma, and quoting the Bible, and then the fat *will* be in the fire." She huffed a sigh. "This *coiffure* will look wrong with that gown. I'll have to start again."

Gemma murmured an apology, but in truth she was not sorry. Her maid's deft, gentle hands working in her hair always soothed her. The tension that had wound like clockwork inside her since Matilda put her head around the door slowly eased. She would be able to meet Scovy again with some semblance of calm, at least.

She smiled, remembering when she gave him that name. *Scovy.* Short for Muscovy duck.

She had caught Sebastian flirting with some of the village girls on the way home from church one Sunday. He must have been seventeen at the time, or thereabouts, very proud of his new striped waistcoat and doing his best to appear the debonair man of the world.

He succeeded well with the other girls, but he could not fool Gemma. Only she noticed the slight awkwardness of his stance as he entertained his audience with tales of Eton. He had not known what to do with his hands, and kept flicking the lid of his snuffbox with his thumbnail. The snuffbox was a ridiculous affectation for a green youth, but his admirers seemed not to remark upon it. Indeed, they hung on his every word.

Teasing Sebastian afterwards, Gemma had dubbed him "the Duck"—all cool, smooth serenity on the surface, but paddling like mad underneath. She could not quite recall where the Muscovy part came in, but he had been Scovy to her ever since.

"There." Dorry finally jabbed home the last pin. "That should hold it."

She stood back, and Gemma scrutinised her reflection.

More braids, arranged in a coronet at her crown this time. A variation on an exceedingly tired theme.

She did not let her smile falter. "Thank you, Dorry." She took a deep breath. "And now, for that dress."

⬥

W HEN Gemma paused on the drawing room threshold in a frothy cloud of white, Sebastian turned away to hide his laughter. She just looked so wrong. All that womanly warmth and sparkle smothered in the fussy trappings of a tremulous debutante. On the pretext of inspecting a Stubbs that hung in sombre splendour above the mantelpiece, he did his best to compose his features.

"Gemma, you're late," barked Hugo, struggling to rise from his chair.

Sebastian moved to place a bracing hand under the old gentleman's elbow. As he looked up, he saw Gemma cast Hugo an anxious glance, but she said nothing, leading the way to the dining room. With gentle care, Sebastian settled his godfather in his place at the head of the mahogany table.

Hugo pounded the table with his walking stick, making the cutlery jump.

"Gemma! Move that infernal lump of tin out of the road, will you? Can't see a damned thing past that monstrosity."

While Matilda mourned her brother's bad language, Gemma signalled to a footman.

"I'll do it." Sebastian reached the epergne first, and hefted it into his arms. The elaborate, silver-gilt ornament represented a jungle scene, with elephants, lions, natives, and—incongruously—the odd pineapple scattered amongst the gleaming foliage. He winced as a native's spear dug into his chest. The damned thing weighed a ton and bristled with sharp objects.

"On that table by the window, I think," said Gemma, her voice quiet, expressionless.

She preceded him to the table and shifted a bowl of blue

hydrangeas to make room. As he set down the epergne, he caught Gemma's flowery scent and his pulse leapt.

A little shocked by his reaction, he did not immediately look at her. There was nothing special about that fragrance to set his heart hammering, was there? Except that it was hers. It wafted from her skin, heated by the lush body under that farce of a gown.

Straightening, he murmured, "What happened to you? A fit of the prims?"

Gemma's lips tightened. She shook her head.

Sebastian tried to study her face but she kept it averted. He frowned. Surely she could not be distraught over that silly little kiss. Perhaps they'd been observed?

"Ah," he breathed, inspecting the epergne with his quizzing glass. "Are we in disgrace?"

"Of course not. Go and sit down."

They took their places at the table.

Matilda fluttered beside him. "Hugo tells me your sister is to be married, my lord. How thrilling!"

Sebastian nodded to a footman, who leaned between them to fill his wineglass with claret. "The arrangement is of long standing, ma'am, so I would not describe it as thrilling, precisely. The respective families are gratified, as you might expect."

Gemma spoke. "And what about Lady Fanny? Is she gratified?"

"Fanny is content with the match, or she would not have agreed to it." He met her sceptical gaze with a bland smile.

Hugo looked up from wrestling with a capon. "You'll find out for yourself how gratified she is when you see her, Gemma."

"It is by no means settled that I am going to Laidley, Grandpapa."

"Oh, yes it is, my girl! I've let you go your own road for too long." He pointed his fork at her. "This time, you'll knuckle under and do as I say." He took a sip of porter and made a wry face. "Chit's barely out of her teens and thinks she can rule the roost."

Seeing Gemma open her mouth to retort, Sebastian intervened. "Ah, these wilful females! I sympathise, Hugo, indeed I do." He shook his head. "How often you must have longed for a quiet little mouse of a granddaughter instead of this firebrand, sir. Someone who'd read you sermons and embroider you slippers when the weather grew chill."

Hugo fell back in his chair with a hearty guffaw. Gemma's eyes crinkled at the corners. She closed her mouth on her heated speech.

Matilda said, "Well, I'm sure I should be pleased to read sermons to you if you'd like it, Hugo. I am always at your disposal if you require religious instruction, you know."

Hugo muttered something that sounded like "wish I could dispose of *you*," and moodily attacked his capon.

"You are fresh from town, Sebastian, I take it?" said Matilda, selecting a portion of veal fricassee from a silver chafing dish. "Did you attend the Regent's fête and all the victory celebrations?"

"I did, yes. Dreadful crushes, all of them."

"I hear Tsar Alexander is a handsome man."

He shrugged. "I believe he is accounted so."

Gemma chuckled. "I have often observed that if you ask one gentleman whether another is well-looking he will never say yes. He might say no, the man is a toad, but he will never pronounce another man handsome. Why is that? If I see a lady who is beautiful, I do not scruple to say so."

"Then you are in the minority of your sex, Gemma," said Sebastian dryly. "I've yet to hear one woman praise another, especially in terms of beauty."

"Perhaps that says something about the company you keep, *my lord*."

Hugo grunted. "What do you know about the company he keeps, miss?"

Gemma widened her eyes. "Only what he has told me, Grandpapa."

Brimming with amusement, Sebastian regarded her steadily over the rim of his glass. He deserved that, for introducing the subject of his amours on the terrace, but he could not let her get away with it. "Gemma told me an interesting thing, today, Hugo. She said she has never been in love."

To his delight, she blushed and bit her lip. "Be quiet, you wretch."

"Love!" Hugo gave a dismissive wave of his hand. "What did love ever do for anyone but make them miserable? Just look at my girl Sybil. Gemma's mother. She fancied herself in love and where did it get her?"

Sebastian saw Gemma stiffen. Her gaze flew to her grandfather. Beside him, Matilda quivered with distress. "*Hugo!* We do not speak of that incident in this house."

"Yes, we do. I'm speaking of it now, aren't I?"

Sebastian wondered if Hugo had been dipping into the burgundy again. He seemed unusually belligerent tonight. "Well, since no one here is in love, I suppose love's dire effects don't concern us." He waggled his eyebrows at Matilda. "Unless you have a fine beau you're not telling us about, ma'am. Come, out with it! Who is the lucky fellow?"

Matilda giggled like a bashful debutante, which was unnerving to watch, but at least it dispelled the tension. He caught Gemma's eye and she mouthed a "Thank you."

He acknowledged her thanks with a quick nod, feeling oddly shaken. Watching her full, delicately curved lips form the silent words, he could not help imagining those lips performing a different function entirely.

He deserved to be flogged. This was Gemma, a gently bred lady, not some bit of muslin. Dragging his gaze away, he drained his wineglass and let the alcoholic warmth seep through his body. The heightened state of awareness that had gripped him since he first saw Gemma again was fast developing into a problem. He needed to regain control before he did something foolish. Something they would both regret.

Just get her to Laidley and get her married, he thought. *She's a beauty and an heiress. How difficult can it be?*

Three

HOT. *So hot.*

A sultry, sizzling siren. Gemma, in his bed.

Her skin scorched his fingertips as he stroked her breasts, her waist, her thigh, and explored the liquid furnace between her legs. But even through the bright, searing agony, he could not stop touching her. Her body glistened, incandescent, slippery with sweat. She breathed steamy sighs in his ear. Her nails raked fire down his back as she twisted and writhed beneath him, wrapped her legs around him, enmeshed him, tangled him in flames.

A faint unease stirred. He should not do this, he should resist. He couldn't remember why, and without a reason, he brushed off the niggling doubt, consigned it to the pyre with what was left of his mind.

He plunged into the inferno, drove himself into her, thrust straight to her molten core. His flesh, his bones, his every fibre blazed with ecstasy, a brief, wild, ultimate joy—

With a shuddering gasp, Sebastian woke, his body damp with sweat. He tried to move and couldn't, realised his limbs were tangled in blanket and sheet. Sunlight lanced through a gap in the curtains. It must be morning, and he was at Ware.

Kicking away the covers, he sat up and dragged his fingers through his damp hair. His throat was parched, his head throbbed, and his muscles protested every movement, as if he'd gone three rounds with Jackson.

What the hell had he dreamed last night?

He shook his head to clear it and shifted to ease the ache in his groin.

Dear Lord, he needed a swim.

A sliver of sunlight fell across the page. Gemma looked up from her work and glanced out the window. Beyond the home wood, the sun peered over the horizon and took its first glimpse of the day. The greater part of the lake remained dark as ink, shadowed by cedars and copper beech, but it beckoned all the same.

She ignored that beguiling invitation, as she'd ignored it every summer's morning since she turned seventeen. She planted her elbow on the desk, sank her brow into her hand, and tried, once more, to decipher Matilda's bookkeeping.

After a few minutes, she noticed that the marks on the ivory tablet she used for rough calculations formed a series of intricate patterns that had little to do with sums. Irritated, she scrubbed the tablet clean, threw down her pencil, and sat back in her chair.

Of course she could not go to Laidley. She'd been mad to consider leaving Ware. The way her mind seemed to move in reverse at the moment, untangling these household accounts would take the best part of a fortnight.

Gemma rubbed her aching temples. How could she have thought for one minute she might go?

But she knew the reason, even as the question formed in her mind.

Sebastian.

Caught up in the joy of seeing him again, she'd been only too ready to set personal inclinations and anticipated pleasure above her duty and the comfort and happiness of people who depended on her. Just like Mama.

She traced the carved scrolls on her chair arm with her fingertips and sighed. She could not go to Laidley, but part of her rebelled against losing Sebastian so soon, and not only because it would mean an end to his easy companionship. A foreign, wanton corner of her heart wished she might experience his kiss once more before he left and the loneliness of life at Ware filled his place.

Loneliness? Gemma frowned. When had she begun to think like that? She loved Ware. She loved being the honorary squire. She loved every inch of her grandfather's land, everyone who lived there. Of course she did.

Ridiculous! She snatched up her pencil and tapped it on the desk. Was she not the most fortunate of females? One whose life meant something beyond the role of daughter or wife or mother or sister? The solid ground of Ware was her reality, and this obsession with Sebastian a fleeting fancy.

And really, there was no point delaying the decision, was there? As if by waiting and dreaming she might hit on some way to get everything she wanted without pain or sacrifice. Life wasn't like that. Or at least, not for her.

Gemma took a deep breath. She would finish the accounts and lock them in her desk. Then she would rise, move one foot in front of the other until she reached the library.

And tell Grandpapa she would stay.

KICKING up hard from the lake's silt floor, Sebastian pulled and stretched through the water until his head broke the surface. He drew the cool, clean air deep into his lungs and brushed away the hair that clung to his forehead.

Turning on his back, he floated, gazed at the feathery

treetops fingering the pale, cloudless blue sky and felt the warmth of the rising sun touch his face.

He imagined for a moment that he could stay here at Ware, in this near-frigid water, for the rest of his natural life.

No responsibilities. No title or dependants. No advisers telling him he must install new drainage systems or sow this field or let that field lie fallow. No interminable speeches in the House during parliamentary sessions. No dignity or lofty position to maintain.

Just him and nature and beauty and . . .

Gemma.

Sebastian groaned. He flipped to his stomach and swam a slow breaststroke. Ploughing the water with his hands, he watched the ripples fan out from his chest, disturbing the tranquil surface.

He'd dreamed of her last night. He knew they'd been erotic dreams, for the tantalising images that flashed across his mind aroused him even now, but he could not remember anything specific, wasn't sure he wished to.

A hot wave of guilt washed over him. Gemma should be sacrosanct, not an object for lurid fantasies. And jaded, unrepentant rake that he was, even he knew better than to pursue well-born virgins. But Gemma was different from any virgin, any *woman* he'd ever known. So powerfully sensual, so provocative, even though she used no feminine wiles, no arts to attract. In his dreams, she'd been everything a woman could be to a man, and more.

A heron shot from the wood and soared low over the lake, skimming its feathered belly along the water. Sebastian rolled and swam a few lazy strokes to shore.

He hauled himself onto the grassy bank. He was a fool. If he managed to persuade Gemma to return with him to Laidley, he'd have to make damned sure he kept his hands off her long enough to find her a husband. Otherwise, he'd end up saying his vows before the summer was over.

And he could not marry Gemma—or anyone. That was certain. He had vowed at his brother's graveside he would never continue his father's line. He was not about to break his word to Andy. He would not bend to his father's will.

Sebastian rummaged through the pile of clothes he'd left under the fronds of a weeping willow. Locating his shirt, he used it to towel himself dry and began to dress.

His drawers and pantaloons clung to his damp skin, but with some contortion and a deal of swearing, he managed. As he hauled one Hessian boot over his wet stocking, he heard his name and looked up.

A footman ran out of the wood towards him. "Lord Carleton! Sir Hugo wishes to see you at once."

"Is he ill?" Sebastian yanked on his second boot, scooped up the rest of his clothes, and strode after the panting servant.

"No, my lord. Nothing of that nature. He is in a fret, but his health is good, considering."

When they reached the sunny terrace, the footman bowed. "In the library, my lord." He indicated the French doors that opened from Hugo's favourite room.

Ruefully, Sebastian glanced down at his wet, half-clad body. He shrugged and entered, pausing on the threshold.

"There you are! Took your time, didn't you?" Hugo motioned for Sebastian to sit down.

Ignoring his godfather's scowl, Sebastian grinned and leaned against the doorframe. "I'm dripping. I'll stand."

The old man squinted up at him. His expression lightened. "Been for a bathe?"

"Yes, sir. In the lake."

Hugo grunted. He gazed past Sebastian into the distance. "Gemma used to swim in that lake."

"Yes, I know."

"Doesn't do it anymore. Matilda saw to that!" Hugo hunched his thin shoulders. "She won't go to Laidley."

Sebastian raked a hand through his hair, showering cold

droplets of water down his back. "How am I to keep my side of the bargain if she won't come?"

"I won't hold you to it." Hugo fidgeted with the fob at his waist. "I sent for you because I thought you might have goaded her to refuse, but I see that isn't the case."

"Well, if I did, you may be sure it was unintentional." He hesitated. "Perhaps I might persuade her yet."

"She seemed pretty set on staying." Hugo's gnarled hands clenched and flexed spasmodically. "I'm out of all patience with the chit. The one thing I've done right in the last twenty years, and she throws it in my face."

Hugo stared out to the lake. "Gemma's unnaturally attached to Ware, you know."

"Well, I knew she was fond of the place—"

Hugo shook his head. "It's more than that. I'm no hand at explaining, but I'll say one thing. It would do her a power of good to get away from here." His jaw set. "And I shall live to see it happen."

With piercing sadness that caught him unawares, Sebastian doubted it. Pain hollowed Hugo's dark eyes, and though his manner and speech remained forceful as ever, he strained for every breath. Sebastian hated to see a man who'd counted among the great amateur sportsmen of his day so weak. Anger flashed through him. Couldn't Gemma see how Hugo suffered for her stubbornness?

And then the realisation hit him. If he could not get Gemma to Laidley, Hugo would not hold him to their bargain.

He was free.

Why, then, did he feel so unexcited by the prospect?

He sighed. Because in fact, this sudden reprieve changed nothing. Hugo was dying, without the comfort of seeing his only grandchild happy and secure before he went.

Sebastian knew he must lift this burden from the old gentleman's shoulders. How he would persuade the head-strong girl to leave Ware, he was not certain, but he must persuade her for Hugo's sake, by fair means or foul. And there wasn't much time. Though he sat ramrod straight in his wingback chair, Hugo looked desperately ill.

"Shall I ring for your valet, sir? Is there anything I can do to make you comfortable?"

Hugo shook his head. "Thank you, no. Go now."

Sebastian turned to leave. On impulse, he looked back, and saw Hugo pass a shaking hand over his eyes.

Sebastian averted his gaze to the long window. "Do you know, sir, I think I shall stay a few more days."

There was a pause. "You will, will you?"

"Yes." He fingered his chin. "I rather think I shall do a spot of fishing."

"Oho!" Hugo's voice crackled with renewed vigour. "Casting out lures, eh?"

Sebastian met the old man's eyes and smiled. "As you say, sir. As you say."

GEMMA needed to tell Sebastian her decision, but knowing the habits of fashionable, town-dwelling idlers, he would not be up for hours. Well, she could not sit around twiddling her thumbs while she waited. There were any number of tasks she could cross off her list before Sebastian's day even began.

But as she stepped onto the terrace, she saw him leaning on the balustrade, studying the formal gardens below.

His back was to her. He was shirtless, his hair wet and tousled. His wrinkled pantaloons clung damply to his thighs.

Gemma stopped short, transfixed. She should go, right now. Eyes primly averted.

But to leave, she would have to walk past him, or retreat the way she had come and leave by the front door. Which would look odd, since she was on her way to the stables. And had she not resolved to go about her regular business, untroubled by thoughts of Sebastian? Once again, he stood, literally and figuratively, in her way.

Faith, he was magnificent, though. Flouting resolutions and maidenly scruples, Gemma let her gaze roam the broad, well-defined shoulders, muscled arms, and trim torso and marvelled at the solid strength his elegant tailoring usually concealed.

On a remote, distant plane, her mind rebelled, shocked at the way his firm, compact buttocks encased in skin-tight wet pantaloons set her own body prickling with heat. He altered his stance and she caught her breath as everything shifted in a harmonious ripple of muscular contractions.

Gemma's sensible brain insisted she walk away. But her insubordinate feet refused to take a step, and in the midst of that heated debate, Sebastian straightened and turned around.

Surprise flickered over his face, but he did not seem embarrassed that she saw him in this state of undress. His sudden look of comprehension sent her heightened senses spinning, even as her mind cringed with shame.

He knew. He knew she had been staring.

He lifted an eyebrow. "Going out?"

"Yes." She cleared her throat, but her voice rasped anyway. "I have much to do this morning."

"I see." He shook out the bundle of clothes he held. He might at least have the decency to put on his shirt, but instead, he laid each garment neatly over the balustrade. "When were you going to tell me?"

For a moment, his words confused her. Then she realised he must have seen Hugo. "I am sorry, Sebastian, I truly am. But you must understand, I am needed here."

He looked up, his eyes a warm, liquid brown. "*I* need you. Very much."

She gripped her hands together in a futile effort to slow the sharp pounding of her heart. "I am sorry. I should never have let you think I might go."

"But you must," he said softly. "I have quite made up my mind about that."

The arrogance of the man! She attempted a scornful laugh. "What are you going to do, drag me off by force?"

He tilted his head, considering. "The notion is strangely appealing."

Gemma suppressed a shiver. *Indeed.*

Before she could dive into those dark eyes and drown like a fly trapped in honey, Gemma lowered her gaze, only to find herself studying the faint sprinkling of dark hair on his chest. Desperately annoyed that she could not control her blushes, she dragged in a breath and looked away.

Sebastian laughed. "Poor Gemma," he mocked, sauntering towards her until he stood uncomfortably close. "Do you want to touch? You can if you wish."

Her head snapped up. She glared at him, suddenly in command of herself. "That won't be necessary, thank you! Now, if you will excuse me—"

"Gemma!" Matilda's cry ripped the air between them. Gemma stumbled back, as guilty as if her aunt had caught her in Sebastian's embrace.

The potted violets Matilda carried crashed to the ground. She stiffened all over, then collapsed on the stone floor and erupted into violent, wracking convulsions amid the pottery shards and scattered earth.

"Good God!" Sebastian started towards her. "Quick, Gemma, send for a doctor."

But Gemma caught his arm and overtook him, hurrying to bend over her aunt. She ripped off her hat and knelt beside the writhing form, trapping one flailing hand in her own. As she chafed Matilda's wrist, she looked up at Sebastian, who hovered anxiously over them both. "There is no cause for alarm. She is not ill, merely hysterical."

Sebastian's expression turned to disgust. "The vapours? Is that all? You cannot be serious."

"You can hardly blame her," said Gemma. "Strange as it

may seem, my aunt is not accustomed to seeing gentlemen without their shirts."

Matilda thrashed and shivered and broke into short, piercing screams. Gemma lifted her aunt's head into her lap and crooned words of comfort, smoothed the iron-grey curls from her brow, tried everything she could think of to soothe her, but Matilda was already beyond reason.

Gemma looked up to see that Sebastian still stood there, naked to the waist and sardonic as a satyr. Exasperated, she raised her voice over the commotion. "Scovy, help me, you idiot! Go and find some smelling salts, or hartshorn or something."

He snorted. "What your aunt needs is a good dose of common sense. What did she think I was doing, raping you?"

"Oh, do be quiet!" Gemma glared up at him. "This would never have happened if you'd the decency to put on some clothes."

A slow smile curled his lips. "You weren't complaining five minutes ago."

Matilda moaned and muttered and twisted as though gripped by a fever.

"An admirable chaperone," remarked Sebastian. "Falls into hysterics at the mere sight of a man."

"Oh, go away if you're not going to help!"

"I could fetch some water," he offered.

Gemma nodded. "Yes, a drink might do her good."

"I wasn't intending she drink it. I was going to dash it in her face."

Ignoring this last remark, Gemma slid an arm under Matilda's shoulders and tried to raise her. "Better yet, help me get her upstairs to her bedchamber. She often takes the best part of the day to recover from one of these spells."

"Good Lord, what a pea-goose."

They tried to assist Matilda to her feet, but she was awkward and uncooperative, struggling one moment, a limp, dead weight the next.

"This is no use. I shall have to carry her." Sebastian swept the afflicted lady into his arms and strode into the house.

Quashing a spurt of envy, Gemma followed.

As they climbed the stairs, Matilda stirred to consciousness. Confronted at close quarters by the very same naked hairy chest that had flung her into hysterics, she shuddered and opened her mouth to scream.

"One more screech and I'll throw you down the stairs," snapped Sebastian.

"Scovy!"

But it had the desired effect. Matilda's eyes bulged, but she gulped and pressed her trembling lips together, and they reached the second floor without further mishap. Gemma directed Sebastian to Matilda's bedchamber and rang for her maid while he laid her gently on the bed.

He did not linger. "Send for me if you need anything. I'm going to cover my shame before the housemaids start swooning."

Gemma curled her lip and watched him go. That teasing boy had grown into the most provoking man.

In the comforting surrounds of her bedchamber, Matilda seemed less agitated, though she still moaned weakly. Gemma took a handkerchief from the bureau drawer, soaked it in lavender water, and pressed the scented linen to her aunt's sweat-dampened brow.

Try as she might, she could not sympathise with Matilda's violent reaction to that scene on the terrace. Even a minor shock seemed to have a cataclysmic effect on Matilda's delicate nerves. She wished she could show her aunt more compassion, more understanding. As a spinster totally dependent on her brother Hugo, Matilda's life could not be easy.

After a few minutes, Hoskins, Matilda's maid, bustled in. She lit a lamp and turned it low, drew the heavy damask curtains shut, and set about making her mistress more comfortable.

Gemma rose to leave, but Matilda groaned and gripped her wrist with surprising strength. Thinking longingly of the tasks she had intended to accomplish that morning, Gemma obeyed the pressure of that clawlike hand and sat down on the bed.

"Gemma."

Gemma patted Matilda's hand. "Hush, now, Aunt. Try to get some rest."

"Promise me," Matilda breathed. In the dim light, her skin appeared clammy and pale against her grizzled ringlets. "Promise me you will never do that again."

Gemma wondered what Matilda meant, what she thought she had witnessed. But she hesitated to ask. She did not wish to trigger another attack of the vapours.

"Do not distress yourself, Aunt." She kept her tone even and soothing. "There is not the least need, you know."

"There is *every* need! The scandal . . ." Matilda closed her eyes. A solitary tear squeezed between her lids.

Please, not again. Even as she thought it, Gemma felt like a traitor, but she could not bear her aunt starting down that well-travelled road.

Matilda's eyes flew open and narrowed. "You knew Sebastian as a boy, my dear, but do not be fooled. He is a man now, and he is a rake."

Gemma flinched. She had always dismissed Sebastian's reputation as a heartless seducer of women. The gossip seemed to concern someone else, not her dear old Scovy. She could never quite believe the things that were said of him.

"Do you want to touch? You can if you wish."

His soft words on the terrace curled through her mind, wicked, seductive. He had guessed what she wanted before she had known it herself. He knew her so well, she had thought.

But did he know her—Gemma Maitland—or was he really a man who knew women as a merchant knows his stock-in-trade? As a skilled hunter knows his prey? She supposed a rake must be like that, expert at gauging a woman's desires, at fulfilling needs she never knew she possessed.

From her prone position, Matilda clutched at the skirts of Gemma's riding habit and worked the dark broadcloth between her fingers. "You must promise me you will avoid being alone with him at any cost."

"But . . . but I have known him all my life." Gemma laughed uncertainly. "I cannot promise that."

Matilda surged up and gripped Gemma's shoulders. "I saw the way he looked at you. Do you imagine anyone will believe you are innocent? Your mama was just like you, reckless of consequences, always expecting people would think the best of her. *Well, they did not.* And look what she has become."

Gemma raised a trembling hand to wipe a fleck of Matilda's spittle from her cheek. Her insides churned.

She knew what her aunt said was true. But to give up Sebastian's friendship when he had only just come back to her . . . "Do not make me promise, Aunt. I will be more careful."

Matilda's voice deepened. "The servants here will not talk. They are a quiet lot, and loyal. But when you are at Laidley, you must promise me that you will not give Sebastian, or any other man, the slightest hint of encouragement."

"But I am not going—"

Matilda laid a finger to Gemma's lips. She was so close, Gemma smelled the faint sourness of her breath. "All the *ton* will be at Lady Fanny's wedding, and they will watch to see what you do. You will never be like other young ladies of your station, free to make small mistakes. You must be above reproach. You must be a thousand times more careful of your honour than the most strictly raised girl. You must remember it every minute of every day you remain under their gaze. *Because you are Gemma Maitland, and they will show you no mercy.*"

❧

GEMMA left her aunt resting and went downstairs, drained and sick at heart. The servants bustled about the terrace, preparing for an *al fresco* luncheon, but she was not certain she could bear to sit there now. She knew she could not eat a bite.

It would be the height of rudeness to give in to her yearning to gallop Tealeaf through the fields until she grew too weary to think. Years of practice at masking her emotions stiffened her spine. She walked out to the terrace where her grandfather sat in his favourite chair, with the lake in clear view.

"Where have you been, miss?" Hugo eyed Gemma from head to toe. "Gallivanting about the place on that flea-bitten grey of yours, meddling in what doesn't concern you, I'll wager."

Gemma dropped a light kiss on his forehead and sat down beside him. "No, Grandpapa, I have been tending to my aunt."

"Had one of her turns, has she? That woman's got more hair than wit."

"In this case, I do not blame her," Gemma said. "She saw Sebastian on the terrace without his shirt."

"Did she?" Hugo's eyes glinted. "And where were you?"

She inspected her knife and rubbed at an imaginary smudge on the blade with her napkin. "I was with him."

"The boy doesn't waste time," muttered Hugo.

Gemma frowned. "I beg your pardon?"

"Did I hear my name?" Sebastian seemed to materialise from nowhere. He pulled out a chair and sat down facing Gemma over a bowl of fruit. There was a devilish quirk to his lips and a challenge in his eye.

Her stomach lurched, but she wrestled her thudding heart to the ground and stamped on it. Throwing Sebastian a dazzling, false smile, she said, "So glad you could manage to find some clothes."

His lips twitched. "Ah, where is your esteemed aunt?"

"Recovering from a horrible shock." Gemma selected a peach from the bowl and began to peel it with her knife. She could not bring herself to eat the fruit, but dismembering it would give her restless hands something to do.

Hugo and Sebastian paid scant attention to her or her hands. They spoke of racing and pedestrianism and prize-fights. Hugo had not entirely lost touch with the world, but he was eager for news of the latest mills and sporting wagers laid in the London clubs.

Gemma scowled. Was it not bad enough that she was obliged to sit down to luncheon with Sebastian? Now she had to listen to him talk about science and form and clever cross-and-jostle work, as if any of it mattered. Anyone would think him an empty-headed gentleman of leisure instead of a landowner with a vast estate to run.

The peach lay on her plate in sixteen neatly dissected segments. Her fingers ran with nectar. She wiped them on her napkin and wished Sebastian would stop talking long enough to put some food in his mouth so the ordeal of luncheon would be over.

But as he employed a handful of unshelled walnuts to illustrate the ingenious placement of fieldsmen in a recent cricket match, Gemma could not help but smile. She had not seen him so animated since he arrived at Ware. He must have combed his hair since their last encounter on the terrace, but it was still damp, curlier than usual, and he paused now and then to brush a stray lock from his brow. He laughed often, joyously, without constraint.

Once again, he was the vibrant boy of those carefree summer days. She longed to grab his hand and run with him down to the lake, as she had done so often before she crossed the threshold to womanhood; before Matilda came to live at Ware and turned her life into an endless series of rules and prohibitions.

Abruptly, she stood. "I must go and see how old Mrs. Lane fares today."

Sebastian rose also, touched a napkin to his lips, and tossed it onto the table. "I'll come with you. If you have no objection, sir . . ."

"No!" The word shot from her mouth before she could moderate her tone.

Sebastian's brows rose. Hugo's shoulders shook slightly, but it might have been a trick of the light.

"I mean, you need not come, Scovy," she amended. "It will be tedious for you, I daresay."

Sebastian bowed with a flourish. "In your company, my dear Miss Maitland, I could never be bored. Besides, if I recall correctly, the younger Mrs. Lane bakes the tastiest currant buns in England. I would not miss them for the world."

"Take him with you, girl," ordered Hugo.

"Oh, very well." Gemma knew she sounded ungracious. "Though I daresay Mrs. Lane will be too busy caring for her mother-in-law to bake currant buns for you, Scovy."

Sebastian just grinned.

INSUFFERABLE! Gemma watched Sebastian eat his third currant bun and wash it down with a glass of cowslip wine. A doting smile deepened the dimples in Edith Lane's red cheeks as she watched him cut a swath through her provisions. Doubtless, she would have made the buns especially if she'd none to hand.

Sebastian did nothing practical to help Gemma minister to the invalid, but his laughter and easy charm wound around them all, like the sweet, warm scent of baking. When Gemma moved away from the pallet bed where old

Mrs. Lane lay, Sebastian immediately took her place. Heedless of the risk of infection, he clasped the invalid's hand and spoke softly to her about nothing in particular. The old lady did not smile, she was too deep in the throes of her illness for that, but her eyes brightened at his touch and the low tone of his voice seemed to soothe her.

Gemma could not quash a foolish glow of pride. He might be doing this to impress her, or because he found it novel, but she could not deny the benefits of his presence. It would have been ridiculous for Sebastian to stand on ceremony with these plain folk who had known him since he was in short coats, but that would not have deterred many men from behaving with new and unbecoming arrogance. After all, the Earl of Carleton was a notable figure. No doubt his London acquaintance would stare to see him eating homemade wine and currant buns and tending to a poor invalid on an estate that was not even his own.

Eventually, the old woman closed her eyes and Gemma and Sebastian took their leave.

Edith Lane accompanied them down the stone path to the gate. As they mounted their horses and prepared to depart, she scowled with mock ferocity up at Sebastian. "And don't you go leaving it another however many years afore you come back, lad, d'ye hear?"

Sebastian nodded and waved, but his smile soon faded once they moved out of sight. He did not like to be reminded of his long absence from Ware, or of its cause. He turned his head to look at Gemma. "Where now?"

"The rectory, if you have no objection."

Sebastian grimaced. "Old Playstead and I were never the best of friends."

"Only because you and the village children used to steal apples from his tree," said Gemma. "Anyway, Mr. Playstead retired. We have a new rector now, a Mr. Vincent. A pleasant man, and young. He married a local woman."

"Oh? Anyone I know?"

Before Gemma could answer, a tall, loose-limbed man with a thatch of straw-coloured hair straightened from his crouching position among the rhododendrons in the rectory garden and called a greeting.

He pulled off his gardening gloves and loped towards them. "Miss Maitland! How do you do, this fine afternoon?"

Gemma edged Tealeaf to the low stone wall that separated them and leaned down to shake hands.

She presented Mr. Vincent to Sebastian, and the rector smiled up at him, one hand shading his eyes from the sun. "Ah, yes. Welcome, my lord. How do you do? You have been to visit the Lanes, I understand." His blue eyes twinkled. "News travels like lightning here, as I'm sure you know!"

The rector tucked his gardening gloves under his arm and gathered his spade and trowel. "Well, Miss Maitland, do let John take your horses round to the stables and go in to Mrs. Vincent. I think you will find she has that receipt for pickled walnuts your housekeeper requested written out for you. I shall be along in a moment when I have put off my dirt."

Gemma and Sebastian relinquished their mounts to the waiting servant and a plump housekeeper admitted them to a small parlour.

Sebastian glanced around him. Comfortably furnished in primrose and white, it was an airy, sunny apartment, perfect for a lady's sitting room. Its occupant put aside her stitchery and rose to greet them.

Suddenly, his crisp surroundings faded to nothing. A pulse throbbed deep in his brain.

Caroline.

The only woman he had ever asked to be his wife.

Four

❧

DIVORCED from the present by some invisible, impenetrable wall, Sebastian watched Gemma's lips move and Caroline mouth a response, and guessed he was being introduced.

He cleared his throat and said something, he didn't know what. Paying no heed to his awkwardness, the ladies sat down on chintz-covered chairs and launched into conversation. Something about sewing new vestments, he gathered, though the details eluded him.

While the women talked about matters domestic, Sebastian's frozen brain slowly thawed to life. He studied his first love. She looked . . . different from the way he remembered her. Older, but that was not surprising. She was five years his senior, and the liaison they had enjoyed ended six years before.

He had enjoyed it. Raw as he had been, he supposed he had done little to make sure she found pleasure in it, too. Even after all this time, he winced at the memory of that eager, callow youth.

But married to the rector! He had assumed she'd used Hugo's money to set herself up in London or Bath and snare a man with better prospects than he, a younger son at that time, had possessed. Her treachery had pained him, but he realised now it was far better than knowing her reasons had not been quite so cynical, that she had rejected him in return for five thousand pounds and this modest, cheerful respectability.

And she was cheerful, he noticed. Cheerful and calm, her once glorious golden hair faded to ash and swept up beneath a plain white cap, her lithe figure now fuller at the breast and rounder at the hips.

This life seemed to suit her. Far more, he guessed, than the position of Countess of Carleton would have done.

Strange, she actually seemed to care about the process of pickling walnuts.

Sebastian realised he was gripping the arms of his chair, so he relaxed his fingers and crossed one leg over the other, feigning a nonchalance he did not feel. Now and then he made some brief comment so as not to appear rude, but he had little knowledge and less interest in the feminine concerns under discussion, so he lapsed once more into silence.

Yes, all things considered, it appeared Caroline had chosen wisely. If the manner in which she had informed him of her choice had been kinder, he might not have hated her so much or for so long.

Looking at her now, he found it difficult to believe this rather commonplace woman had taken him to such heights of joy and depths of torment. What had been so special about her? Merely that she was the first woman he had been intimate with?

Delving into memories he'd worked so hard to bury, Sebastian fell deeper into the past, until Gemma's sharpened tone cut through his brooding.

"Isn't that right, Sebastian?"

He blinked. "I beg your pardon?"

Gemma frowned at him. "I was telling Mrs. Vincent you are fond of Alexander Pope."

When had they moved from pickled walnuts to poetry? "Oh, ah. Yes."

Poetry. With an effort, he stopped his eyes seeking Caroline's. She possessed firsthand experience of his talents in that direction. His ardent verses praising her beauty had been flung in the fire long ago, but not before she had read them. Not before she had laughed.

"Do you still write, Sebastian?" Gemma turned to Caroline. "I always think poets must be terribly clever, don't you?"

Sebastian managed a strained smile. "Oh, I don't know about that. Just look at that Byron fellow."

Gemma chuckled. "You are jealous because he makes all the ladies swoon."

"I don't need poetry to do that, m'dear."

He spoke flippantly, without thinking, but Gemma choked, pink tingeing her cheeks. When Caroline glanced curiously from her to him, Sebastian knew he must get out of there.

He stood, just as Vincent bounded in.

"Come and see the church!" The rector spread his arms wide as if to shepherd them along, his extended frame too large for the tiny parlour. "Miss Maitland is already acquainted with our new addition, but I cannot pass up an opportunity to command your admiration, Lord Carleton. I think you will find it a marvel, indeed I do." He looked at his wife. "Will you join us, my dear?"

Caroline smiled and shook her head. "No, Henry. Baby Jack is teething and I promised Nurse a rest. She has been up all night and is worn to the bone, poor soul." She turned to Gemma. "You will excuse me?"

She has a baby, thought Sebastian. *They have a baby. Probably several of them tucked away somewhere.*

"Of course," said Gemma, rising. "You will be anxious

to go to him. Sebastian, you must come and be suitably impressed by our new treasure, if you please. Good afternoon, Mrs. Vincent."

Caroline curtseyed and finally, *finally*, a look came into her eyes that signified something more than the polite interest of a hostess in her guest. Not regret, of course, never that. Not even wistfulness. Nostalgia, perhaps?

It was something, and he knew it was all he would get.

The next instant, Caroline straightened and the cheerful, calm expression fell back in place.

So that was that. With an ironic bow in her direction, Sebastian turned on his heel and left.

Gemma took Mr. Vincent's arm and chattered to him as they walked the short distance to St. Margaret's Church. Sebastian strolled alone through the avenue of red-berried yew trees, past the mossy headstones of parishioners long dead and forgotten. The newer graveyard lay on the west side of the church. Morbidly, he wondered whether anyone he knew rested there. After all, death could have come as easily as new life to those he had left behind.

He would ask Gemma about it. But not today, not yet.

When they reached the church door, Gemma turned to Sebastian, her face radiant with anticipation. She looked just as she had as a girl when she had made him shut his eyes and hold out his hand for something precious, like a robin's egg or a smooth, flat pebble, perfect for skimming on the lake.

Ever so slightly, the darkness around his heart receded. He felt his own mouth lift at the corners in response, even though he could not imagine what might be so wonderful about the interior of a church.

The rector flung the church door wide open and Sebastian had his answer.

She soared high above the altar, serene and invincible, a figure of astonishing, unearthly beauty rendered in stained glass. She wore a pearl-studded coronet and held a crucifix aloft in her right hand. The green palm leaf of the martyr hung in the air beside her head, its hue echoing the emerald robes that fell about her in graceful folds and disappeared into the split belly of a prone, vermilion dragon. Strangely, the dragon gazed up at the human it had just disgorged with adoring eyes, reminding Sebastian of nothing so much as a friendly spaniel.

But her face . . . Her face was fascinating. Dark blond hair clustered in tight, fat curls around her head, the odd ringlet lifted sideways by an imaginary wind. The day had turned cloudy, but even without the benefit of strong sunlight, the figure's oval face glowed, as if lit by some intrinsic, mystical power.

"Do you know who it is?" Gemma's lowered voice thrilled through the empty church.

"St. Margaret? Extraordinary." Sebastian dragged his gaze from the martyr and looked at Gemma. "Where on earth . . . ? Never tell me this was the original window?"

She nodded, beaming back at him. "We found her buried behind the stable yard at Ware, of all places. Mr. Vincent thinks the villagers probably removed her for safekeeping when Cromwell's soldiers rampaged through the district during the Civil War. The soldiers stabled their horses in churches, you know, and vandalised the buildings shamefully."

Sebastian walked farther up the aisle and craned his head back to look at the martyr. He wanted to be closer to the image, to touch it, though he knew the window was best viewed at a distance. "But this must date back centuries. It's medieval isn't it?"

Vincent came up and hovered behind him, his excitement almost palpable. "Yes, we think it is probably the work of a craftsman known as the Master of Exeter Cathedral. We cannot be certain, of course, but she does have the distinctive hair, a thick mass of curls, and those heavy-lidded eyes and full lips bear a close similarity to known examples of his work. A pity we cannot see her feet—he usually made them triangular."

The rector overtook Sebastian, sprang up the altar steps, and bounded over to the window. "Just observe the detail here!"

As Vincent reached up to run his fingers over the vivid dragon scales, Sebastian wondered if there were some merit in the Protestant prohibition of idolatry. This glorious creature must surely distract the congregation from proper worship.

Without taking his eyes from her, he sat down in a nearby pew. "St. Margaret. What was her story again? Something about being swallowed by a dragon? I remember that much."

It was Gemma who answered him. "Margaret was the daughter of a pagan priest, but her nurse was Christian and she raised Margaret as a Christian, too. The local Roman prefect saw Margaret and fell in love with her beauty, but she refused to become his wife—or concubine—we are not certain exactly what he proposed. He cajoled and threatened her, but she preferred to dedicate her virginity to God."

Gemma moved to stand next to Sebastian, her hand resting on top of the pew at his back. Immediately, he became conscious of the hard wood of the pew connecting them. An odd sensation crept over him, a tingle of awareness mixed with a curious sense of peace. Had it only been ten minutes ago that he fought for air in Caroline's sunny parlour?

Gemma continued, and the keen sense of drama he remembered so well stole into her voice. "When Margaret would not agree to his wishes, the prefect threw her into prison. It is said Satan appeared to her there, first as a handsome young man, to tempt her astray. When she refused to renounce her faith, Satan came to her in the form of a dragon and devoured her whole. She still held her crucifix, however, and its presence irritated the dragon's belly so much, it split open and disgorged her."

Vincent nodded. "There is another variation of the story, in which Margaret overpowered the dragon with her crucifix and used her girdle to lead the tamed beast where she willed."

Gemma chuckled. "The former version is more dramatic, of course, but I confess I prefer the latter."

Sebastian glanced up. At the sparkle in her eyes, he began to sympathise with the dragon. "So how did she become a martyr, then?"

"Oh, the prefect tortured her for a bit, then tried various means of killing her—all unsuccessful—and ended by chopping her head off," said Gemma. "Charming man, wasn't he? I think she was about fifteen at the time."

The door to the south porch opened, catching Gemma's attention. Sebastian looked around to see two ladies enter the church, each with a large wicker basket of chrysanthemums, lilies, and assorted greenery in hand.

On catching sight of the present occupants, the ladies stopped short. The thread of their conversation snapped, as if sliced by a knife.

They appeared discomfited, and Sebastian could only assume it was his presence that affected them. Of course they guessed who he was—everyone in the village would know what he had eaten at breakfast by now. He repressed an exasperated sigh. Even at Ware he could not escape his wicked reputation.

"Good afternoon, Mrs. Whitton, Mrs. Briggs." Vincent's lively good cheer smoothed over the awkward moment. "Have you come to arrange the altar flowers? Lovely!" The rector's smile embraced Sebastian. "We are fortunate, my lord, to have two such talented ladies among us."

Neither the tall, dark woman nor the plump one with pale blond ringlets seemed familiar. Sebastian rose and bowed and hoped that they were, indeed, strangers and he had not simply forgotten them. The rector made the introductions, relieving him of that concern. Both ladies had settled in the district upon their respective marriages, well after his time.

His initial impression turned out to be incorrect, however. Far from holding themselves aloof from such a notorious rake, the ladies were all flattering attention. But as they inquired politely about the length of his stay and where his own home was situated, Sebastian sensed Gemma's subtle withdrawal and wondered at the cause.

Did she dislike them? But Gemma liked everyone. And they seemed pleasant enough women. They were young, elegant, and well-bred. Lacking in spice or any sort of natural vibrancy or charm, but inoffensive enough, surely.

The rector soon excused himself, pleading parish business. Gemma bade him a warm farewell, then pressed her lips together and did not speak again. Mrs. Whitton and Mrs. Briggs barely acknowledged Vincent's departure, and continued to watch Sebastian like sparrows expecting a crumb.

He smiled and threw them one. "I have been admiring the new arrival." He gestured to St. Margaret. "Magnificent, is she not?"

Mrs. Whitton pursed her lips and exchanged a sideways glance with Mrs. Briggs. "Indeed."

The cool response puzzled him. How could anyone remain unaffected by such transcendent beauty?

Surprise must have shown in his face. Mrs. Briggs raised her fine, dark brows and answered his unspoken question. "You do not think the window a trifle vulgar, my lord? So . . . so *colourful*. I am afraid it is not at all to my taste. And quite out of keeping with the traditions of our unpretentious little church, if I may say so."

Sebastian wondered if the woman knew it was the original window. Or, indeed, if she knew anything at all about church traditions. In earlier times, the walls of this church would have been covered with brightly coloured murals from floor to vaulted ceiling.

Mrs. Whitton nodded her agreement. "We—Mrs. Whitton and I, and the other *ladies* of the parish—had grave reservations about the propriety of restoring the window." Her gaze flicked to Gemma, then returned to fix earnestly on Sebastian. "Indeed, we wonder that the bishop allowed such a thing."

A challenge rang in her tone. Until this point, Gemma had appeared uninterested in their discussion, but now her lip curled in a look of disdain Sebastian recognised. She stared past Mrs. Whitton's left shoulder and said nothing. Sebastian steered the conversation down other avenues, hoping Gemma would join in, or at least that they might retire gracefully soon.

When Gemma began to fidget with her riding gloves, Sebastian judged he had wasted enough time exchanging pleasantries. He held out his arm to her and made their excuses. Before they could leave, Mrs. Whitton fluttered her hands to detain him.

"If you mean to make an extended stay at Ware, you must call on us at Pilgrove, my lord. Mr. Whitton will make you most welcome." She glanced at Gemma. "I daresay you simply pine for genteel company."

"Do you indeed?" The grip on his arm tightened and Sebastian smiled, showing his teeth. "I fear I am fully engaged for the rest of my stay, ma'am."

Mrs. Briggs's brow furrowed. "But did you not say you were uncertain how long you would remain in the district, my lord?"

Sebastian let his smile widen, until the angry flush in Mrs. Whitton's cheeks showed she understood him perfectly—that no matter how long he stayed at Ware he would not choose to call on her.

"Ah, yes," he murmured. "So I did."

As soon as they cleared the village, Gemma spurred Tealeaf to a canter. Spying an open meadow, she veered off at a sharp angle and slowed her mount to jump the hedgerow that separated the meadow from the road. Picking up speed, she galloped Tealeaf along the flat, green ground, scattering a flurry of nervous sheep in her wake.

She heard Sebastian call out, and seconds later came the thunder of hooves behind her and more confused bleating. She did not bother to glance around; he would be with her soon enough. At that moment, she wanted to be alone and racing. She loosened the reins and let Tealeaf fly, the mare's action so smooth Gemma barely felt her hooves touch the ground.

As she had predicted, Sebastian drew level with her. She held Tealeaf at a steady gallop and waited for him to surge ahead, but he matched his pace to hers.

"Pass me, confound you!" she muttered, but of course he did not hear. He did not seem interested in winning this race.

They cleared a low hedge together and her hat whipped off as they hit the ground, its pins ripping at her hair. For an instant, Gemma wondered what Matilda would say if she returned home in Sebastian's company, bedraggled and without her hat, looking for all the world like a blowsy damsel who had been tumbled in a barn. She laughed, a wild, tearing sound borne away on the wind, but she slowed the mare's pace and after a few hundred yards, reined in.

"What the devil was that about?" demanded Sebastian.

She wheeled Tealeaf and set off again at a sedate trot. "I must get my hat."

Sebastian brought his horse into step with hers. When they reached the ditch below the hedge where her hat lay, he dismounted and threw his reins to her to hold while he retrieved it. He dusted the curly brimmed beaver with his handkerchief and gave it back.

Gemma thanked him and met his concerned gaze as she passed back his gelding's reins. She looked away, resisting the urge to pour out her humiliation and resentment. The relief would only be temporary, and she despised people who wrung their hands over things that could not be mended.

As they moved off, Sebastian blew out an audible breath. "Do you mind telling me why you look like a thundercloud or must I endure these sulks for the rest of the journey home?"

"I am not sulking. I never sulk."

He stared at her for a few moments, then shrugged. "As you say."

They continued without speaking until they reached the narrow stream that bordered the Ware land.

Sebastian gestured towards it with his riding crop. "I'll wager these beasts are thirsty after that ride. Shall we?"

Gemma assented and dismounted before Sebastian had a chance to help her. She let him take Tealeaf and sat down on a sunny spot while he watered the horses. He left them lipping the long grass at the stream bank and came to sit beside her.

With a contented sigh, he stretched out on his back, tipped his hat over his eyes, and looked for all the world as if he would fall asleep.

"Why did you do that?" Gemma burst out.

Only his lips moved. "Do what?"

"You know very well what I mean. You were unpardonably rude to Jenny Whitton just now."

"She was unpardonably rude to you. She deserved a setdown, and I dealt her one as you seemed reluctant to do so." He flicked up his hat brim and squinted at her. "Why should you suffer insolence from that woman?"

She smoothed the skirt of her riding habit and dropped her hands in her lap. "I don't know what you mean."

"What can you have done to inspire such malice?"

A bitter laugh escaped her. "I? *I* have done nothing."

There was a pause. "I should have guessed. It's your mama, isn't it?"

His swift comprehension struck a blow to her stomach. Gemma pressed her lips together and shook her head.

He rolled onto his side and propped himself on one elbow, brow furrowed. "It is, isn't it? Those cats turn up their noses at you because you're Sybil Maitland's daughter."

He looked so troubled, and at the same time so boyish and dishevelled that she wanted to kiss him for his concern and cry her eyes out at the same time.

Instead, she focused on a solitary blade of grass bending and lifting in the breeze; listened to the soft, chattering rush of the stream, the sweet, desultory chirp of birds grown lazy in the summer heat. She tried her best to bring her turbulent emotions under control.

Her throat tightened with the effort. "You are mistaken."

"Am I?"

He lay there watching her for the longest time, it seemed. She did not meet his gaze, but his regard surrounded her like some invisible force, pressing her to confide. She plucked at the blade of grass and resisted the urge to give in.

Pride was part of it, but that was not the only consideration that kept her silent. With Sebastian, she could imagine she was the girl she had been before she realised it did not matter what she did or how she lived her life, she would always bear her mother's shame. She had never let women like Sarah Briggs and Jenny Whitton bother her, for they needed no excuse to belittle others and she was by no means their sole victim. She found it far more difficult to shrug off slights from good, respectable people who genuinely feared her corrupting influence. Usually she would not even notice Jenny and Sarah's poisonous barbs.

But when they needled her in front of Sebastian, it was different. She could be herself with him because he believed she still was that carefree girl he knew years ago—not some sad little dab whose neighbours shunned her, not some feeble maiden who needed rescuing from dragons in jockey bonnets.

And what could he do to help her anyway? In a few days he would be gone, perhaps for another six years.

Perhaps for good.

Sebastian sat up and stretched out to clasp her hand, crushing the blade of grass between their joined palms.

"Come back to Laidley with me."

Even through gloves, she felt his warmth. It spread through her body, enveloping her. "You think I am a coward, that I would run away?"

"No, but why should you stay?"

"Ware needs me."

She realised how improper it was for him to keep her hand and tried to disengage herself, but he held it fast.

He looked down at their clasped fingers. Slowly, he said, "That is not the real reason you won't come, is it?"

"What? Of course it is."

He shook his head. "No, you are afraid and you are using Ware as an excuse. You *are* running away, but not from Ware. You are running away from life."

She yanked her hand free and scrambled to her feet. "And what life is that? A shallow existence full of spoiled Society darlings like you?" She brushed at her grassy skirts and started down the bank towards Tealeaf. In a flash, he followed and caught her elbow, spinning her to face him.

"It would be so easy for you to hide here and think you have a full life, wouldn't it, Mistress Squire? You have the household and the estate and your charities, and no doubt you think you are blessed to have such purpose. But don't forget, Gemma, there is more to human existence than that."

He took her face between his hands and looked into her eyes. "You are so damned beautiful," he breathed. "You deserve to be loved."

She thought he might kiss her then, and suddenly it was too much. She gripped his wrists and wrenched his hands away, stumbling back a step as she threw them off. "You left me, Sebastian, remember? You only came back because Grandpapa summoned you. And now you think you can waltz in and turn my life upside down? If you cared so much about what happened to me, you wouldn't have left!"

She broke off, appalled at what she had said, aghast at his ravaged expression.

They stared at each other, and Gemma turned cold in the sunshine. She had meant never to reproach him with this. Why had she done so now?

"I wrote to you," he said at last.

"Yes, you did." It had not been enough.

His gaze slid away from her and he stared into the distance. "The reason I stayed away from Ware had nothing to do with you."

Strange, that hurt almost as much as if she had somehow caused his absence. She put her hand to her temple, then waved it dismissively. "Your brother died, and then your father, shortly afterwards. You were busy, first at Laidley, and later leading a fashionable life in town. I understand, there's no need to explain."

"That wasn't it."

She decided then that she must be a coward, because suddenly she was terrified of hearing his explanation. But the look on his face told her he needed to say it, so she made herself ask. "What, then?"

He gave her one of his old, sweet smiles, but after a moment the smile twisted and vanished. He gestured to the path that wound away from the stream and took her arm. As they walked, Gemma gleaned what comfort she could from his closeness. She had the strangest notion he was slipping away from her, in a sense that had nothing to do with the physical.

Sebastian paused to kick a rock out of Gemma's path.

He wanted to tell her everything, but it was scarcely the act of a gentleman to reveal the past he and Caroline shared. Particularly now she was the rector's wife and eminently respectable.

Abruptly, he said, "Mrs. Vincent. How well do you know her?"

He sensed Gemma's bewilderment at the apparent change of subject, but he did not look at her. He gazed into the distance, where the path ended in a quiet glade littered with bluebells.

"Not very well," answered Gemma slowly. "I never had much to do with her until she married Mr. Vincent. I like her. She is . . ." Gemma frowned, searching for the word. "Comfortable. Easy to talk to. She does not disapprove of me like the others."

Sebastian snorted and Gemma said, "You may scoff, but there is no escaping the fact that hereabouts I am considered quite beyond the pale. Mrs. Vincent treats me with the same kindness she shows to everyone."

Kindness! Sebastian grimaced. Caroline had changed very much if that were the case. At least she was not a hypocrite. If his former mistress had dared to turn her back on Gemma like all those other sanctimonious females, he would take the utmost pleasure in making her regret it.

He looked down at Gemma, and all impulse to explain his sordid past flew away as she stared up at him, a curious mixture of innocence and sensual beauty.

That warm tingle of awareness he had felt in the church returned tenfold, without the accompanying sense of peace. Because it was there, no matter how determined she was to deny it, no matter how much that prissy aunt of hers tried to smother it in white muslin and dire warnings. Something beyond mere physical perfection; something elusive but powerful that must draw men to her like the moon draws the tide. By all accounts, her mother possessed this magnetism;

he knew very little of Sybil Maitland, save that she was very lovely and she had abandoned her only child.

But he could understand why people associated Gemma so closely with her errant parent, and perhaps it also explained why other women of her class were so determined to despise her. Because she had it, too, this mysterious quality that made men forget propriety, obligations, even honour itself—a quality that incited them to think of sex whenever they looked at her.

As he was thinking of it now.

Five

SEBASTIAN realised they had halted amongst the blue-bells and Gemma stood very, very close. Her hand slid up his arm. An innocent touch on her part. He knew it, but the breath caught in his throat and refused to reach his lungs.

"Tell me what troubles you so," she whispered.

He watched, fascinated, as her mouth formed the words. Her lips were not red, but a more subtle shade, like the rosy blush on a peach—full and lush and ripe, with two, delicate, delicious peaks on the upper lip, and a small indent in the centre of the lower.

He raised a hand and brushed the tiny cleft with his thumb, his fingers curled under her chin. "I remember how you got that scar. Do you?"

Her eyes widened, but she did not shrink or protest at his touch.

"Yes." Warm breath stole over his thumb. Her lips parted and closed against its tip as she spoke the word. His body tightened, aroused by the soft caress.

With light, controlled pressure he rolled his thumb

downwards over the scar, pulling her lip into the mere hint of a pout to expose the moist, tempting flesh within. He ached to taste that flesh, to explore every inch of her mouth with his lips and teeth and tongue.

Why didn't she stop him?

"Does it still hurt?" he heard himself say.

She swallowed, and her voice shook. "No, that was years ago."

He tilted her chin until her gaze met his, and fell into those fathomless eyes. "But some wounds never quite heal, do they, Mistress Squire? And some heal, but the scars may still be tender when touched."

Gemma's eyes sparked and smoked, pulling him deeper. "Do you mean my scars or yours?"

The question caught him by surprise. He had thought her dazed, enraptured as he was, but she'd managed to disconcert him as she always did. Suddenly, he felt as if he were not the one in control, as if he teetered on the edge of something disastrous.

Desire, almost painful in its intensity, left him as swiftly as it had come. He broke their gaze, let the hand that grasped her chin fall to his side, and told himself his willful imagination had conjured the passion in Gemma's eyes. She was his friend. She showed him a friend's tender concern for his troubles, that was all.

"We should go home or your aunt will send out a search party." His words came out clipped and harsh. He did not take her arm again, or even look at her, but started back along the path.

"Scovy, wait!"

He heard her call out, but strode along the cool, shade-dappled path until he reached the sunny spot where their horses grazed. What the devil was wrong with him? Without even trying, Gemma had tempted him to folly twice in twenty-four hours.

Lord help him if she ever set her mind to it.

He felt like a besotted schoolboy; as if he were reliving in agonising detail every last moment of his infatuation with Caroline. Only this time it was Gemma, and the stakes seemed infinitely higher than they had those many summers before.

It was this place. He was never himself at Ware. Once he quitted the warmth and sunshine, once he was back in the cold, relentless grip of Laidley—in his own milieu with his family and friends hedged about him—he would be his own man again, in control. He would know how to deal with Gemma.

Sebastian had untied the horses by the time she caught up with him. Though he knew a craven wish to mount his hunter and gallop away, he stood next to her mare and waited to throw her into the saddle.

Gemma said nothing—so rare for a woman to know when it was not the time to speak—but as she set her boot in his clasped hands, she shot him a worried glance tinged with speculation. He ignored it and launched her upwards.

She had barely settled in the saddle before she was off, throwing a challenge over her shoulder to race. He vaulted onto his horse and shot through the trees in hot pursuit, glad he did not have to think again or talk to her for a while.

He won, of course.

Eyes shining, Gemma pulled up beside him and pinched her finger and thumb close together. "A mere hairsbreadth," she panted. "I shall come about, never fear!"

It was her old catch-cry. Sebastian grinned as his hunter danced beneath him.

Gemma laughed back at him from sheer exhilaration. She knew perspiration sheened her face and her hair tangled down her shoulders, but for the moment she did not care to be a lady. There would be time enough for that when he was gone.

Their gazes caught and Gemma suffered the slight shock

of awareness, the dart of heat through her centre that was becoming all too familiar to her now. Without another word, they turned into the arbour that led to the parterre garden at the east side of the house. They rode in a silence that should have been companionable. To Gemma, it seemed fraught with renewed tension.

She bent to stroke Tealeaf's neck and shot Sebastian a covert glance. What on earth had that interlude in the bluebell glade been about? She wanted to think they had returned to a semblance of their close friendship, but she could not deny her old playmate unsettled her in a new and powerful way. Every time he touched her, whether it was running his thumb over her lip with breathtaking intimacy or simply setting his hands under the sole of her boot, a cloying, sweet warmth stole through her body, melting her bones, dizzying her mind.

She had to admit it, if only to herself: She wanted more.

Sebastian muttered something under his breath. She followed his gaze and saw John Talbot in the distance, astride his tame chestnut, waiting patiently in the forecourt outside the Hall.

Gemma reined in. "Oh, bother! I forgot I was supposed to meet John."

Sebastian quirked an eyebrow. "Shall we turn around and sneak off in the opposite direction?"

She was tempted, and not just because she wished to avoid the tedious company of her neighbour. She could not compound her rudeness by playing truant, however. Stolid and condescending he might be, but he did not deserve such cavalier treatment.

Gemma urged Tealeaf forwards. "Of course not. I have had enough riding for today, though. We shall ask him in for tea."

They emerged from the arbour and rode past the parterre garden filled with bright annuals laid out in geometrical patterns and bordered by clipped box-tree hedges.

"Is he enamoured of your expectations, do you think?" Sebastian still gazed after Talbot's distant figure.

She made a face. "What a vulgar thing to say! And scarcely complimentary to me."

"On the contrary. I simply don't credit him with such discernment."

"Yes, I believe I am what is called an acquired taste," she said dryly. "Thank you so much for pointing it out."

Gemma spurred her mare forward, leaving Sebastian to follow at a walk. As she neared the house, she heard the crunch of wheels on the crushed seashells that formed the carriage drive and turned her head to see who approached.

She did not recognise the carriage that bowled around the chestnut-lined bend towards her. And she rather thought she would have recognised it if she had seen it before.

Drawn by a team of glossy, black Thoroughbreds, the body of the chaise was an improbable turquoise, trimmed in gleaming ebony. The bright panels were innocent of a crest and thick curtains at the windows remained closed against prying eyes, but the carriage was clearly the property of someone wealthy and eccentric. In addition to the liveried coachman and postilions, three outriders and two Dalmatians made up the entourage.

As the chaise slowed and swept into the forecourt, Gemma wrinkled her brow. The colour of that carriage seemed familiar.

She knew she had never seen such a vehicle, but the unusual shade reminded her of something. As she rode on to meet their unexpected guest, she searched her memory.

The chaise halted outside the front door and it came to her, with a shocking inevitability that made her wish she had not been so quick and curious, that she had indeed turned around and galloped in the other direction as Sebastian had proposed.

Because the panels of that celestial chariot exactly matched Sybil Maitland's eyes.

With a queer clench in her stomach, Gemma dismounted and handed Tealeaf's reins to a waiting groom. Vaguely, she was aware that John Talbot loomed above her on his chestnut gelding. She passed by him without a glance. She could not deal with John now.

"Darling!" Her mother glided—there was no other word for the way she moved—down the carriage steps and drew Gemma into her arms.

Bemused, Gemma suffered the warm, scented embrace and fought the sudden urge to weep. What had come over her? She usually bore her mother's lightning visits with a calm sense of tolerant amusement. This time, she felt fragile as glass, and equally transparent.

"Mama."

Sybil stepped back, hands sliding down to draw Gemma's arms outwards. "Let me look at you. Ah, but you are charming, my dear!"

It was hardly the truth. Gemma knew she appeared a perfect romp, yet somehow one always trusted the sincerity in those fascinating eyes. But then Sybil Maitland could convince the sun that night was day.

"Now, here is a sight to gladden a man's heart." Sebastian's lazy drawl sounded behind them. "Two matched beauties together." He dismounted and bowed. "Your servant ma'am."

Sybil swept a dignified curtsey. "My lord."

"You are acquainted, then?" Gemma looked from one to the other. "How can that be?"

Sebastian answered. "We met once, in London. I did not expect to have a place in your memory, ma'am."

"Did you not?" Sybil's gaze ran over him and a slow smile curved her lips. "But how could I forget my daughter's dearest friend?"

She turned away and flourished an elegant hand, beckoning to one of the horsemen.

Gemma had assumed he was an outrider in the employ

of whatever besotted unfortunate owned that outrageous vehicle, but upon closer inspection, she noticed he was dressed like a gentleman. The quick, confident surveillance of his surrounds as he approached proclaimed he was no servant.

Sybil beamed. "My lord, my dear, may I present Charles Bellamy, who has been so kind as to escort me. Charles, the Earl of Carleton and my daughter, Miss Maitland."

Something about the set of his shoulders spoke of a sudden unease, but the impression was fleeting. The gentleman bowed and murmured greetings in a low, pleasing tone.

Gemma watched him and wondered if he could be real. Bellamy was almost tragically beautiful, if such a word could be applied to a man. Thick chestnut hair curled beneath his hat. Large, soft hazel eyes with long black eyelashes gazed limpidly from under its brim. His mouth formed a red slash across his sun-tanned face. A strong, angular jaw and a well set up physique saved him from appearing girlish.

Gemma did not admire that particular cast of masculine countenance, but as her mother watched Bellamy with rapt approval, it became shockingly clear that Sybil Maitland did.

Good God, what did Mama mean by bringing her youthful lover to the Hall? The scandal of it would be enough to send Aunt Matilda screeching to Bedlam and back.

A loud cough reminded Gemma that John Talbot still lingered, and she quickly drew him into the circle and made introductions. Under the cover of polite conversation, she threw Sebastian a look of entreaty.

He quirked an eyebrow, clearly intrigued by this new development, but when she frowned at him, he grimaced and took the hint. "Bellamy, Talbot, Sir Hugo is indisposed and unable to come down to greet you as he would wish, but I believe I know the way to the drinks cabinet. Shall we?"

"Capital idea!" An appreciative grin split Bellamy's face

and Gemma wondered how she had ever thought his looks tragic. He bowed, with a special smile for Sybil. "Ladies."

Talbot hesitated, but Sebastian took his elbow. "Best not get involved, old man. Leave the ladies for a bit."

Gemma watched them go, then turned to see her mother regard her escort's retreating back with a doting smile.

"Have you run mad, Mama?"

"Mad?" Sybil considered. "I do not *believe* so. Or no more than usual, at any rate." Her eyes crinkled at the corners and she patted Gemma's cheek. "Come! We will go up to my sitting room for a comfortable coze."

Just as if it had been a week and not a year since they had last seen each other.

Reeves admitted them and they crossed the great hall and climbed the winding staircase to the apartments set aside for Sybil's sporadic use.

Sybil took off her bonnet and tossed it on the counterpane, smoothing her copper hair. "And Hugo. Is he well?"

Gemma sighed. "His gout pains him, I think, though he insists he is spry as ever. Grandpapa resents my interference on the estate, but truly, he is past being bothered with such things." She paused. "Perhaps with the warmer weather his health will improve."

Sybil cast her a quick, acute glance but said merely, "I shall see him when I have restored myself a little. We have much to discuss, your grandfather and I."

That sounded ominous. Gemma waited hopefully for an explanation, but Sybil's conversation skipped off in another direction, to the Allied victory and the exile of Bonaparte to Elba. She twisted a stick of scent and dabbed at her wrists. "My dear, I cannot fathom how the French tolerated such a dirty little man. The creature changes his linen but once a month, only fancy!"

As if *toilette* were the only criterion on which a leader of nations should be judged. Upon reflection, Gemma admitted her mama had a point.

Gemma listened to her mother's tales of abroad with a touch of wistfulness. She had always secretly envied Sybil's freedom. When she was a girl, she had dreamed of flying with her mother to distant lands on a magic carpet, but alone she had never got up the gumption to venture more than a few miles from Ware. The real world had always seemed enormous and hostile, yet Sybil made foreign travel seem tediously commonplace and wildly exotic at the same time. The short journey to Laidley that had so daunted Gemma only that morning paled in comparison with travels to Brazil, the Indies, and the Levant.

She watched her mother drift around the boudoir, rearranging cushions and spindle-legged furniture, tracing a fingertip over the blue-and-gold damask counterpane on her enormous tent bed. There was an air of suppressed excitement, a restless energy about her that made Gemma think it would not be long before she left for some new and distant corner of the earth.

"Where will you go next?"

A brilliant smile lit Sybil's features and Gemma caught her breath. No wonder men bought Mama carriages to match her eyes. Even Gemma felt the power of her beauty.

"Next?" Sybil picked up a Meissen figure and turned it to the light as if to study it, but Gemma sensed her mind was not on porcelain. "Oh, I have done with my wanderings."

Hope surged in Gemma's chest. She could not mean it! She was coming home?

But Gemma had suffered cruel disappointment on her mother's account so very many times before. Ruthlessly, she tamped down her excitement until it tightened in a thick band around her ribs. She clasped her hands together in her lap and waited.

Sybil moved to the window that overlooked the shrubbery and the patchwork of fields beyond. In full light, her hair flamed to life, a fiery sunset, a glorious dawn.

"I have bought a pretty little house in Kensington. It is out of the way—deeply unfashionable, in fact—and I shall trouble no one there."

Her gaze flicked to Gemma and down to the worked cloth on a small round table by the window. She fingered the linen with wonder, as if it were the finest silk. "When one has been away so long, one begins to appreciate the comforts of home."

Then come home! Gemma wanted to shout. Why settle in England and not be at Ware?

But suddenly, she knew the reason. Charles Bellamy. Her mother could not carry on a liaison with him under Hugo's roof—not with Gemma and Aunt Matilda there. And Gemma realised there could be no other reason for this about-face, for her mother's unprecedented wish to settle quietly in her native land.

After all this time, Sybil Maitland had fallen in love with an Englishman—an Englishman half her age.

The pain of it took her breath away. Bellamy's love could keep Sybil by his side when Gemma's own love never had. Tendrils of jealousy curled around her heart.

Yes, Sybil wanted Charles Bellamy. If Gemma knew her mother, neither Society's disapproval nor any sense of propriety or dignity would prevent her grasping what she wanted with both hands.

In a strange way, Gemma envied her this, too. Sybil had shrugged off the shackles of duty and ignored the standards of her class to pursue love, not once in her life, but twice. Perhaps many times. Gemma doubted she would ever experience a love like that. And even if she did, she would never find the same courage to pursue it.

She was not her mother's daughter, after all.

Without warning, the door opened and Matilda popped her head around it. "May I come in?" She simpered, belatedly tapping a crooked knuckle on an oak panel.

Sybil's dreamy expression vanished like chalk wiped

from a slate. A dazzling smile in which she seemed to show every one of her even, white teeth took its place. Sleek and bright and deadly, she regarded Matilda like a tigress contemplating her dinner.

Shocked at this sudden transformation, Gemma's instinct was to protect her great-aunt, who reminded her of nothing so much as a scrawny nanny-goat tied to a stake. But after a moment of fearful confusion, a gleam of pure cunning stole into Matilda's eyes. Seeing it, Gemma remembered that Matilda's weapons of choice, though less direct, were no less effective than Sybil's.

She would not interfere, but she could not be at ease. Sybil and Matilda had never dealt well together, but this was something else. This was no prelude to witty setdowns, polite sniping, or severe homilies. Animosity, almost primal in its naked, raw force, thickened the air of the elegant boudoir.

Nerves taut, Gemma rose and made an effort to avert whatever crisis was upon them. "I must go down to our other guests. Won't you join us for tea, Aunt Matilda? Mama?"

Sybil tilted her head back and viewed Matilda through half-closed eyes. Turquoise deepened to green.

"No, darling," she purred. "You run along. Aunt Matilda and I need to have a little talk."

Six

❦

GEMMA tracked the gentlemen to the billiards room and found Sebastian playing a stroke with deft precision. Bellamy looked on, propping his chin on the top of his cue.

"Where is John?" she demanded as the balls clacked together.

"We got rid of him for you." Sebastian spoke over his shoulder as he moved around the table.

She frowned. "What?"

"We thought it was time he left." Bellamy's face was grave, but his golden eyes twinkled.

How dared he even speak to her, much less tease her in that familiar way? Gemma favoured Bellamy with a blank stare, then turned to Sebastian. "Scovy, what did you do?"

"Do? I? Nothing."

Sebastian bent over the table to line up his shot. A wavy lock of hair dropped over his eyes. "Oh, did you want him to stay?" he asked innocently, looking up at her through his flopping fringe. He made the shot with a fluid stroke of his cue, missed the carom by the merest whisper, and straightened.

Gemma could not help giving him a satisfied smirk, but when he rounded the table and made as if to hand her his cue, she backed away, warding him off with her palms. "I do not wish to play."

"No?" Sebastian slid a glance at Charles. "Bellamy, I believe Miss Maitland is a chicken-heart."

When had these two become bosom-bows? Gemma scowled and put her hands on her hips. "Stop trying to distract me. What did you say to make John leave?"

"Sadly, he has not left the premises, only this room. He has gone to pay a call on your grandfather. Most probably wangling an invitation to dine." Sebastian took her hand and closed it around the cue. "Now play."

Sullenly, Gemma obeyed.

At least bending her mind to the game kept her from speculating about the battle of wills proceeding without her upstairs, or torturing herself over Sybil's plans for the future. She could even hide a smile as Sebastian goaded the younger man into making all sorts of preposterous wagers, backing himself against her.

She shrugged off a momentary qualm. She should not feel sorry for Bellamy. His confidence might be well placed.

As it turned out, she and Bellamy were fairly evenly matched as far as skill went. But Gemma ruthlessly exploited her superior knowledge of her grandfather's table and its peculiar quirks. Soon, she drew ahead.

"The wood is a trifle warped just there," she pointed out, repressing a triumphant grin when Bellamy's carefully placed shot spun away at a crazy tangent.

His handsome jaw tensed and he appeared to redouble his efforts. As he learned the table, he made fewer mistakes, and Gemma did not doubt that he would equal or even beat her in time.

However, that time was not yet upon them. She finished

ahead by two games. Bellamy scribbled a vowel for Sebastian and handed it to him, laughing with easy good nature at
his downfall, and this made Gemma like him in spite of herself. But when he held out his hand to her, as if he would
shake it like a man's, she remembered abruptly that she did
not like him, and that to encourage any familiarity would be
to place her own reputation in jeopardy. She snatched back
the hand that had moved automatically towards his.

Bellamy flushed, but pretended not to notice the slight.

Sebastian looked on with lazy amusement, as if he were
watching the tantrum of a favourite child. Gemma ignored
him. She would make no scenes, but he could not expect her
to go beyond the merest civility to her mother's lover. Sybil
should never have put her in such an awkward position.

Then Gemma remembered the scene upstairs. She shivered, wondering what the outcome of that discussion would
be. For the first time in her life, she wished her mother
gone. Ware was far more comfortable without her.

WHATEVER had occurred in Sybil's bedchamber, no
trace of discord appeared between Matilda and Sybil at
dinner. In the drawing room afterwards, Gemma dispensed
tea and the others played whist while Sybil and Bellamy
sang duets at the pianoforte. Their voices blended superbly,
a glorious whole that transcended the mere sum of soprano
and tenor. All ballads and love songs, of course.

Gemma glowered at Bellamy as he tra-la-la'ed away.
He stood entirely too close to her mother, one hand resting
on the back of her chair, the other on the pianoforte, poised
to turn the pages of her music. Gemma plonked a full cup
down by his hand and the steaming tea slopped in its
saucer. Only sorry she had not scalded his sun-bronzed fingers, she stalked back to the silver tea urn.

Sebastian's gaze, alight with laughter, caught hers. When
no one else was looking, he waggled his eyebrows, as if he

were still a naughty schoolboy trying to make her giggle in church.

Despite her efforts to maintain it, Gemma's frosty glare slipped. Splaying his hand of cards like a fan, Sebastian fluttered his dark eyelashes and sent her a message using the language of the fan: *You are cruel.*

She turned away to fight a chuckle. Sybil had taught Gemma the flirtatious signals the belles of her day used to communicate with their beaux at balls and parties. Not an indiscreet word need be spoken aloud if one had command of this silent language of the fan.

Gemma had thought it a great joke and taught Sebastian in turn. How had he remembered, after all these years? Had he used the coded language with his ladies? The idea made her grip falter and slip on the teapot handle. She gasped and snatched her hand back as the heat burned her knuckles.

She looked up, but it seemed no one noticed the clatter of the pot on the tray. Composing herself, Gemma distributed more tea to the card players.

John Talbot thanked her, but paid her little heed. He was single-minded and competitive, and suffered the severe handicap of partnering Matilda, who dithered over her discards and maintained an inane running commentary on the play. Talbot snapped his cards down when she said something particularly foolish, and hissed reproofs at her when she heedlessly threw away trumps or failed to take a trick she should have won. Gemma stole several glances at Sebastian, but his attention was focused on the play.

If only this night would end! As she bent over her grandfather, Gemma glanced up at Sebastian to see if he shared her boredom. Absently, he held his cards splayed half-open, pressed to his lips. *You may kiss me.*

The breath caught in her throat. Heat raced through her body. She straightened, but she could not drag her gaze from his mouth, could not stop herself imagining . . .

Sebastian leaned forward to trump Talbot's ace and swept the trick towards him, wholly absorbed in the game.

Gemma shook herself. He had meant nothing by it, of course.

The performers reached the end of the recital and their audience broke into applause. Bellamy clasped Sybil's hand and raised her to make her curtsey, kissing her fingers and then her cheek. Sybil turned to cup his jaw in her palm, holding it as though it were fashioned of something smooth and rare and precious.

Sickened and wretched, Gemma moved to the window and fought envious tears. She rested her brow against the pane and wished she could turn the clock back to a time when she did not doubt who she was and where her place should be.

A moment later, a voice spoke behind her. "You look heated, my little fire-eater. Care for a stroll on the terrace?"

His breath stirred the curls at her nape, sending an anticipatory shiver down her spine. Gemma turned and glanced past Sebastian's shoulder at her aunt, but Matilda was too focused on the hand being dealt her to notice. Bellamy had taken Sebastian's place at the card table with Sybil stationed beside him, a neat reversal of their positions at the pianoforte.

"Yes, please." Gemma took his arm.

As they moved towards the French doors that opened onto the terrace, Gemma caught her mother's sober regard. Gracious! Did Sybil actually disapprove of her going apart with Sebastian? Sybil Maitland preaching propriety. Wonders would never cease.

Gemma lifted her chin and marched out on Sebastian's arm into the moonlit night.

"You are very severe," he said.

She released him, folded her arms and quickened her pace, heading towards the stone steps that led to the gardens. She wanted to run.

"I have reason to be severe!" she said over her shoulder, as he lengthened his stride to keep up. "They all behave as though it were an everyday occurrence for my mother to bring her . . . her *cicisbeo* to Ware. What is the matter with them? Even my aunt remains in the same room with him, playing whist, of all things! Why on earth . . ." Gemma gasped and her hand flew to her mouth. She halted and faced Sebastian. "Oh, no."

He bent to look level into her eyes. "What?"

"Scovy, she is going to marry him. Charles Bellamy is going to be my father!"

Sebastian straightened, a smile playing about his lips. "Lord, won't that set the cat among the pigeons?"

"Oh, do be serious! He cannot possibly want to tie himself to a woman so many years his senior." She curled her hand into a fist and struck her palm. "He must be after her money."

Sebastian leaned against the balustrade and considered her. "I doubt it. Your mother is a desirable woman and will continue to be one at any age, I suspect."

Gemma fell silent and stared out at the glimmering lake. She swallowed the lump in her throat. "Yes, she is very beautiful."

He pushed away from the balustrade and moved towards her. "Well, there is beauty, and then there is that indefinable something about a woman that will make her desirable regardless of how regular her features are. True, your mother is very lovely, but even when the angles of her face blur and the colour of her hair fades, there will always be something about her that entices men to . . . make fools of themselves over her."

He stood very close. There was a shaft of moonlight between them but nothing more and suddenly, she had the oddest feeling he was not really talking about her mother.

Sebastian's gaze traced her face, her throat, flickered to

her breasts, then returned to fix on her mouth. She rather thought she should feel embarrassed or ashamed, but instead she felt drawn. In the back of her mind, she wondered whether women would still make fools of themselves over Sebastian twenty years from now.

Probably.

He bent towards her. She couldn't breathe. "Don't you wonder what it would be like?" he whispered, so softly, in her ear.

"It?" She hardly dared imagine what he might mean.

He drew back and smiled, that old, sweet smile. "If I kissed you, would you punch me on the nose?"

"Gracious," she breathed, alarmed, elated, mildly triumphant. Her nerves jangled and clamoured, threatening to jump out of her skin. "No. No, I don't think I would."

"Well, then."

His bent head blocked the moon, then his mouth drifted over hers, gossamer-light. Gently, he tugged her bottom lip, and she exhaled a shivery breath. She hesitated, unsure of what to do, her pleasure in his touch tempered by anxiety. Then his lips settled to a tantalising rhythm, and apprehension drowned in a flood of pure delight. She kissed him back, and he angled his mouth over hers, not touching her at all except with those warm, skillful lips.

Her hands lifted of their own accord, but when he still made no move to put his arms around her, she let them fall by her side, anxious to follow his lead, desperate not to give herself away.

Her body ached to sway to his, her fingers trembled with the effort of keeping from his thick, wavy hair; from trailing over his shoulders; from cupping the back of his head; pressing his mouth harder against hers.

All of these things she concealed from him, while she melted and thrilled and quivered inside. Just from a kiss.

Vaguely, she recalled she had told Sebastian she was

accustomed to kisses. Was this why he had been so bold? Or had he perceived that tonight she needed this, even if she had barely known it herself?

It hardly mattered. Perhaps when he stopped, it would, but at the moment, it didn't, and she was glad.

His hands touched her then, bracketed her face, threaded fingers lightly through her hair. Her entire body shuddered at that simple caress. The urge to abandon herself to him was so strong, it frightened her.

She placed her palm against his chest, uncertain whether she meant to push him away or feel the hammer of his heart. On a groan, Sebastian deepened the kiss and the sudden hardening of the mouth devouring hers made the ground swing beneath her feet. She swayed and his strong arms closed around her. She opened her mouth to him and his tongue swept past her lips to touch hers.

She gasped and jerked back at the flagrant intimacy. He raised his head and released her, his breathing fast, a little harsh. "Come to Laidley with me."

She blinked, trying to clear the fog.

"Why?" A disingenuous question, she supposed, but she wanted to know if this time, the invitation was connected to this kiss in his mind as it was in hers. And whether there would be more where that one came from.

He reached out and grazed the line of her jaw with his knuckles. She shivered, though the night was warm. He did not answer her, and in the half-darkness she could not make out the subtleties of his expression, but the gentle sweep of his fingers told her what she needed to know.

He wanted her. How and why he wanted her, she knew not. But it was so very long since she had felt wanted.

Everything had changed at Ware. Hugo loved her in his own way, but he believed he did not need her to run the estate. He was wrong, of course, she knew that. But the way he had publicly demonstrated his views by employing an agent to take over her duties had hurt her heart and her pride, as well.

Add to that her mother's obvious devotion to Bellamy, a devotion Gemma had craved from Sybil all her life, and suddenly, her existence at Ware had become almost too painful to bear. If she stayed, she would be obliged to bear it, goodness knew for how long. Perhaps until the next London Season drew Sybil back to town.

Yet, here was Sebastian, making her feel desirable, necessary, *alive* as she had never felt before. Tantalising her with kisses. Asking her to come away, to leave the pain of Ware behind.

She stared up at him, so tall and darkly handsome in the moonlight, and an unfamiliar yearning tinged with excitement rose within her. She wanted to go with him, she realised. Just for a handful of short weeks to prolong this wonderful feeling. Was that so wrong of her?

As she stood there, wavering, Sebastian dropped his hand to the small of her back and pulled her closer. The warmth of his breath fluttered over her cheek.

"Say yes." He turned his head and swiftly recaptured her mouth.

The kiss ended almost as soon as it began. But in that brief contact, his lips scalded hers, and the heat swelled and crashed through her body, firing her yearning to a desperate need, incinerating her doubts.

Before she could change her mind, she answered.

"Yes."

Gemma sensed, rather than saw his satisfaction. It was a fleeting impression, but it bothered her. She jerked her head away and stepped back.

Fighting to regain her balance, she cleared her throat. "Well, now that's settled, shall we go back inside? There is much I must attend to before I leave. Shall we say, the day after tomorrow?"

She was breathy and babbling like some silly innocent. Sebastian's teeth gleamed in a smug smile that made her want to hit him.

"But of course." He bowed and followed her close until they slipped back inside.

Sybil gave them a sharp glance when they returned. Gemma could barely meet her mother's eye. Her cheeks warmed with embarrassment and that made her scowl. Why should she hang her head at her mother's disapproval? Sybil had done far worse, and at a younger age.

Gemma glanced around to see whether anyone else had noted their absence, but the turn of the cards held the others in thrall, just as Sebastian had held her on the terrace, in the moonlight.

She sighed. True romance had not come her way very often. She had not attended public assemblies since her teens, and the great houses neighbouring Ware proliferated with married men and spotty youths down from Eton or Harrow. Some of the latter had been disposed to admire her, but it was calf-love, and Gemma knew how to turn that potentially dangerous emotion into friendship. She liked men, and if their wives did not guard them so jealously she might have enjoyed more of their company.

She had not understood why the local matrons were so vigilant against her, until she received a grossly improper offer from one woman's husband. Though the shock of it had left her sick and mortified, she had handled the situation as best she could. But she learned a valuable lesson. The men in the district considered Sybil Maitland's daughter fair game.

And that was why it seemed like the outside of enough for Sybil to preach propriety to her now. She had no precise knowledge of her mother's misdemeanours, but she had suffered for them all her adult life. More, perhaps, than Sybil herself, and certainly with less justification. Now, Sybil stood at Bellamy's side watching the cards, one delicate hand resting on his shoulder. She appeared serene and happy, without a care in the world.

As the evening progressed, and Sybil's affection for Bellamy grew ever more marked, Gemma thanked the stars she had agreed to go to Laidley. Though Sybil had spoken of taking up residence in Kensington, the house would not be habitable for another month or two. The interior was at present receiving a complete refurbishment. Sybil would not set foot inside until all was finished, the smell of new paint gone, and a full staff complete with majordomo and French cook installed awaiting her pleasure.

"I have quite a menagerie, too," she added with a bland smile. "The Duchess of York sent me a pair of sloths to breed from, only fancy! What I shall do with a litter of the creatures, I have no idea. They just seem to hang about doing nothing all day. Not the sort of life I should choose. . . ." A fluttering hand alighted on Gemma's knee. "But you must come and visit me when you are in town, my dear. I should like it above all things!"

Not if he *is going to be there.* "I should be charmed, Mama, but I do not expect to visit London in the near future."

Sybil glanced at Sebastian. "Oh? Well, one never knows what the future may bring."

Gemma shook her head. "My future is here."

※

"So now you may tell me what you are up to, if you please." Sybil's polished fingernails drummed the balustrade. She did not glance at him as she spoke.

Sebastian raised an eyebrow. Once Talbot had left and everyone else retired to bed, he had drifted out to the terrace. He told himself it was to think, but really it had been to relive that amazing kiss.

"Up to?"

She turned and looked him in the eye. "What do you want with my daughter?"

Here was plain speaking. Well, two could play that game. Sebastian shrugged. "What do you want with yon sprig Bellamy?"

She laughed, a harsh, mirthless sound. "You have no business asking me that. I am Gemma's mother. I have a right to know what you mean by her."

He regarded her for a moment. "But I am her friend, ma'am," he said softly. "And it seems to me you forfeited that right many years ago. Furthermore, I would not see her hurt, nor drawn into the company you keep. You should not have brought Bellamy here."

Sybil's eyes darted fire.

Strangely, this woman was magnificent, patently beddable. But she did not come close to touching his emotions. Not like her daughter did.

Sybil's eyes narrowed to slits and her lips thinned. Her teeth flashed in the dark. "You know nothing, *nothing* of me!"

Her voice was a low whisper, but the vehemence in her tone intrigued him. He would never have guessed such strength lay beneath that fragile shell of femininity.

"I may not always have been here, but I know my daughter, my lord." She pointed a slender finger in his face. "And if you hurt her, Sebastian Laidley, so help me I will kill you."

Seven

GEMMA spent the day before they left Ware preparing for her absence. She banished all thought of Sebastian's kiss.

But the memory returned from exile at the most inconvenient moments—while discussing a new roof for the piggery at the home farm or approving an order of coal for the coming winter. Even the difficult question of evicting a drunken lout of a tenant whose rent was shamefully in arrears could not entirely absorb her. Her grandfather's agent must have coughed himself hoarse, he cleared his throat so often to recapture her wandering attention.

Despite her fractured concentration, when Mr. Porter left her, Gemma felt as confident as she could that all was in hand. The harvest was well under way and the men knew what followed better than she did. She chewed her lip and stared out the window at the fields. This would be the first harvest feast she had missed since she was thirteen.

After anxious consideration, she decided to entrust the

household accounts to Mrs. Jenkins. The housekeeper surprised her by saying Reeves had taught her how to figure, and together they would muddle along somehow in the months their mistress was away.

All at once, Gemma felt superfluous, but the afternoon brought with it a number of difficulties and disputes to resolve in the village and that made her worried about the effects of her absence all over again. She spent the remaining hours torn between the fear they would never cope without her and the greater fear that they would.

With these matters arranged to the best of her ability, Gemma paid her final call on the Lanes. Satisfied that old Mrs. Lane seemed improved, though still pitiably weak, she accepted the Lanes' good wishes for a safe journey and left the cottage.

As she closed the gate behind her and set off for Mainwaring Hall, Gemma saw John Talbot standing by an elegant phaeton a little farther up the road. She did not need to see their faces to realise the occupants of the phaeton were Sarah Briggs and Jenny Whitton. They had turned their backs on her so many times before.

When she reached the group, she greeted the three of them with a determined, friendly smile. "I was just saying my last farewells. I leave for Lord Carleton's estate in the morning, you know."

The two ladies raised their brows and exchanged knowing glances, but made no comment.

Talbot cleared his throat. "Yes. Yes, I did know." His gaze darted away from her as he spoke and his shoulders tensed. He looked poised for escape.

She tilted her head to study him, trying to discover the source of his discomfiture. "Is everything all right, John? Are you well?"

Pink flooded his face, making his shifting eyes seem a brighter blue. Fidgeting with his watch chain, he stared at a point behind her left ear, as if she did not exist. "Perfectly, thank you. Good day to you, Miss Maitland. Ladies." He tipped his hat, spun on his heel, and strode away.

Gemma stared after him, at a loss. Had she offended him? He had seemed his usual self the previous evening. Now, he did not seem to want to acknowledge her acquaintance. What had happened in the meantime?

"Your aunt is before you with the news, Miss Maitland," cooed a voice from above her. Gemma looked up, to see a smirk on Jenny Whitton's china-doll face.

"So your infamous mama has arrived at Ware to stay." Jenny slid a sly, sideways glance at her friend. "And brought a handsome young . . . ah . . . *friend* with her, too."

Sarah Briggs inclined her head, her thin lips quivering. "How fortunate you are in your connections, Miss Maitland. So *colourful*." The two ladies tittered as they drove away, allowing Gemma no opportunity to answer. Which was probably fortunate, because the many retorts that sprang to mind were grossly impolite.

With a last, murderous look after the retreating phaeton, Gemma turned and walked briskly in the other direction. She should have guessed how it would be. Having panted after her like an eager puppy for months, John had all but cut her acquaintance. One whiff of her mother's past, thoughtfully embellished by the bonneted dragons, and the coward took to his heels.

It was a wonder he had not heard of Sybil Maitland before, but John was a recent arrival in the district and it took the people of Ware years before they warmed sufficiently to newcomers to gossip with them. No doubt this morsel had been too juicy for Jenny and Sarah to keep to themselves.

Gemma ripped off her hat and swatted at a fly that buzzed round her as she trudged the two-mile walk back to the Hall. She had not wanted John Talbot as a suitor. In fact, she had tried her best to hold him at a distance, but his rejection hurt more than she had thought possible.

Why did she keep hoping things might be different? By now, she should know not to put her faith in human nature, but she kept falling into that same trap. And she was disappointed every time.

Gemma blew out a shaky breath. She could almost be glad she was leaving Ware.

On a small rise, she paused to look down at the golden expanse of her home, as she had done so many times, with a thrilling sense of ownership and pride. But she had no real stake in Ware, and little hope of ever convincing Hugo to give her one unless she showed him how much Ware needed her. Rising profits, the good heart of the land, and the general contentment of its people had not convinced him. Perhaps her absence would.

For once, she shortened her walk and cut through the fields. She fitted her hat on her head and climbed over a stile that led to a meadow. Raising a hand to greet the workers cutting wheat in the next field, she tramped through the sweet-smelling grass. Her habit was a trifle heavy for this weather. The grey broadcloth absorbed the sunshine and its high military collar itched her throat. By the time she reached Mainwaring Hall, she felt hot, thirsty, and considerably bruised in spirit.

As she sipped the sweet, tart lemonade Reeves brought her, Gemma realised she looked forward to her journey to Laidley. Since Sebastian arrived, her ordinary life at Ware had begun to seem a little stifling, if she must be honest.

She traced through the droplets of moisture on the outside of her glass with one gloved finger. Was it very stupid of her to want to be with him a little while longer? She did not mind being alone, but she did not want to end up alone and lonely, dissatisfied and bitter like her aunt.

She could not rely on her mother for companionship, that much was clear. Gemma set her glass down and removed her York tan gloves, easing them off one finger at a time. Sybil seemed further distanced from Gemma than she had ever been, despite her intention to remain in England. Aside from that first discussion upon Sybil's arrival, Gemma had not caught the chance to speak with her alone. Bellamy shadowed Sybil's every movement, as though he could not bear to let her out of his sight. Perhaps he did love her, after all.

Or perhaps he did not wish to give Gemma the chance to present a case against him.

She handed the butler her empty glass. "Where is everyone, Reeves?"

"Sir Hugo is in the library, miss. His lordship and Mr. Bellamy have gone riding, and Miss Mainwaring is paying calls."

"And Mama?"

"In the rose arbour, I believe."

"Thank you." She jabbed her hairpins through the hat, handed it to him with her gloves, and walked out onto the terrace and down the steps. Rounding the corner, she followed the gravel path to the walled garden, where her mother sat on a rustic bench, twirling a Pomona green parasol and staring with a faint frown into the distance.

"Stop that, Mama, or you will give yourself wrinkles." Gemma walked towards her and inhaled the sweet scent of roses. Sybil was like a rose. Soft, fragrant, heart-wrenchingly beautiful, but try to hold her too tight and she pricked your hand.

Sybil laughed. A merry, musical laugh, not the artificial titter many ladies affected. But then, the graces other ladies studied with anxious diligence came as easily as breathing to Sybil Maitland.

"Who cares for wrinkles?" Sybil patted the seat next to her. "Come sit by me, darling. Isn't this sunshine glorious? Who could be out of sorts on such a day?"

Gemma suppressed a sigh. This mood did not augur

well for the discussion she had in mind. She sat next to her mother and tried to frame a sentence introducing the subject of Bellamy, but the words would not come.

"Darling, I am glad you are here because I think we should have a talk." Sybil's hand fluttered over Gemma's. "I am worried about you."

The world suddenly spun in reverse. "*You* are worried about *me*, Mama?"

"Yes, and I must speak before you go. You do not mind, do you darling? Only, I could not let you leave with Sebastian if I did not warn you."

Gemma put up a hand to forestall her. "I know what you are going to say. Sebastian is supposed to be a terrible rake, but—"

"No, that was *not* what I was going to say. I am quite sure you are up to snuff and you know he did not get a reputation like that from sitting at home twiddling his thumbs. But reputations can be misleading, my dear. No one knows that better than I."

A large, brown grasshopper sprang onto Sybil's lap. She did not even flinch, but brushed it off with the handle of her parasol and watched interestedly as it flickered its wings and flew away.

Gemma frowned. Her head began to ache. "Are you warning me that Sebastian may turn out *not* to be a rake?"

Sybil laughed. "Good God, no! Just that seduction is not the only thing you must be wary of, that is all. Sebastian has led a certain mode of life for a few years but his character was formed much earlier than that. The face he shows to the world is not the real one. I am persuaded he is not as careless as he seems."

"But isn't that a good thing?"

"Well of course not! Oh, lud, I am making a mess of this." Sybil sighed. "What I *mean* to say is that regardless of how he behaves with all his *ton* friends, Sebastian is a young man of deep, strong passions. Do not play with fire, my dear, unless you are sure that you wish to be burned. And I do not mean lovemaking—I know you are too sensible to let it go that far. But I also know he kissed you on the terrace last night."

Gemma felt herself flush, pink as the roses climbing the wall behind her, no doubt. "How—"

Sybil grimaced. "I recognised the look on your face. Goodness knows I have seen it often enough on my own. But it would be folly to follow my example, you know. And I should be criminal if I did not advise you against it."

She snapped her parasol shut. "Now, that John Talbot seems a solid sort of fellow, and his land marches with ours. I should think he would make you an excellent husband."

Yes, but he knows who you are and now he does not want me.

Sybil observed Gemma with a faint smile, reached over and gently stroked her cheek. "Have your fun at Laidley, my dear. Lord knows you have had little enough of that buried alive in this place. But make sure at the end of it you can forget this foolish link with Sebastian and be content without him. Because you can never be comfortable with a man like that. It is all uphill and down-dale with them."

"Whereas Mr. Talbot is a nice, smooth, flat road," said Gemma.

Sybil beamed. "Exactly so! Believe me, you will be less likely to come to grief if you choose that course." She paused. "You will have to marry someone, you know, darling. Hugo will never make you mistress of Ware."

The familiar pain burned Gemma's chest. "Everyone says that, but I have no idea why it should be. I have given Ware my all and still, it is not enough."

"That is not the issue. You have done an excellent job of helping your grandfather with the estate. But Hugo wants to see you happy with your own family about you." She clasped Gemma's hand. "He is a stubborn old man, my dear, but in

this I think he is wise. You must not close your mind to marriage."

Gemma looked away. It was impossible to confront
Mama with the truth. That no gentleman would marry the
daughter of a notorious *femme fatale*. He might have other
uses for her, but giving her his name would never enter his
plans. Gentlemen saved marriage proposals for ladies with
reputations and pedigrees above reproach. And if Sybil
now meant to create more talk by marrying a man more
than twenty years her junior, there would be even less hope
for Gemma than before.

"I do not see you taking your own advice, Mama," she
said lightly, trying to turn the subject.

For an instant, Sybil's smile froze. Then she gave her
slow, sensual smile. "Oh," she said. "You may be sure, my
dear, that I have never been lonely."

She dug the point of her parasol into the gravel at her
feet and rose. "Do let us go in. I must change my gown before Charles comes back."

INVIGORATED after their strenuous ride, Sebastian left
Hugo's well-kept stables with Bellamy and strolled up to
the house.

He had shown the younger man all of his and Gemma's
old haunts as they hacked about the neighbouring countryside. Revisiting them was like stepping back to his youth,
to a time when he had not thought beyond the moment.
Now, everything seemed planned, controlled. Even the
lighter side of his life followed a pattern almost monoto-
nous in its predictability. He anticipated the end of each affair before it began, and his *amours* grew ever shorter and
more frequent. He did not believe he had broken any
hearts, though. He preferred his women without them.

But Gemma owned a heart as big as the sun, so what
had he been about last night? He hardly knew. She had

looked so lost and angry standing there at the drawing room window, his first thought had been to take her mind off a kind of misery that simply did not have a place in her life. He should not have kissed her, had not meant to advance the kiss further than a brief, chaste touch of the lips. But her response had been so free, so quintessentially Gemma, desire had flamed within him and he could not let her go.

He remembered Gemma telling him she had experience of kisses. Had she kissed other men like that? Sebastian hacked his whip at a blameless daffodil. He did not want to think about it.

He could not let it happen again. She had disturbed something in him he had thought was dead and buried, something he had been content to let rest. He did not want her rousing it further. He must leave her be.

They reached the south lawn, and Bellamy's voice broke his thoughts. "Now this is a pleasing prospect! Is that a Roman ruin on the other side of the lake?"

Sebastian followed the direction of his gaze. "The folly? Nothing so romantic, I'm afraid. I believe Sir Hugo's father had it built. We used it as a boathouse."

"Such gentle countryside, so green and welcoming," murmured Bellamy. "Yes, I believe I *could* live here."

Sebastian's brows snapped together. "What do you mean, you could live here? There is no question of you living here."

Bellamy turned to face Sebastian, then his gaze shifted and slid away. "It was merely a figure of speech. I meant, of course, that I could quite easily live in the English countryside. Countryside like this."

Sebastian did not believe him. It was time to get to the bottom of this mystery. "But aren't you removing to a little house in Kensington in a month or two?"

"Oh, no, I . . . Well, that is to say . . ."

Sebastian cocked an eyebrow. "Prefer to keep separate lodgings, do you? I admire your forethought."

Bellamy stiffened. "I do not take your meaning, my lord."

Smiling, Sebastian balanced on the balls of his feet. "Easier to come and go more freely that way, wouldn't you say? Always a sound policy to have more than one string to your bow when it comes to women."

When Bellamy's fist flew towards him, he was ready for it, and dodged. The boy must mean marriage, then. Gemma would soon call Bellamy "Papa."

"Good Lord!" Sebastian stepped back out of range and held up his hands in a conciliating gesture. "I see I've entirely misjudged the situation. Pray accept my apologies and forget I mentioned it." He bowed and turned, ready to continue on their way.

"Am—am I to call you a coward, my lord?"

Sebastian froze. Slowly, he turned back. "I beg your pardon?"

Fear darted across Bellamy's bronzed face, but he stood his ground, fists clenched by his side. "I believe you heard what I said. Are you a coward?"

Softly, Sebastian replied, "If you cannot tell the difference between a sincere apology and cowardice, then I might just have to show you. Take off your coat."

Bellamy's fingers already fumbled at his buttons. He yanked one arm free. "With pleasure, my lord."

Stripping was no easy feat for either gentleman. If Bellamy had not been white-lipped and shaking with rage, Sebastian could have laughed at the sheer ludicrousness of them both struggling out of their tight-fitting coats before having at one another on Hugo's lawn.

He eyed the younger man critically. Perhaps the lad's prettiness had misled him, for now as he looked closer, he realised Bellamy was well up to his own weight. Sebastian pulled off his gloves, blood rushing at the prospect of a good fight.

His challenger barely waited for him to throw down his hat before charging at him with far more energy than science.

Sebastian blocked and feinted and sparred, gauging his op-
ponent's skill, giving Bellamy time to master his fury. This
youth's obsessive passion reminded him of himself at that
age.

"Keep your head still, for pity's sake," he ordered, when
Bellamy took another wild swing.

He had meant it as friendly advice, but his words acted as
a goad. Bellamy's golden eyes flashed and he rained blows
on Sebastian, blows that met with nothing but air and fists.

A shout came from the terrace. "Scovy! What on earth?"
Distracted, Sebastian's gaze flickered upwards and Bellamy landed a glancing punch to his cheekbone.

Sebastian staggered and palmed his stinging cheek.
"Damn it, Gemma." He ducked another of Bellamy's swings,
and put up his guard. "Go away! Can't you see we are sparring? Bellamy here is just getting the hang of it, but he is
glaringly abroad. Hardly a sight for ladies."

"Scovy, stop! Right this minute."

"Go into the house, Gemma." Sebastian wanted to end
it, but he did not wish to do that while Gemma stood by.
She always turned queasy at the sight of claret and he had
a mind to draw Bellamy's cork. Letting some of that hot
blood might calm him down a trifle.

As Sebastian wove and jabbed, he heard nothing more
and assumed that for once, Gemma had obeyed him.

Until a pair of small hands caught his upper arm and
hung on with all their might.

As Sebastian pivoted to regain his balance, Bellamy's
flailing right hook connected with his jaw and knocked
him clear off his feet, sending Gemma with him.

They landed on the turf with a double "Oomph!"

Sebastian tasted blood, and his jaw screamed agony. He
opened his eyes to the blue sky and groaned.

"Miss Maitland, are you hurt?" Bellamy's anxious voice
sounded above them.

"No, I'm perfectly well," said Gemma. Panting, she

wriggled from beneath Sebastian's arm and raised herself on one elbow. "No, don't help me up. I just want to stay here for a moment and catch my . . . catch my breath."

Out of the corner of his eye, Sebastian watched her do just that, with a pleasantly heaving bosom and her wondrous, bright hair snaking about her shoulders. She glanced at him and their gazes melded and time stood still. He could lose himself forever in those midnight eyes.

Bellamy's voice snapped Sebastian out of his trance. "My lord, I am truly sorry. I did not see Miss Maitland there, or I would not have . . ."

Sebastian squinted up at him. For the moment, he'd forgotten the fellow was still there. "Oh, the devil, go away! Haven't you done enough?"

"With all due respect, my lord, if you had not impugned the honour of the sweetest, most blameless lady, I should not—"

Gemma gasped. Sebastian felt her wide gaze upon him. "Scovy?"

He dragged his palm down the good side of his face and mumbled something deliberately incoherent. The prospect of confessing he had insulted Gemma's mama did not appeal. Wincing at the throb in his jaw, he slowly raised himself to a less supine position. "I trust you are satisfied, Bellamy. Or shall I ask my friends to wait on yours?"

"A duel won't be necessary, my lord. If you do not require my assistance, Miss Maitland, I shall bid you good afternoon."

Sebastian watched Bellamy collect his accoutrements with shaky dignity and stalk towards the house. Avoiding Gemma's gaze, Sebastian collapsed, closed his eyes . . .

And waited for the next blow to fall.

A tender hand touched his cheek. "Your poor face! I'm so sorry, Scovy. I did not think."

Relief made him wheeze a laugh. Always expect the unexpected with Gemma. "Oh, don't mention it! I doubt

Bellamy is proud of milling me down with a woman's help. He certainly could not have done it without you."

"Are you so good, then?"

"No, he was truly awful."

"Hmm." And I suppose if I ask you what the fight was about, you will say it is none of my affair?"

He should have known he would never be safe. Gloomily, he replied, "That is the line I should like to take, but I doubt it would do any good."

"None at all," she answered cheerfully. "But it can wait, I daresay." She patted his arm. "Let's get that pretty face of yours seen to."

"Pretty?" He grimaced. "I'd prefer ruggedly handsome."

"Mm, no."

He quirked a brow. "Devilishly attractive?"

She grinned and shook her head. "Your jaw looks like a squashed plum. I shall put some ointment on it if you like."

He rose painfully to his feet and followed her.

Gemma as ministering angel. The idea struck him as delightfully erotic. Watching the slight sway of her hips as she walked ahead of him towards the terrace steps, the devil in him wondered if he could persuade her to tend to *all* his aches.

He groaned. Of course not. Gemma was a gently bred lady, not some light-skirt in the green room at Drury Lane. If he did not stop thinking of her that way, he would compromise them both, and then he'd have to marry her.

Ironic, that. Marriage would be the perfect damper for this charge of attraction fizzing between them. Delight would turn to duty the moment he said "I do."

As they mounted the steps, he recalled the interview he had denied his steward in London before he left for Ware, all the myriad obligations awaiting his attention once he returned to Laidley. His mother's troubled, confused face rose before his mind's eye and a mixture of guilt and defiance washed over him. He was not responsible for the way things were between them. Any chance they had to make things right was lost when Andy died.

He sighed. He had no wish to go back. He almost wished Gemma had not relented so soon.

He paused at the top of the stairs and gazed over the patchworked fields with their neat hedgerow borders, to the lake all golden and glittering in the afternoon sun.

Frowning, he ran a hand through his dishevelled hair. He had not given much thought to how Gemma would survive her months at his ancestral pile. London in the Season would have been better, infinitely so. The house in Berkley Square had somehow escaped his father's bitter taint. In town he might have left the task of snaring Gemma a husband in his sister's hands and not spent more than one evening in ten at home.

But Laidley was different. He could not leave Gemma to fend for herself there. He could not count on a ready supply of suitors eager to pluck the newest heiress from the marital tree. He would have to apply himself to the task of finding her a husband. Once she was safely betrothed and out of his sight, he might then apply himself to the task of forgetting her.

The thought made him clench his jaw.

A blade of pain sliced through him, punishing him for his folly. Putting his fingertips to the hinge of his jaw, he opened and closed his mouth a few times, almost relishing the pain the movement caused.

He needed to stop this growing obsession with Gemma, nip it in the bud before it burgeoned out of control. Perhaps a stay at Laidley was exactly what he needed—a blanket of gloom to smother this blossoming tenderness, damp down this flaming desire.

Gemma waited for Sebastian to take his last look at a Sussex sunset and wondered what he was thinking. His shoulders bowed a little before he straightened and walked towards her. Her brow furrowed in concern.

The truth was, she felt utterly mortified at what she had done. Interfering in a fight? She knew better than that. Only, for some stupid reason, when she saw Sebastian coolly toying with Bellamy, the need to protect the younger man had made her launch herself at Sebastian without thinking.

Grandpapa would be disgusted. *She* was disgusted. How did she think to step into Hugo's shoes if she could not observe the gentlemanly code? She should have known neither man would thank her for her interference.

She saw Sebastian working at his jaw. "Does it pain you very much? Come down to the kitchens. Cook will have something you can put on your face."

"No need," he said, brushing past her. "I will attend to it myself."

His brusque tone winded her like a punch to the stomach. Obviously she was not forgiven. "Scovy!" She hurried after him, into the dim hall. "Scovy, I said I was sorry. I will not do it again."

"What?" He had set one foot on the stair, but he turned at that, looking at her oddly. "Oh. The fight." He hesitated. "Well, just see that you don't."

FORTUNATELY, no one carried the tale of that afternoon's doings to Aunt Matilda, or she would have dealt Gemma a severe scold. Gemma had hoped Matilda would be too caught up in her silent battle with Sybil over household tasks to remember her duty and accompany Gemma to Laidley. However, when Gemma joined the other ladies in the drawing room after dinner, it became clear that Matilda had not forgotten.

"Sebastian most *particularly* desired me to accompany Gemma to Laidley," said Matilda in a quavering voice that bordered on the shrill. "There can be no *question* of sending only her maid."

Sybil raised her brows and smiled. "I believe I know what

is best for my daughter, Aunt Matilda, dear. And just think, who will run the household while Gemma is not by if you do not? Hugo needs you. Dorry is a steady, sensible woman, perfectly adequate protection for the journey, and Sebastian's mama will chaperone Gemma while she remains at Laidley. I do not think there is any more to discuss."

"But Sebastian—"

Sibyl gave a delicate laugh. "Oh, Matilda! If you mean to hold up Sebastian Laidley as the arbiter of what is right and proper, I must begin to fear for your wits."

"All the more reason for me to go with her," hissed Matilda. "That man is wicked, depraved. He cannot be trusted with our dearest girl."

The debate went on, but Gemma took no part. She did not doubt the outcome. Snatching up her embroidery, she stabbed her needle through the linen, thinking it really did not matter who chaperoned her, they might place absolute trust in Sebastian keeping the line. He had not spoken a syllable more than necessary to her all through dinner, and when she had attempted to joke him out of the sullens, his bruised, handsome face could have been fashioned from granite for all the response he gave.

By contrast, his manner towards Bellamy bordered on brotherly. Incomprehensible, the ways of men.

It was not just her interference in the fight that bothered him, Gemma thought, as the rumble of deep voices heralded the gentlemen's entrance. There was something else, but what?

Sebastian tried to appear unaware of the dusky blue eyes that followed him as he moved around the room, but ever since he had resolved to stay away from her, his wayward senses did nothing but seek Gemma out. The cadence of her voice wove through the general chatter and ripple of the pianoforte to caress his ear. Her scent, the fresh scent of spring, seemed to surround him, even when she was not near. He could not look at her without wanting to touch her, to soothe that troubled crease from her brow, trail his fingers over her lips, and throat.

He closed his eyes.

The best effort he could make at self-preservation was to place a buffer between them, but soon he realised his attempt to thrust Matilda into the breach had not met with success. Sybil Maitland watched him assimilate this with a smile of delicious satisfaction, like a cat presented with a brimming pot of cream. What was the woman playing at? Was she unaware of her daughter's danger, or did she think she had scared him off with her warning last night?

Feigning interest in the sonata Matilda played with surprising skill and feeling, Sebastian tried not to remember Gemma's kiss, the sheer rightness and delicate power of her embrace. How could he be so comfortable with a woman and yet so excited by her at the same time? In his previous experience, the two had been mutually exclusive.

Why try to analyse it? There was no future for them together. If he could turn back the clock, undo every decadent, reckless folly he had committed since Andy died, they might still have a chance. But he had moved far beyond that innocent, ardent boy she thought she knew. That boy no longer existed, and a hardened, heartless rake had taken his place. She would not heed the rumours, but she would find out soon enough for herself. Sebastian gazed at that untouched, vibrant beauty, and his black heart bled for her, for one day she would realise that everything they said about him was true.

❦

LATER that evening, Gemma put her head around the library door. "Grandpapa?"

Hugo sat in his favourite wingback chair by the fire, a book open on his lap, though he did not appear to be reading it. He turned his head to look at her, and his rare smile clutched at Gemma's heart. In the preparations for her departure, she had almost forgotten she would be leaving him, as well as Ware. A rush of affection flooded her. She ran to sit in a flurry of muslin skirts at his feet.

They remained like that in silence, staring into the flames. For so long, it had been just the two of them, together against the world. Gemma had a notion that for better or for worse, that was about to change. This last night, she wanted to tell him how much he meant to her.

He was the only one who had never left.

But she could not put it into words, and knew he would not want to hear them even if she could. It was enough to sit quietly with him in the firelight, to sense that he understood.

After a while, Gemma began to drowse. Vaguely, she wondered whether she should go to bed, when a trembling hand touched her hair.

"Gemma."

She tilted back her head to look at him. "Yes?"

The hooded dark eyes held a faint frown. His free hand clenched and unclenched. She laid hers upon it.

"What troubles you, Grandpapa?"

His mouth twisted. "Maudlin nonsense, that's all."

She smiled and brought his hand to her cheek. "I shall miss you, too, Grandpapa."

His trembling fingers clenched around hers. "Gemma, you're a good girl. Young, beautiful. You should not be tied to an old man." He paused, before muttering, "I just hope to God I've done right this time."

After Sebastian's recent coldness, Gemma could have echoed that hope on her own account. But she raised her chin, not allowing a shadow of her doubt to cross her face. "It was my decision to go to Laidley, Grandpapa. Please, do not fret yourself. I shall write to you, and you have Aunt Matilda and Mama and—and Bellamy to keep you company. I shall be back before you know I am gone."

Eight

❦

Storm clouds gathered in a dense mass low on the horizon. As Gemma's chaise rounded a bend, the clouds seemed to thicken, solidify, and resolve into a hulking expanse of grey stone.

Laidley. The Earl of Carleton's principal seat.

The chaise bowled under the arch of a crenellated gatehouse and down the straight, chestnut-lined drive. On either side, the jewel-green lawns of the park sprawled forever, and a scattered herd of deer gently raised their heads to watch the intruders pass.

There was a faint, salt tang in the wind that buffeted Gemma's bonnet as she let down the window. Ignoring Dorry's protest, she leaned out a little way to study Sebastian's home.

Imposing. Vast. Sombre.

Benighted, more like. Laidley stood closed and impenetrable, as though it had hoarded dark secrets for hundreds of years. She sat back against the cushions and tucked her wind-whipped hair back under her bonnet. A shiver ran down her spine, despite the day's warmth. Gemma chuckled and cursed her penchant for gothic romance.

Sebastian had ridden ahead to warn of their arrival. He had barely spoken to her beyond strict necessity since they left Ware. Not for the first time, Gemma wondered why she had travelled all this way and left Ware, her bright, beloved home.

For what? she would like to know. To show Hugo how much Ware needed her? To help with Lady Fanny's wedding? Or on the faint, illusory promise of a kiss?

The carriage swept around the circular drive, then slowed and drew to a gentle halt.

As the footman opened the carriage door and folded down the steps for her to alight, Gemma tried to quell the uneasy fluttering in her stomach. Not an auspicious beginning. None of the family was there to greet her, not even Sebastian.

They will show you no mercy.

Remembering her aunt's words, Gemma realised she had given little thought to any of the inhabitants of this place besides her old playmate.

Sebastian only had one sister, Fanny, who was about to be married. Andrew, the eldest, had died in a sailing accident off the Cornish coast. Sebastian had rarely spoken about his family, even as a child, so Gemma did not know what to expect. Would she be welcome in this house? She had never been invited here before.

Dorry trudged up the steps as though marching into battle, the ribbons of her sensible grey bonnet fluttering like standards in the brisk wind. She clutched Gemma's dressing case in one mittened hand and muttered to herself, no doubt holding the household up to scrutiny, finding it lacking, and planning a complete rout of the enemy by teatime.

Still, no one came to open the door.

Gemma glanced around and hesitated, as if setting foot on the first step would commit her irrevocably to stay—as if she had not been committed from the time Sebastian had kissed her, whispered that heated plea against her lips, made her promise to come.

Suddenly, the door flung open and he stood above her, looking as grim as the Cornish-quarried stone that framed him. He still wore his riding garb, leather breeches and an oilskin coat, though his head and hands were bare. Had Gemma been a fanciful heroine of a gothic romance, she would have called his appearance sinister. As it was, she squared her shoulders, jammed her bonnet more firmly on her head, and summoned a jaunty grin.

"Gracious, Scovy, had I known you were lord and master of all this, I would have paid more heed to your consequence. But now I see it is all a façade, and you are in fact reduced to performing the duties of your butler."

Sebastian's lips twitched as he jogged down the steps towards her, and she exhaled the breath she had not realised she'd been holding. He flourished a bow and extended his hand. "Welcome to my far-from-humble abode."

She laid her hand in his large, warm one. He smiled at her, and that smile gave her the courage to face whatever lay ahead.

As they entered the house, Sebastian said, "Mama would have been here to greet you, but she has met with a . . . an unfortunate accident. She asks that you excuse her for the moment. My sister is with her, but she will join us directly."

Gemma was too well-bred to inquire further, even of Scovy, about his mother's "accident," so she said nothing and allowed herself to be handed over to a flustered housemaid and conducted to her bedchamber.

The exterior of the house had prepared Gemma somewhat for inside. A heaviness pervaded the great hall, no doubt a result of the bare flagstones, the paucity of windows, and the dark tapestries smothering the walls. To her left, two suits of armour guarded a display of truly barbarous looking weaponry. Swords and axe-heads gleamed dully in the dim light.

Even the atmosphere seemed weighted down, thick with dust and . . . and smoke? Gemma sniffed the air and frowned. If there was one thing she could not abide, it was a smoking chimney. But why would they need fires here in the daytime at the height of summer? Was there an invalid in the house?

She and Dorry followed the maid up the steps and turned left at the landing, where the stair branched in opposite directions. As they continued to the gallery above, a door opened at the top of the stairs across the way.

A billow of smoke rolled into the hall. A man wearing the green livery of a footman shot into the passage, slamming the door behind him. He bent over and put his hands on his knees as he gasped for air.

Gemma stared, but on catching sight of her, the footman straightened, righted his powdered wig, and continued on his way with a majestic, measured tread. His dignity might have been restored completely were it not for the scorch marks on the ragged tails of his coat.

Dorry threw Gemma a glance signalling her intention of discovering the whys and wherefores of this strange behaviour at the first available opportunity. Gemma bit back an answering smile. This was all most intriguing—hardly what she had expected from Sebastian's family. From the scant details he had let fall, she had always imagined them to be pompous and stiff.

However, now was not the time to investigate. They hurried to catch up with the maid, who had continued on, oblivious. After a brisk journey through a series of galleries and corridors, they reached the chamber set aside for Gemma's use.

Gemma ran a critical eye over her new living quarters. She found nothing that could not be fixed with a little concentrated effort. Well, quite a lot of concentrated effort, really, but she had no doubt she and Dorry were up to the challenge.

The rolling burr of the little housemaid's speech broke into her plans for improvement. "Begging your pardon, miss, but there weren't the time to prepare . . ." It was a good thing Sebastian had often indulged his talent for mimicking the local accent, or Gemma would not have made out one word the girl said.

"No, that's quite all right," she said briskly, stripping off her gloves. "As long as the bed linen is well aired and I may have hot water for my bath this evening, that is all I require for the moment. Will you return in half an hour and show my maid to her quarters?"

"Yes, miss." The girl bobbed a curtsey and left.

Gemma inspected the woefully shabby room. Wallpaper peeled away in two corners and damp patches bloomed on the outer wall. Carved nymphs and demons and goodness knew what else cavorted up and down the heavy mahogany posts on the ancient, canopied bed. Holes riddled the drab brown velvet curtains until some parts resembled cobwebs. Gemma met Dorry's horrified gaze and burst out laughing.

"Oh! Do you think it is our presence that has thrown this household into disarray or is it always like this?"

"I don't know that, Miss Gemma, but I shall find out," said Dorry, her lips set in a determined line.

"Now, don't you go upsetting everyone below stairs. I shall do perfectly well, once we have made some changes. We must proceed with caution and tact." She glanced about her with satisfaction. "Only think! I expected I should be bored to tears here, but already I have been presented with a mystery and a muddle. What could be better?"

Gemma gingerly drew back the curtains and uncovered a dirt-encrusted diamond-paned window that obscured more of the scenery than it revealed. Stifling a sneeze from the dust she had dislodged even with that circumspect movement, she tried to force one open, but it resisted her attempts as surely as if it had been nailed shut.

Taking a handkerchief from her reticule, Gemma rubbed a patch of grime from the thick glass and peered out. On the horizon, the storm clouds seemed to have cleared, revealing an expanse of pale sky that deepened into blue-green sea. In the foreground, grass of an impossible chartreuse spread from beyond the sheep pastures right to the cliffs' edge, broken now and again by purple smudges of heather. Squinting, she could even make out a small, sheltered beach, nestled at the foot of the cliffs.

An exploratory ramble was clearly in order.

Gemma eyed the ragged bell-pull doubtfully and decided she would find her own way to the drawing room, where Sebastian said he would await her. Instructing Dorry to restrain her natural impulse to set the household by the ears, Gemma tidied herself and prepared to brave the corridors beyond.

❦

SEBASTIAN watched Gemma climb the steps to the first floor, dazed with an emotion he had never experienced before and did not really recognise. He could not believe she was here, inside this grim cavern of a place he avoided calling home. Far from the dark atmosphere dimming her shining presence, it was as if a beacon had entered the house. His own mood had lightened at the first glimpse of her merry smile.

He shook his head and took a deep breath. An acrid smell filled his nostrils, recalling his mind to the pressing matter of his mother. He waited until Gemma was out of sight, then took the stairs three at a time and strode the short way down the corridor to his mother's sitting room.

The damask curtains hung in charred ribbons, fluttering like ghostly fingers in the sharp breeze that gusted through the open window. After a swift survey of the apartment, Sebastian glanced up at the moulded ceiling, and noticed thick swirls of grey curled lovingly around blackened plaster cherubs and doves. He would have to get someone up there to clean the soot when everything settled.

He cursed under his breath as servants hurried past him, removing Buhl tables and Sheraton chairs. Perhaps a few of the sturdier furnishings away from the seat of the fire could be saved, but the delicate, eggshell-blue-and-grey stripe of the upholstered pieces was singed, smoke damaged, or blurred and disfigured by watermarks.

The ancient wall hangings depicting a momentous battle fought by one of his ancestors had survived intact.

"More's the pity," Sebastian muttered, stepping aside for a pair of footmen to remove the charred remains of an occasional table that had once been a handsome, burnished walnut.

Clearly, the room would have to be cleaned and refurbished before his mother could return. He sighed. He had no idea of such matters, and Mama . . . well, he did not want to trouble her with such matters at the moment.

She had changed since his father's death. Had she loved him so much, that she would turn into this lost, remote stranger once he was gone? And worse, the mere sight of Sebastian seemed to pain her. He had stayed away because of the stark despair he saw in her eyes when she looked at him too long.

He sighed. He did not know what to say to her. He never had been able to please her, not since he was a small boy. It was too late to begin again.

When the servants had finished mopping the water used to douse the flames and swept up the worst of the debris, Sebastian dismissed them and moved to gaze out the window.

"Gracious, what on earth happened?" Gemma's clear voice chimed from the doorway. "Was anyone injured? Do you need help, Scovy?"

His head snapped around. He barely managed to stop himself from snarling at her. Furious that some idiot had left the door open for her to see, Sebastian strode forward to block the way. He whisked her along the gallery and down the steps before she could do much more than stutter a protest.

By the time they reached the hall, Gemma seemed to have remembered her manners, for she tucked her hand under his arm and said composedly, "Well, now! It is bidding fair to becoming a glorious afternoon. Will you not show me the gardens, Scovy?"

After a silent few moments, he regained his own composure. "You must be famished after the drive. I've ordered a cold collation to be served in the south parlour. This way."

He tried to infuse his voice with his customary nonchalance, but knew he failed. Was there anything more unfortunate? That she should arrive when the household was in an uproar over another of his mother's antics?

Gemma would not rest until she had ferreted the truth out of him. But she had grown more subtle than she had been in her youth. Now, she bided her time before she pounced.

"Oh! This is a charming room," said Gemma when they reached their destination.

"Is it?" He looked around, mystified at what Gemma could find in the dim parlour to admire.

Gemma threw a smile at him over her shoulder as she moved to the window and thrust the curtains open. Watery rays of sunlight shafted through the glass and danced patterns on the bare stone floor.

"Yes, don't you see? The aspect is particularly lovely and the proportions just right. A few . . . improvements and it will be perfect."

This caught his attention. "Improvements? Now, listen, Gemma—"

She raised her brows. "You are the Earl of Carleton, are you not?"

"I fail to see—"

"And forgive the vulgarity, but you are not precisely purse-pinched, are you?"

"No." His honoured Papa had made certain of that.

"Then why," she demanded, "does this place look as though it is like to fall down around our ears? Have you *seen* my bedchamber?"

He shifted. "No, of course not, and I don't—"

She counted the items off her meddling little fingers. "One, the ceiling plaster is cracked and likely to fall on my head as I sleep. Two, there are damp patches on the walls and the paper is peeling away. Three, the curtains are moth-eaten and threadbare. Four—"

Mortified, Sebastian interrupted her. "You must have been shown to the wrong chamber, in the old part of the house. Leave it to me and I will see you bestowed more comfortably."

The Lord only knew where. Perhaps he could cozen Fanny into giving up her room.

She regarded him thoughtfully. "No, that won't be necessary, thank you. Dorry will do what is required to make it habitable." She paused. "Is your Mama . . . *well*, Scovy?"

"Yes, of course. She is perfectly well. Never been better," he lied. "Oh, you mean the accident! She burned her hand and the doctor has told her to rest. She will be recovered in no time, I'm sure."

Gemma seemed to accept this. "Well, I do hope so."

She placed a hand on the back of a chair as she spoke. Grateful for the distraction, he skirted the table to pull it out for her. "Won't you sit down?"

"Thank you."

He took the place opposite her, wishing Fanny would make good her word and join them and bring the inquisition to a close. But she did not appear, and his wayward servants seemed to have made themselves scarce, so he served both of them himself. They ate in uncomfortable silence.

Sebastian selected an apple and gave it his undivided attention. He had peeled, cored, and quartered it before he realised he really did not wish to eat the damned thing.

What he wished to do was put off his dirt, wallow in his bathtub for the next three months, and pretend that the problem of catching Gemma in parson's mousetrap by the end of it did not exist.

He offered her the plate and she took an apple quarter.

Sebastian watched her bite into the crisp white flesh, then selected his own. Trying for a light note, he said, "Do you know, I've never tasted an apple better than the ones we used to steal from old Playstead's garden?"

She grinned. "Spoils of war always taste sweetest. Do you remember when he caught little Tommy Burke and you insisted on owning up to the crime so he would not give Tommy a thrashing?"

"Yes, and then he thrashed Tommy anyway because he could not lay a finger on an earl's son but he needed a target on whom to vent his spleen." He snorted. "A most Christian gentleman! The rectory tree was laden with fruit. Year after year those apples lay rotting on the ground before the old curmudgeon would pick them, yet he begrudged the smallest pippin to those village brats."

"They often asked after you, you know," said Gemma, and he sensed her watching him as he sliced his piece of apple into small, precise cubes. "Tommy and Jonas and the others. They were forever wondering when you would be back."

That old reproach. He was so tired of feeling guilty, of answering to everyone, most particularly to Gemma. Knowing the feeling was unreasonable and unjust—she thought she was at Laidley to do him a favour, after all—he wiped his hands on a napkin and pushed away from the table. "If you are finished, I'll introduce you to Fanny, shall I?"

Gemma agreed, wondering what on earth had possessed her. First, she had criticised his mama's housekeeping and then she had nagged him over his prolonged absence from Ware. That was no way to promote amity between them. Why could she not stop needling him, challenging him?

Gentlemen abhorred bossy females, wasn't that what Aunt Matilda always said?

As they turned into a narrow corridor, Gemma glanced out the windows and saw a green courtyard, colonnaded on three sides and open on the fourth to terraced gardens. Tiers of fountains played lazily, their fine spray glittering like diamond tiaras in the sunlight.

It was all very formal and grand and imposing, but at least the grounds appeared in better condition than the house. She longed to breathe fresh air. "May we not walk outside, Sebastian?"

He halted and followed her gaze. "My apologies, I have business to attend to. Fanny will be pleased to walk with you, if you like. I shall send her to your bedchamber directly."

SEBASTIAN found his mother sitting ramrod straight in her bed, her back not quite touching the pillows banked behind her. Her bandaged right hand lay limp on the counterpane. A cup of tea and a small glass of cloudy fluid stood on a tray on the bedside table.

Fanny put her embroidery frame aside when he entered the bedchamber and moved, soft as a wraith, towards him, her dark eyes anxious.

"How is she?" he murmured.

"I don't know." Fanny flicked a glance at the bed. "I have dressed her hand but the skin will blister badly I am sure. She refuses to see the doctor. Laudanum would dull the pain, but I cannot persuade her to take it." She searched his face. "The fire has been put out, I assume? Where is our guest?"

He nodded. "Gemma is in her bedchamber, awaiting you."

"I will go to her at once. I do not believe there is more I can do here, and Mama prefers Shelby to attend her anyway."

Sebastian frowned. "I still cannot fathom how it happened. What was she thinking of, lighting a fire herself, and in August, of all months?"

Fanny shook her head, glancing again at the rigid figure in the large, canopied bed. "Not a fire," she breathed. "A cigarillo."

"What?"

"I am perfectly well, Sebastian. Thank you." The precise, surprisingly forceful voice stopped him asking Fanny for more detail.

Sebastian moved to the bed, in which his once formidable mother appeared fragile, even a little lost. He reached to take her good hand in his, but remembered just in time and let his hand fall. She had never liked touching him.

She watched the futile movement, and a bitter smile flitted over her face as she turned her head away. But after a moment, her chin came up. With a small shake of her shoulders, she seemed to shed her air of frailty like a discarded cloak.

"I believe I should like to get up now."

Was that wise? Sebastian sent a questioning look to Fanny, who still hovered by the door. Almost imperceptibly, she shook her head.

"No, no!" He tried for a jovial tone but it clanged a false note. "Why, I have only just arrived and you mean to dismiss me, ma'am. Will you not stay awhile and let me keep you company?" He cringed inside at the hypocrisy. When had she ever desired his presence?

"Company?" Her thin eyebrows buckled. Her good hand plucked at the crisp linen sheet.

Sebastian swallowed and averted his gaze, searching the room for inspiration. A slim, leather-bound volume lay on a table at his mother's bedside. He stared, taken aback. His cold, rigidly principled mama, the woman who had never touched any of her children either in love or in anger, kept Byron as bedtime reading?

An idea occurred to him with such force that he blurted it out. "Would you like me to read to you, ma'am?"

Instantly, he regretted the offer, knew her answer would annihilate him as her cold dismissals of his overtures always had. *Never let down your guard, you fool.*

She tried to answer, but seemed to have difficulty swallowing. Pressing her hand to her breast, she began to cough. Perhaps the smoke had affected her lungs?

Silently closing the door on his emotions and throwing the bolt, Sebastian picked up the tumbler of diluted laudanum and offered it. "Drink this, Mama. It will make you more comfortable, I assure you."

Without speaking, she took the small glass in her good hand and slowly drained it, choking a little as she swallowed. She handed him the empty tumbler, settled back against her pillows, and closed her eyes.

"Yes, Sebastian. Read to me. That would be pleasant."

FANNY'S smile wavered to uncertainty and deepened to horror as her gaze travelled around Gemma's chamber. She looked as though she had never set eyes on the disreputable room before and rather wished she had remained in blissful ignorance.

Gemma chuckled. "My thoughts precisely. But it shall all be set to rights in the shake of a lamb's tail, never fear."

Fanny wrenched her stunned gaze from a pair of hideous bronze eagles on the mantel and wrinkled her patrician nose. In a low-pitched, slightly husky voice, she said, "What is that smell?"

"Damp? Dry rot?" Gemma hazarded. "Oh, you mean the camphor." She moved to shut the clothes press and the pungent odour receded.

"Moths," she explained when Fanny continued to look perplexed. "Camphor does wonders to eradicate the little pests."

Gemma surveyed her visitor with interest. She was remarkably like Sebastian, with the same dark, strongly marked features. But her chin was pointed, not square, and her soft lips the antithesis of her brother's chiselled masculinity. "Thank heavens you are beautiful," said Gemma with satisfaction. "You will make an exquisite bride."

Fanny started and flushed. "Oh, but—"

"Now, about your wedding." Gemma waved aside the embarrassed interjection. "Leave everything to me. All you need do is tell me your requirements, and I shall engage to fire you off in grand style."

Fanny blinked. She drew her Norwich silk shawl close around her and half turned away. "Good Lord! Er, that is to say . . . Good Lord, what a predicament."

Realising the dingy surroundings had appalled her companion into incoherence, Gemma tucked her hand in Fanny's stiffened arm and tilted her head to scrutinise her face. Her new friend was rather tall for a female. "Should you object to continuing this discussion outside? If we stand about in here much longer I fear one of us will fall into strong convulsions. Do come along," she coaxed, drawing Fanny towards the door. "I simply pine for fresh air."

"Yes, of course. In a moment." Fanny stepped away from her. She lifted her chin in a gesture that held a deal of defiance and gave her something of the look of Sebastian when he turned mulish. "Miss Maitland, before we go any further, there is something I must tell you."

"Yes? Please, call me Gemma."

Fanny inhaled deeply through her nose, then let out a short breath. "I am very much afraid my brother has brought you here on a fool's errand. I . . . Gemma, I must apologise. There is not going to be any wedding."

Nine

———— ⚜ ————

"No wedding?" Gemma plumped down on the threadbare counterpane. The ancient bedsprings groaned and wheezed.

Fanny shook her head.

Gemma eyed her companion and waited. She did not wish to pry, but she had travelled a long way with the best of intentions and she rather thought she was entitled to some sort of explanation for the sudden abortion of her mission.

She frowned. "Do you mean Sebastian has brought me here under false pretences?"

"Not false pretences, no." Fanny sat beside Gemma and her gaze slid away. "Well, not entirely. You see, I *was* betrothed."

"Oh."

"But now I am not."

"I see." Gemma considered this statement. "Do you mean you broke the engagement?"

Fanny inclined her head, a queenly gesture. "Yes. It was high time." She straightened, her neck and spine extending until Gemma wondered that anyone could manage such perfect posture without a backboard.

Staring at the wall opposite, Fanny went on in her cool voice. "Mama entered into my feelings completely, which surprised me. She has always been such a high stickler. But she has finally seen what I have been trying to tell her since the start of this sorry engagement. We simply do not suit."

"We?"

"Lord Romney and I." Fanny smoothed her cambric skirt over her lap.

"Romney?" Gemma had heard of his lordship, a notorious libertine and boon companion of Sebastian's. "Did Sebastian arrange this match?"

Fanny flicked a piece of fluff from her shawl. "No, Romney and I have been betrothed forever. Our respective parents simply refused to believe the match was unsuitable." She curled her lip. "I fear I am far too staid a creature for Romney's taste."

Gemma could well believe it. By all accounts, the poet Byron's famed excesses were nothing to Romney's, though Romney boasted his affairs were conducted with greater finesse. "If you dislike him so much—"

"Dislike him? I *loathe* him. His mode of life disgusts me." Fanny launched herself from the bed and began to pace, redistributing quite a bit of dust in the process. This animation suited her.

Overcome by dust, Gemma sneezed. She crossed to the dresser to unearth a handkerchief. "Well, it seems you have extricated yourself from the engagement, so that is what signifies. Though I know it will not be pleasant to be branded a jilt, it is better than living the rest of your life with a man you despise."

Fanny paused. "Of course. Of course it is." She resumed her pacing. "But you don't understand, Gemma. The battle is just begun." She whirled about. "Can I count on you to stand by me? I can, can't I? I know you would not suffer me to marry such a man."

"Well . . ." The faint echo of an alarm sounded in Gemma's head. Something about the tension in Fanny's slender frame sent a warning. "If your mama approves of you breaking the engagement and you have written to Lord Romney, I do not quite see why you need my support."

Fanny's eyes blazed, grew almost wild. She pressed Gemma's hands between her palms. "Do not fail me! I cannot tell you all, but you must help me."

Gemma blinked. "Oh, well then. Ahem. Yes. Yes, of course I will."

"THE wedding is off?" Sebastian thrust away his list of eligible bachelors and rounded the big oak desk. "Gemma, did you have something to do with this?"

Her mouth fell slightly ajar. "Of course not. How could I? I've only just arrived."

Recognising the illogic of his accusation, he raked a hand through his hair. This was all he needed on top of his mother's problems, to have his sister embroiled in a scandal. Then he paused. Perhaps the prospective groom had something to answer for.

He sighed. "What has Romney done this time? Please tell me I don't need to call him out."

She folded her arms. "Fanny has disliked the match from the start. I would have thought her reasons for breaking the engagement obvious. Even I have heard of Lord Romney's reputation. Opera dancers and such."

Sebastian narrowed his eyes. She stood there with her straight little nose in the air, the prim expression of moral outrage sitting oddly with all that lush, ripe beauty. His temper commenced a slow burn. "You don't know what you're talking about. Romney is a capital fellow, well suited to my sister."

"Your sister does not wish to be tied to a rake."

He remained impassive, though for some reason her words stabbed his chest. Silkily, he replied, "Is that so? In my experience, it's the rakes women find attractive."

She sucked a breath between her teeth, but then her mouth twitched into a smile, as though she were faintly amused. She shrugged. "Rakes are well enough for dalliance, I daresay. *Not* as a life sentence."

Fury ripped through him, an emotion that had little to do with his sister's predicament and everything to do with Gemma's implied dismissal of the whole race of rakes, more specifically of him, Sebastian Laidley, society's rake extraordinaire. Was that how she viewed their moonlit kiss? Mere dalliance? A pleasant way to pass an evening?

He did not understand her.

He had grown up with certain assumptions about what ladies did and didn't do, and how they were to be treated. If one toyed with a virtuous female of one's own class, one paid the penalty by marrying her. Ladies did not give their kisses lightly and gentlemen did not take them without serious intent.

But Gemma represented a strange force of nature that confused his gentlemanly instincts and blurred the line between untouchable lady and available woman. Though a lady by birth and upbringing, she possessed a vital, fresh sensuality that was all the more alluring for being unconscious. And her easy attitude to kisses did not tally with what he knew of *ladies*.

For the first time, Sebastian faced facts. Had Gemma attached any significance to their encounter on the terrace at Ware, they would be betrothed now. In all honour, he should have asked her to marry him that night. When he hadn't, she should have demanded his ring on her finger. So why hadn't she?

He gripped her wrist, feeling nineteen again, hurt, angry, ready to lash out. "And you are quite the expert on dalliance, aren't you, Miss Maitland?" He stared at her mouth, at that plump lower lip with its tiny, ridged crescent of a scar, and wished she were any woman but a gently bred lady, a guest in his house.

Any woman but Gemma.

Her breath came fast, a little harder. "Let go of me. *I* am not one of your opera dancers."

He dropped her wrist. "I thought we were talking about Romney."

If only she were some nameless *fille de joie*, he could work off this ridiculous obsession. He could take her right now on the desk and . . .

His voice rasped. "I think you should go now."

She frowned. "But what about Fanny?"

He clasped his hands behind his back, fighting for control. "That is hardly your concern."

Chagrin, disappointment, and something else he could not identify clouded her face for an instant, then disappeared.

Slowly, she nodded. "No, I suppose it isn't. In fact, none of it is my concern. This house, your mama, your sister . . . *You*, Scovy, are not my concern."

She spun on her heel and stalked towards the door.

"And where do you think you're going?"

She turned back. "My coachman is staying overnight before he leaves for Ware tomorrow. I must tell him he will have two passengers for the return. After all," she said, staring him straight between the eyes, "according to Fanny, there will be no wedding. My services are not needed here."

Gemma saw Sebastian pale and tried to ignore the twinge of conscience that whispered *he* needed her, even if he didn't know it. Even if he insulted her, he needed her to stay.

She wanted to help Fanny, too, but she could not do it if she made good her threat and left. Loath to back down, she waited.

"On the contrary," drawled Sebastian. She'd no idea he could sound so arrogant. "The wedding will proceed as planned. I wish you to undertake the more onerous duties of hostess, as you promised." He arched his brows in high-bred insolence. "I trust you are not about to renege on our agreement."

His voice was light and calm but she read strain in the clench of his fist, in the tense set of his shoulders. One hand dived into his coat pocket and unearthed his snuffbox.

In that instant, Gemma decided to stay. But she did not intend to make her capitulation explicit.

"Do you ever take that?" She moved to peer at the contents of the box.

"Snuff?" Sebastian's eyes searched her face, then his features eased. "Very seldom." He held it out to her. "Care to try some?"

"Ugh! No, thank you."

He watched her for a moment. Then a slow smile spread. "Chicken."

Gemma grimaced. She was not about to fall for that old chestnut. Reluctant, but willing to play along for the sake of peace between them, she plunged finger and thumb into the powder.

"No, stop!" Laughing, Sebastian dealt her knuckles a light slap so she released the powder back into the box. "Inhale that much and you will sneeze from here to Scotland. The merest fraction will do. Look." He laid the snuffbox on the desk. Taking a tiny pinch, he deposited it on the inside of his wrist below his shirt cuff. "Try that."

Suspicious of his dancing dark eyes, Gemma regarded him for a moment, then lowered her gaze to his upturned hand. Why had she never noticed how strong and fine his hands were? Suddenly, inhaling those few tiny grains from his wrist seemed unbearably intimate and daring.

Before her bravado ran out, she gripped his hand, dipped her head, and sniffed. She heard his breathing hitch. Quickly, she straightened and wrinkled her tingling nose.

"How do you like it?" Sebastian watched her intently.

"Not much." She fought a sneeze and her eyes watered with the effort. "But thank you for the experiment."

Sebastian's dark gaze held hers as he took another pinch from the snuffbox. "May I?" Swiftly, he caught her hand, dropped the snuff on her wrist, bent, and sniffed.

The faint rush of air sent whispers of sensation up her arm. His lips brushed the delicate inside of her wrist, and the blood sparkled and fizzed like champagne beneath her skin. She gasped and closed her eyes, scarcely able to believe the effect of this simple touch.

Lord, she was weak! Completely at his mercy, any time he chose to exert this strange power he held over her. If she did not stop this, soon she would not know herself, or have any will left to resist.

She curled her fingers around his jaw, and felt the beginnings of stubble rasp against her fingertips as she raised his face to her level. His eyelids drifted shut and he angled his head slightly, as if to accept a kiss, black lashes lying short and thick against the hard plane of his cheek. The masculine scent of leather and sandalwood surrounded her as his mouth drifted towards hers.

"Sebastian?" Gemma murmured, trying not to inhale him.

"Mm?" His brow creased slightly when she continued to hold him off with the gentle press of her fingers. Slowly, his eyes opened, their dilated pupils shrinking in the light.

"Scovy, if I am to stay here, I shall want *carte blanche*." He jerked back. *"What?"*

Heat swarmed to her cheeks when she recognised the double entendre. "No, not *that* kind of *carte blanche*, you stupid man! I mean I want free rein with the household. You must allow me to make whatever changes I see fit to prepare for the house party. I suppose that will proceed, at least."

He stared at her a moment, then sighed and turned away to gather papers from his desk. "Whatever you wish, my dear. Just rack everything up to me."

She nodded. "Thank you. You may be sure I shall not

outrun the carpenter, but there is much that needs doing. Have you decided on the guest list? Do you wish me to send invitations?"

Sebastian leafed through his papers. He drew out one sheet and frowned over it. "No, I have not yet decided. I will give you the list tomorrow morning."

He looked up. "Would you be so good as to tell Fanny I wish to speak with her?"

Gemma stood her ground. "And the wedding?"

He waved the paper impatiently. "You don't understand how it is with my sister and Romney. They have these ridiculous spats at least once a month. It never comes to anything."

"Once a—" Gemma gasped. "But Fanny has written to terminate the engagement. She told me your mama lends her full support. I don't believe any lady would do such a thing lightly. You must be mistaken."

His mouth twisted at her confusion. She was innocent in so many ways. "You don't know much about passion, do you, Gemma? People affected by powerful emotion don't always behave rationally, you know."

Just look at me, he thought. *I should avoid you like some virulent, deadly disease, yet I can't keep my hands off you for five minutes.* "I don't care what Fanny told you. That pair will marry in the village church in two months' time with all the pomp and ceremony we can muster."

He smiled. "Unless they kill each other first."

THE next morning, Gemma started awake, felt hands squeeze her shoulder and shake it. She sat up, peering through sleep and surrounding gloom at Fanny's face.

"Gemma, please get up! Quickly, you must dress."

"Wha—?" Brushing her hair away from her face, Gemma rubbed her eye with one knuckle and tried to haul her dream-fogged mind into the present. "Whatever is the matter, Fanny? Are you ill?"

Fanny waved a hand impatiently, sending lavender wafting through the air. "Get dressed," she hissed. "Please, you must help me. He is here."

"Who? Romney?"

Fanny nodded. She left the bed and flung open the curtains. A wad of fabric came away in her hand.

She stared at it, then tossed it on the dresser and began rummaging through drawers to find Gemma's undergarments.

"Now just a minute!" Gemma scrambled out of bed and plucked her shift and stockings from Fanny's fingers. "You must calm down, Fanny. Have someone send my maid to me and I'll—"

Shaking her head, Fanny said, "No, there's not time! He is here, I tell you. He is here!"

"Well he'll just have to kick his heels and wait until we are ready to receive him, won't he?" Exasperated, Gemma folded her arms and glanced at the mantel clock. "It is seven o'clock. What sort of time is this to pay a call, anyway? I cannot believe the fuss you are making over it."

Fanny threw open the clothes press, dragged out a sprigged muslin gown, and tossed it at her. "Quick, there's no time. Oh, do hurry along, or Lord knows what might happen."

Suddenly, Gemma saw that Fanny's gown was fastened all wrong, she wasn't wearing a corset and her lustrous dark hair was piled on her head in strange loops and falling down around her ears. She wore slippers but no stockings.

"Fanny?" A deep voice rolled down the corridor towards them. A door creaked open, slammed. Then another, and another.

Gemma's horrified gaze met Fanny's. "When you said he was here, I thought you meant—"

"Fa-anny!"

Gemma dived for the silk wrapper that hung over a

chair, dragged it on and fumbled at the tie. "Is he mad? How did he get past the servants?"

Fanny listened at the door and whispered, "I don't know. I think he knocked at least one of them down. He came to my bedchamber, but there is a secret way, a servants' corridor. I escaped, so now he is ransacking the house to find me." She eased the key around until the lock clicked, drew it out, and set her eye to the keyhole.

Gemma snatched up a fire iron from the hearth, ready to do battle. "What will he do when he finds you? Is he violent?" How could Sebastian force Fanny to marry this brute? She would have a few choice words to say to him if she made it out of there alive.

Still crouching at the door, Fanny sent her an impatient glance. "Don't be ridiculous! Romney would never offer physical violence to a female." As the heavy footsteps drew nearer, she stood and backed away.

The footsteps stopped. The doorknob turned. The door did not open. Muttered curses ripened the air outside. "Fanny, I have ridden a long way. Open. The door."

Fanny shot Gemma a glance and put her finger to her lips.

"My lady," said a soft, dangerous voice. "If you do not open this door, I shall kick it down. So you might wish to stand clear."

"Now that is the outside of enough." Gemma shoved the fire iron back in its stand. She wrested the key from Fanny, unlocked the door, and flung it open. Six foot two of tawny-haired, fuming male stood before her. She fumed right back at him.

"You, sir!" She poked his hard chest with her finger. "What do you mean by coming here, pounding on my door—and at this hour? Shame on you, rousing respectable people from their beds!"

Romney blinked. The high colour drained from his face. Gemma almost laughed at the ludicrous transformation from leonine ferocity to sheepishness.

She bit her lip, but kept her voice stern. "Well? What have you to say for yourself?"

"Yes, I should like to know the answer to that question." Sebastian's voice sounded behind Romney, cold steel in his tone.

Romney raised his gaze to the ceiling, closed his eyes, and breathed hard through his nose. He did not turn around. "Fanny. I thought she was here."

Sebastian spoke close to his friend's ear. "I don't care if you thought the Queen of Sheba was in that room. You do not come into my house, terrorise my servants—whose wits are addled at the best of times—and tear the place apart looking for my sister. Do I make myself clear?"

He glanced at Gemma, and his mouth tightened. "Go and cover yourself, Gemma, for the Lord's sake. You—" he collared Romney and propelled him down the corridor. "—Go down to the breakfast room and wait for me. By the time I join you, I might have reconsidered the urge to beat you to a pulp."

Romney shrugged from his hold, sent him a glare over his shoulder, and stormed off.

Sebastian turned back to Gemma, who seemed in danger of succumbing to a fit of giggles. Relieved, he reached out and flicked her cheek. "Are you all right?"

She grinned. "Oh, perfectly, thank you. I was sending him to the right-about when you arrived. What a—what an impetuous man your friend is."

"Yes, that's one word for it." He looked past her, expecting to see Fanny, but the room was empty. "You should not have opened your door to him. An incident like this could destroy your reputation if anyone heard of it."

"Well, I did not have much choice, since he threatened to break it down if I did not. But pray do not make it a matter for fisticuffs, Scovy. I am persuaded he has learned his lesson." Her eyes twinkled. "If only you had seen his face when I opened the door!"

Sebastian managed a strained smile. Only a shock such as Romney had suffered could make a red-blooded man think of anything but bundling all that rumpled femininity straight back to her bed and making love to her for the rest of the day.

Her glorious golden hair curled and waved around her face, tumbling down to caress her breasts. Without the constraint of a corset, those breasts seemed even fuller than he'd imagined. The peach silk wrapper was a frivolous contrast to the plain, sober garments she usually wore. She looked rosy-cheeked and soft-lipped and utterly delicious.

He cleared his throat and shifted his stance. "If you're quite sure—"

"Oh, yes." She waved a hand, making parts of her move in the most distracting way. "Do go down and see if you cannot drum reason into the poor man. Is he a little touched in the upper works, do you think? Perhaps he suffers from some affliction of the nerves?"

No, just thwarted desire, thought Sebastian. *And I know exactly how the poor sod feels.* He sighed. "I'll do what I can. But don't you go working Fanny up any more than she is already. She's playing with fire as it is."

"Fanny wasn't the one creating a ruckus up and down your corridors, if you recall," retorted Gemma. "I suggest you tell your fiery friend to go and throw a bucket of water over his head before someone else does it for him."

She pulled her wrapper tighter around her and shut the door in his face.

❧

"WOMEN!" uttered Romney in a voice of loathing as he loaded eggs onto his toast. "No, scratch that, make that *ladies.* Women, I understand. Love women. Ladies, on the other hand, are a plague and a pestilence, a cruel joke on mankind."

Sebastian was inclined to agree, but he clapped his friend

on the shoulder as he crossed to the sideboard. "Well, stop dancing to Fanny's tune. You know she only sent you that note to bring you running. And here you are, roaring around my house like a lion with a prickle in its foot. Get a hold of yourself, man."

He forked ham onto his plate and looked around, narrowing his eyes at Romney. "And I don't want Gemma caught in the middle of your ridiculous tomfoolery again."

One tawny eyebrow lifted. "Gemma?"

"Miss Maitland to you."

Romney gave a low whistle. "Lord! I thought she looked familiar, but in the heat of the moment, I couldn't place her. Are you telling me you have Sybil Maitland's daughter under your roof?"

Sebastian gave him a long, cool look. "No. I am not telling you anything of the sort. Miss Maitland is a virtuous young lady and she will be treated as such."

Romney put down his knife and fork. "Have you forgotten I'm betrothed to your sister?"

"That's not what she says."

"Well, I am. Till death do us part and all that rot."

Sebastian smiled. "I think you'll find that's marriage."

Romney swallowed a mouthful of toast. "Y'know Sebastian, when I agreed to take Fanny on I'd no notion what it would mean. It's supposed to be a marriage of convenience, for God's sake, and yet it's been the most *in*convenient damned thing that's ever happened to me."

Sebastian finished his selection and came to the table. "If you take my advice, you'll leave her alone. Wait for her to come about."

"Can't do that." Romney contemplated his buttered eggs.

"Why not?"

He shifted in his chair, but kept his eyes on his plate. "I can't, that's all. So you'll just have to live with me awhile longer."

Ten

GEMMA turned back to an empty bedchamber. "Fanny?"

Still clutching her wrapper around her, she scanned the room. It was so sparsely furnished, there were few places Fanny could hide. The large fire screen concealed no secrets, and anyone lurking behind the threadbare curtains would be clearly silhouetted against the pale morning sunlight.

Gemma knelt and lifted the skirt of the coverlet to peer beneath the ancient four-poster bed. Nothing. Not even dust—Dorry had made sure of that.

Then came a click and a soft whine. Gemma scrambled to her feet and started towards the sound. She froze, and watched, open-mouthed, as a large panel in the wall beside the fireplace swung open to reveal her friend.

"Gracious, is that where you went? I thought you'd vanished like Banquo's ghost."

Fanny stepped into the room and turned to close the secret door behind her.

"Wait." Gemma crossed the floor towards her. "Show me how that works."

"Oh, it's quite easy," said Fanny. "You just press in-wards, like this. And *voilà*! It opens."

"You say that as if I ought to be pleased." Gemma tried it herself. A sharp jab of the fingers, and the door sprang open with daunting alacrity. She caught the panel, closed it again, and frowned at the apparently innocuous wall. "Where does this lead? Can one lock it from the inside?"

"The corridor runs past the principal bedchambers," said Fanny. There's an old set of stairs that leads to the ser-vants' quarters on the floor above and to the kitchens be-low. The servants don't use it anymore because we no longer require them to add invisibility to their other duties and it is less convenient than using the back stairs. I think everyone but me has forgotten it's there. Why should you wish to lock it?"

Gemma glowered at her. "Perhaps so I might get some sleep. I did not intend to keep cock-crow hours here."

She took Fanny's elbow and propelled her towards the conventional door. "Now, Fanny, be a dear! Do go away while I dress. I'll see you in the breakfast parlour presently."

"I shall breakfast in my room," said Fanny with affected unconcern. "I do not wish to see him."

Gemma rolled her eyes. "Yes, you have made that abun-dantly clear. Something tells me, however, that Romney will not be denied. You might as well give him his march-ing orders face-to-face, before he tries some other hare-brained trick and ruins your reputation. Then you'll have no choice but to marry him."

Delicate colour rose to Fanny's fine-boned cheeks. "You are right. He will not stop at that small reverse." The tip of her tongue touched her lower lip. Her dark eyes glinted with speculation. She traced the blond lace edging Gemma's sleeve with her finger. "I wonder how he will go about it. There is a sturdy trellis beneath my window."

Gemma threw up her hands. "You are incorrigible! I'm beginning to believe Sebastian's right. You and Romney are well suited." She looked at Fanny curiously. "He seemed very upset. Are you positive he does not care for you?"

Fanny snorted. "Oh, don't let his barbarian ways fool you. Romney sees me as his possession, and he will move heaven and earth to have me, but once I am his he will lose interest. The minute I succumb, he will be off chasing the next thing in skirts that looks at him twice. I know his sort exceedingly well."

"Do you indeed?" Gemma marvelled at Fanny's certainty. She herself found it impossible to fathom the ways of men. She supposed that came of largely disregarding them, of missing the London Season, and of steadfastly ignoring her mama's frequently dispensed gems of worldly wisdom.

But Fanny, it seemed, experienced no doubts. "Yes, and I'll tell you one thing, Gemma. My brother is no different from Romney. They are hell-born babes, the pair of them."

Gemma smiled at the expression issuing from Fanny's lips, but unease prickled her nape. The memory of Sebastian's mouth teasing hers, the devious way he had lured her into taking snuff from his wrist, flickered a warning. "Scovy—I mean, Sebastian—is not so bad, surely?"

Fanny's eyes rounded. "Worse! When our brother Andrew died, Sebastian turned wild. I believe Papa would have disinherited him if he could, but the entailment means Sebastian gets everything." She paused, tilting her head. "Why do you call him Scovy?"

"Oh!" Gemma tried to look innocent. "I don't really remember."

Wistfully, Fanny said, "I never knew Sebastian as you did. He was rarely here. Always, he was at school or at Ware. Now he makes his home in town." She smiled. "I used to dislike you intensely, you know. Sebastian was my favourite brother, and yet I hardly ever saw him, only sometimes at Christmas. He was always with you."

Guilt clawed inside Gemma, but she refused it purchase. "You must have known that was not my doing."

"Yes, but I detested you all the same. Silly, isn't it, the way children think?" Fanny laughed and tucked her hand in Gemma's arm. "Now I have met you, it is quite different. You are charming, and I have made up my mind to find you a husband while you are here."

The quick change of subject startled Gemma. She broke free of Fanny's hold. "A husband? Oh, no."

"Why not? You cannot have met anyone eligible at Ware or you would be married already. You are quite the most . . . well, I was going to say *beautiful* but that's not right, is it?"

Fanny observed her through narrowed, assessing eyes. She sighed. "You, dear Gemma, are ravishing." She held up a hand at Gemma's protest. "Yes, *ravishing*, that is the word. It describes you perfectly. Now, I am accounted handsome among the *ton*." She wrinkled her nose. "Such a lowering description, as if I were a barouche or a yacht or something." She caught Gemma's wrist and coaxed her to stand before the cheval glass. "But together we make quite a pair, don't you think?"

Gemma was reduced to incoherence by this frankness. She could only stare at their reflections, one slender, dark, and elegant despite the deficiencies of that morning's *toilette*; the other fair and disarranged, slightly blowsy, if she must be honest. Like a milkmaid or some bosomy tavern wench with a rather expensive taste in lingerie.

"A pair?"

Fanny bestowed a smug smile on their reflection. "Yes, indeed. We shall form a two-pronged attack."

Gemma did not doubt that in the battlefield of love Fanny would prove a formidable general, but she had no taste for strategic manoeuvres, no desire to wed. The last thing she needed was a husband.

All she wanted was Ware.

ROMNEY stared at Sebastian's proposed guest list as though comprehending plain English were a feat beyond his powers. "Algernon Mosely? Gervase Stone? What is this, a list of England's most boring bachelors?"

Sebastian leaned back in his chair. "Respectability does not necessarily equate with tedium."

"But it all too often does." Romney flicked the paper with a spatulate finger. "Why are you inviting a load of Friday-faced parsons to Laidley? And why aren't there any females on the list?"

"Ah. I thought you might be able to help me there. I need . . ." Sebastian frowned and ran the feather of his pen through his fingers. "I might as well tell you as long as you promise to be discreet. I am trying to find Gemma a husband."

Romney started in surprise, then a smile burst over his face. "Oh, by God, that's rich! Sebastian Laidley, confirmed bachelor, throwing his hat in the ring with the matchmaking mamas. And Miss Maitland is acquainted with this plan of yours?"

Casting him a glance of loathing, Sebastian grunted. "No."

"I see." Romney's grin spread wider, if that were possible. "Well, your Miss Maitland is a filly with a good dose of spirit in her. I can't picture her bedding down with any of those wet blankets you've picked out."

Sebastian's nostrils flared. "You will refrain from speaking of Miss Maitland in those terms, if you please."

His friend held up his hands in a surrendering gesture. "Oops. Beg pardon, wasn't thinking. Here, let me have a try."

Reluctantly, Sebastian handed over paper and writing implements. Romney pulled his chair closer to the other side of the desk. He reached over to dip the pen in ink, blotted it and tickled his stubbled chin with the feather as he thought. "What about Pinkerton?"

Sebastian snorted. "That fribble! She would have nothing to say to him."

Romney raised his brows as he wrote. "He's a viscount and full of juice besides. Most women wouldn't look further than wealth and title in their choice of a mate."

"Well, this one does! Or she will if she knows what's good for her." Sebastian gritted his teeth. "And she would never so much as glance at Pinkerton."

"Oh, I don't know. Ladies seem to take to him very well, don't they? Always fluttering about him whenever I've attended any of those dashed dull affairs at Almack's. Well, I've put him down, anyway. Now. Who else . . ."

Romney slapped his knee. "My cousin, Brooke. The very one! Now, you can't say he's a fribble, Sebastian. Dashed fine figure of a man. Top-of-the-trees Corinthian and wealthy to boot. His maternal grandmother died last year. Left him very plump in the pocket."

This discussion was not proceeding as Sebastian had planned. "Look, forget about the men. I have them sorted already. I want some females, but I need ones who aren't . . ." He broke off, floundering under Romney's ironic gaze.

"What?"

He sighed. "Competition. I need Gemma to stand out and I don't want any diamonds competing with her."

Romney's hazel eyes brimmed with laughter. His shoulders shook from holding it in. "So, you want hideous crones who have no money, no prospects, and no connections?"

Sebastian brightened. "Do you know any?"

Romney burst out laughing. "Oh, Lord! I suppose I could prune a couple from the family tree, but why? Your Miss Maitland would outshine the greatest beauties of the day."

At this praise, Sebastian fought an odd sense of pride. Coolly, he said, "She is past price, isn't she? Not your classical beauty, but all the same, she has an abundance of charm."

"Yes, I noticed her, er, abundance."

"What?"

"Oh, nothing. Just that I noticed her charms."

Sebastian half rose from his chair, then made himself sit back. "Listen, Romney, I don't need to tell you that I consider you still bound to my sister. Furthermore, if you think to pay court to Gemma, I shall have no compunction in kicking you down the stairs."

A sardonic smile played about Romney's mouth. "Not to mention your sister would have my guts for garters. No, I thank you. I agree that your Miss Maitland is a highly finished piece of nature, but my appreciation is purely aesthetic. If she has a sizeable dowry, you'll have no trouble firing her off. But why should it be left to you? Doesn't she have family?"

Knowing his friend would think the joke too rich for words, Sebastian omitted the history of his bargain with Hugo. "Her grandfather also happens to be my godfather."

"The one who is dying?" Romney gave a silent whistle.

Sebastian sucked in a breath. Hearing it out loud was more painful than he had thought possible. "Yes, but Gemma doesn't know that. I promised him I would find her a husband, and that's what I intend to do."

Romney swung a booted leg over the other. "Which begs the question: Why don't you marry her?"

"*I?* Certainly not."

His companion shrugged. "Seems the simplest solution to me."

"No, it is the worst possible solution. Please keep your mind on the task at hand. Females." He counted down his list. "Twelve of them. Including chaperones, I suppose. Fortunate, that. We need only invite half the number of unattached ladies to even the numbers."

"You're really serious about this, aren't you?"

Sebastian looked at him.

Romney shrugged. "Invite Brooke, then. He's hanging out for a wife."

R ELUCTANTLY, Gemma decided to postpone her exploration of the Laidley estate in favour of taking stock of the house. She donned an old dark blue round gown, perfect for household chores. Lady Carleton had not rejoined them yet and Fanny showed a high-bred disdain for domestic matters, so Gemma rang for the housekeeper to attend her in the south parlour, where she and Sebastian had taken luncheon the day before.

Having awaited the woman at the appointed place for more than fifteen minutes, Gemma's temper rose. After a prolonged search, she found a maid daydreaming over her work polishing the banisters on the central staircase and inquired where the housekeeper might be found.

"In 'er sittin' room, miss," came the bewildered reply.

Grimly, Gemma requested directions, thanked the maid, and stalked upstairs to Mrs. Penny's room.

When she knocked on the door, a rich, deep voice bade her enter.

Mrs. Penny was a shiny-faced, rounded individual, her generous girth suggesting she was unaccustomed to moving quickly, or, perhaps at all. Like the housekeeper herself, her surroundings were ample and richly appointed. A handsome burgundy carpet sprawled over the floor and several overstuffed armchairs ranged around the hearth in a cosy circle. The hangings were old and faded, but free from dust. The curtains that framed a charming view of the formal gardens were crisp, clean, and, most important, intact.

Gemma's eyes widened as she sat down. No wonder the house was in such a poor state. All of Mrs. Penny's effort seemed directed towards looking after herself.

Gemma introduced herself to the woman and explained Sebastian's instructions on the matter of the house party.

She smiled. "Of course there has not been the necessity to prepare for a party of this magnitude at Laidley in many years. I believe the former earl did not care for company, but with Lady Fanny's wedding day approaching, we must make ready for a large number of guests."

Mrs. Penny beamed at her and nodded with native Cornish charm. "Oh, yes, miss. Never you mind your pretty head over that, never you mind. I shall see to it, miss. Oh, yes."

Gemma smiled back. "But you see, Mrs. Penny, Lord Carleton charged me specifically with minding my head over the arrangements. That is why I am here. Now, I wish to inspect the guest bedchambers first. Once we have taken note of what needs doing there, we will move on to the staterooms."

Ignoring the housekeeper's blank look, she went on. "I shall also require all the counterpanes, rugs, and hangings beaten and washed where possible, the furniture polished, the linen bleached and mended, and I should like an inventory of the still-room and the storerooms and larder."

Mrs. Penny blinked. "May I offer ye some cake, miss?" She waved her hand, indicating a sumptuous array of cakes and savouries on a small round table by the window.

"No, thank you, I have just breakfasted. Now, about those bedchambers—"

"What about a nice samwich, then? I've salt beef or ham?" The kindly blue eyes crinkled at the corners. "Bonny lass like you needs your susteynance. Tea?"

Gemma eyed the silver tea urn, a more handsome specimen than she had seen in the breakfast parlour that morning. She wondered what the lady of the house made of Mrs. Penny's lavish notions of what was due to her. She suspected Lady Carleton remained ignorant of the housekeeper's practices. That raised intriguing questions, but Gemma lacked the leisure to mull them over at that moment.

Not many more minutes spent in her company convinced Gemma that Mrs. Penny regarded the position of housekeeper as purely nominal. Short of lighting one of Whinyates' infamous rockets under her, there seemed to be no way of moving her from her comfortable roost.

Gemma tilted her head, considering. She could simply order the woman to cooperate, but that would only incite resentment. She would have to do her best on her own. Once Lady Carleton was fit to see her, she would assess the strength and will of the mistress of this ramshackle establishment and from there consider her best strategy.

She left the housekeeper's domain and decided her first port of call might as well be the room that required the most extensive refurbishment—the burnt-out shell of a salon where she had found Sebastian the day before.

Gemma opened the door without knocking, not expecting to find anyone within. A tall woman, her jet-black hair streaked with grey, turned swiftly on Gemma's entrance. She stood at the window, framed by tendrils of tattered curtains patterned with filmy sunlight.

"So foolish." She put a bandaged hand to her cheek. Her dark gaze wandered the room, then came to rest on Gemma. "Only look what I have done. How my lord would have berated me."

And then she began to laugh. She brought up one hand to cover her mouth like an errant schoolgirl, but her dark eyes glistened with tears of mirth.

Lady Carleton. It had to be. Gemma moved to take the lady's uninjured hand. She urged her to sit on a small sofa that had escaped damage.

Lady Carleton pressed a handkerchief to her lips. Slowly, the shudders that ran through her slender frame subsided.

She seemed to draw herself up, the lines of her body tensed, as if she needed to exert control over each and every muscle to stop herself disintegrating.

She even managed a polite, social smile. "I am so sorry. What a terrible way to greet a guest. You are Miss Maitland, are you not? I am Lady Carleton. Forgive me for not welcoming you before now."

Gemma regarded her with concern. "Should you not be resting, ma'am? I am persuaded you are not yet recovered from your indisposition."

"Oh, I am quite recovered, thank you. You must not trouble yourself about me." She stared hard at Gemma, as though searching for something.

At length, she said, "You are very like your mama."

"Thank you." Gemma had learned to take such double-edged compliments at face value. Feeling as though the anticipated ordeal by social torture had begun at last, she waited for the next strike. Lady Carleton's expression remained perfectly benign, but Gemma knew not to trust the smiling character assassins of the *ton*.

"Sybil was a great friend of mine, you know," said Lady Carleton unexpectedly. "We both made our come-outs in London in the same Season. I'm afraid after Sebastian was born we lost touch. I had hoped that making Sir Hugo Sebastian's godfather would . . ." She sighed. "But it was not to be."

Had Lady Carleton not turned her back on Sybil, then? If that were the case, she must be unique among the ladies of her class. Gemma knew well that high sticklers did not tolerate Sybil Maitland. Aunt Matilda had described in luxuriant detail the treatment meted out to fallen women of the *ton*, a fate that could so easily befall Gemma if she did not take scrupulous care of her reputation.

Gemma had always supposed Hugo to have been friends with Sebastian's father. They were much of an age, for the earl had married late in life.

However, it appeared the connection was on Lady Carleton's side. Why had Sybil never contacted her friend? Perhaps she had not been sure of her welcome. Despite her vagaries, Sybil was unflinchingly proud.

Smiling, Lady Carleton touched Gemma's hand. "At all events, you are here now, and that is the main thing!"

Perhaps she should raise her reason for coming to Laidley. The time seemed as opportune as any. "Sebastian mentioned Lady Fanny is to be married, ma'am, and I do so love weddings. I wondered if you might grant me a favour? Would you let me help with the arrangements? I am used to being occupied and I cannot bear to sit about plying my needle all day. I must be up and doing."

Lady Carleton's face lengthened. "Oh, my dear! Didn't Sebastian tell you? The wedding has been cancelled."

Gemma hesitated. "Sebastian thinks Fanny may well relent towards Romney, my lady."

"Oh, no. Sebastian is quite wrong. Fanny told me herself." With the air of repeating something learned by rote, Lady Carleton said, "Fanny would rather be boiled in oil and sold into slavery than marry that inconstant blackguard." She chuckled. "I must say, I thought it most spirited of her to end the betrothal."

Gemma spread her hands. "Sebastian seems to believe Fanny will change her mind, and I must admit, I am coming round to that view myself. You do not think it would be as well to continue with the preparations regardless? There is to be a house party, I gather, and—"

"A house party?" Lady Carleton squeezed her hands together and pressed them to her lips. "Oh, yes! But we don't need the betrothal as an excuse to have a party. Not anymore."

Eleven

SEBASTIAN visited his mother's bedchamber, intending to see how she did, but Shelby informed him her mistress had already breakfasted, dressed, and sallied forth.

As he hurried along the corridor in search of her, he heard voices in his mother's sitting room and ducked his head around the door to investigate. He saw Gemma and his mother enjoying what looked like a comfortable coze.

"Mama!" He strode in, annoyance sharpening his tone. "What are you doing here? This room is not fit for you yet." Stiffly, he bent to plant an awkward kiss beside her mouth.

"I was becoming acquainted with our guest, Sebastian." His mother looked into his eyes and her smile faltered. She gestured to the devastation around her. "But you must think me odd to keep you sitting about in here, Miss Maitland." She gathered her skirts and rose with careful dignity. "I shall bid you both good morning."

Sebastian stared after her as she left the room, then turned and caught Gemma regarding him with a troubled expression. He sighed. How could he explain his mother's behaviour when she confused him as much as she confused everyone else?

"You were not very kind, were you, Sebastian?"

"Kind!" He gave a harsh laugh. "How kind do you think it was to pack a six-year-old boy off to stay with relatives, friends, school, anywhere but his home, where he wanted to be?"

He shook his head and turned away to gaze blindly out the window. "Don't—*don't* feel sorry for her, Gemma. You simply do not know."

With a feminine rustle of skirts, he heard her approach. Though she did not touch him, her warmth surrounded him, drew him in.

"You are right," she said softly. "I don't know about the past. But perhaps your mother has changed, Scovy. I sensed deep remorse in her, though I could not guess why. Perhaps she feels sorry that she treated you so."

Sebastian exhaled a sharp breath. "She has infinitely more to be sorry for than that."

"What do you mean?"

He closed his eyes. He shouldn't have said it. Now Gemma would pester him in gentle ways until he told her, just as she always did. But some wounds were too raw even for her tender touch. He waved a dismissive hand. "Never mind."

Her attention caught by the movement, Gemma looked at the slim volume he held with interest. "What is that you are reading, Scovy?"

"What? Oh, nothing. *Childe Harold's Pilgrimage*." He squirmed under her candid gaze and tossed the book onto the sofa. "If you must know, I've been reading it to Mama."

Gemma's eyes gleamed approval. "Now, that is more what I would expect from you." She hesitated, then put her hand on his arm and tilted her head towards the window. "Shall we walk outside, Sebastian? Will you not show me some of the estate?"

Grateful for the change of subject, he clasped her hand briefly. "We would need to ride to see it properly, but I can show you the gardens and the park if you like."

"Yes, please. And then we shall ride early tomorrow, before breakfast. Will you wait in the hall while I fetch my bonnet? My skin has a dreadful tendency to freckle, you know."

With a quirk to his lips, Sebastian watched her go. He found this small vanity in the usually practical Gemma endearing. Who would have thought she cared for freckles?

Which brought his mind to another consideration. If what he had seen of her wardrobe was any indication of the remainder, Gemma needed new gowns before the house party started. He must find a way to broach the subject soon.

He considered the matter as he jogged down the stairs to wait for her. He would only entrust Gemma to a top London *modiste*, but the logistics of fulfilling such a commission would be a challenge.

He smiled cynically. Madame de Cacharelle would oblige him, no doubt. She had received many similar commissions from him in the past—for less respectable women, of course, but to the avaricious Madame it was all the same, as long as her bills were paid.

When Gemma reappeared, she had changed her gown for a more becoming pale yellow muslin and added a chip-straw hat with a wide ribbon in the same shade as her dress. She looked like sunshine. The only thing left to do was to get rid of those dreadful braids.

"Charming!" He offered his arm. "Shall we?"

They descended the front steps to the drive and he paused. "Now, where shall it be? The cascade? The rose arbour? The maze? We have an Elizabethan knot garden, after the style of Tradescant, which sports a particularly fine herbaceous border. Or perhaps sculpture is more to your taste? I believe my grandsire plundered most of the principal classical monuments to amass the rather fine collection that litters the paths in the Grecian walk."

Gemma wrinkled her nose at his flippancy. "You must show me all your favourite haunts, of course! I did not come with you for a tour of the grounds as if I were a visitor on public day."

"Favourite haunts?" He grimaced.

"Yes, of course. There must have been trees you climbed as a boy, lawns you played cricket on with your brother, a shrubbery where you played hide-and-seek." She wrinkled her brow. "Are you telling me you have no fond memories of Laidley at all?"

He shrugged. "I was hardly ever here. All my favourite places are at Ware. You know that."

Gemma stared up at him with the sun in her eyes and slowly shook her head. "Poor little boy."

Sebastian decided he did not care for her sympathy. He paused for a moment, as if to think, then snapped his fingers. "Ah! Now I remember. There *was* a tree." He caught her hand. "Let us see if we can find it."

He strode off and Gemma tripped along beside him in a flurry of skirts and ribbons, holding on to her hat with her other hand.

The tree was entirely apocryphal, of course. He owned not one memory of Laidley free from the poison of his father's relentless ambition, but if she wanted childhood reminiscences, childhood reminiscences she should have.

They crossed the drive and cut through the lime walk. When they reached the depths of the park, he picked an old oak at random and halted before it. "That's the one. I used to climb this tree."

He looked down at Gemma. The dappled sunlight shifted and played over her creamy complexion. A strong breeze tugged at her hat and ruffled the edges of the gauzy tucker she wore at her bosom.

She moved to examine the trunk. "But how would you find a foothold here? It is quite a way to the lowest branch."

"What?" He inspected the tree. She was right. "Well, I was always tall for my age, you know. And . . . and the tree has grown since then, I daresay."

She glanced at him oddly, but all sense and reason seemed to have flown from his head. He had wrestled most of the morning with his list of eligible bachelors, his mind filled with images of Gemma walking out of a church to the tune of pealing bells, with her delicate hand tucked under the arm of one man or another of his acquaintance— one man or another with the right to stroke the tender flesh of her breast; one man who would taste her lips night after night, feel her move beneath him, surround him . . .

"No, that's not the tree at all. I was mistaken," he said huskily. "We should go back."

Gemma's hand came to rest on his chest, restraining him. He hoped she did not feel his heart thump in response, as if trying to leap into her palm. He fought to calm his breathing. "Don't."

"What?"

"Don't touch me, Gemma. We should not be alone like this. I can't keep seeing you and not touch you. It's driving me insane."

Her eyes widened in shock. She tilted her head and incredibly, a smile slowly curved her lips, like heat and sex and sunlight all rolled into one.

With a strangled sound, Sebastian gripped her wrist and pulled her into his arms. In the same motion, he swooped under the brim of her hat to capture her mouth. One arm encircled her waist, one hand tipped her hat off her head. He kissed her ear, the corners of her eyes, her throat. She gasped, so he kissed her neck again, and worked his way back to her mouth, hungrily making a meal of all that lush softness.

This time, when his tongue touched hers she did not retreat. Triumphant, he deepened the kiss, stroking into her mouth, pressing her harder against him, feeling her, lush and inviting. She tasted so sweet.

He groaned and the hand at her waist moved upwards of its own accord to trace the outline of her breast, rub her taut nipple through layers of muslin and shift and corset. He'd wanted to do this since he first laid eyes on her again, and finally he had and she was letting him.

A small hand plunged through his hair and settled at his nape. She held him close and their kisses grew ever more heated, and the longing to lay her down on the soft grass and love her thoroughly coursed through him like a fever in his blood.

In all of his experience, nothing compared with this. Their first kiss had been light and tentative. Now, Gemma demanded as much as he. Her lips burned, she shifted and stretched under his hands and moaned softly in her throat, but she did not tell him to stop.

Could he stop? He didn't know. He didn't care. All he wanted was Gemma. To make his mark on her and brand her as his before some other man . . .

Oh, God. He wrenched his mouth away and stepped back, catching her questing hands. Her lids fluttered open. She was flushed and breathless. One edge of her tucker drifted loose while the yellow ribbon of her hat caught in a knot at her throat.

Sebastian muttered a curse. If anyone saw them like this, he could wave his comfortable existence good-bye. He adored Gemma, he craved her, but he would never make her—or any woman—his wife. Let his cousins beget heirs to the title and the estate. He wanted none of his father's legacy, no hand in perpetuating such an abomination, such an affront to Andy's memory.

"Gemma, I'm sorry. I shouldn't have—"

She bit her lip and did not meet his eyes as she set her gown to rights. "No, that's quite all right. I shouldn't have, either, but the fact remains we did."

The fingers that retied the ribbons of her hat trembled. "Perhaps from now on we might agree not to kiss anymore," she said huskily. "It does terrible things to my brain, kissing you, Scovy. I don't know why I keep doing it."

He cleared his throat awkwardly, like a callow youth engaging in his first dalliance, and looked away. "Perhaps . . . perhaps the affection we feel for each other, our old friendship is confusing us." He sighed and brought his gaze back to hers. "When I'm with you, I feel sixteen again, innocent and young and free, as if anything is possible. But it's an illusion, Gemma. I am who I am, and I'd be criminal to pretend otherwise."

She searched his face. "You should not need me to feel free, Scovy. The only pretence I see in you is the uncaring face you show to the world. It is not you, this . . . this reckless disregard for your duty, this cynical indifference."

Her words stung like brandy on a raw wound. He bared his teeth at her in a smile and saw her recoil at his vicious expression. "If you knew the things I had done, you would not say that, my dear. If you knew the things I want to do to you, you would run screaming for the hills. Oh, no, Gemma. Make no mistake. What you see is the real Sebastian Laidley, a depraved, idle rake." His jaw clenched. "And you would do much better to stay the hell away from me."

She gasped. "Scovy, don't!"

But he ignored her, turned on his heel, and strode back to the house—to pack.

H E *had his hand on your breast!* In the safety of her bedchamber, Gemma tried to shut out the voice of her conscience. But the voice of her conscience sounded like Aunt Matilda, and was equally difficult to ignore.

Gemma stood before the mottled cheval glass in her dingy chamber and saw the flush that still blazed in her cheeks. Her breast tingled, raw and aching, as if the ghost of Sebastian's palm still stroked it, as if the tender flesh longed for more.

She raised trembling fingers to her lips and sank onto the bed, gripping the carved bedpost for support.

What did he mean by kissing her like that? Sebastian Laidley, the most determined bachelor in Christendom could not mean marriage. Even John Talbot, a respectable gentleman farmer, had balked at courting someone with her background.

More to the point, what on earth had *she* been about, letting him take such liberties? Inviting them, revelling in them like the veriest wanton. She had no more desire to marry than Sebastian. If she married him, she would have to leave Ware.

Her conscience tittered at her naivety. *He is a rake. You are Sybil Maitland's daughter. What do you* think *he means by kissing you?* She groaned and leaned her forehead against the ugly carved mahogany of the bedpost. Even when he had mocked her and warned her against him, it had not *felt* like those other times when men tried to take what they expected would be easy pickings.

Perhaps the only difference lay in her.

She had to admit it: Sebastian moved her, excited her in a way no man had ever done before. Even now, her body craved his touch. Heat flashed in her belly every time she thought of his large hands moulding her curves, his firm lips, his unrelenting mouth ravishing hers.

Her cheeks burned hotter. Perhaps she was her mother's daughter after all. Hiding away at Ware, she had never strayed from the path of virtue, but then, she had never been tempted. One look, one kiss from Sebastian had been enough to steer her frighteningly off course. What had happened to her? Why didn't she have the strength—the will, even—to fight this dangerous attraction?

Her mind shied away from pursuing that line of

thought. She took a deep breath. Sitting there thinking about it, reliving the encounter in her imagination would do nothing to restore her calm.

So she did what she always did when she did not want to think. She changed back to her shabby blue gown, donned her old baize smock, and threw herself into work.

As she left the last bedchamber in the house some hours later with a list of required repairs and purchases, Gemma almost collided with the butler. A lanky stick-insect of a man, Ripton loomed over her, the grey eyes in his angular face shifting under woolly eyebrows. Gemma opened her mouth to greet him, but he pressed a long, bony finger to his lips and beckoned her into a small saloon. Biting back a smile, she followed.

"Miss Maitland, may I say how happy I am to see you here?" Ripton's softly spoken London accent was a direct contrast to the housekeeper's rollicking Cornish burr.

Surprised, Gemma inclined her head. "Why, Ripton, I'm flattered."

He made a harassed gesture. "You must have guessed how it is at Laidley, miss. I do not like to speak out of turn, but it makes my heart ache to see the old house so rundown as she is. It's the mistress. She's not well, and there are those who've taken sore advantage of her indisposition. There are those who will try to put a spoke in the wheel of your house party, miss."

Mrs. Penny. That had already been made clear to her. What remained clear as mud was why Mrs. Penny should wield such power. In Gemma's household, such insubordination would be dealt with summarily.

"I wish you to know, miss, that I shall assist you in any way I can. Even had my lady not required it, I should have offered you my services."

She smiled at him. "Splendid! Let us start, then, with this list. You will know who in the village might assist us. We need a seamstress and a carpenter, at least, and a few more girls to help in the house, especially the kitchens. We will use what materials and labour may be provided locally and send posthaste to London for the rest."

Ripton permitted himself a smile. "Thank you, miss. I should be delighted."

EARLY the following morning, Gemma summoned Dorry to help her dress in her charcoal riding habit. She was still trying to decide whether to keep her appointment with Sebastian when Fanny walked in.

"Now that is fortunate! I was just about to go for a ride myself," said Fanny.

Gemma raised her brows. "You have decided to venture out of your self-imposed exile, then?"

"I have it on excellent authority that Romney and my brother made sharp inroads on the brandy last night and we'll not be seeing either of them before noon. I shall be quite safe."

So, it appeared, would Gemma. She did not know whether she was entirely happy about that.

She told herself she wanted to see him again to clear the air that had suddenly turned hot and thick between them, to recapture their former, easy friendship. But part of her knew there was no going back. Part of her longed to feel his arms about her, his mouth fitting so perfectly over hers.

"Are you coming?" asked Fanny, turning back at the doorway.

Gemma started. "Oh! Yes. Let me get my hat."

THE glossy black mare that awaited her on the drive made Gemma cry out in delight. Sebastian had judged her taste to a nicety. She spent some time becoming acquainted with her new mount before she allowed the groom to assist her into the saddle.

While the groom attended to Fanny, Gemma let the mare dance beneath her, shaking off her fidgets. The horse had just settled when a large post-chaise bowled around from the back of the house and pulled up before the front steps.

Gemma recognised Sebastian's crest on the panel. The front door flung open and three footmen laden with baggage descended the stairs in a stately procession. Gemma exchanged a puzzled glance with Fanny.

Sebastian emerged, clad in a caped greatcoat, gleaming Hessians and beaver hat. He looked crisp and elegant, as if he had never heard the word brandy spoken. Romney followed, his appearance considerably more disreputable.

"And just where do you think you're going?" demanded Fanny. Gemma was glad of her friend's forthrightness. It was exactly what she wished to know.

Romney inclined his head in an ironic bow. Sebastian answered. "London. I have urgent business there." He turned his head to regard Gemma, and the first inkling of his overindulgence the previous evening showed in a strange glitter about his eyes. "How do you like Black Dancer? She seems to like you."

"Very much, thank you." Gemma found it difficult to be as cool as she wanted when he had lent her such a prime piece of horseflesh. His gaze trailed fire over every line of her body, a heated reminder of her folly the day before.

Her pulse fluttered. She cleared her throat. "You will be back for the house party, I presume."

His mouth quirked in a half smile. "Oh, yes. Well before that. Write to me at Laidley House if you need anything. I shan't be away too long."

SEBASTIAN sat in Madame de Cacharelle's cream-and-gilt showroom and calculated he had been celibate for precisely twenty-seven days. No wonder he could not control himself with Gemma. Having endured the good-natured teasing of Madame at the change in measurements from his last commission, he recalled, for the first time since he left London for Ware, that Eleanor might be wondering where he was.

Relieved to have discovered the source of the strange discontentment that had been plaguing him, he decided to stroll round to Mount Street to call on his latest paramour after he'd finished with Madame de Chacharelle.

That settled, he put her out of his mind and concentrated on the *modiste*'s suggestions for Gemma's new wardrobe. He had asked Fanny to winkle Gemma's dimensions from that fierce maid of hers and presented them, together with an exact description of Gemma's colouring, to Madame.

De Cacharelle *tsk*ed and *tutt*ed and *oh la la*'ed. Having explained what an impossibility it would be to design clothes for a lady she had never seen, she rapidly drew sketches and ordered her girls to model various costumes. At the end of a dazzling parade of gauzes, muslins, lustrings, merinos, satins, and silks, she shot him a look of birdlike inquiry. "Why so secretive, milor'? This new *amour*, she is special, no?"

Sebastian stared at her impertinence, but Madame rattled on gaily, unabashed. "Oho! So coy. But we must let you have your secrets, *non*?"

"Just so, Madame."

"And now for the more intimate apparel, *hein*? I shall show you my *pièce de résistance*. Only for my most favoured customers, you understand." Madame bustled off to the back room and returned with a filmy concoction of peach gauze and cream lace, a dashing peignoir fit for a high-class courtesan.

Sebastian gazed at the garment and swallowed hard. He could not stop imagining how Gemma might look inside it.

Wrenching his mind from a fantasy he would never realise, he said carelessly, "Oh, very well. Throw that in, too."

Madame would only grow more suspicious if he declined such a ravishing ensemble for a woman she assumed was his mistress. He would have the boxes sent directly to him and remove the offending garment before it reached Gemma.

Having completed his transaction with Madame to her patent satisfaction and his considerable expense, he left the elegant showroom. With a sense of grim determination hardly commensurate with his amorous purpose, he strode around to Mount Street.

Eleanor kept him kicking his heels downstairs for a long time, no doubt making certain preparations. He smiled to himself when the butler bade him go up. With Eleanor, at least, one did not have to waste time talking.

"Darling." In a sinuous movement, she wound her arms around his neck, gusting him with Eau de Nuit, a scent he had purchased for her, but now found slightly overpowering.

He drew back a little and explained about the house party, the reason for his absence.

Not that she would care. Eleanor never asked him to explain himself. If she took other lovers, he did not demand the details. A perfectly convenient, amicable relationship. But then why did her embrace feel like a stranglehold?

"A house party and I am not invited?" The delicate, skilled hands slid to his shoulders. Her lips formed the slightest pout, as if she knew very well how tempting her mouth looked in that pose.

On the pretext of taking out his snuffbox, he disentangled himself. "Just a dull affair full of cousins. You would not be amused, my dear." He looked up. "I am surprised you would wish to attend."

Eleanor shrugged and turned away. He watched his high-born mistress drift around her boudoir, and for the first time, he noticed the artifice behind her sensual movements, the cosmetics carefully applied to emphasise her features, the way every inch of her *dishabille* had been designed and draped to enhance her figure. Surely he had known all that before, thought it a cultivated elegance, valued her none the less for it.

Irritated at this sudden twinge of dissatisfaction, he said, "Well, why not? You will undoubtedly enliven what promises to be the most tedious affair. I shall include your name among the invitations."

Eleanor inclined her coiffed dark head. "Thank you, my lord."

She seemed to be waiting for something, though he had no idea what. She opened her mouth to speak, but apparently thought better of it. She smiled, and her teeth showed very white against her rose-tinted lips. "I am afraid I am not at leisure this afternoon, Carleton." She held out her hand. "Until Laidley, then."

Almost relieved, Sebastian took her proffered hand and raised it to his lips. "Until Laidley, my dear. I shall live in anticipation."

SEBASTIAN had meant only to stay in town long enough to wait for Gemma's gowns to be made up, execute some trifling business with his solicitor, and call on the few of his friends who happened to be in London still when the rest of the *ton* had removed to Brighton or their country estates.

But he lingered, and Romney lingered with him. He did not visit Eleanor again, noting that she had not wished to see him until the date of the house party. He wondered why he should consider it in the nature of a reprieve.

Still less could he fathom what idiotic whim had led him to invite her to Laidley. Eleanor was discreet, the widow of a baronet. No one would question her presence at a *ton* party, and he believed few knew of their connection anyway. But he would know, and for some reason it made him uncomfortable to think of her in his home, mixing with his mother and sister and meeting Gemma.

"How about Crockford's?" Romney swung his Malacca cane idly as they strolled along St James's after dining at their club.

"Crockford's?" Sebastian raised his brows. "Don't think I've heard of it."

"It's a new hell. Play is deep, but the wine's tolerable."

Sebastian grimaced. He had not much taste for gaming, but Mortimer's suggestion of visiting Fatima's House of Pleasure in Covent Garden held little appeal either. He had an inkling of why that should be, so he said, "I vote for Fatima's. Lead on, Mortimer."

A stifling mix of heat and cheap scent assailed him as he handed his coat to the attendant. The establishment was not one of the more exclusive ones Sebastian had ever patronised, but the women made up in exuberance what they lacked in refinement.

After a brandy or two, he had begun to convince himself that a cheerful tumble with an uncomplicated young whore was precisely what he needed, but when a rosy brunette thrust her generous bosom in his face and demanded in ringing tones whether he fancied some, he could barely conceal his disgust.

Romney sat at a corner table, drinking steadily and snarling at anyone unwise enough to approach him. Mortimer had his hands full with twin redheads, the undisputed attraction of the house.

As if from a vast distance, Sebastian surveyed the tawdry, tragic gaiety that frolicked around him. He felt like an outsider, a stranger to the riotous life he had led since Andy died.

Quietly, he finished his drink and slipped away.

Twelve

———— ❧ ————

AFTER a month, Sebastian returned to a house transformed by a whirlwind of light, fresh air, and excellent taste. Laidley, which could once have earned a starring role in one of the hoarier gothic romances, now appeared elegant, comfortable, and welcoming—at least on the inside.

The great hall remained essentially the same, though plush red Turkey carpets sprawled over the flagstones to lighten the atmosphere and a couple of Sheraton tables supported huge Imari vases full of crimson roses. Armour and medieval weaponry conceded their places to a magnificent collection of Meissen porcelain, which used to grace the long gallery, if he remembered correctly. The air smelled of beeswax and lavender, and even the tapestry hangings on the walls looked fresh, rejuvenated by skilled, careful hands.

Faint sounds of sawing and hammering disturbed the tranquil setting. The work was not yet done.

Sebastian turned on his heel, jogged up the stairs, and strode along the corridor, eager to see what transformation Gemma had wrought in his bedchamber.

He stopped short on the threshold.

The room had been altered along the same lines as the great hall, but with one significant difference: Suspended from the pelmet of his four-poster bed, glittering with gilt and scarlet embroidery, was a cobalt-blue silk hanging depicting the family crest.

Sebastian's jaw clenched. "Ripton!"

In a few moments, the butler's measured tread approached. "My lord?"

"Find Miss Maitland for me, will you, and ask her to attend me here."

Ripton hesitated. Sebastian shot him a searing glance.

The butler bowed. "Yes, my lord. At once."

In a few minutes, Gemma joined him, smiling a welcome. He was too irritated to return the smile, even though the vision of her sweet face had haunted him since he left Laidley.

He jabbed a finger at the hanging. "What is the meaning of this?"

Gemma glanced from him to the abomination behind his bed. "The crest? That was my idea. Don't you like it? Fanny told me all your predecessors hung it over their beds."

Sebastian gritted his teeth. "Not this one."

"Oh? Well, I shall have it removed, then." Gemma's matter-of-fact tone made him feel as if he'd overreacted.

And he had, hadn't he? Churlish of him to pinch at her for the one thing she had done that was not to his taste. He should be on his knees thanking her for her efforts in his absence.

"Was that all, *your lordship*?" The irony in her voice told him she agreed with his silent assessment.

He turned to her. "I'm sorry, Gemma. I don't like to be reminded—"

"That you are the earl? But you are, you know. And you cannot continue trying to escape it." She started for the door.

Keeping a tight rein on his anger, Sebastian followed her. "Forgive me, but you do not know the circumstances."

Gemma kept walking. "I know that it is not in your nature to shirk your duty, Sebastian. I wonder why you insist upon pretending you don't care."

Irritated at having to address her straight little back as she marched along the corridor, he stalked after her. "Where are you going?"

"To a quiet place where we may talk."

"Marvellous!" That's just what he needed—a quiet place to wring Gemma's interfering neck.

She led him downstairs in silence, through the heavy oak door to the east wing of the house and on past the state rooms—grand, richly decorated salons; the principal dining room; and the ballroom. All had been stripped of their Holland covers and appeared repaired, refreshed, polished, dusted, and ready for use.

Sebastian glanced through doorways as Gemma led the way down the corridor. "Never say my staff did all this?"

"Not all of it," said Gemma. "I hired a lot of help from the village, but your servants set to with a will, Sebastian. They are excited about the prospect of entertaining again."

They continued to the end of the wing. Gemma passed through the double doors with a look of mingled mischief and triumph on her face. "Now, you will be surprised!"

She led him through the music room and flung open a pair of doors. Sebastian pulled up short and stared around in amazement.

A small oasis of lush green foliage and bright flowers arranged in beds and urns and hanging baskets met his appreciative gaze, all set under a dome of panelled glass to catch the sun. A fountain tinkled in the centre of the stone courtyard. Love seats were scattered about, flanked by potted orange trees and palms. On the other side of the conservatory, long windows opened to a sprawling green lawn beyond.

"You did all this in four weeks?"

Gemma nodded. "It is not quite finished, but well enough

for our guests. The glaziers were not precisely dagger-cheap, but the result is magnificent, don't you agree?"

Sebastian swallowed, humbled and sick with guilt at having left Gemma to do all of this. He'd had no idea what lengths she had meant to go to, or he would not have stayed away so long.

"Gemma, I . . ." Words failed him.

She smiled, understanding what he wanted to say. "Now, about the hanging over your bed, Scovy."

"Never mind."

"No, you are right. I should not have taken such a liberty." She sat down on a love seat and regarded him with her open, candid gaze. "Fanny told me you did not wish to take over your father's apartments when he died."

Sebastian inspected a stone urn spilling geraniums. "That is correct."

"Yes, well, I thought you ought to have something in your rooms to indicate that you are master here. Perhaps even a reminder of your heritage?"

Sebastian barked a laugh. "Gemma, I don't need a reminder. My position here hangs about my neck like poor Coleridge's albatross. I cannot escape it."

"Much as you might try?" Gemma's dark blue eyes were serious, penetrating. She saw too much. "Sebastian," she added, "I need to speak to you about the estate."

He nipped a crimson geranium from its trailing stem and leaned over to tuck it behind Gemma's ear. He smiled down at her, though it was an effort. "Don't let us quarrel. I am really not in the mood, and these delightful surroundings aren't conducive."

She raised her brows. "Why must a discussion about the estate necessarily be quarrelsome?"

He sighed. "Because you wish me to act as you would, and I simply don't have the stomach for playing lord of the manor. It is as much as I can do just to *be* here, Gemma.

Don't ask any more of me. Not now. Let us face the hurdle of this house party and the wedding, and put the rest aside for the moment, shall we?"

Gemma plucked the geranium from behind her ear and twirled it between her fingers. "It is highly doubtful whether there will be a wedding, Sebastian. I know what you said about Fanny and Romney, but he has not helped his cause by racketing about London with you these past weeks."

"Which just shows the irrationality of women," remarked Sebastian. "When he tried to speak with Fanny, she would not even grant him an audience." He sighed. "If it's any consolation, we did not racket about town. We were models of propriety, in fact."

"Oh? How gratifying." She did not believe him, and he supposed he could hardly blame her. She rose and shook out her skirts. "Now, I must go and make sure everything is in order in the kitchens."

"Gemma . . ." That she thought so poorly of him stung. "Leave the crest where it is. I daresay I shall get used to it."

She smiled. "Yes, Scovy. I daresay you will."

❧

FANNY strolled in the shrubbery with no sense of impending danger until large, firm hands caught her waist and swung her into a hard embrace.

She melted into him, met his lips with feverish intensity to match his own, and when he finally raised his head and looked into her face with those fierce, wild eyes, she licked her lips so she could taste him again.

Remembering where he had been these past weeks and how he must have spent them, Fanny tried to summon her previous righteous anger, but her knees were the consistency of syllabub and the comfort of Romney's strong arms around her proved too strong to fight.

"This does not mean I will marry you," she said weakly, fingering his coat lapel.

"Ah." He bent his head and nipped her earlobe. "Then I shall have to compromise you further. Perhaps an obliging gardener might happen upon us when my hand is up your skirts."

She gasped and tried to thrust him away. "You are supremely vulgar. No wonder I hate you."

"*Methinks she doth protest too much.*" Romney's light tone belied watchful eyes and a determined set to his jaw. "Fanny, this nonsense has gone on long enough, don't you think? Come, you know you must marry me."

She tried to avert her head. His hot breath tickled her throat and thrilled her down to her toes. " 'Must' is a dangerous word to use to a Laidley, my lord. I will not marry a man of your inconstant, profligate character."

He traced her lips with a fingertip. "Now *you* are being vulgar, little Fanny. Virtuous ladies, my dear, should know nothing about that side of a man's life."

Fanny's eyes grew hot with tears. She blinked them back. "Well, we both know I am not virtuous," she whispered. "And I won't play second fiddle to your other women."

He laughed and caught her closer. "Don't you think you could hold me, Fanny? Do you think I would stray?"

"A leopard does not change his spots, or so I am led to believe." She struggled to maintain her composure as the hard length of his body pressed against hers and the glint in his eyes told her he was hot for her. The thought set her blood racing and scrambled her thoughts, made her body ache for his. She wanted to believe in the fairy-tale ending, but she was too pragmatic to trust in a rake's reform.

He growled in her ear. "Fanny, I have made love to you. You could be carrying my child—"

"No!" She said it more sharply than she'd intended. Quietly, she added, "There is no child. And now I have been granted that reprieve, I do not mean to indulge in such folly again. I've been given a second chance and I intend to take it. I would only end up miserable married to you."

He exhaled a sharp breath, as though her words were a blow to the stomach. But how could that be? "There may be no child, but I have ruined you for any other man. You must allow me—"

Fanny snorted. "What nonsense you speak, Romney. There are any number of gentlemen who would turn a blind eye on their wedding night for the price of my dowry and connections."

Romney stared at her, and his arms dropped to his sides. "Indeed? I'd no notion you were such a little cynic, Fanny. I fear, my sweet, that your worldly wisdom surpasses even mine."

He went quiet a moment. Gazing into the distance, he said, "I can make promises, but I do not have a window into the future. I cannot offer you proof of my good intentions. It is something that must always be taken on trust between a woman and a man. And because of my past, you cannot trust me." He looked at her. "There is nothing I can do to convince you, is there?"

His sober words set her objections in stone, when before they had just been nebulous, doubts that might have been overcome in the heat of passion or by his confident reassurance.

Wretched, knowing he spoke perfect sense, Fanny shook her head. "No, nothing."

Romney turned away and his voice was remote. "Then our betrothal is at an end. I shall inform your brother and send the notice to the papers. Good day, Lady Fanny."

SEBASTIAN dragged a hand through his hair. "You cannot be absent from a house party in your honour. Good God, why did you have to have this conversation with her now?"

"I am desolated that my timing was so inconvenient. In future, I shall take care to consult you before I allow myself to be jilted."

"Sorry." Sebastian sighed. "She loves you, you know."

"Does she?" Romney's sarcastic smile twisted. "I thought so at one time."

Neither of them spoke for some minutes after that. The westering sun streamed through the library window. Sebastian squinted at the horizon until his eyes smarted and streaks of light danced before his eyes. Then he lit the lamp on his desk and moved to draw the heavy curtains shut.

Romney drained his glass and set it down with a decisive snap. "I must show her. I must reform."

Sebastian repressed a smile. "Well, it's worth a try. How do you propose to go about it?"

"I don't know. Perhaps I should model myself on one of those virtuous bores you intend for Miss Maitland—attend church on Sunday, keep regular hours, indulge in healthful exercise, prose on about crop rotation and sheep-breeding techniques, that sort of thing."

"Lord, you'll be driven to suicide in a week."

"No. I can do it. I will do it. I must."

❧

THE sung Eucharist on the Sunday before the house party was enlivened by an extraordinary occurrence. Two elegant male personages graced the Laidley family pew, clutched their hymnals, and raised their bass voices in surprisingly tuneful song.

The rest of the congregation spent most of the service craning their necks to obtain glimpses of the earl and his friend. Though the earl received the vicar's sermon about the sins of the fathers with a saturnine expression, his companion attended with rapt concentration.

"He is nodding and smiling now. What can he mean by it?" Fanny whispered a running commentary in Gemma's ear. "Do you think he will do something shocking and embarrass me before the congregation?"

Under her breath, Gemma answered, "Perhaps he came to pray for divine mercy since you will show him none. Really, Fanny, you must stop tormenting the poor man."

When the service ended and the parishioners gathered outside to gossip, Gemma and Fanny waited for the gentlemen to join them.

Romney paused to chat with the vicar and his wife. Sebastian stood by, with a slightly ironic expression that boded ill for the shiny-faced little vicar's attempts to include him in the conversation. Nevertheless, the two gentlemen left the vicar beaming.

They approached Gemma and Fanny and bowed. Romney spoke. "Ladies, we are invited to tea with the vicar. I undertook to accept the invitation on your behalf."

With courtly correctness, he offered Fanny his arm. Clearly bemused, she took it, and they walked on towards the vicarage.

Gemma glanced at Sebastian as they passed through the lychgate. "What is all this about?"

He shrugged. "Romney's idea, not mine. And I shall not be prolonging the experience. Come on."

He led Gemma away from the vicarage to the common. No children played there, as it was the Sabbath. The green landscape was silent, but for the odd birdsong and the salt breeze hushing through the trees.

"But what about the vicar?"

"Hang the vicar. He should know better than to preach his sermons at me."

Gemma considered. "The sins of the fathers? But your father was a very upright man by all accounts." She hesitated, choosing her words. "When one is feeling guilty, one tends to interpret the most innocently motivated words as a reproach."

Sebastian stared at her, hard.

Gemma lifted her chin. She owed it to him to tell the truth. "When I mentioned the estate the other day, Scovy, I did not mean to pinch at you. I wanted to tell you I am concerned. Your steward is ill and failing, but he is too proud to ask for help."

"What? Wilks is only one-and-sixty, not in his dotage. Fit as a flea, old Wilks. I rely on him utterly. You must be mistaken."

Gemma shook her head. "Since I have been here, I have noticed things. All is not as it should be." She paused. "Do you review the ledgers yourself, Scovy?"

"No, Wilks does it. Why?"

"I was provisioning for the house party and naturally wished to study the household accounts. There are . . . discrepancies which neither your housekeeper nor Mr. Wilks could explain to my satisfaction. I fear that if you check your other account books, you might find similar ones."

He was silent for a moment. "Are you telling me Wilks has been skimming the profits? I don't believe it."

"No, I suspect it is Mrs. Penny who is the culprit, but Mr. Wilks should have noticed, don't you think?"

A flush of mortification swept over Sebastian's lean cheeks. Stiffly, he said, "Thank you. I shall look into it."

Gemma laid her hand on his arm and they walked on. She decided she had said enough on that subject for the time being. "Now, tell me about all of these people who will be coming to the party."

He shrugged. "I'm not sure what I can tell you. You will meet them soon enough."

Typical man! "When I meet them, I want to be prepared. If you describe them to me, I might remember their names more easily. I might know what to talk to them about."

He eyed her with amusement. "Meeting new people makes you nervous, doesn't it?"

"Of course not. I am always meeting people. Just . . . just not ones of your world, Scovy."

He sighed. "I suppose this is about your mother. Gemma, she is hardly Harriette Wilson. She is not well known in London, because she spends most of her time abroad. I doubt many of our guests would connect you with her, and even if they did, they would not care. My mother is sponsoring you, my sister and I acknowledge you. That is all that will matter to them."

"Perhaps you are right," said Gemma, not believing it for a second, but loath to debate the precise level of her mother's notoriety. "Still, I would prefer to stay in the background. You are kind to include me, but I am far happier keeping things running smoothly. I don't wish to dine with you, or—"

"For God's sake, Gemma, stop mouthing fustian like some deuced governess. You will join in the entertainments and that's the end of it. You insult my friends by assuming they will not welcome you." He grinned down at her. "The men will welcome you with open arms."

She flushed. The prospect did not entice her. A fortnight of dodging stray hands and extricating herself from surreptitious embraces held little appeal.

But Sebastian went on, oblivious. "Oh, I almost forgot. I took the liberty of purchasing a new wardrobe for you in town."

She halted. "You did what?"

He raised his brows. "As the *de facto* hostess, you will need to be suitably attired, and I thought the expense should be mine."

Was he out of his mind? "You bought gowns for me? I never heard of anything so outrageous. You know I cannot accept them, Scovy."

He sighed. "Look, no one need know I bought them and I certainly don't expect anything in return. Take it as a gift in thanks for your fine work here. I never did thank you properly." He caught her hand and raised it to his lips. The warm light in his eyes told her he wanted to do more.

Ruthlessly, Gemma thrust aside a similar desire and drew her hand away. She kept walking, her heart beating a little faster. He fell into step beside her.

She stole a glance under her hat brim at Sebastian's chiselled profile. Why did her instinct always tell her to trust him? He was a rake, a heartless seducer of hapless females. He had never pretended otherwise. Yet when he produced a truly ridiculous justification for doing something that would ruin her if the gossips got hold of it, she believed him. Couldn't help it. He was still Scovy to her.

When they passed under the canopy of a huge oak, Gemma stopped and turned to him. There was something she desperately wanted to know. "The day before you left for London . . . when you kissed me. Why did you do it?"

His lips twisted, a touch rueful. He reached past her and ran his fingers down the tree trunk. "It was your smile, princess. I could not resist."

She tried to ignore this new endearment. "But if I were a lady of irreproachable virtue, you would have resisted, wouldn't you? If I were not Sybil Maitland's daughter—"

Sebastian threw his head back and laughed. "Oh, by God, that's rich!" He put his hands on her shoulders, sliding them down to grasp her wrists. She stepped back, but he moved with her, backing her slowly until her hat brim buckled against the tree trunk and her shawl caught on the bark.

Impatiently, he shook his head. "You silly little fool. Don't you know if I thought you were fair game we would be lovers by now?" His voice grew husky. "We would have been lovers before we left Ware."

Her cheeks flamed. Her heartbeat grew frantic. She must be like her mother after all, because the idea of being Sebastian's lover was like a lightning strike through her body, melting her from the inside out. Her knees buckled. She managed to choke out, "I believe I might have had something to say to that."

"Oh?" The set of his shoulders reeked of masculine arrogance. Still gripping her wrists, he smiled, a flash of white teeth. "Then you do not want me? You let me put my tongue in your mouth and my hand on your breast—out of friendship, perhaps?"

Furious at his crude conceit, she wrenched her wrists from his hold, but she was trapped between his large, solid body and the tree trunk. Before she could slide free, he took her face between his hands and stared deep into her eyes, his wayward dark fringe flopping over his brow.

"I may be many things, Gemma, but don't accuse me of not valuing you as I ought. It is only your honour that has prevented me from making you mine."

Slowly, he bent towards her and stopped, his mouth inches from hers.

For a long, tense moment, she thought he would kiss her again, and—spineless idiot that she was—she wanted his kiss, craved it more than life. Her whole body trembled with the effort of remaining still, of keeping her own wayward lips to herself.

But only his warm breath whispered over her mouth as he spoke. "Don't offer me a challenge I can't resist."

Thirteen

THE first day of the two-week house party dawned grim and grey. By mid-morning, a howling wind whipped the surrounding trees to a frenzy and rain hurtled against the window panes in clattering waves.

As Gemma hurriedly revised her plans for the guests' entertainment that afternoon, the weather seemed both an ill omen and an accurate reflection of her mood. That her black-edged humour might stem from the fact that Sebastian had *not* kissed her the previous morning was a thought she refused to countenance.

But her mind continually absented itself from her task. Her body thrummed with restless energy, a powerful force inside her clawing, twisting, thrashing to break free. She felt wrong in her skin, as if that external layer concealed something wild and dangerous, something that might consume her if it could not find release.

The notion gripped her so hard that she went to the looking glass, only to see her perfectly normal reflection staring back.

Ridiculous! She smiled at her stupid fancy. Surely, this restive turbulence must be the result of missing her morning exercise because of the inclement weather. Resolving to ride out the following day—even if it stormed, she paced the floor of her bedchamber, waiting for Dorry to come and help her change her dress.

With complete disregard for Gemma's protests, Sebastian had sent mountains of bandboxes to her bedchamber. Only the twin considerations of the wasted expense and the scandal it would cause stopped her pitching them out the window into the rain.

When Dorry finished helping her into her best morning gown—her *own* best morning gown—Gemma ordered her maid to put the illicit purchases away, claiming that her mother had sent them. She hoped she would not be caught out in the lie.

"I'll say one thing for your mama, she has exquisite taste. Just look at the lace on this gown." Dorry laid the azure lustring carefully in the clothes press and ripped open another bandbox. "Oh!"

"What is it?" Gemma moved towards the bed. "Dorry, you are quite pink. Let me see."

She snatched the garment from Dorry's grasp and held it up to the dim, watery light. A diaphanous concoction of peach silk, lace, and gauze, designed to tantalise and reveal, to hint at what riches might lie beneath.

Gemma stared. She had never seen such a thing before in her life, had never imagined something like that existed.

The realization that Sebastian had presented her with this shocking creation crashed over her.

"Ooh!" She hurled the peignoir onto the bed. "Just wait till I get my hands on—that mother of mine. What can she be about, to send me such a thing?"

She choked on a laugh at Dorry's horrified expression. Breathless and hot, with a sickening flutter in her stomach, she picked up the garment and shook it out. "I—do you know, perhaps there has been a mistake. Yes, that must be it. I shall send it back to Mama. Thank you, Dorry, that will be all."

Fanny wandered in as Gemma stood gazing at the silly piece of peach fluff in her hand. She quickly stuffed the peignoir back in its bandbox before her friend saw.

But Fanny's thoughts were elsewhere. "I cannot believe it. He has invited Lady Russell—*Eleanor* Russell—to a party in our house." She eyed Gemma. "Why are you wearing that old thing?"

Gemma looked down. The sage green cambric was new this summer, neat and simple. Unexceptionable, she had thought. "What is wrong with it?"

"I supposed you would wear one of those marvellous creations Sebastian bought from de Cacharelle." Fanny grinned. "I took a peek earlier."

Gemma turned to her dressing table. "Surely you know it is the height of impropriety for your brother to be buying me clothes."

"Well, there is that, I suppose. Can't you pretend they are from Mama?"

"No. I can't. And what is wrong with my clothes anyway?"

Fanny waved a hand. "Nothing, darling. It is just that they are not precisely *à la mode*. When one must face the likes of Eleanor Russell, one should be armed with all the fashionable arsenal at one's disposal."

Gemma took a comb and began to tidy her hair, which didn't need tidying. "Who is Eleanor Russell, and why should I be locked in sartorial combat with her?"

There was a pause. Gently, Fanny said, "Lady Russell is Sebastian's mistress."

Gemma froze. After a blind, blank moment, she realised she gripped her comb so tightly its teeth bit into her palm. She uncurled her fingers and stared down at the angry red depressions on her skin. An ice-cold hand clenched around her heart.

But as the shock of Fanny's revelation gradually eased, Gemma wanted to shake herself for her stupidity. Hadn't she known such a woman as Lady Russell might exist? Must exist? And why shouldn't Sebastian go elsewhere for a bed partner when he could not get what he wanted from her?

But despite these reasonable, logical questions, talons of jealousy raked her heart.

"There is still time to change," said Fanny.

Part of her was sorely tempted, but such petty behaviour would gain her nothing. As if what she wore could change anything that mattered.

"No." She plastered a bright smile on her face. "Let us go down."

The guests arrived in a steady stream throughout the afternoon. Gemma greeted them like a polite automaton while an awful sadness weighted her heart and tied her stomach in knots.

"You are doing splendidly," Sebastian murmured in her ear as he paused beside her.

"Thank you." She made herself look at him, and marvelled that the familiar, dark features remained the same, though the world had rocked on its axis since last they spoke.

Images of Sebastian kissing a faceless, skilled, *willing* woman the way he had kissed her in the park swirled through her mind. But it wasn't just kissing that he and this Lady Russell indulged in, was it? That was the whole point.

Sebastian muttered a curse under his breath. Gemma turned in the direction of his gaze. And knew this woman instantly.

She was a beauty. Of course. Any mistress of Sebastian's

would be. But more than that, she was exquisite, from the soles of her Roman sandals to the dark hair curled *à la Meduse* under her dashing plumed hat.

Lady Russell posed for perhaps ten seconds on the threshold, waiting for all eyes to flock to her, before she undulated into the room.

I could never do that. Gemma let out a controlled breath and fought to keep her expression neutral.

Fanny greeted the newcomer with a chill hauteur that gave Gemma a crazed desire to laugh. Sebastian bowed as if he and this poised, elegant piece of feminine perfection were the merest acquaintances. "Ah, Lady Russell. The Chilterns are here and James Putney, too. Shall I take you to them?"

Lady Russell's pencilled brows flexed. "But will you not make your friend known to me, Sebastian?" With a delicate wave of her slender hand, she indicated Gemma.

Gemma's stomach lurched. Sebastian looked resigned, even a little bored. "But of course. Lady Russell, may I present Miss Maitland?"

"Lady Russell." Gemma curtseyed and shook the paragon's outstretched hand. "How do you do?"

The sparkling dark eyes assessed her. "Oh, I am sure we shall be friends. After all, any friend of Sebastian's . . ." She threw him a teasing, sidelong glance and laughed with her pretty mouth closed. A musical little hum.

The knots in Gemma's stomach pulled tighter. For two weeks until this house party ended, she would have to listen to that smug little laugh. Two whole weeks.

Gently, Gemma eased her hand free and forced an answering smile.

"You wished to see me, my lord?" Wilks bowed his grizzled head and entered the library.

Sebastian motioned for his steward to sit down. This

would not be easy. He had never been obliged to interfere in the running of the estate before. Wilks was a good man and a proud one. Though he might cling to certain of the late earl's practices with which Sebastian heartily disagreed, Sebastian had never cared enough to try to change things. But now he would have to step in, and he cursed the need to do so.

He frowned and ran a finger down the ledger in front of him. "Wilks, a serious matter has come to my attention. It appears someone has been falsifying the household accounts."

Wilks straightened in his chair. "My lord!"

"Of course I don't accuse you. I trust you implicitly, as my father did. But . . . Miss Maitland took an inventory of the larder, storerooms, and stillroom, and what she found there was considerably less than had been listed in the household expenses for this quarter. The household cannot have consumed so much in that time. You see my dilemma?"

"Of course. I shall have words with Mrs. Penny at once." Wilks seemed a trifle breathless. He swallowed convulsively.

Sebastian hastened to reassure him. "Of course, I do not attach any blame to you, Mr. Wilks, but I would like this sorted out as quickly as possible. If you see the need, you have my leave to dismiss Mrs. Penny." He sighed. "Goodness knows she does little enough around the place, so there's not much chance she'll be missed. It's the last thing I need in the midst of a fortnight-long house party, but you'll see to hiring a replacement as soon as may be, won't you? Good fellow."

"Yes, my lord." Wilks appeared to be gasping for breath. "Might I trouble you for some water?"

"Yes, of course." Sebastian moved to the drinks tray and poured a whisky tumbler full of water. He handed it to Wilks, watching him with concern. "Are you quite well?"

"It's nothing, my lord." Wilks shook his head and lowered

it to drink, then licked his moist lips and set the glass down on the desk with a trembling hand.

He stood, straight as a die, and bowed with his usual correctness. Picking up the ledger Sebastian had shown him, he said, "I shall study these figures and see Mrs. Penny. You may leave the matter in my hands, my lord."

Sebastian smiled. "Thank you, Wilks. I can always depend on you."

WITH the ordeal of welcoming everyone over, Gemma thought she might safely retire into the background. All the more reason *not* to wear any of those scintillating gowns Sebastian had bought her.

But she was woman enough that she could not resist stealing another look at them when she retired to her bedchamber to dress for dinner. Dorry had taken charge of seeing that the ladies' maids and valets were properly housed and provisioned, so Gemma had agreed to share Fanny's maid that evening.

Waiting for Charters to finish with her mistress's *toilette* gave Gemma leisure to finger her forbidden wardrobe. There were rich silks and satins, gauzes and muslins in a stunning array of shades—gold, jonquil, aquamarine, cobalt blue, and creamy magnolia—all selected to flatter her colouring. Not a frothy white ensemble to be seen.

Had Sebastian chosen these, imagining what she would look like in them? A shiver ran through her at the thought.

As she trailed her fingertips over the embroidery on a lustrous silk bodice, some dormant feminine urge sprang to life. An insistent murmur in her heart tempted her. What harm could it do to wear one of these gowns? Surely, it was a far greater crime to let all that shimmering loveliness go to waste.

But besides the moral implications of accepting clothing from Sebastian—she might as well accept his *carte*

blanche—dressing finely always seemed to beg for trouble.
She hated being the focus of attention, especially attention
of the masculine variety, which so often brought feminine
disapproval in its wake. If she wore her own modest, coun-
trified clothes, the men might leave her alone, and perhaps
among the women she might even find a friend. With a sigh,
Gemma shut the clothes press on a beguiling dream.

When Fanny's maid raised an insolent eyebrow at her
old sapphire silk, Gemma paid no heed. She sat at her
dressing table. "I want braids, please."

Charters pressed her lips together in disapproval, but
she arranged her pins and brushes in silence and set to with
a will.

The result, when Gemma finally paid attention, was out-
rageously becoming. Instead of scraping her hair back
hard from her brow, Charters had coiled and twisted it into
a soft, loose knot, from which one thin, looped braid hung
in a horseshoe shape behind, the smallest possible conces-
sion to Gemma's orders. Fine, curling tendrils whispered
about her forehead and temples. Her eyes looked impossi-
bly large and blue.

"Ravishing, miss, if I may say so."

That word again. Nervous anticipation spiked through
her, though she could not have said why.

Charters gathered up the sapphire silk. She hesitated.
"If you will permit me, miss, the high neckline of this
gown does not show to best advantage with your coiffure.
Perhaps . . ."

"Nevertheless, I shall wear it." Gemma smiled to soften
her words. "Come, Charters, help me. I want to be down
before the others arrive."

IN the drawing room before dinner, Gemma circulated
among the guests, making sure her arrangements met with
their approval.

Alistair Brooke answered her polite inquiry with an amused quirk to his lips. "Thank you, Miss Maitland. Every attention has been paid to my comfort."

He gestured with his quizzing glass. "But tell me, do you think my cousin has turned queer in his attic, or is there some spark of wit in Miss Taylor's conversation I have yet to discern?"

Gemma glanced at Romney, who gave the appearance of listening to the garrulous debutante with careful attention. Gemma sympathised. She had suffered the girl's inane chatter for half an hour that afternoon.

She laughed. "Yes, Lord Romney is quite a reformed character. He took tea with the vicar yesterday, you know."

"Good God! Is he ill?" Brooke's thin lips quirked upwards. "But of course not," he murmured. "One need only *cherchez la femme*."

She followed the direction of his gaze and saw Fanny flirting desperately with Mr. Joyce, tossing a glance like a challenge at Romney over her shoulder. Gemma frowned. Hardly just reward for Romney's recent efforts to win her.

"You look very fine this evening, Gemma."

She jumped. Sebastian stood close behind her. Too close. Any closer, and he might have rested his chin on her head. The heat from his body warmed her back. She did not care for the possessiveness of his stance and stepped away from him, nearer to Brooke.

Sebastian's gaze raked over her gown. "Very fine, indeed."

"Thank you." Gemma gave him a tight smile.

To Gemma's dismay, Brooke seemed to sense the discord between them. With exquisite tact, he inclined his head in a slight bow and moved on.

Sebastian prevented Gemma from doing the same by clasping her wrist. Softly, he said, "You are mulish, Gemma. Why will you not wear any of the gowns I sent you?"

Gemma offered him another taut social smile. Her lips

barely moving, she said, "This is hardly the place to discuss it, my lord. And you know my objections. We need not belabour the point." She tugged to get free of his hold, but without success. "Please remove your hand."

He released her. "I never thought you, of all people, would be so missish."

Gemma subdued a flash of temper. "I, of all people, must be especially *missish*. With my background, I cannot afford to be careless of my reputation."

"Oh, that old chestnut! No one *cares* about your mother, Gemma. Look around you. Has anyone here tonight slighted you or treated you differently?" His dark eyes glinted. "If you do not wear one of those gowns tomorrow, I shall come up and dress you with my own hands."

The feigned smile calcified on her face. Out of the corner of her mouth, she breathed, "You wouldn't dare."

His jaw hardened. "Try me."

Ripton announced dinner, preventing her reply. Sebastian bowed and stalked away.

Gemma took a deep, calming breath. With relief, she recalled that Alistair Brooke was to be her dinner partner. She took his proffered arm and they followed the rest of the company filing into the vast state dining room.

Despite her agitation, she could not help glancing around with a twinge of satisfaction at the products of the servants' labour. The table shimmered and blazed with candelabra, delicate crystal, and gleaming gilt plate. Confections of sugar and marzipan in the shape of fruit bowls and fairy-tale castles ranged down the centre of the table to dazzle the senses. The rich scent of game and subtle Continental sauces flowed around them, as footmen entered bearing the first course—a far cry from Gemma's first meal at Laidley.

The dishes were plentiful and varied, a blissful marriage of local specialties and French cuisine. Wine flowed freely. It was a young set of people, for the most part, and exuberant chatter filled the room, checked now and then by a chaperone's quelling frown.

At one point, Gemma caught Sebastian watching her. Unobtrusively, he raised his glass in a silent toast, reminding her of his earlier challenge. A surge of warmth flooded her cheeks.

In the past few days, the atmosphere between them had altered, fairly crackled with tension born of repressed desire. She no longer felt at ease in his presence. With a pang, she realised that she missed their former friendly interaction. Just meeting his eyes across a crowded dinner table caused a wild flurry in her stomach, as if it contained a swarm of angry bees. The knowledge that she only came a tepid second to Lady Russell in Sebastian's affections made this uncomfortable reaction even more humiliating. She could not wait for the house party to end.

At a nervous cough beside her, she dragged her gaze away from her tormentor and focused on the gentleman to her left. A Mr. Tilney, whose bobbing Adam's apple and shock of red hair made him rather awkward, poor fellow.

She smiled at him and led him to speak of his favourite subjects, which appeared to be hunting, shooting, and fishing, in no particular order. Mr. Tilney's descriptions were decidedly too graphic for the dinner table, and Gemma's susceptible stomach squirmed. She refused the dish of veal olives a footman offered her. Her neighbour's conversation had quite banished her appetite.

Fortunately, an eager young miss on his other side captured Tilney's attention, and Gemma turned to her right to see Alistair Brooke observing her.

He did not leer, but his blatant admiration put her on guard. She returned his gaze with a hint of ice.

One side of his mouth lifted in a self-deprecating smile. "Forgive me for staring, Miss Maitland. Beauty such as yours does not often come my way. May I say what a pleasure it is merely to sit and look at you?"

His careless tone made light of the compliment. Against her will and common sense, the words soothed her wounded spirit like a balm.

She could not resist returning that rueful grin.

❦

By the time Sebastian led the gentlemen to join the ladies in the music room after dinner, he had almost exhausted his admittedly limited store of polite restraint. Most of the talk over port and cigars had been the usual ribald palaver and political discussion that attended any male gathering, but subtle hints and queries about the lovely Miss Maitland convinced him his matchmaking plan was working well.

Damn it.

And there was Brooke now, murmuring in Gemma's ear, charming her with his lazy assurance. A delicate colour tinged her cheeks and her deep blue eyes danced. How could she be taken in by such obvious tactics?

Nauseated, Sebastian turned away with an inward, cynical laugh at his own naivety. When it came to the game of love, women were all the same. Every successful rake knew that.

Even Gemma, it seemed, was no exception.

There was music, there were card games, there was conversation, there was tea. Sebastian had no taste for any of it, though he circulated among his guests, never stopping for too long in any one place and doing his best to avoid Eleanor.

It wasn't until Gemma excused herself to attend to some matter, that Ripton whispered in her ear that he saw his chance to get her alone.

Sebastian planned to waylay her in the corridor on her return, but then he stopped short. To do what? Seek reassurance? Probe her feelings for Brooke? Kiss her witless and make her admit she wanted him, and him alone? And what then? His mind foundered at that question.

What he should do was keep his distance, not corner her at every opportunity, trying to make her admit to her desire. For where would that lead? To her ruin and his. He would have to ask her to marry him. For the first time, he realised he was not at all certain what her answer to that impossible question might be.

He reminded himself he should do his best to deny the attraction between them, for Gemma's sake. He should stand aside and allow one of those other, better men claim her.

And they were better men, weren't they? While Miss Taylor sang a plaintive ballad, he propped himself against the wall and reviewed his male guests.

Brooke had made himself useful to some government minister or other before his grandmother obligingly died and left him her fortune. He had bought an estate, in Derbyshire, Sebastian thought. And according to Romney, he'd openly declared he was ready to take on a wife.

Yes, Brooke was a worthier man.

Young Tilney was a waste of the air he breathed, his mind paltry and his figure skinny, but he stood heir to a baronetcy and owned a tidy estate in one of the shires. Gemma could rule the roost in his house, which would be to her taste, no doubt. A sure point in his favour.

Sir Gervase Stone and Algernon Mosely were both cut from the same cloth—fustian perhaps. Dull and worthy—either would make a solid, if unexciting husband for Gemma.

Lord, what was he thinking? He couldn't bear to see her with either of those prune-faced bores. Imagine looking at that over your steak and kidneys every morning.

He passed several other gentlemen under review and concluded glumly that Brooke really was the pick of them, damn his steely grey eyes.

And Brooke was hanging out for a wife.

As the evening wore on, Sebastian watched Gemma unfurl like a blossoming rose under Brooke's smooth flattery and felt a primitive urge to smash something—preferably Brooke's smiling face.

But he needed to do what was best for Gemma. And right now, it looked like Brooke was it. Sebastian sank his chin into his cravat and observed the two fair heads bent close together, the faint smile on Gemma's lips as she listened to whatever honeyed words Brooke poured into her ear.

Truly, a perfect match.

He sighed. It was only a matter of time.

❧

"Did you see Romney tonight, Gemma? He actually drank tea!" Fanny brushed her dark hair with short, vigorous strokes.

Gemma smiled. "Yes, and entertained all the shyest ladies in the party, too, and made himself agreeable to their mamas. You must be proud of him, Fanny."

"Ha! He did not even speak to me."

"Well, words have not worked so far with you, have they? I believe he means to show you he knows how to behave himself."

"He actually drank tea."

"*Greater love hath no man than this . . .*" murmured Gemma. She stood behind Fanny's chair and watched her friend's disconsolate reflection in the glass. Tucking a stray lock of hair behind Fanny's ear, Gemma said, "Darling, don't you think it is time you put him out of his misery?"

"But I have! I did. I told him I could not trust him not to pursue his fancy women after we are married. He accepted that our betrothal is at an end. But now he has formed this stupid scheme to win me, and I never wanted him to become all prosy and boring. I just—" She broke off, biting her lip.

Gemma dropped her hands to Fanny's shoulders. "Do you know what my mama once said to me?" She smiled. "I do not usually take my mother as a model, but you may be sure that she is a woman who knows a great deal about men."

"What did she say, then?"

Gemma met Fanny's eyes in the looking-glass. "She said that a rake in love makes the best kind of husband."

✥

LONG after the ladies retired, the gentlemen played cards, drank, smoked, and generally disported themselves in a manner unbefitting the presence of said ladies.

Sebastian remained unusually sober. He wondered if Romney's leaf-turning had rubbed off on him. And then Brooke strolled up and started on about Gemma.

"Marvellous," muttered Sebastian.

"I beg your pardon?"

"I said, yes, she is marvellous, isn't she?"

"Sublime," Brooke agreed. "There is an openness, a freshness to her that is intensely appealing, don't you think?"

"Appealing, yes," said Sebastian.

A long silence passed, and Sebastian was damned if he'd break it. He knew it was his duty to bat hard for Gemma, since she would do none of the work herself. He shrugged and tossed off the rest of his brandy. He didn't feel like matchmaking tonight.

"You have an interest there, perhaps?" Brooke's mouth was grave but his eyes mocked.

"My only interest is in Miss Maitland's happiness and well-being," answered Sebastian stiffly. "Her grandfather consigned her to my care."

A warning. And not a very subtle one.

Brooke swirled his brandy. "Did he, indeed? A wise gentleman. Well, I am sure you will not disappoint him."

Sebastian inclined his head. Suavely, he said, "Oh, you may be sure of that." He smiled through gritted teeth as Brooke strolled away.

He then proceeded to get thoroughly foxed.

Romney sauntered over later, teacup in hand.

Sebastian blinked up at his friend from his sprawling position in a comfortable leather armchair. "Taking this to extremes, aren't you, old fellow?"

Romney stared glumly at the innocuous beverage. "Don't think I've been sober at this hour since I was in short coats."

"Your cons— your consti— your liver will thank you for it."

Romney made a face and put down his cup. "Your sister is a flirt."

"Yes."

"I never noticed that before."

Sebastian smiled. "That's because she always flirted with you."

"Did she?" Romney grimaced. "And how fares your scheme to marry off the lovely Miss Maitland? M'cousin seemed very taken with her."

"Yes, he is. He told me so." Sebastian frowned in an effort to remember. "Believe I warned him off."

Romney's eyes quickened. "Did you, now? And why would you have done that?"

Sebastian grunted and stared into the depths of his glass. "You know why. Brooke knows why."

His friend waited.

"Want her for myself, of course." He flailed a hand, spilling brandy over his coat sleeve. "Well of course I want her. Any man in his right mind would. But it's more than that. She knows me too well. I feel comfortable with her, and yet—"

"And yet every time she looks at you it's like a kick in the guts," finished Romney.

"Lower."

"Hmm, nasty."

Silence.

"Would it be so terrible to marry her yourself?"

"Yes. No. Perhaps. I don't know." He clutched his friend's sleeve. "One thing you could do for me, if you will, Romney."

"What's that?"

"Keep Eleanor away from her."

Fourteen

───────── ❧ ─────────

WHEN Gemma answered the summons to Lady Carleton's boudoir early the next morning, she found her hostess sitting pensively at her dressing table, wearing fashionable *dishabille*, her dark hair swept up beneath a pretty lace cap.

"Gemma, my dear." She held out her hand.

"Oh, you look so much better today, ma'am!" Gemma crossed the room, took her outstretched hand and pressed it. "Will you not come down to dinner this evening? Everyone asks after your health. I am sure they would love to see you."

Lady Carleton gave a faint smile, but did not answer. She gestured for Gemma to sit on a spindle-legged chair at her side. Fiddling with a pot of cream on her dressing table, she said, "Are they kind to you, Gemma? Are the young ladies agreeable company?"

Gemma blinked. "Why, yes. They are kind." In fact, Sebastian had been right. No one referred to her background or slighted her because of her mama. Their behaviour perplexed her. She wondered if Sebastian had anything to do with it.

She discovered she had little in common with any of the females of the party, but that was the fault of her unusual upbringing, not theirs. Ladylike pursuits always made her impatient, and with no riding or other outdoor activity to be had during three solid days of inclement weather, this dawdling existence threatened to suffocate her. But she would not tell Lady Carleton that.

"And the gentlemen? I hear you have many admirers."

Gemma repressed a grimace. "They are also kind."

"I understand Alistair Brooke has taken particular interest in you," pursued Lady Carleton, watching her out of the corner of her eye. "A most eligible gentleman."

Oh, dear! Now Lady Carleton had decided to play matchmaker, too. Her experience with John Talbot had shown her that no respectable gentleman would ever want her. She shook her head. "Mr. Brooke is charming, but he has no serious intentions towards me. And besides, I do not wish to marry."

"Not marry?" Lady Carleton gasped. She swivelled in her chair to face Gemma full on, her dark eyes avid. "If that is so, I admire your courage, my dear. What do you mean to do if you do not wed?"

Startled at Lady Carleton's enthusiasm, Gemma almost laughed. She had never in her life met with such a reaction to her ambition. Even Sebastian, though understanding her reasons, seemed to treat her plans as belonging to the realm of fantasy. "I wish to run the Ware estate. That way, I would be a burden to no one, because Hugo would not have to pay an agent to do the work."

"Remarkable!" Lady Carleton gripped her hands together. "But do you not think you might be lonely without a family of your own? Do you not wish for children?"

Children. The word was like a blow to her chest. A moment passed before Gemma could summon the breath to speak. With difficulty, she answered, "I have long since given up the thought of children of my own."

She hurried to change the subject. "At all events, Hugo is against the idea of me running Ware, so it will all come to nothing if I cannot persuade him."

"And what will you do if he refuses?"

Gemma shrugged and gave a rueful laugh. "I shall remain at Ware and keep meddling until I am sent away, I suppose. After that . . . I don't know. Perhaps I might live with Mama in Kensington."

The thought of cohabiting with Sybil and her young lover in a townhouse far from her beloved Ware filled her with gloom. "I trust it won't come to that. I must convince Hugo I am right."

Lady Carleton regarded her seriously. "Well, if that is what will make you truly happy, my dear, I hope very much that you do."

ON the first fine day they had enjoyed since the house party began, most of the young people went out riding, while the older ladies paid calls or gossiped in the drawing room. Though itching for a good gallop herself, Gemma stayed behind to organise activities for the following day. Lady Russell had proposed an archery tournament, so Gemma sent servants to ransack the attics for bows, arrows, and targets.

Cook took the change of plans to *al fresco* dining in her stride, but the fierce head gardener objected to a parcel of nobs playing merry hell with his lawns, so Gemma negotiated a compromise. Finally, they agreed to hold the tournament in a large clearing in the park.

She was leaving to run some errands in the village when Hugo's carriage drew up outside, bearing Matilda and enough trunks and bandboxes to last a month.

Gemma called a welcome, hoping her aunt did not intend

to stay that long. But together with the usual exasperation came a warm feeling of familiarity. She realised she was glad Matilda had come. Perhaps now she might glean news of how the estate went on in her absence. Letters from Ware had not told her the things she most wanted to know.

"Aunt! How do you do?" Gemma hurried down the steps to meet her, rapidly reviewing and discarding vacant bedchambers for Matilda's use. She took her aunt's lilac-gloved hands, kissed her withered cheek, and led her up the steps.

Ripton met them at the door and bowed a welcome.

"The rose room, I think, Ripton, don't you? Will you have a tea tray sent to my aunt's chamber, please?"

Matilda fluttered. "Oh, no, Gemma. I shall join you downstairs directly. You will wish to make me known to everyone before dinner." She looked around her with interest. "What a noble house! It is not at all as I imagined. What is through here?"

She scurried towards the door that led to the library, Sebastian's retreat. Gemma ran after her. "Aunt! That is private." She caught Matilda's elbow and drew her to the staircase. "Do come up and refresh yourself. I am sure you would like to change your dress after your journey."

By the time Matilda had complained about her chamber's dimensions, décor, and aspect, the softness of the bed's mattress, the hardness of the pillows, and the room's distance from Gemma's bedchamber, Hoskins and the rest of Matilda's baggage had arrived. As the maid arranged Matilda's grey locks, Gemma peppered her aunt with questions about Ware.

"And is the harvest in yet? Did Mr. Porter follow my advice about the new fencing?"

"I'm sure I know naught about that side of things," said Matilda pettishly. "The estate runs itself without any help from me. Yes, the harvest is in, but as for Mr. Porter, he is a very capable man—Hugo says so—and far above taking advice from the likes of you, miss!"

Matilda sprinkled lavender scent on her handkerchief. "But all our neighbours ask after you, and the tenants as well, until I'm tired of telling them how you go on. You should write more, Gemma, so I have more to say. I am sure you never tell the sort of things *I* most wish to know."

A wave of homesickness struck Gemma. Until now, she had been too busy to indulge in longing for Ware. What a pity Sebastian would not take her advice or lift a finger about the Laidley estate. There was so much she could do here. Already, despite the ramshackle household and the strangeness of Cornish ways, she found herself attached to the place. But for all that, Laidley wasn't Ware.

When Hoskins was finished, Gemma led Matilda downstairs and introduced her to the matrons of the party who had not accompanied the younger set on their excursion. Satisfied that her aunt was fast making new friends, Gemma slipped away to the village.

When she arrived, she found the square bustling with people in high spirits carrying garlands of wheat and flowers, trestle tables, benches, and barrels of ale. It seemed they planned a celebration.

In the haberdasher, Gemma met Polly, one of the girls she had hired to help prepare for the house party. "What is going on, Polly? Is it the harvest feast?"

"Oh, yes, miss," said Polly. "The harvest be almost done, so they will hold the crying of the neck this afternoon and there'll be a church service, and dancing after. Why don't ye come along?"

Gemma's blood tingled at the prospect. How she longed for plain country fare and dancing after the stuffy restraint of the last few days. But could she manage to slip away? Or better yet, perhaps the whole party might enjoy such a merry evening.

WHEN she returned to Laidley, she tracked down Sebastian in his library. He rose hastily at her entrance and bowed, seeming ill at ease. She gave him a teasing smile and dipped a formal curtsey in response. Only when his thoughtful gaze ran over her old habit did she recall his promise to dress her himself if she did not wear the gowns he had bought.

A faint shudder ran through her. She hoped the sudden heat in her cheeks did not show itself in a blush.

A little short of breath, Gemma broke the silence. "I have been to the village. There is a feast tonight, and dancing to celebrate the end of the harvest. Do you think we might make up a party and join them?"

He quirked an eyebrow, snapping closed the small book he held. "They invited you?"

"Why, yes. I have become acquainted with many of your people while I've been at Laidley. Why should they not invite me?"

He smiled, though the smile did not reach his eyes. "Why not, indeed? It seems wherever you go, people love you, Gemma. It is your particular gift."

She was almost sure he did not intend that to be a compliment. More of an accusation, though she could not guess why. She tilted her head and moved to rest her fingertips on his desk. "You know, Scovy, it would be the perfect way for you to become better acquainted—"

He cleared his throat and tidied some papers. "Thank you, but they all go on perfectly well without me. My presence would only cast a pall on their amusement, I daresay."

He blinked rapidly. When he lifted his gaze to hers, his dark eyes were turbulent, but she could not quite bring herself to feel sorry for him. It was within his powers to endear himself to his tenants if he wished. He managed well enough with the people at Ware. But Sebastian was stubborn, and she did not know how to move him from this uncharacteristic resolve to shun his responsibilities. Why it should matter so much to her, she could not have said.

"I don't understand you, Scovy," she whispered. "Not at all."

He shrugged. "People change, Gemma. I am not the boy you remember. Perhaps I never was."

The silence stretched until she realised he did not intend to say any more. That was the end of the matter.

She made an effort to smile. "Well, then. You won't object if I ask the others, will you?"

He took a hasty step towards her, one hand slightly lifted. He stopped, letting the hand fall. "No. You may go with whomever you wish."

But when she proposed the outing that afternoon, the other guests instantly dismissed her suggestion. The gentlemen had agreed to attend a prizefight in nearby St Just that evening. Gemma frowned. Despite his impassive expression, she suspected she had Sebastian to thank for that sudden decision.

Gemma appealed to the rest of the party ladies, but Lady Russell could imagine nothing more tedious than hobnobbing with a load of rustics over the corn stubble. All the other ladies agreed. Miss Taylor proposed parlour games, and her suggestion was endorsed by the rest of the guests who stayed behind.

With a sigh, Gemma resigned herself to another evening of boredom.

❧

ROMNEY clutched the side of Sebastian's curricle and held on to his hat as they swept round a bend. "Steady on, old man. We're not dragging, y'know!"

Sebastian threw him a sidelong glare and drove his greys faster out of the turning. "Love sent you soft, has it?"

Romney snorted. "Not soft in the head, at least."

"And just what are you implying?"

"If you can't guess, then you're further gone than I thought. For God's sake, slow down, man, or you'll overturn us. What has she done now?"

"Nothing. I'm driving fast. I always drive fast. Why should it have anything to do with her?" Sebastian flicked his whip so it cracked in the air, just above the leader's left ear. The curricle surged forward.

Romney threw up his hands, grabbed for his hat again, and raised his voice against the wind and rattle of the carriage. "I've half a mind to back you against the champion tonight. You can work off some of your spleen on his hide instead of near-killing me on the way home. Why are we going to this mill, anyway?"

"I needed to get out. That place is suffocating me." Sebastian concentrated on the road. A deer bounding out, a vehicle coming the other way—anything could happen and they'd end up smashed to pieces if he did not react in time.

Damn her. Why was she always right? An annoying trait in anyone, but in Gemma, infuriating. If he behaved badly, everyone else just shrugged and said, well, what would you expect from a rakehell like Carleton? But Gemma gave him no quarter. She expected as much from him as she expected from herself.

She expected too much.

He had squirmed under her reproachful gaze when he'd refused to go to the crying of the neck. Bright memories of harvest feasts at Ware filled his mind, but he blocked them out. At Laidley, it wouldn't be the same.

They would not welcome him, anyway. His parents had never attended such festivities. His father, the old earl, had thought them beneath his dignity. His father . . .

Sebastian let out an oath. He had too much regard for his horses to yank on the reins, but he slowed them and brought them to a halt. He looked at Romney. "I have to go back."

"Eh? But we're halfway there!" Romney stared at him as if he'd run mad.

Perhaps he had. He gave a crack of laughter and slowly backed the curricle to the crossroads, where there was enough space to turn it.

"Sorry, old man. There's something I have to do."

❧

INSTEAD of whirling past in a flurry of dancing and good cheer, the evening crawled by. Gemma had no patience with silly children's games, charades, jackstraws, and the like. They seemed pointless to her, a way of eking out an evening doing nothing to the purpose.

She realised that many ladies spent all their lives in futile pursuits like these. Not for the first time, she reflected that at least her work made a difference to the people of Ware.

She longed to be transported back there, if only by proxy, joining in with the celebrations in the village.

And why not? she thought. *What is stopping me, besides dreary convention and Sebastian's pig-headed disapproval?* Gemma looked around at the other guests, all preoccupied with lottery tickets, speculation, and whist. No one would even notice if she slipped away.

Gemma found her aunt sitting in the music room listening to Miss Taylor play the harp. In a low voice, she said, "I shall retire, I think. It has been a long day."

Matilda clutched at her hand. "Oh, my dear! You are not sickening for something, I hope . . ."

"Just a touch of the headache, ma'am. You know I am never ill. A good rest and I shall be well by morning."

Matilda made as if to rise. "Shall I come up with you?"

"No, no, Aunt. Please don't trouble yourself. I shall go straight to bed. Good night." She patted Matilda's hand and left before she could make more fuss.

Gemma hurried up to her bedchamber to change.

Dressed in a plain blue round gown, a light merino cloak, and sturdy boots, she glanced in the looking glass. The rigid restraint of her hairstyle struck a discordant note with her reckless mood. With the thrill of rebellion skittering up her spine, she ripped out the pins that held the coil of braids twisted in a knot atop her head, and raked her fingers through her hair until it clouded about her face. She smiled in delight. She felt like a girl again.

Crossing to the secret door Fanny had shown her, Gemma pushed the panel sharply to open it. She crept along the corridor by the light of her bedside lamp and set it down on the landing, before picking her way down the stairs. She let herself out a small side door covered with trailing ivy, and stole into the night.

❧

LADY Carleton stared out her window as shadows lengthened over the landscape in the wake of the setting sun. She had dined in her room the past few evenings. With the best will in the world, she could not make herself go down and face them all.

But the cloaked figure with bright gold hair flitting along the side of the house and on towards the stables caught her eye. She wondered, at first.

Then she remembered. The crying of the neck. A lovely old tradition celebrating the end of the harvest. And feasting and dancing afterwards.

What fun.

❧

WHEN Sebastian arrived at the harvest feast, the celebrations were well under way. At first, his tenants looked at him askance. They greeted him politely enough, but turned away and muttered amongst themselves, their teeth clamped over small, clay pipes.

Sebastian gave a cynical smile and stared into the snapping inferno of the bonfire. He had known it would not be easy. A just punishment for his neglect.

He could simply walk away. But he would be master here for the rest of his sorry life. If he did not make amends now, with Gemma's cheerful support bolstering his courage, he never would.

He stood there alone, considering his strategy, until someone clapped him on the shoulder and thrust a tankard of home-brewed ale into his hand. The foam slopped over the lip of the tankard as he turned around, to see a tall, lanky man with sandy hair and a tanned face beaming at him.

"Pendargon, you old devil!" Sebastian laughed and shook hands with his gamekeeper, the man who had taught him to track deer and tickle trout in the stream. "How are you?"

"Oh, none so bad." Pendargon's eyes crinkled at the corners. His face was a map of wrinkles, but he glowed with health from the outdoors. "Come and meet everyone, lad." He winked. "They're a dour lot, but they won't bite."

After that, the evening progressed at a rollicking rate. Sebastian listened to the men's observations on life and drink and women, and spun a few yarns and told bawdy jokes of his own. The dancing was in full swing inside the barn, with lively music and much laughter and clapping and stamping of feet. He supposed he should go and do his duty by the local women—they would be easier nuts to crack than the men. But . . . he sighed. He wished Gemma was there.

And then, as if he had conjured her from his thoughts, she appeared.

For an instant, he thought he'd imagined it, for she seemed a creature of the flames, her cloak whirling around her as the sparks showered from the bonfire and warm lights flickered in her unbound hair.

But her eyes were only for him, dark as midnight, large and stark against her pale, moonlit skin. *Cream and brandied peaches,* he thought, and stepped involuntarily towards her.

"You came!" She smiled up at him, her joy vibrant, unclouded by that awareness that seemed to rise between them like a Hydra in the preceding days.

Still stunned by her presence, it was a moment before he replied. "Yes. I did not think to see you here." He pitched the end of his cigarillo into the bonfire.

She looked around, her face alight with interest. "Isn't it wonderful? I am sorry to have missed the crying of the neck, but I could not slip away until now."

"No one knows where you are?"

Gemma shook her head. "But why concern ourselves with that? I have ample chaperonage in all these good people."

He took a deep breath. "Your trust in me is ... humbling. Particularly after what has passed between us in recent days."

Her gaze slid away. "Why should I not trust you? You would never do anything to hurt me."

With a bitter twist to his mouth, he held out his hand. "Come. Dance with me, then."

It amazed him, though he knew it shouldn't, how rapidly Gemma had made friends with the people of Laidley. As they moved into the barn where the feasting and dancing took place, Sebastian marvelled at the warmth in the greetings she received.

"Good evening, miss, and happy we are to welcome you to our party." Trengarry, the carpenter, a burly man with a wiry curl to his hair offered her his place on the rough wooden bench that ran along an enormous trestle table.

Gemma dipped a curtsey. "Thank you, Mr. Trengarry, but we thought we might join the dancing. You will save me a dance, won't you?"

Shyly, the man ducked his head. "Aye, miss, thank you. That I will."

"You have made the poor fellow blush," remarked Sebastian as he led her to the floor. "I was hoping you'd save all your dances for me."

She smiled, but said nothing and they took their places in the set.

This company danced with far more vigour and less restraint than might be seen at the sedate balls of the gentry, but Gemma seemed to enjoy herself. She laughed and clapped and jigged about with verve, yet her every movement retained that innate grace that was peculiarly her own.

Sebastian could not take his eyes from her. The rosy cheeks and flying, burnished hair; her plain blue gown swirling about her voluptuous figure as she moved. The country dances did not allow partners to remain together for long, and he resented every separation, though he smiled and exchanged greetings with the wives and daughters of his neighbours and tenants as he went.

They ate hot pasties and drank ale and cider. Trengarry even reenacted the crying of the neck for Gemma's benefit.

He mimed cutting the last sheaf of corn in the field and tying the bundle with twine. "Then he raises it in the air and holds it to the east, the south, and then the west, and cries, 'I have'n, I have'n, I have'n.' "

"What have 'ee, what have 'ee, what have 'ee?" the others called in reply.

"A neck, a neck, a neck."

"Hurrah, hurrah, hurrah!"

Gemma clapped her hands. "Oh, very good. Thank you, Mr. Trengarry. That was wonderful."

They danced again many times, together and with other partners. At the end of another set, someone tapped Sebastian on the shoulder.

It was a footman from Laidley. "My lord, you must come quick! Mr. Wilks has had a nasty turn."

Sebastian frowned. He had not set eyes on his steward all evening. "What sort of turn? Where is he?"

"In his cottage, my lord. He felt poorly so he did not come tonight. The doctor's been sent for, and Mrs. Wilks asked that you come, too."

"Of course." He looked at Gemma. "Will you be all right here?"

She shook her head. "I'm coming with you."

He should have protested, but he was too grateful. He knew next to nothing about tending the sick, but Gemma was skilled at such work.

They fetched their cloaks and hurried out to their horses.

Outside, Sebastian saw a familiar figure hovering by the bonfire. He pulled up short. "Mama."

His mother started and whipped around. In an instant, she regained her poise and inclined her head. "Good evening, Sebastian. I am surprised to find you here."

Icily, he replied, "I thought it was about time someone showed our people we are not merely their overlords, to be feared and obeyed."

Gemma put her hand on his arm. "Scovy."

He shook her off. "No, Gemma. I won't apologise for speaking the truth. My father's despotism will take time to erase, but I'm determined to do it. And I won't have you come here and question my actions, ma'am."

His mother's face remained expressionless, but her hands fidgeted with her cloak. "Sebastian, my dear—"

"I don't have time for this." He turned and strode to the rail where the horses were tethered.

"Scovy!" Gemma hurried after him.

"Just leave it, Gemma."

As soon as he spoke the words, he cringed and lifted his gaze to the darkening skies. Why did he have to bite her head off like that? But he couldn't talk about it now. "We must get to Wilks."

They rode the short way to the steward's cottage, a handsome house built from the same grey stone as Laidley.

The housekeeper let them in and took them straight up to Wilks's bedchamber. The room was dark but for the pale circle of light cast by a lantern on a table set apart from the bed where Wilks lay. Sebastian could hardly discern the figure lying strangely still under the covers, but Wilks's laboured breathing filled the room.

Mrs. Wilks, a tall, thin woman with salt-and-pepper hair, rose and hurried to meet them at the door. "He is sleeping," she murmured, her grey eyes shadowed and anxious. "Will you come into the sitting room, my lord?"

They followed her into the small parlour. Sebastian said, "I am deeply sorry, Mrs. Wilks. Has the doctor been?"

"Yes, he has just left. It is my husband's heart, of course. The doctor told him months ago he must not work himself to the bone as he does, but he would not listen." Her gaze flickered to Sebastian. "I do not know if he will ever be well enough to take up his duties again as your steward, my lord. I fear Mr. Wilks is no longer suited to such heavy responsibility."

A responsibility that was partly his master's. Shame crashed into him like a wave. It was all his fault. If he hadn't been so determined to turn his back on Laidley, he might have noticed what Gemma had seen as soon as she arrived. Wilks had not been coping.

Gemma murmured words of comfort. Mrs. Wilks dabbed at her eyes with a handkerchief, her thin shoulders shaking.

More grateful than ever for Gemma's presence, Sebastian remained silent, remorse lashing his conscience. As steward, it was Wilks's job to run the estate, but he should never have had to bear the burden of making every decision. He had tried to involve Sebastian in the process, but Sebastian had not wanted to know. Wilks must have been bewildered by this *laissez-faire* approach after the controlling attitude of the late earl. And now, his very life hung in the balance because of Sebastian's neglect.

Sebastian cleared his throat and addressed the overwrought woman. "When you judge Mr. Wilks is well enough, send me word and I will return to speak with him about the future. In the meantime, tell him he must not worry. I will do all that needs to be done until a replacement can be found."

Gemma glanced at him and rose. "If circumstances change, or if there is anything we can do, you will send word to the house, won't you?"

Mrs. Wilks stood, gripping a fold of her apron in her hands. She raised a fearful gaze to Sebastian's. He managed to smile at her and take her hands in his. "Do not fret, Mrs. Wilks. I shall see your husband gets the best possible care."

She clung to him and her lips quivered. "He will worry so. About the estate, I mean."

Sebastian saw doubt in her eyes. She did not believe him competent to take over her husband's duties. Well, she might be right, but for all their sakes, he would do his utmost to prove her wrong.

Gently, he said, "Tell him he need not worry about anything, save getting well." He paused, trying to find the right phrasing, knowing how important it was to preserve the Wilkses' pride. "I shall speak with him myself about what will happen after that, but you may be sure I shall not forget your husband's many years of faithful service to our family."

The gratitude in the woman's eyes made his stomach twist. "Thank you, my lord. Indeed, I will tell him."

He and Gemma left the cottage and rode away in silence.

Quietly, Gemma said, "You must not blame yourself."

He did not answer her. Somehow, her absolution made it worse, but beneath the shame at the damage his past behaviour had wrought ran a determination to rectify it for the future. That was the only thing that could ease his guilt. He would do better now.

Then he remembered: By righting that wrong, he would break a promise to someone he loved.

Andy.

The pain of it stopped his breath, as if a hundred-weight had slammed into his chest.

A sudden need gripped him. Instead of taking the road back to the house, he wheeled his gelding and headed towards the cliffs.

"Where are you going, Scovy?" Gemma sounded apprehensive as she urged Black Dancer into a trot to catch up.

"I've remembered somewhere," he said, looking across at her in the half-light of the moon. "Somewhere I used to be happy. Will you come?"

Gemma did not hesitate. "Yes, Scovy. Of course."

CRUSHED to her soul, Lady Carleton slowly turned away from the barn. She watched the bonfire, the men sitting around drinking and smoking their pipes, the children running wild and free and happy.

She had never been one of them. Foolish to come here. Doubly foolish to let Sebastian go before she could explain her presence. Soon, he would have retreated far beyond her reach.

"My lady? Is it you?" Betty Grimes, the midwife who had delivered all three of Elisabeth's children, peered into her face. "It is! Oh, do come in, my lady, and have summat to wet your whistle."

Her first impulse was to decline. But then a fiddle struck up a lively jig and the music called to her, and she thought of warmth and fun and *people* and she said, "Why, thank you, Martha. I'd love to."

She whirled in the dance with half a dozen partners, and

knew the flush in their cheeks and the bright light in their eyes were reflected in her own. How wonderful it felt to be alive and dancing!

But in the midst of her delight, she knew her people could not really give themselves up to frank enjoyment while she was by. They were on their best behaviour. One evening would not change the fact she was their mistress. So after an hour of freedom, she reluctantly said her farewells and made her way back to the house.

As she walked alone in the moonlight, through cricket song and the rustle of stirring leaves and scurrying night-creatures, she thought of how her lord, the earl, would have despised her actions this night.

And she hummed an air, and performed a light step-dance along the winding path.

THEY came to a tiny cottage at the top of a cliff over-looking a small, protected cove and the deep, glassy darkness of the sea.

"Here?" Gemma brushed her wind-blown hair from her eyes and searched Sebastian's face. She could not make out the slightest nuance of expression. The clean lines of his nose and jaw seemed fashioned of marble, pure and stark in the moonlight.

They tethered their horses to a rail outside. He opened the door for her and she went in. As Sebastian located a lamp and a branch of candles and lit them with brisk efficiency, Gemma looked around.

A great stone hearth dominated the single room. From a rack above it hung pots and pans and a big, blackened kettle. A table and a couple of shabby chintz armchairs stood at right angles to the hearth, and a small bed huddled in the corner. Everything was faded, but the cottage was neat and airy, the floor swept clean of dust.

Gemma turned to Sebastian, a question on her lips.

"I came here to get away from him," he said.

She stripped off her gloves and lowered herself onto the bunk, never taking her eyes from his. "Tell me."

Exhaling a long breath, Sebastian sat on a tattered armchair and leaned forward, clasping his hands together between his knees. A tangle of dark hair skimmed over his brow.

He stared at his hands. "This was my old nurse's cottage. I used to come here to escape. She always took me in, though she could have lost her pension and this cottage for her pains. Eventually, she did lose them." He looked up at her. "What a selfish young cub I was, Gemma. I endangered her by being here and yet I could not stay away."

"What happened?"

"The earl found me. If it had been one of the servants, they would have lied for her. But *he* found me, and that was the end of it."

Gemma's heart clenched to hear Sebastian speak of his father as "the earl." "What happened?"

"He evicted her on the spot. I had concocted some tale explaining my presence, but he brushed me off like a speck of dust from his sleeve. He sent her away with only the clothes on her back. I never saw her again. He made sure of that. No one dared tell me where she was, and when I grew old enough to make my own enquiries, I discovered she'd died in a workhouse."

Gemma's eyes pricked with tears. "Poor little boy."

"No. Don't feel sorry for me, Gemma. It was my fault."

"Oh, Scovy, you were a little boy. How could it have been your fault? What had you done to make the earl so angry?"

He shrugged. "Nothing. I did not have to do anything to incur his wrath. At the time, I thought he hated me. Looking back, I think he was merely irrational and a bully— perhaps a little mad." His eyelids flickered and he drew a ragged breath. "My mother had given me a volume of poetry. Pope, you know."

Gemma waited for more. "I don't understand," she said. "Why would that make him angry with you?"

Sebastian shook his head. "As I said, he was irrational. He never paid any heed to me at all when we were small. Andrew was the heir. Fanny and I were nothing. But as I grew older, he seemed to become resentful of my very existence. He took all of his resentment out on my hide. And when I turned to my mother for help, she sent me away."

"Perhaps she thought it best," said Gemma softly.

There was a long pause while he looked down at his hands. Then he met her gaze and his dark eyes burned with loss and anger. "I would have suffered a thousand beatings, just to know she loved me."

"Oh, Scovy." Gemma knelt before him and reached up to touch his cheek. "She *does* love you. I know it. She always did."

He clasped her hand and held it. "It's too late, Gemma."

"It can't be. While you both still live, it can never be too late."

"It is too late for Andy. He will never come back."

Bewildered, Gemma stammered, "But your brother's death was an accident."

Sebastian's grip on her hand tightened painfully. "No. Andy killed himself. He left me a note."

Shocked, she searched his face, and the raw pain in his eyes was too much for her to bear. Her tears spilled over and rolled down her cheek. He wiped them away with his thumb and made a pathetic effort to laugh. "Don't cry, princess. You weren't to know."

He reached for her then, and it seemed the most natural thing in the world when he drew her onto his lap and into his arms. He stroked her hair with a tenderness that made her throat ache, as if she were the one who needed comforting. And his strong, masculine warmth was a comfort. He smelled clean and fresh, with a faint, pleasant hint of hops.

"Why did he do it?" she whispered.

The hand stroking her hair stilled. At first, she thought he would not answer, then his voice spoke softly to the night.

"My brother was a sensitive youth. We did not have much in common growing up. The fact that my father favoured him made me keep my distance, and in later times I saw him rarely. He was at home with tutors, while I was sent away to school. But there was a bond between us, nevertheless."

He shifted, gently pressing Gemma's head to rest on his shoulder. She settled against him, and felt the words vibrate in his chest.

"I should have realised what a strain it was for him to always please my father. I should have realised it was too much—the weight of responsibility, of the earl's ridiculously high expectations. He was determined to groom Andy to be the next earl, but he was impossible to please. If Andy showed eagerness, he was accused of wishing my father dead so he could step into his shoes. If he displayed indifference, the earl harangued him for his poor attitude. Laidley and his position here obsessed my father. He would have taken them to the grave with him if he could."

She looked up. "Is that what the note said?"

Sebastian leaned his head back against the chair. She watched the ripple in his throat as he swallowed. "He wrote that he would never be good enough. That he despaired, and could not go on."

"And when Andy died, the earl turned to you."

Sebastian gave a hard laugh. "Yes, but by that time, I was old enough to tell the old fellow to go to hell. Saving your presence, princess."

Gemma remained silent. She saw it all now, the reason Sebastian despised his position at Laidley. His father's obsession had driven his brother to his death. The business had given Sebastian only unpleasant memories of his home and a supreme reluctance to take up the duties his father prized so highly—prized above life itself.

Sebastian cleared his throat and pulled away a little. "I vowed at Andy's graveside that I would never marry, never continue our father's precious line, never fulfil his overweening ambition by taking an interest in the estate. But I realised tonight that I have not been hurting my father by failing in my duty. The only ones I hurt were Wilks, my people, and perhaps myself. Andy would not have wanted that."

He fell silent for a moment. "You were right about Wilks. I must make up to his family for my neglect. And Gemma, I'd be grateful for your advice about the estate." His hold on her tightened. "I would rather not do this alone."

She marvelled at the courage it must have taken to admit that to her and ask for her help. Slowly, she said, "You do not have to do things his way, you know. Just be the kind of landlord you want to be. Change will take time, but it will be worth it in the end."

She smiled up at him and stroked his cheek. "I am so glad, Scovy."

He stared deep into her eyes, and when their lips met, the kiss seemed inevitable, overpowering, endless. She sank into him and his arms tightened around her, and still she could not get close enough to all that hard, masculine strength. His tongue stroked into her mouth and she tangled hers with it, drunk on his intoxicating heat.

With fumbling fingers, he loosed the strings of her cloak and smoothed it away. His hand slipped over her breast and she gasped, and the gasp turned into a long, low moan of pleasure. A faint, inner voice said this was wrong, an outrage to convention and morality, but she ignored it. Her conscience had no place here tonight.

"Gemma, please," Sebastian whispered against her lips. She had no clear idea what he wanted, but she kissed him hungrily and rode the deep dark wave of sensation. His fingers stroked and squeezed one tight nipple until she grew mindless with need. Just as she thought she couldn't bear any more, his hand slipped down her waist, down beneath her skirts, and skimmed up her stockinged calf to trace the garter above her knee.

The heat spread low in her belly, and lower, and thrills from his fingertips brushing her thigh shot straight to her loins. "Oh, what are you doing to me?"

"Gemma, let me. Say yes."

"Oh! Yes."

His fingers circled higher and his mouth drifted lower, and a hot current ran between them. His lips trailed down her throat and skimmed above the line of flesh along her bodice, making her shiver with desire.

He raised his head and murmured hot words into her neck. "Gemma. Open your legs for me."

Utterly shameless, throbbing with need, she opened to him, and he teased the throb to a pound and shimmer and rush. There was a hiatus, where it seemed she floated on a cloud of rapture, and then a storm of hot sensation took her, wrenched and shook her, overwhelmed her in shudders and gasps.

As she sank back to earth, he gripped her face between his hands and kissed her fiercely. As if he, and not she, had just touched heaven and he was thanking her for it.

Gemma drew back from his kiss and tugged at his cravat. He helped her rip it away, and she kissed his jaw, and then his throat. He groaned, and she unbuttoned his waistcoat and opened it, slid her hand beneath his shirt and spread her palm across the muscles of his chest.

A fine sprinkling of wiry hair rasped under fingertips. When she found his flat nipple, she circled it with one experimental finger, and his throaty gasp and hot eyes emboldened her to continue. How wonderful to do this for him, to return the exquisite pleasure he had given her. She trailed her lips down to his collarbone, splaying her hand over his heaving chest, and relished the effect of her touch.

He gasped and shifted his hips. "God, that feels so good."

Gemma felt the hard bulge in his pantaloons beneath her thigh and hesitated. She knew what that meant. Sybil's discussions had always been frank. She turned her forehead against his shoulder, breathing hard. "Scovy, I'm not sure . . ."

A hand stroked her hair. "Hush." His deep voice was strained and husky. "This was for you, Gemma. No consequences."

He bent to her again. His lips burned, sliding over hers, his tongue stroked possessively into her mouth, but she sensed the hard tension in his body. He trembled with it, so she stopped again.

"Is there nothing I can do for you?" she whispered in his ear.

"Oh, Lord!" He shuddered. "No!" Quickly, he rose, lifting her with him and set her on her feet at a distance.

Without looking at her, he snatched up his cravat and hastily retied it. If she did not know better, she would have thought she'd done something wrong. With a small sigh, Gemma picked up her gloves and cloak.

After a moment, she said, "Thank you, Scovy. That was a precious gift."

He laughed without the slightest vestige of mirth. "You should not thank me, Gemma. The last thing you should do is thank me."

No consequences. Gemma groaned under her breath as she eased open the rusty-hinged door, pushed tendrils of ivy aside, and slipped into the house. How could he say that when he had just turned her whole life upside down?

Grateful for the lamp she'd left burning on the small landing above, she set her hand on the iron rail and slowly climbed the stairs.

Until now, she had believed she could live a contented,

full existence without a man. And the truth was, she still believed that. She did not need a man to complete her.

But she wanted Sebastian.

Not as a master or guide, but as an equal, to share happiness and sorrow, to give each other comfort, warmth and passion, as they had done tonight.

But how could she have Sebastian and Ware, too? And did he really care for her—want her to be part of his life—or did he see her merely as a convenient object for dalliance?

Sebastian had said he'd held off seducing her out of regard for her honour. He could have taken her tonight. She had not been thinking clearly. She had wanted him to make love to her. With the slightest persuasion from him, she would have succumbed. But he had retained enough sanity for both of them and stopped.

She should be glad of that.

But her heart, ridiculous organ that it was, was not glad. In her heart, she knew what she wanted, and the mere idea was scandalous enough to steal her breath. She paused at the top of the stairs, gasping, and contemplated the path her foolish heart urged her to take.

The primrose path, they called it. Following in her mother's footsteps, her aunt would say. Well, perhaps she was her mother's daughter after all.

Voices in her bedchamber roused Gemma from her thoughts. The voices were muffled. She could not discern what they said or who was there, but she had a fair idea.

Panicked, Gemma clutched her cloak tighter round her throat and flew back down the narrow corridor. Without knocking, she eased into Fanny's room.

Bedclothes rustled. "What? Who's there?" said Fanny. "Oh, Gemma, is it you?"

"Yes, it's I." Gemma hurried forward to set her lamp on Fanny's bedside table.

Fanny squinted against the light. "What is it? What's wrong?"

Gemma whispered, "Listen, you must help me. I went out tonight. To the crying of the neck, and when I returned just now, I heard voices in my bedchamber. I think my aunt has discovered I am missing. Can you say I was with you all this time?"

"I could," said Fanny, "but—"

"Oh, thank you, dearest!" Gemma stripped off her cloak and bundled it under the bed. She began to tidy her hair, and Fanny watched her, owl-eyed and blinking.

"But Gemma, you don't understand. She has already been here. Your Aunt Matilda, looking for you."

Fifteen

———— ✦ ————

FANNY dragged herself up on her elbows. "Oh, dear! If I'd known what you were doing I might have been able to make up some story, but—"

"I am sunk." Gemma plumped down on the bed. Her stomach pitched sickeningly. Her mind refused to work. She was trapped. She had never been good at lying, and in any case, she could not think of an excuse for her absence that would be acceptable to her aunt. The best she could hope for was to keep Sebastian's part in her escapade quiet.

Fanny gripped her wrist. "What will you do?"

Gemma gazed up at the moulded ceiling, fighting despair. She took a shuddery breath and blew it out.

"Tell the truth, I suppose. I am of age. Aunt Matilda cannot punish me for going against her wishes." Her lips twisted. "There will be an unpleasant scene, but I suppose I've brought it on myself."

Fanny threw back the covers. "I'll come with you."

Buoyed though she was by Fanny's support, Gemma put a restraining hand on her arm. She managed a smile and shook her head. "You are a dear, but there is no point in you suffering my aunt's scolds. I shall go and face her."

She gathered her cloak, pressed Fanny's hand and left by the conventional door.

Gemma made her way to her bedchamber, her steps weighted by dread. Why had she not stopped to consider the consequences of her actions this time? Had the evening been worth the coming disgrace?

She paused outside her door to gaze at a candle still flickering in its sconce, throwing its soft glow over the crimson Spitalfields silk that covered the wall. She thought of Sebastian and how much he'd needed her tonight, to be with him when he fought those dark, bitter memories, to hold him and listen and comfort him. She remembered how much she had craved his warmth and his touch, the way he had brought every part of her alive, set every inch of her alight, and the memory burned inside her like the glow of that lone candle. She might never experience such a wealth and force of feeling again.

Yes, it had been worth it. So whatever came now, she would not repine, but bear it, secure in the knowledge that she had given what Sebastian needed her to give.

Taking a deep breath, Gemma squared her shoulders, put up her chin, and opened the door.

Matilda whipped around to stare at her with narrowed eyes but Gemma kept her head high. *Let Matilda screech.* She refused to be ashamed of what she had done.

Suddenly, she noticed they were not alone. Before she could speak, Lady Carleton rose from a wingback chair with a serene smile and glided forward. "Ah, there you are, my dear. I was just telling your aunt what a lovely time we had at the party in the village. To be sure, it was very naughty of me to prevail upon you to accompany me, but I was persuaded you would enjoy it."

Gemma tried her best to mask her shock. "Oh, er, yes. I did. Thank you, Lady Carleton, for inviting me."

Approval flashed in those dark eyes. "And did you ask Gertie to warm me some milk before bed? Thank you so much, my dear." To Matilda, she added, "Milk always helps me sleep, you know."

Gemma cleared her throat. "Gertie will be up with your milk shortly, ma'am." She forced herself to speak calmly, though she could have whooped with relief.

Matilda's tightened lips conveyed her scepticism, but she could not openly brand Lady Carleton a liar. No doubt she would have something to say to Gemma when their hostess retired.

Perhaps Lady Carleton sensed it, too, for she linked arms with Matilda and drew her towards the door. "Now, we must all get our beauty sleep. Time for chatter in the morning. Come along, Matilda, dear."

And with a twitch in her eye that might, in a lesser person, have been construed as a wink, Lady Carleton shepherded Matilda from the room.

SEBASTIAN tossed back his third bumper of brandy and cursed himself for a blackguard and a fool.

What had he said to Gemma when she arrived at that party? *Your trust in me is humbling.*

He smacked his brow with the heel of his hand, slid his fingers through his hair, and laid his head back against the chair. He could still smell her, feel her, taste her, even through the brandy. How could he have resisted? And yet, how could he have done that to her, robbed her innocence, left her with no assurance of his intentions or his regard?

Even his mistresses fared better than that. At the very least, they knew where they stood. He had never, not once, pretended he cared.

But where did Gemma stand? Sebastian grimaced. Squarely on his vital parts, was the answer his aching body gave. But she was so much more than an object of desire. So much more than any woman he had ever known.

He had never given pleasure without taking before. He had never thought there could be such overwhelming gratification in watching a woman climax, feeling her quiver and tremble in his arms, knowing that he had done that to her, and he alone. Gemma's abandoned response had fired him almost to the point of explosion, but even as her mouth pleasured his burning body, she never lost her innocence, her fresh, dazzling appeal. He had wanted her to the point of insanity.

And yet, he had held back.

Because she was special. Precious. As far above him as the princess he called her. Ultimately unattainable.

Yes, it was that which made him chary of examining his intentions towards Gemma too closely. Even after all they had been to each other, there was still a part of her he could not reach. He had seen it, the distance in her eyes as she surveyed her territory, on that first day he arrived at Ware. The remote, untouchable beauty of her spirit, an innate sense of duty and belonging, a sense he had never known.

She deserved better than to be tumbled in an old cottage, far better than he, with his wasted, tarnished heart could give her.

And yet . . .

And yet, he could not let her go.

❧

"A word?" Alistair Brooke cocked his head towards the library.

"Of course." Sebastian opened the door and followed him inside.

Choosing a leather easy chair by the fireplace, Alistair folded his long body into it and crossed his legs before him. Sebastian threw his hat and whip on the table and flung himself into the chair opposite, wondering what the fellow could have to say that required privacy. There had been any number of opportunities for them to speak during their cross-country ride that morning.

Brooke inspected his nails for a moment, then looked up. "It transpires that I have some business in town and I shall not be at liberty to attend your ball at the end of the week. I regret the discourtesy, but it is something which cannot be put off, unfortunately."

"Indeed?" Sebastian raised his brows. "Nothing serious, I trust."

Brooke smiled. "That remains to be seen. At all events, away I must, but there is something I wished to ask you before I go."

"Yes?"

"You stand *in loco parentis* to Miss Maitland, do you not?"

"I?" Sebastian stared at him, appalled.

Brooke rubbed his chin with his York tan gloves. "Yes, I'm certain you mentioned that her grandfather had consigned her to your care. Perhaps I misunderstood. But in any case, you have made her welfare your concern while she is at Laidley. I thought it appropriate for me to discuss this with you before I approach her grandfather."

Suddenly, the world fell away and Sebastian's vision narrowed to focus on the thin-lipped mouth forming those fatal words. He knew what was coming and raised a hand as if to stop the rest being spoken, but it was too late.

"I am greatly taken with Miss Maitland and wish to court her in form," continued Brooke. "Do you think her grandfather would look on my suit favourably?"

Sebastian drew out his snuffbox while his inner self scrabbled to collect the tiny fragments of his mind and paste them back together. Brooke would ask Gemma to be his wife.

His voice rasped. "This is . . . sudden. Have you any notion that Miss Maitland returns your . . . regard?"

Brooke tilted his head. "I think—I hope Miss Maitland is not indifferent to me. Beyond that, I could not say."

He smiled, and there was a light of anticipation in those grey eyes that made Sebastian want to lunge across the space that separated them and pummel the urbane, smiling face until its teeth fell out.

Oblivious, Brooke continued. "I would, of course, court Miss Maitland in the proper manner before I pressed my suit. She is a lady who deserves every delicate consideration. Don't you agree?"

"Oh, yes. Beyond question." *And if you lay one lily-white hand on her, I'll kill you.* An image of Gemma draped across his own knee, flushed and panting as he touched her in every forbidden place flooded his mind's eye. He banished the thought.

With a nod, Brooke rose. "Well, that settles it, then. I leave for London this afternoon."

Unable to restrain himself, Sebastian said, "Then you will not speak to her before you go?"

Brooke regarded him thoughtfully. "Only to say *au revoir.*"

THE rest of that week, Sebastian behaved strangely, sometimes paying Gemma absurd, flowery compliments that made her bite her lip against a chuckle. At other times, he spoke to her curtly or didn't speak to her at all. And Aunt Matilda clung to her like a burr.

Even on her early morning rides, she could not escape. Matilda ordered the mare with the most docile temperament in Sebastian's stables to be saddled ready for her to chaperone her great-niece whenever she ventured out. Clearly, Matilda did not believe the story Lady Carleton had concocted about the crying of the neck. She seemed determined not to be caught napping again.

With a sigh of frustration, Gemma matched Black Dancer's pace with the gentle gait of Matilda's mount. She had not told Sebastian how close they came to discovery on the night of the harvest feast, worried he might think she expected a marriage proposal. She wondered if Lady Carleton had mentioned the incident to him, but dismissed the idea. Sebastian's behaviour was not such as to encourage a confidence from his mother. Gemma chewed her lip. There must be something she could do about that.

As for Sebastian himself, she tried to imagine putting into words the riot of emotions rampaging through her since their encounter in the cottage, and failed. Such a scandalous declaration would shock him even more than the need to make it shocked her. She could barely admit it to herself, this primitive need to take every forbidden delight Sebastian had to offer. She would never feel the same way about any other man. She would never want to do those things with anyone but him. She had never felt closer or more connected to any human being than she had to Sebastian when he'd held her and kissed her and pleasured her to the brink of heaven in that tiny cottage on the cliff.

She frowned. The distance Sebastian had set between them might be due to Aunt Matilda's vigilance, but she doubted it. His reticence indicated he regretted what they had done in that cottage, but she could not. A new world had opened to her, a whole Pandora's box of sensation and intense emotion she had never imagined she might experience.

She could not turn her back on that now.

Perhaps, instead of telling him, she might rather show him what she wanted. *But how?* They were never alone together—Aunt Matilda made sure of that. Even when Sebastian invited her to inspect the plans for the new row of tenant houses he planned to build in the village, Matilda had come to the library with her and interrupted their practical discussion with a string of vapid inanities.

So if she wanted to attract Sebastian back to her it must be done subtly, and in public. Perhaps at the Laidley ball?

Gemma fingered her lips. It was going to be a challenge.

⚜

THE last day of the house party finally came, and more guests arrived for the ball after luncheon. Gemma greeted them and saw them conducted to their rooms to rest before the evening's entertainment.

Having handed the Chilterns over to the butler's care, she was about to return to the house to attend to last-minute preparations for the ball, when that outrageous, turquoise travelling carriage swept around the circular drive and came to a smooth halt under the portico. She gasped. What was Mama doing here?

"Darling!" Sybil threw her arms around Gemma and hugged her close.

For a bare instant, Gemma buried her face in her mother's shoulder and breathed in her light floral scent. Feeling oddly strengthened by that warm embrace, she linked arms with Sybil and led her to the house.

At the top of the stairs stood Lady Carleton. "Squib!" she breathed, her face lit like a spring day. She held out her hands.

After a slight hesitation, Sybil slipped from Gemma's hold and moved to greet her friend. She drew Lady Carleton close and kissed her cheek. "Lissybet." There was tenderness in Sybil's smile.

Watching them, Gemma's heart felt as though sunlight had poured into it. She sensed these two women had much to say to one another. "I shall leave you to have a comfortable prose."

Sybil looked an inquiry at her friend. Lady Carleton shook her head. "No, come with us, Gemma. You are the cause of our reunion, after all."

They adjourned to Lady Carleton's sitting room, newly refurbished in cheerful blues and yellows. Gemma had urged Lady Carleton to rid the walls of those sombre hangings, historically significant though they might be, in favour of charming Chinese wallpaper, a handsome pier glass, and her favourite family portraits.

Lady Carleton rang for tea and they sat down, regarding each other in silence. Then Sybil burst into her rich laugh. "Oh, we are as shy as schoolgirls! How ridiculous we are. Elisabeth, how are you? What have you been doing since I saw you last?"

Lady Carleton opened her mouth and closed it again, as if she did not know where to begin.

Sybil fluttered a delicate hand. "I heard Carleton died and I meant to write to you, but I could not think of what to say. Condolences would not have been appropriate, would they? You must be utterly *thankful* he is gone."

"Mama!" Gemma gasped. Even for Sybil, this was outrageous. Gemma had the guilty feeling she was not meant to see her elders like this, speaking frankly about the past, but she was fascinated all the same.

Lady Carleton choked, and it was not a sob but a laugh that escaped her. "Oh, Sybil! You always liked to shock people, and now you have scandalised your own daughter." She leaned forward to press Gemma's knee. "But your mama is perfectly right, Gemma. I do not mourn the earl's loss as perhaps I should. He made us all very unhappy, you see."

She gazed earnestly into Gemma's face. "No doubt you have wondered at my behaviour since you arrived here, my dear."

She clasped her hands together, seeming to search for the right words. "When my husband died, I was like . . . oh, like a bird set free from a cage. Filled with exhilaration and revelling in my sudden independence. But he had kept me captive for so long, I could not cope easily with the outside world. Like one of those pathetic creatures dashing its head against a pane of glass, I kept testing my wings, flying at freedom, only to fall."

She blinked a few times, and a sad smile touched her mouth. "Those stupid, petty rebellions—smoking the cigarillo, permitting Fanny to call off her engagement, attending the crying of the neck—each one of them seemed to go wrong. But I needed to break free from that cage, Gemma, and find my own way, once and for all. And now, with your help, I think I have finally done it. But it took a long time for my lord's influence to wane. He has controlled me, you see, even from the grave."

Sybil grimaced. "We neither of us made the best bargains with our husbands, did we? Only I chose mine, flew in the face of Hugo's good sense, whereas you were forced to marry a man thrice your age. It was criminal."

"Yes, I still recall you urging me to rebel, but I hadn't half your spirit." Lady Carleton sighed and gave a brief grimace, as if to hold back tears. Her voice trembled. "If only I'd had the courage to stand against my husband, our dear Andrew might still be alive."

Sybil exchanged a concerned glance with Gemma, but the tea tray arrived before either could respond. Lady Carleton passed a hand over her eyes. "Gemma, would you? I don't think . . ."

"Of course." Gemma made them strong, sugary tea, a buffer against the shocks she anticipated lay in store.

Sybil moved to the sofa, where her friend sat and took her hand in a comforting clasp, her bright hair haloed by the sun streaming through gauze curtains. "Elisabeth, you must not blame yourself. Carleton was stronger than you and he had not an ounce of chivalry or respect for those he should have been sworn to protect. No amount of spirit could have prevented him from behaving exactly as he chose." She lowered her gaze. "Wives have so little power, even where their own children are concerned."

Gemma stared. Sybil's tone contained a bitterness she had never heard from her mother before.

"Sebastian will not forgive me," whispered Lady Carleton. She raised her teacup to her lips and gazed into the distance, into the past.

With meticulous care, she set down her cup. "He was supposed to be mine, you know. Andrew was the heir, handed over to nurses and nannies and tutors. But when Sebastian came, I thought he would be mine."

Her face started to crumple, but she fought it, and soon her features smoothed. She took a shaky breath. "I nursed and cared for Sebastian myself, as I was never allowed to do with Andrew. I loved him so dearly, but over the years my devotion became a source of disgust for the earl. It reached the stage where he punished Sebastian for some minor transgression whenever I took the slightest notice of him. So, I had to pretend I did not care for Sebastian at all."

Gemma caught her breath. She had known there must be some explanation for Lady Carleton's cold behaviour towards Sebastian when he was a lad. The kind, generous woman Gemma had come to hold in deep affection could not have treated that small boy cruelly by design. If only Sebastian knew, surely he could not continue to hold a grudge.

Sybil squeezed Lady Carleton's hand. "That must have been painful for you, my dear."

Choking back tears, Lady Carleton nodded. "I never realised how I hurt that little boy. I sent him away as much as I could, because I could not bear to see his small body covered in marks from his father's whip."

Gemma winced. Her stomach churned at the thought of what Sebastian had endured. No wonder he had hated Laidley so much.

Sybil spoke. "You sent him to Ware and he was happy. There was nothing else you could have done."

Lady Carleton looked up through her tears. "Yes. Yes,

there was," she whispered. "I could have told him I loved him."

AFTER an hour, Gemma slipped away and left the ladies together. She was glad Lady Carleton had invited her mother to stay. Sybil seemed to give such comfort to her old friend. Gemma wondered if her mother might even persuade Lady Carleton to attend the ball.

The thought of the ball that night made her shiver with excitement. An involuntary smile of anticipation tilted the corners of her mouth as she checked over the final arrangements.

Despite turning the matter over in her mind almost every waking moment, Gemma had not yet hit on a plan to break down the wall of exquisite politeness Sebastian had built around himself. She had been formulating and rejecting all kinds of wild, improbable scenarios. While these imaginings heightened the nervous excitement singing in her blood, they made no practical contribution to solving the problem at hand.

Her heart knew what it wanted, and repeated its demands with insistent, powerful clarity. Mutual, complete surrender—nothing less. Her body cried out for Sebastian's touch, the warm pressure of his mouth on hers, his hands on her body. Her mind still held sway, but only by the merest whisper, that sensible voice warning her if she obeyed her body and her heart, she would risk everything she held dear.

By the time she went upstairs to her bedchamber, her thoughts and feelings jangled in a discordant clamour. She was supposed to be resting, like all the other ladies, but she could not sit still, much less sleep. She made her *toilette*, then paced the floor restlessly, waiting for Charters to help her dress. Dear soul though Dorry was, tonight, Gemma did not want braids.

She glanced at the bed. Following Gemma's earlier instructions, two dresses lay on the counterpane, pressed and ready for wear. One, her sapphire silk, modest and plain. The other, the *pièce de résistance* of Sebastian's chosen gowns, a creation so delicate and evocative of hidden desire, only looking at it made Gemma giddy. She had never worn anything like it in her life.

Ridiculous, but she knew with utter certainty that her fate rested on her choice. Gemma closed her eyes. Mind, body, or heart—which of them would win the almighty battle waging inside her?

But before she could make her selection, Charters bustled in and decided for her, without so much as a by-your-leave.

Scarcely glancing at the sapphire silk, the maid picked up the gown Sebastian had bought and threw it over Gemma's head. The fabric draped and swirled over her body as it settled into place. Although designed along classical lines, the sea-green gauze clung daringly to her curves. How had Sebastian judged her measurements so perfectly? A stab of excitement pierced her at the thought.

Seduced by this tantalising new vision of herself, Gemma did not heed the voice of her mind and conscience telling her wearing this gown would be the most dangerous thing she had ever done. When he saw her in this dress, Sebastian could be left in no doubt she wanted him. Wearing his gown would mean accepting that their friendship had stepped into another realm.

She should take it off. She should wear the sapphire silk and hold on to her virtue like a survivor clinging to the wreckage of a lost ship. But when Charters sat her down at the dressing table and brushed the braids out of her hair, she did not protest. She acquiesced without thought, almost without volition.

This time, Gemma made no mention of braids. With intense concentration, Charters dressed her hair in a unique variation of the Grecian style: a riotous, wanton disorder, with one fat, burnished ringlet brushing the sensitive, bare flesh where her throat met her shoulder. She picked over Gemma's jewel case and drew out her gold Roman coin necklace and matching gold earrings with something almost approaching a satisfied smile.

When Charters's work was done, Gemma inspected herself in the looking glass. She had never worn so little in public in her life before. She felt quite naked except for the soft whisper of gauze against her legs, and the firm support of her stays, thrusting her breasts into an enticing display. Her skirts fell in a slender column to the ground, and the layered gauze gave the illusion of being translucent, as if by concentrated effort, the viewer might see something underneath he wasn't meant to see.

Fanny came in and stopped short on the threshold. "Ravishing! Did I not tell you?" She eyed Gemma speculatively. "I wonder why you decided to wear that gown tonight?"

Gemma frowned at her and pointedly thanked Charters for her services.

Fanny, who treated servants like furniture, glanced around. "Yes, Charters, you may go." She dismissed her maid with a flutter of her hand and turned back to Gemma, her expression eager. "Now, tell me. Whom do you have in your sights tonight?"

Gemma surrendered to the inevitable. "Sebastian. Who else?" She traced the low neckline of her gown with her fingertip and smiled.

Fanny clapped her hands. "Aha! I guessed as much, but I did not think you would tell me. Well, Gemma, only smile like that and you will have all the gentlemen at the ball at your feet."

A knock sounded on the door and Gemma bade the visitor enter. Sybil stood on the threshold, projecting restrained beauty in emerald satin. Behind her hovered Aunt Matilda.

Sybil caught Gemma's eye and shrugged. "She would

come with me, my dear. Ah! And you must be Fanny." She moved to embrace the girl. "So like your mama at that age," she murmured.

Fanny gazed, wide-eyed, from Sybil to Gemma.

Gemma grinned. "Lady Fanny, my mother, Mrs. Maitland."

"Oh, call me Sybil, everyone does."

"Gemma!" While these civilities were exchanged, Matilda had been standing, frozen, at the bedchamber door. Now, she marched forward and twitched the skirts of Gemma's gown. "Gemma! What on earth are you wearing?"

"Doesn't she look delicious? Quite simply edible." Sybil smiled beatifically. "Never say Dorry is responsible for that creation, darling. Who dressed your hair?"

"Fanny lent me her maid," said Gemma. She straightened and held herself proudly under Matilda's horrified gaze.

Matilda's mouth worked into a prune of silent outrage. Then, she erupted into speech. "You cannot wear that abomination! People will say you are no better than—"

"Oh, do but look at the time!" interrupted Fanny, no doubt sensing imminent danger. "I, er, I must go and see if anything needs to be done downstairs. Pray, excuse me." Fanny scurried from the room.

Sybil's eyes sparked, but Gemma stepped between the two women. This time, she would fight her own battle.

She tried to steady her voice. "Aunt Matilda, for more years than I care to remember you have slandered my mother and warned me against becoming like her. Well, I made a discovery today, though I have known it in my heart all along. My mother is a loyal and loving creature. I should be honoured to be likened to her."

Matilda and Sybil gasped as one, but Gemma was in the grip of something hot and consuming, something very much like rage. It came to her in a flash, as if her burning anger had seared away blinkers she had worn for too long—the reason no one at Laidley had treated her like a pariah, though Matilda had assured her she would be an outcast; the source and fuel of rumours about her and her mother at Ware. What had Jenny Whitton said that day in the village? That her aunt had been before her with the news of Sybil and Bellamy's arrival. It all made horrible, sickening sense.

She advanced on her aunt. "It's been you all along, hasn't it? Your gossiping, meddlesome tongue! *You* have been responsible for keeping an old scandal alive in the minds of our neighbours. *You* have caused them to shun me, not Mama."

Matilda opened her mouth to speak, but Gemma silenced her with a glare. "I think you know what I am talking about. Your predilection for scandal-broth is renowned, but not much of note happens in our little corner of the world, does it? You have used my mother and me to provide cheap entertainment for our neighbours for years. Lord, what a fool I have been! It's taken me this long to discover what was behind it all."

Matilda began to gasp for air. Uttering a wordless cry, she stumbled backwards and clutched her chest.

"And don't try any of your hysterical fits on me, ma'am," said Gemma. "Recollect, if you succumb now, you will miss the greatest opportunity for scandal-mongering that has come your way. You will miss the Laidley ball."

Suddenly, she felt deflated, as if that speech had taken all her energy. She felt her mother's hand on her shoulder, a warm, strengthening touch.

"Bravo, my dear," murmured Sybil. To Matilda, she said, "I think I may safely speak for Hugo in this. You will not return to Ware. *Ever.* You will leave here tomorrow in Hugo's carriage and you will go to Aunt Gertrude in Bath. No doubt Hugo will be generous enough to make you a comfortable allowance, but after this night, Matilda, all correspondence between you and my family will cease. And if you do not want me to hunt you down and make you sorry, you will keep your busy mouth shut about me, and most especially about Gemma. Do I make myself clear?"

White-lipped and stiff with outrage, Matilda stared at them, open-mouthed. She made a furious, strangled sound and stalked from the room, slamming the door behind her.

Triumph and pride surged through Gemma, and a huge lump formed in her throat. That her mother would come to her defence so swiftly, so decisively, was more than she could have wished for. She had been prepared to fight this battle alone, as she had fought so many others. But her mother had been there, standing by her when she needed her the most.

Sybil gazed after Matilda and shook her head. "What a foolish, destructive woman." She turned to Gemma. "Darling, I am so sorry. I had no idea."

"I can scarcely believe it myself. But it all fits." Gemma paced the room, her hands twisting. "It's the hypocrisy of it that makes me so furious. She was forever warning and lecturing and condemning my free manners. And all the while, she secretly fuelled the whispers behind my back."

Gemma wrapped her arms around herself against a sudden chill. "I did so want tonight to be special, Mama. I am afraid she will spoil it, the same way she has spoiled everything else."

Sybil was silent for a moment. "I suppose I can guess what you are about. I understand Sebastian bought gowns for you in London. That was not well done of him." She hesitated. "Are you certain you know what you are doing, darling? I don't want to pry, and God forbid I should preach, but is this what you really want?"

Gemma took a deep breath. "I don't know what I want to come out of all this, but I do know that I have to do it. I have hidden away for so long, Mama, and it was all for nothing. Don't you see? I just want to be free."

Sybil searched her face, then nodded slowly, as if she understood. She rose and moved to the door. "In that case, I have something for you. Wait here while I get it."

Staring after Sybil's retreating form, Gemma wondered what her mother might have to give her. Some new piece of jewellery perhaps? Or a silk shawl to complement her gown?

But when Sybil returned and shut the door behind her, she held a small, misshapen parcel, wrapped in brown paper and tied with string.

Perplexed, Gemma received the parcel and turned it over to slide off the string.

Sybil reached out and put her hand over Gemma's. "You need not open it now, but I want you to promise me you will use this if the occasion arises. There is a pamphlet inside to show you how." She paused. "It is to prevent pregnancy."

Gemma flushed with embarrassment more acute than any she had known. "Mama, I really don't think—"

With a light touch of her forefinger to Gemma's lips, her mother silenced her. "Whether or not it comes to that will be your decision, darling. But it is always wise to be prepared."

Staggered that her mother could place such confidence in her judgment, Gemma stammered, "But . . . then you approve?"

Sybil snorted. "Are you mad? You are my daughter. I love you. Of course I don't approve. I would have you wait for your marriage bed, as any mother would."

"Then why . . . ?"

Sybil regarded her with an expression both shrewd and kind in her remarkable eyes. "Do you *want* me to forbid you, Gemma? Someone told me I had forfeited that right long ago." She tilted her head. "Perhaps he was right. In any case, you will go your own way, my dear, but I don't want you to tread blindly. There is far too much at stake."

Suddenly, Gemma realised another truth, something she had doubted until this moment: Her mother loved her. Perhaps Sybil had not been there to share everyday trials and mundane joys, but she cared deeply for her daughter in her own, unique fashion. Gemma looked down at the package in her hand, not knowing what to say.

She raised her eyes to Sybil's. "Thank you," she whispered.

Smiling, Sybil traced Gemma's cheek with her fingertips. "The best way to attract a man, the right man, is always to be yourself, Gemma. Listen to your body. Listen to your heart, and you will know what to do."

SEBASTIAN lurked in the great hall, unsure what he was waiting for. He should be in the drawing room greeting his guests, yet the need to see Gemma first kept him loitering there, hoping to catch her before the crowd swallowed her.

He had taken out his quizzing glass to inspect the maker's mark on the base of a small, Chinese vase, when he heard a step above him. He looked up, to see a vision that stole his breath.

The quizzing glass dropped from his hand. After a moment, he realised his mouth hung open and he shut it. Gemma stood there like some goddess—Venus, perhaps— or a water sprite, her figure tantalisingly revealed by the fine, clinging fabric of her sea-green gown.

One of the gowns he had bought.

Too stunned to contemplate the implications of her choice, he drank his fill of the creamy expanse of her bosom, two delicious mounds framed by frothing green, like a pristine beach caressed by waves. His mouth was so dry, he could not speak. He simply stared.

With a slow, feline smile that shot the blood to his loins, she descended the stairs. Her cheeks flushed pink, but that was the only sign that she might not be entirely comfortable in this new guise.

Before she even reached the foot of the stairs, he took her hand and raised it to his lips. "Gemma, you look . . ." He couldn't find an adequate word to describe the mixture of knock-out beauty and sensual appeal. He settled for, ". . . breathtaking."

"Thank you." Her gaze travelled over him, and her eyes sparkled with approval. She put her hand on his arm. "Shall we?"

For an instant, Sebastian considered sweeping her back upstairs to his bedchamber and forgetting the ball entirely, but of course he couldn't do it. He all but groaned as he led her towards the state apartments.

Why had she dressed this way, tonight of all nights, when he had resolved to woo her gently, as Brooke had reminded him a lady of quality ought to be wooed? He did not know how he would restrain himself over dinner, let alone all night.

As they moved, he caught her scent. Something floral, but elusive, heady, intoxicating. He breathed her in, and wished with all his soul they did not have company tonight.

When they reached the drawing room, Sebastian was surprised to see his mother there, in close conversation with Sybil Maitland. Another surprise. He did not recall seeing Gemma's mama on the list of guests for this ball.

Shrugging, he greeted Sybil and resigned himself to impatience until he could see Gemma alone.

By a pure stroke of genius, Romney had decided to rearrange the place cards so that he sat next to Fanny at the vast dining table.

If anyone noticed they had not been seated strictly in order of precedence, they gave no sign. Conversation buzzed. The guests seemed delighted at the chance to enter Carleton's illustrious abode. It had been many years since they had attended a ball at Laidley.

Romney slid a glance at Fanny, who chattered to her neighbour with the appearance of enjoyment. A pretence he knew was false, because he had taken care to put that prosy bore, Gervase Stone, on her other side.

When Stone turned in response to a remark from the lady on his left, Romney moved in.

"Fanny, why, exactly, is this ball going ahead? We are not betrothed anymore."

Fanny did not look at him, but she jerked a thin shoulder in a shrug. "How should I know? Ask Sebastian. He seems to have a most touching faith in the match." She stabbed a piece of chicken fricassee with her fork. "Does not Gemma look well tonight?"

"Hmm?" Romney cast a cursory glance in Gemma's direction. "Oh, yes."

"You are not bowled over by her beauty, then?"

"I prefer brunettes." He leaned to whisper in her ear. "One brunette in particular."

And at the gleam in her eyes, the happy blush that rose to her cheeks, he knew then what he should have known all along.

Surreptitiously, he slid his hand beneath the damask tablecloth and rested it lightly on her knee. She gasped and choked on a morsel of chicken. He smiled, raising his wine glass to his lips.

"My lord!"

"My lady?"

"Please remove your hand."

"I can't. Regrettably, it is attached to my body."

She gritted her teeth. "I mean remove your hand from my knee."

"Right you are." He grinned and slid it higher.

Fanny jumped and her face flushed darker. She threw him a venomous glance tinged with something hotter and turned away to pursue a laborious discussion with Stone.

Romney continued to sip his wine, and traced a winding pattern with his fingertips on his lady's thigh.

Sixteen

———————— ❦ ————————

FOR the first time in her life, Gemma revelled in the knowledge that the man of her choice desired her. Sebastian partnered all of the highest-ranking ladies in quadrilles and cotillions and reels, fulfilling his obligation as host. He did not approach Gemma, but she felt the hunger in the heated, dark gaze that rested on her as she moved around the room. She smiled to herself. She would bide her time.

She danced with many gentlemen and conversed with them easily, but she did not flirt. Except for a newfound confidence in her body, she behaved with her usual, cheerful friendliness to everyone. She did nothing that might set malicious tongues wagging, though if those sharp-eyed matrons knew the wickedness of her thoughts, they would banish her from good society forever.

She let the magic of music and champagne seep through her. For once, she allowed herself to enjoy masculine attention. Now that her aunt's grim warnings had proved to be nothing but air, the gentlemen's admiration neither threatened nor discomfited her. A strong, purely feminine power coursed through her, hers to wield as she pleased.

Her blood hummed with anticipation, but she did not seek Sebastian out or even attempt to plan their next encounter. The sense of expectation was heady and delicious, a savoured treat, almost an end in itself.

Would Sebastian make the next move? A thrill shivered through her at the thought.

"I say, are you cold, Miss Maitland?" Lord Granton hovered over her. "Allow me to fetch you a shawl."

"I shall fetch it," said Mr. Tilney, flushing to the roots of his flame-coloured hair. "Miss Maitland has promised me the next dance, so I should be the one to fetch her shawl."

Mr. Brandon smiled lazily from his superior height. "I have a notion. Why don't you *both* fetch the shawl and leave the lady to me?"

Tilney and Granton exchanged chagrined looks.

Gemma laughed. "No, no, I am perfectly comfortable, thank you, gentlemen. I've no need for a shawl."

"Amen to that," murmured Brandon, his gaze lingering at her *décolletage*.

Granton raised his quizzing glass. "I say, who is that old trout over there regarding us so balefully? Do you know her, Miss Maitland? Looks like she don't approve of the company you keep."

Turning her head, Gemma saw her great-aunt watching her. Matilda's stare glinted with resentment. Gemma instantly regretted confronting Matilda with the knowledge of her malicious gossiping. By the look in her eye, Matilda intended to make a vast deal of trouble for Gemma before she was exiled to Bath.

Surely, she would not be so vindictive. Surely, she would realise that besmirching Gemma's reputation would also reflect badly on her. But that had not stopped her before.

The throng shifted and Gemma lost sight of Matilda,

but she could not shrug off a sickening sense of unease. The ballroom grew stuffy and hot. Gemma danced and drank more champagne, trying to recapture her previous mood, but the sour taste of Matilda's malevolence lingered.

When she saw her aunt deep in conversation with a group of matrons at the side of the room, her stomach clenched.

Several curious glances shot her way. She began to wish she had worn something a little less striking, that she had not drunk so much champagne. She held her head high, but as Matilda flitted from one group of matrons to the next— like a bee taking pollen from bloom to bloom—Gemma's ears filled with a strange buzz. The jabbering crowd in the ballroom seemed to press in, threatening to suffocate her. She imagined them all turning to point accusing fingers, condemning her with shocked, self-righteous faces. In the middle of a conversation with Romney and Fanny, she excused herself abruptly and pushed her way towards the door.

"Gemma." Lady Russell seemed to rise out of the polished floorboards, blocking her path. "You look divine this evening."

Even through the sick giddiness that threatened to engulf her, Gemma saw a dangerous light in Lady Russell's eyes, a tautness about her rosebud lips. All she could manage in reply was, "Thank you."

Lady Russell gave one of her irritating closed-mouth laughs and indicated her own ensemble, a lyric in oyster satin and silver lace. "De Cacharelle is a genius, is she not?"

If she did not get away, she might cast up her accounts all over that oyster satin gown. "Yes. Yes, she is." Gemma forced the words past her lips and fought rising nausea.

Lady Russell drew breath through her teeth with a hiss. "It's true, then. I might have known. Carleton bought that for you, didn't he?"

Panic shot through the nausea. Gemma's cheeks burned with a hectic flush. "Sebastian? No! No, of course he did not."

But her agitation betrayed her. Lady Russell's stare became glacial. Gemma licked her lips and tried to swallow, but her mouth was too dry. This could not be happening. If Lady Russell knew she had accepted a gown from Sebastian, it would be all over the ballroom in the blink of an eye. She would be ruined, if Aunt Matilda had not already blackened her reputation beyond repair.

Lady Russell's fine eyebrows peaked as if she awaited an explanation. As if she was entitled to one.

"There you are!" Romney stepped up to them and Gemma sagged with relief. She had never been happier to see anyone in her life.

Romney bowed. "Lady Russell, I believe this is our dance."

Lady Russell continued to stare at Gemma. "No. It isn't."

"Of course it is. What a pitiful memory you have, m'dear." He took her hand and tucked it firmly in his crooked arm. "Come along, now. Don't dawdle. The sets are almost made up."

Gemma did not wait for Lady Russell to argue further. She jerked a curtsey to them both and escaped.

Outside the ballroom, the cool air hit her face like a slap. She dashed down the corridor, not stopping until she reached the empty conservatory. Two branches of candles cast sinister shadows, transforming the pleasant courtyard into a mysterious jungle filled with wild, exotic scents.

Clutching her midriff, Gemma hurried to the long windows and threw one open. She leaned on the window frame and drew the fresh night air into her lungs. Her nausea had abated, but her mind revolved in a dizzying whirl.

For a long time, she stared out to the vast, rectangular lawn bordered by clipped yew trees, her mind numbed by dread. The night was warm, the fountain still and silent, its clear pool reflecting the star-scattered sky. She tilted her face and let the full moon bathe her in milky light.

What had she done?

She retreated from the doorway and sank onto a stone bench, trembling. Her thoughts tangled together. Impossible to separate each strand, to think logically about what she should do.

Ruined. After she realised the extent of her aunt's mischief, she had hoped she might one day win back her good name. But between them, Lady Russell and Matilda had ripped respectability from her grasp once more.

Why had she hoped it might be different this time? Why did it matter so much to be accepted? She had never sought social acceptance before. She had never liked being an outsider, but Ware had been consolation enough. Why had everything changed?

She thought about going back to the ball and shuddered. How could she face them all again?

"Gemma."

She looked up, and saw Sebastian's tall figure silhouetted against the doorway. His face remained in shadow, but his snowy linen gleamed pure in the uncertain light. A diamond pin flashed in the folds of his cravat.

His voice sounded husky. "Is something wrong? Why did you leave the ball?"

What to say? She could not tell him about Lady Russell. She plaited her fingers together and forced out the words. "My aunt. She has been busy this evening. Telling everyone her poor opinion of me, no doubt. By now, the story of my mother's disgrace will be everywhere. Comparisons will be drawn, and it will start all over again."

"I see." He hesitated. "Gemma, there have been many rumours, much gossip about me in recent years. You have heard some of it. Does that make you feel differently towards me?"

Arrested by this unexpected question, she thought for a

moment. "No. But then I've known you forever, Scovy. And you are a man. It is not the same."

He moved closer, pushing aside a trailing stem of geraniums as he passed. Flipping the tails of his black coat out of the way, he sat on the bench beside her. "Gemma, do you care about the approval of someone who will judge you lacking without knowing you?"

She sucked in a breath at his nearness. Despite her distress, her body reacted to him on an elemental level, a level far beyond her control. She took another deep breath and focused on answering his question. "When you put it like that, of course not." She bit her lip. "Yes, I do, though. I can't help it, Scovy. I want people to like me. I don't want to hide anymore, or have to hold up my head and smile while they whisper about me."

"But I have heard only the highest praise of you," said Sebastian. "Your beauty, your charm. All the old cats think you're a delight. You may depend on it that the shrewd ones will see the spite behind your aunt's tales. With my support and my mother's, we can brush through this, you'll see." He took her hand and kissed it. The shock raced up her arm. "Come back to the ball and waltz with me."

Tingling from his touch, she made herself shake her head. It was far, far worse than he realised. After Lady Russell said her piece, Gemma would never be able to face those people again. She pressed his hand and tried to smile. "No, you go. I do not wish to return just yet."

He stood and bowed over her hand, watching her through the lock of hair that fell over his brow. "Then I shall have to dance with you out here."

His firm grip and intent gaze melted her defences. A terrible longing flooded her. She wanted him to hold her so much it hurt to breathe. She succumbed to the insistent pull of his hand and rose.

His arm encircled her waist. She placed her left hand on his shoulder and felt the steely strength beneath. Their other hands clasped, an electric connection even through virginal white gloves. Her heart bounded as he swept her into the waltz.

She wanted to urge him closer, but he held her at the proper distance, a vast, respectable chasm between them. Faint strains of music filtered from the ballroom. Her dancing slippers whispered in three-quarter time over the hard, stone floor.

Negotiating flower beds and urns instead of other whirling couples, Sebastian held her gingerly, as if he thought she might crumble. She hungered for the warm, hard length of his body against hers, wanted him to make love to her until she forgot who she was and why they must be apart.

Looking back, it seemed inevitable that they would come together like this. From the time he returned to Ware, from the time he dipped his head and gave her that teasing kiss, everything had led to this moment. How she wanted him! She craved his heat and his masterful, gentle touch.

She locked gazes with him and threw all that longing into her eyes. His breathing hitched and his steps faltered. The depths of his eyes smouldered and the circle of his arm grew rigid, but he did not pull her closer.

Her lips parted, so sensitised with desire, even the faint rush of air between them sent shivers down her spine. If he kissed her now, she'd go up in flames.

Sebastian held himself in check, though she saw the tension in the set of his jaw, felt the rigid restraint of his carefully impersonal embrace.

Did she dare kiss him? What if he repulsed her? She did not think she could bear that. Not tonight. She stared at his lips and willed them to meet hers.

One kiss.

He halted abruptly, his chest rising and falling as though he had run a great distance. "God, Gemma, when you look at me like that, I can't think straight. Why are you doing this? What do you want from me?"

It was now or never. On a spurt of brazen daring, she reached up and curled a hand around his nape, spearing her fingertips through his thick, dark hair. "I want you to kiss me, Sebastian," she whispered. "I want to feel your arms around me, your mouth, your hands on my body."

His hand clamped her wrist with a grip that was almost painful. "Gemma, what are you saying?"

"I'm not sure how I could put it more plainly." She forced her lips into what she hoped was a seductive smile. "I am wearing one of the gowns you gave me."

His hands released her and dropped by his sides. In the cold light of the moon, his face could have been chiselled from stone.

"You were right," he said finally. "I should never have bought you those gowns. I don't know what I was thinking." A pulse ticked in his jaw. "We should return to the ball before we are both missed."

A powerful mix of emotion filled her chest: shame, disappointment, and above all, excruciating hurt. Scarcely able to breathe, Gemma turned away. She had lost her only chance. Tomorrow, she and Sybil would leave for Ware.

"Please make my excuses to your Mama," she whispered. "I—I think I shall retire." Blindly, Gemma pushed past him and hurried to the door.

"Gemma, wait!"

She stopped, bowing her head, unwilling to look at him. Shakily, she said, "I must go."

But shameless longing made her turn back, and she saw with a sudden, staggering clarity what it cost Sebastian to hold himself in check. His mouth was a hard line, his arms rigid by his side, his hands clenched into fists. Only the scorching heat in his eyes could not be restrained. He wanted her—as badly as she wanted him.

How could she break that grim resistance?

Before she knew what she was saying, the words came out, sounding not seductive at all, but ridiculously arch. "If you change your mind, Sebastian, you know where to find me."

YOU know where to find me.

The rest of Sebastian's evening passed in a blur of half-heard conversations. He did not dance again. Gemma was absent, so there seemed no point.

He watched Romney revert to his old self, murmuring wicked things in Fanny's ear to make her blush. How silly all their bickering seemed when compared with the intricate maze he trod with Gemma.

That whispered invitation echoed through his mind. He thought of her lying in her bed upstairs waiting for him, imagined giving in to temptation—taking everything she offered. But how could he make her his mistress? How could he turn her into a woman like her mother, something Gemma had fought all her life not to become?

"My dear? Sebastian, did you hear what I said?" His mother smiled slightly at his blank look. "Where is Gemma? I have not seen her since supper."

"Oh, I beg your pardon, ma'am, I forgot. Gemma asked me to make her excuses. She was not feeling quite the thing."

His mother's brows knitted with concern. "Should I go to her, do you think?"

"No, no. She would hate to cause a fuss. A slight headache, I believe. She has worked hard for us, you know."

His mother sighed. "Yes, she is a dear girl. So like her mother."

She raised her brows at his confusion. "Did you not know that Sybil and I were bosom-bows? It was why I made Hugo your godfather."

"No, I . . ." Sebastian frowned. He had never thought about it. Just that Ware had been his home.

But not anymore. Becoming reacquainted with Laidley, the land he had loved as a small boy—planning improvements, involving himself in the day-to-day business of the estate as his steward's convalescence continued, he'd come to a realisation almost blinding in its simplicity. This small piece of England had existed long before his father walked the earth, and would continue long after the old earl's death. The earl's dark reign was but a wrong stitch in the rich tapestry of time, a miserable aberration. Sebastian had resolved that the true pattern of existence would begin again with him. And with that decision, he found a new sense of belonging, an affinity with the place of his birth.

But Gemma belonged at Ware. She would never give up that dream. If he understood her unprecedented behaviour in the conservatory, she was prepared to take him without his ring on her finger so she would not have to abandon her dream of running the estate.

The knowledge made his stomach churn. He could almost laugh at himself—the worst rakehell in London, balking at taking a willing woman he desired without marriage. Was he mad?

He needed time. He needed to think.

Sybil Maitland glided up to them with a slight frown marring her exquisite features. "Sebastian, where is Gemma?"

"She has retired with a headache, ma'am."

Her frown deepened. "A headache? That is most unlike her." She cast him a shrewd glance, then turned to his mother. "That wretched Matilda has been spreading stories again. I have put a stop to it, but I very much fear the damage is done."

His mother's face froze in a disdainful expression he knew from old. "Indeed? Well, we shall see about that."

Linking her arm through Sybil's, she threw her thin shoulders back and marched off into the fray.

HE wanted her. She knew it. But he would not come. Gemma gripped her hands together as she paced her bed-chamber. She felt like a caged animal, raging to break free, desperate to go to him. But the ball still whirled below. The chatter and music and laughter swelled beneath her feet.

By now, everyone would be whispering that she was Se-bastian's mistress. By now, her name would be a byword, thanks to Aunt Matilda's scandal-mongering and Lady Russell's elegant malice. She would never get her reputa-tion back, so what was there to lose in doing what she wanted, what every cell in her body urged her to do?

She should have been more ruthless, less hesitant. She should have hammered at his resistance until she smashed it to pieces and felt his lips hot on hers, his hands roaming her body, making every inch of her skin tingle and burn.

What sort of sorry excuse for a rake was he, anyway, to have a fit of conscience now? He'd already done such inti-mate things to her it made her body blush all over just to glance at his hands with their clever, magical fingers. In the eyes of Society he had already ruined her. Why hesitate to finish what he had started?

A shudder ran through her at the memory of that night in the cottage. Heat pooled low in her stomach and her loins seemed to melt. The sensations made her heart ache. There would never be another man for her. She would go to her grave without ever knowing such pleasure again. Lonely, dried up, and bitter—like Aunt Matilda.

Unless . . .

Gemma slowly moved to stand in front of the cheval glass. She untied the belt of her wrapper and shrugged out of it, letting it fall to the floor. In her night rail, now, she ran her palms down her body, learning the shape of it, assess-ing the strength of its appeal. Her legs were adequate, she supposed, her waist slender but not scrawny. Her neck was neither too short nor too long. Everything seemed in proportion, except her overlarge chest. She turned to look at her reflection side-on, smoothing her lawn night rail down her stomach so that the curve of her breasts was clearly defined.

She had always been ashamed of her bosom, deeming it more suitable for a *chère amie* than a respectable female, but Sebastian seemed to like it. Her cheeks burned at the memory of his hands stroking and teasing her through the fabric of her gown. What would it be like to feel him, skin to skin?

Listen to your heart. Listen to your body. Her mother's words whispered in her ears. For the first time in her life, Gemma shut her mind, closed her eyes, and simply let herself feel. The exhilarating sense of feminine power she had first experienced in the ballroom surged through her again, igniting her blood, making her heart pound a wild, primitive beat.

She swayed and opened her eyes, suddenly imbued with a desperate sense of purpose. Crossing to her dresser, she took out the brown paper package.

She knew what she had to do.

"SEBASTIAN, I wish you would explain something to me." Restlessly, Eleanor paced the small, curtained alcove.

Sebastian had accompanied his mistress to this secluded spot against his better judgment. There was a dangerous glitter in her eye that he greatly mistrusted. He had never taken the trouble to fathom the inner workings of Eleanor's mind, but he knew her well enough to realise that she was in a towering fury—and she was about to unleash it on him.

Her lips thinned. "What is Miss Maitland to you?"

The cold, staccato words pierced his chest like shards of ice. He betrayed no reaction, but inwardly, he flayed himself for making his preference for Gemma so blatant.

He stared down his nose at her. "I don't know what you're talking about."

"Don't lie to me!" Her voice trembled slightly. "That girl is wearing a gown designed by de Cacharelle. To your order, I make no doubt. She as good as admitted it, the little whore."

Fury ripped through him. He took an involuntary step towards her before he made himself stop. If she'd been a man, he would have hit her for speaking of Gemma that way. Slowly unclenching his fist, he did his best to look amused. "I'd be careful whom I called hard names if I were you, my dear."

A hiss of outrage escaped her, and immediately, he knew he had said the wrong thing. He needed to put a stop to this, before Eleanor's temper made her throw discretion to the winds and spread the story far and wide. Then it would not be Eleanor alone, but the entire *ton* who labelled Gemma a whore.

Gemma would never be able to hold her head up again if it were known he had bought gowns for her, and from the same *modiste* patronised by his mistress. He could not let that happen.

Taking his time, Sebastian removed a piece of lint from his coat sleeve. He met Eleanor's gaze coolly. "My mother commissioned Miss Maitland's wardrobe, not I. You may ask Lady Carleton yourself if you don't believe me. And she will tell everyone else the same if you are stupid enough to spread this scurrilous gossip about a gently bred lady in her charge. I guarantee you, Eleanor, you will only make yourself look foolish if you take this further." In a voice that cloaked steel with softest velvet, he said, "For your own sake, my dear, I beg you will not risk it."

A subtle threat, but she was intelligent enough to take his meaning. It was one thing for a widow to have affairs, as long as she was discreet. It would be quite another for

Sebastian to openly acknowledge Eleanor as his mistress. It was not the act of a gentleman to threaten her with exposure, but he would fight fire with fire to preserve Gemma's good name.

Eleanor sucked in a breath. She was defeated, and she knew it. Even at the height of her fury, she would not ruin Gemma at the expense of her own reputation.

Still, Eleanor lifted her chin, dark eyes flashing. She was a magnificent creature, there was no doubt about it. But even as some corner of his mind acknowledged her beauty, he realised she had lost the slightest power to move him.

He inclined his head. "I need not tell you, of course, that our . . . *friendship* is at an end."

Her lovely eyes sheened with tears before she swallowed and lowered her gaze. The sight disconcerted him. Did Eleanor really care for him? She had never given the slightest indication of it.

"You are in love with her, then," she whispered, turning away, her slim shoulders heaving. "I might have known."

In love? With *Gemma*? The notion flashed through his mind like a lightning bolt across a darkened sky, dazzling him with its brilliance. He made no effort to stop Eleanor when she swept from the alcove in a swish of oyster satin.

As the heavy curtain swung shut behind her, he stood, still staring, rooted to the spot. Had he been that transparent? Did everyone know? Did Gemma?

He had stumbled about like a player in blindman's buff, trying desperately to marry Gemma to someone else, yet wanting to kill every man who glanced twice at her. He had rejected all she had offered him so sweetly tonight, pushed her away, when what he really wanted was to keep her with him forever. He had tried to tell himself it was pure desire, or mere friendship that he felt for her.

But no. Eleanor was right. He loved Gemma. And he wanted her to be his wife.

ONCE his valet had assisted him in removing his boots and his tight-fitting coat, Sebastian dismissed the man and dropped into his wingback chair with a brandy in hand.

There was no question in his mind. He had stopped Eleanor's tongue for the moment, but he would not be easy until he could protect Gemma from malicious gossip by giving her his name. Once she was the Countess of Carleton, none would dare say a word against her.

The more he thought about this marriage business, the more he wondered why he had been so adamant against the institution for so long. He had vowed to discontinue his father's line in punishment for the earl's treatment of Andy, and he had held that vow sacred. But the oath itself had been an adolescent reaction to stunning grief, one he now realised he had carried into adulthood with little further reflection. Perhaps because it had suited him to do so.

Perhaps, all it had taken was the right woman to convince him he was a marrying man, after all. The right woman was Gemma, beyond doubt. Exhilaration pounded through him. Now he had made that decision, he could not wait to make her his.

With a considerable effort of will, he stopped himself charging down the corridor to hammer on her door. He wanted to do this properly, treat Gemma with the respect she deserved—even though it might kill him to do it.

A click and a wheezing creak sounded from the far corner of the room.

Sebastian started up. "Who's there?"

For the second time that evening, she robbed him of speech. Gemma, dressed—no *undressed* was the word—in a peach gauze peignoir.

The candlelight gleamed and leaped in her unbound hair. Every soft inch of her extended an invitation. Though the negligee covered her more completely than her evening gown, the filmy wisp of lacy nothing showed clearly the outline of her breasts, the dark rose pink of her nipples, and the slender curves of her waist and hips. His gaze travelled down her legs—long, smooth, shapely perfection. Her feet were bare.

Hot blood shot to his groin, but he forced himself to stay where he was. If he touched her, he was lost.

She advanced into the room, head held high like a queen. "I thought you might like to see another of your gifts."

"*What?* I didn't . . ." Then he recalled de Cacharelle pressing that last item on him. He'd meant to get rid of it before the boxes were delivered to Gemma. Why hadn't he remembered?

"*Ravishing,* isn't it?" Gemma smiled and drifted closer, with a sultry sway far removed from her usual purposeful stride. "It is a little tight across here." She swept her fingertips lightly across her bosom and smiled. "But I am sure it matters not."

She kept her hand on herself, fiddling with a silly little bow at the side of her neck. He wanted to flick her fingers away and put his mouth there, rip the bow apart with his teeth, but he held back, dragged his gaze away.

He forced the words out. "You don't want to do this, Gemma, not now."

Her light voice tormented him. "But now may be our only chance. Since there is no wedding to plan for, I return to Ware tomorrow." She twisted a red-gold lock around her finger, pulled it taut, and let it spring back into place.

Panic flared along with the heat. He closed his eyes. She held a gun to his head. He could follow her to Sussex and begin his campaign to court her, but once she was back there, he knew he would lose her to Ware's thrall. His hand clenched. Damn that place to hell! And damn her ridiculous obsession.

This was his last chance to win her, and suddenly, he

knew he could do it. She thought she could just take him to bed and then walk away. But she was wrong. This time, there would be consequences.

Consequences. He rose and spoke carefully. "Have you considered what would happen if I got you with child?"

He heard a faint gasp. "I believe there are ways to prevent that."

Sebastian tried not to show his shock at her knowledge. "They are not reliable."

"I'm willing to take the chance. If it happens, I shall be discreet. You need not worry."

"If it happens, you will marry me."

"Sebastian!"

"Your word on it, Gemma, or I won't do this."

She stared at him for a long time, her midnight eyes huge and unblinking in her fine-boned face. "All right. If, against all precautions I get with child, I shall marry you." She paused. "And I will live with the child at Ware."

The words were spark to tinder. Ablaze with hurt and limitless passion, Sebastian gripped her arm, jerked her against him and kissed her hard. For an instant, incredibly, he sensed her fighting him, in a duel of tongues and lips and teeth. He tightened his hold, crushed her breasts against his chest, and assaulted her mouth with all the power and skill at his command.

Suddenly, she sank into him with a soft murmur in her throat, and all that warmth and woman moulded around him and he nearly died.

His fingers traced patterns of lace at her bosom and shoulder, whispered through gauze as he kissed her and stroked down her body, running his hands over all that lush softness. He was hard, throbbing, and oh, so ready for her, but he needed to take it slowly, pleasure her to madness, until she could not even think of saying good-bye.

Her hands were busy at his waistcoat, his neckcloth, his shirt. He yanked the shirt over his head and threw it on the floor. When he stood bare-chested before her, her gaze feasted on him, and the blatant satisfaction in her eyes made him savage with desire.

She skimmed her fingertips along his shoulders. "So hard." Her lips whispered over his chest.

He gave a hoarse laugh. "Everywhere." He caught her hand and brought it to the bulge in his pantaloons. She drew back. Her eyes lit with fascination, then she closed them and stroked him gently. "Does that feel good?"

"That feels . . ." He groaned as she gripped him a little harder. Seizing control, he picked her up, a fragrant soft bundle, and threw her on the bed, following swiftly to loom over her.

Gemma watched Sebastian transform from reluctant, honourable gentleman to the graceful, stalking predator above her. She almost purred in satisfaction. She flicked the heavy weight of her hair from under her, aware of his gaze on her uplifted breasts. Her nipples hardened, pricked with anticipation.

He sat on the edge of the bed and leaned down to ravish her mouth. His kiss seared her, made her skin burn for his touch. Could she ever get enough of him? Could she ever leave him, as she planned to do?

She reached up to pull him down to her. He resisted the tug of her arms, and she felt the strength of him then and revelled in it.

"Slowly, Gemma." He gave her a lazy, wicked smile. "We've a long night ahead of us."

A responsive shudder ran through her, right down to her toes. With one hand at her nape, he drew her to a sitting position. Then he kissed her with thorough, tortuous deliberation, until her bones melted and her flesh liquefied and her mind drifted away.

Still kissing her, he undid the row of tiny pearl buttons that ran down the centre of her negligee. His fingers lingered in their task, touched her intimately as they worked to undress her, shooting darts of pleasure through her, as he did wondrous things with his lips and teeth and tongue.

She kissed him back, telling him everything she could not say—how much she needed him, how much she wished they could be together always, not only these moments, not just this night.

When his mouth left hers, she felt bereft, but he speared his fingers through her hair and tangled in it, tilting her head back to expose her neck, his lips trailing a sizzling path along her jaw. He nuzzled her throat as if to breathe in her scent, then lightly nipped the tender skin. She gasped at the potent mix of pleasure and pain, and moaned as he bit deeper. The negligee gaped open down her front, now, exposing her belly and the valley between her breasts to the night air.

He slid his hands beneath the silk, skimmed them over her sensitive, swollen breasts to smooth the garment away. His palms were hot on her skin where the air had been cool, and she shivered at the delicious contrast. He pushed the garment off her shoulders so it slipped down her arms with a soft hush. Then he raised his head and stared.

"Oh, my God. Gemma."

She tugged her hands free of the negligee, but she took a deep, ragged breath and fought the urge to cover her nakedness. There was no turning back now.

Sebastian studied her with those heated, dark eyes. "I've dreamed of this," he whispered.

"Y-you have?"

He nodded. "But my dreams came nowhere near reality."

He ran his palm over her breast and down her waist, tracing her shape, trailing fire in his wake. He let his hand rest on her thigh and the blood beat in her loins, a burning, thrilling ache.

As he bent to her breast, she licked her lips. "Now you." She wanted no barriers between them this time.

He hesitated, then, with a faint groan, drew back. Gemma

closed her eyes and took another deep breath, trying to
calm her hammering heart and slow the blood that
pounded through her veins. His weight lifted from the bed,
and when she opened her eyes again, he stood with his
back to her, removing his pantaloons, stockings, and finally, his drawers.

As the linen dropped past his buttocks, Gemma forgot
to breathe. In that moment, she wished she could sculpt
him from marble, shape the broad, muscular shoulders
with their sharply defined blades; the long, gently curved
torso; the narrow hips, tight, rounded buttocks and thick,
powerful thighs. Not just to capture his masculine strength
and beauty, but so she could keep him like this with her forever. She lay back and watched the muscles in his arm flex
as he flung his clothes onto a chair. A fierce, shocking wave
of possessiveness swept over her. *Mine, mine, mine,* chanted
a primitive voice inside.

And then he turned around.

She blinked. For the first time, her courage wavered.
She knew the mechanics of what they were about to do, but
the dimensions staggered her somewhat.

He watched her with tender amusement. "Having second thoughts?"

Sitting on the edge of the bed, he took her hand and
leaned closer for a warm, slow kiss. "Just relax. Everything
will be all right, Gemma. I promise."

Against his lean cheek, she whispered, "Of course,"
though her mouth dried and her nerves thrummed with tension.

He stretched out beside her and moved down her body,
kissed her earlobe, her throat, the swell of her breast. She
gasped, and when he drew her nipple into his mouth, suck-
led and tongued it with firm, steady strokes, all power of
thought and doubt flew away. She dug her fingers into his
back and writhed under the insistent, drawing pressure.

He lingered there, as if worshipping her breasts was an

end in itself. Finally, he descended lower still, kissed her stomach in a sudden movement, and she squirmed, couldn't stop the laughter that escaped her. She felt his lips spread in a smile at her reaction. His tongue moved in lazy whorls around her navel. He kissed her belly and parted her legs with one large hand.

Delicious thrills shot to her loins, even though his hand had merely brushed her sex. His mouth feathered kisses down her hipbone, drifting slowly inwards. She tensed, strung tight with anticipation. He couldn't. He wouldn't . . . would he?

He did.

In one, swift motion, he gripped her inner thighs, gently parted her folds with his thumbs and sank his head between her legs. Gemma gave a startled cry, shocked by this new sensation. His mouth was hot and wet and he found the place he had worked to a fever that night in the cottage. His tongue swirled, flicked and kneaded, flooding her body with pleasure. Panting, burning, she threw her arms above her head and surrendered to mindless rapture.

A distant earthquake rumbled, sending faint tremors through her body. She opened her eyes and looked down, and the sight of Sebastian's dark head moving rhythmically between her thighs spiked her with excitement. Frenzied, gasping, lost to shame, she ran her fingers through the thick waves of his hair, pressing him harder against her. The faint stubble on his chin rasped her sensitive flesh. A prickling, hot, frantic sensation built in her spine, down her thighs, along the soles of her feet.

While his mouth pleasured her beyond control, he slipped one finger to stroke inside. Her body swirled like a river of fire with hot, surging currents and ripples of intense pleasure. She bucked and moaned, even tried to push him away. His hands clamped down on her thighs, trapping her beneath him. Burrowing down, he took the swollen nub of flesh between his lips and sucked, until the searing currents swirled and clashed and exploded at her centre.

She cried out, convulsing and shuddering helplessly. He kept touching her, gently prolonging the sweet agony, until waves of ecstasy swelled and broke again and again, and she heard her own voice whimper a plea for mercy. With a harsh exhalation, he finally left her throbbing, twitching loins to ravage her mouth.

She tasted her own essence on his tongue as she kissed him back hard. In some effort to convey the wild joy inside her, the frantic need, she ran her hands over him, raked her nails over the broad, muscled back she had coveted in secret so long ago at Ware.

"Gemma, touch me." Sebastian's voice sounded ragged, pleading even, all his suave sophistication stripped away.

Without hesitation, she reached down and curled her hand around his erection. "Like this?"

A soft groan escaped him. "I'm your slave, princess. Do with me what you will."

Impatient, yet intrigued, she gave him a little push so he lay back on the bed. She knelt and reached for him, ran her fingertips along his erection, gasping when it sprang up at her touch. The skin there was smooth, soft as a rose petal, but there was a thrusting, jutting strength to that hard ridge of flesh that intimidated her. Gathering her courage, she took the shaft in a firm grip and explored its tip with her fingers. She heard him moan. His chest heaved. A glance at his face showed his features drawn in a slight grimace, as though he were in pain.

Not what she wanted at all. She wanted to drive him mindless with desire, pleasure him as he had her, but she had not the slightest notion how. Frustrated at her inexperience, she admitted it. "I'm sorry, Scovy. I don't know what to do."

Laughing, he surged up, tumbling her beneath him. In a

voice roughened with passion, he said, "I want you now, Gemma. We'll play those games some other time."

Sebastian made an effort to speak calmly, but he did it through gritted teeth. Holding back while she teased him with such curious, inexpert innocence was pure torture. With the fixed notion that if he didn't get inside her right now, he would explode, he reached down and positioned himself at her entrance. She was hot and wet, pliant and ready as a virgin ever could be for such an invasion. The thought of her virginity nearly made him lose control. To be the first man, the only man Gemma had ever had— would ever have, if he had anything to say about it— aroused him more than he'd thought possible.

Grimly restraining himself from ramming into her like some oafish adolescent, he stroked the head of his erection up and down the slick folds of her sex. He leaned in to kiss her, and as she reached up to slide her hands over his shoulders, he pushed in a little way, then eased a little farther into that searing, moist sheath and stopped.

"How peculiar," breathed Gemma.

The muscles in his neck and shoulders corded with tension, he was sweating with the effort of restraint, and all she could say was "how peculiar"?

He just managed to grind out, "This will hurt," before he surged in and thrust deep.

She gave a strangled cry and her face spasmed with pain. He lowered his head to kiss her with what gentleness he could muster, forced himself to remain still inside her until he felt her relax around him.

"All right?" he whispered against her lips.

"Yes."

He ran his hand over her breast and down her silken, sweat-dampened body. "God, you are perfect."

Shyly, she smiled into his eyes. "So are you."

Sebastian froze. In an instant, that bright, trusting smile cracked the shell of cynicism that had taken so many years to harden around his heart. Her warmth and light ripped through him and for one, glorious moment he thought, *This is love.*

But he was a man inside the body of a woman he had desired forever, it seemed, and this strange epiphany only heightened his need.

There was no more talk after that. He stroked into her smoothly, endlessly, relished her sweet responsiveness; the soft, moist heat that encompassed him, gripped him, drew him on and on. Her breath came sharp and gasping in his ear as he moved inside her, and then she began to move, too, catching his rhythm, sending him spinning in a white-hot whirlpool of desire.

He thrust into her again and again, lost himself in the scent of her, in the cadence of her sighs.

She strained against him, and he tilted her hips to stroke deeper. She gave a throaty moan, a siren song luring him to the edge. In a convulsive thrust, she broke the rhythm and cried out, arched and trembled beneath him. He gripped her hips and plunged into darkness, and the blinding, searing release shook him with a ferocity he'd never imagined. He pumped his seed into her with a harsh, guttural groan and collapsed, a shuddering, breathless weight sprawled over her lovely body.

Closer than ever before.

Moments passed before he realised. He had not withdrawn in time. Barely able to summon the strength, he rolled away.

Too late.

Somehow, he found his voice. "Gemma. Please, you must marry me."

She turned her head and the shock in her eyes mirrored his own. He could hardly believe the words had come out of his mouth as a plea. Yet it felt so utterly right, that they should be together like this for the rest of their lives. And so wrong if what they had done was for mere physical gratification. To him it meant much more. But how could he put it into words?

Quietly, she said, "Don't."

He gripped the hand that rubbed agitatedly at her throat. "But I have to. Don't you know how much I need you?"

Gemma glanced away. "I only came to Laidley as a temporary measure. My place is at Ware."

He raised himself on his elbow and looked down at her tumbled golden beauty, her full lips bruised from his kisses. She was everything he wanted, and it seemed incredible to him that they had made love. After all these years, who could have guessed it would be Gemma Maitland who held his heart, his future, in her small hands?

"Gemma . . ." *I love you.*

He couldn't say it. He couldn't say it, knowing she would never say it back. She would not laugh, as Caroline had done so many years ago. But she would gaze at him with those deep eyes full of pity and remorse, and that would be infinitely worse.

He flung himself onto his back, clasped his hands behind his head, and stared at the canopy above them the same fathomless blue as her eyes. He had meant to spend the whole night loving her, but now he could not even glance in her direction. Something inside him was shattering into tiny splinters and he couldn't find a way to stop it.

Sebastian hauled himself out of bed and padded to the brandy decanter. He had never known such miserable indecision. This was what came of a lifetime of letting no emotion touch him, of shrugging off others' sensitivities. He had not the slightest clue how to appeal to the woman in his bed. With Gemma, neither suave love talk nor a display of prowess between the sheets would work.

Her soft voice broke his thoughts. "You are very kind, Scovy. It is truly noble of you to feel you must marry me, but don't you see? I am Sybil Maitland's daughter. No one would expect it of you."

His fingers clenched so hard the brandy balloon cracked. Slowly, he opened his hand and let the shards fall onto the drinks tray, hardly aware of a small, stinging cut on his palm. He turned back. "Don't *ever* say anything like that to me again."

Gemma sighed. "Sebastian, you want to believe that I am a gently bred lady to be set on a pedestal, but I'm not. I'm just a woman." With a scintillating smile, she stretched her arms above her head. His groin tightened at the sight of those luscious breasts thrusting upwards, her slender torso arching as if in the throes of passion.

"Please, Sebastian. Make love to me again."

He wrenched his gaze away. "And that's all I am to you, is it? Someone to warm your bed. Well, I want more than that, Gemma. I want marriage."

Sebastian rolled his eyes in disgust. He could not believe he had just said something like that, something a *woman* would say. But he meant every word.

She shook her head. "It's not possible. You know it isn't. You must marry a high-born lady with an unblemished reputation. I am not that. Certainly, not anymore."

He closed his eyes. It was not an accusation, she said it almost with relish, but guilt swept over him. He should have been strong, resisted temptation. Now he had ruined her, and she would not let him make the only reparation possible.

"Sebastian." Her voice was smoke and honey. "We might not have a future, but we have tonight. Come to me."

Unwillingly, he opened his eyes and watched her, the tantalising half-smile as she twirled a bright lock of hair around her finger, the heat in her eyes pulling him towards certain destruction. What had happened to Gemma tonight? It was as if she'd suddenly discovered every feminine wile ever practised on mankind and invented a few more.

He cleared his throat. "No. We need to talk about this sensibly."

She blinked, but continued to smile and twist her long,

silky hair. "Oh, by all means. Do let us be sensible, dear Scovy."

"It might be better if we dressed."

She sighed theatrically, and her lips trembled with a suppressed amusement that galled him. "Very well. Would you fetch me my peignoir, please?"

He shot her a dark glance and tossed her his dressing gown instead. He found a shirt and breeches and put them on while she donned his robe. The mannish garment concealed her body, but it threw all that heavy-eyed, tousled femininity into startling relief. She rubbed her cheek against the satin lapel like a cat, lowered her thick, dark lashes and sniffed, as if she scented ambrosia.

The provocative sensuality of her movements roused him to blind, cold fury, even as his body raged to take her. She rejected him for the most altruistic reasons, no doubt, but it was still rejection, and the excruciating pain of it was killing him inside. She had ripped away his cynical, protective shell, and for that brief, explosive paradise in her arms the rawness of exposure had been worth it. But against her indifference, he now had no defence.

Softly, she said, "Sebastian, I know you mean to be honourable and gentlemanly, but there is not the least need . . ."

She had flayed him with her talk of Ware and now she rubbed salt into his bleeding flesh. Deliberately, he lashed out, wanting to hurt her, desperate to prove he could.

"Oh, but there is. You see, I promised Hugo I would marry you."

Seventeen

❧

"YOU promised?" Gemma stiffened. "What nonsense is this?"

In the twin grip of jagged, savage agony and cold, numbing rage, Sebastian answered with a lift of his brows. "Can't you guess? I gave my word to Hugo if I didn't find you a husband in three months, I would marry you myself. That is what all this has been about."

"You did . . . all this to fulfill a promise? I don't believe it."

Gemma leaped from the bed and marched over to him to search his face, trying to read him. Even in her fury, she looked wildly desirable, but despite his reluctant admiration he kept his expression cynically amused, gave nothing away.

With a frustrated growl, she turned and paced, all slender, lithe energy, even as his dressing gown gaped about her and dragged on the floor behind her heels.

She pivoted to face him, realisation sweeping her features. "So this visit to Laidley was just some little plan you cooked up with Hugo to lure me away from Ware?"

He simply looked at her, couldn't believe that after all they'd done, after the poison-tipped arrow he'd aimed squarely at her heart, her first thought was still for Ware. His emotions slammed shut.

She bunched her fists in his shirt. "Answer me, damn you!"

From behind a wall of ice, he replied, "Hugo did not inform me of his plans."

She released him and struck her fist on her palm. "Oh, I should have known better than to leave Ware."

He said nothing. Realising beyond doubt there was no hope for them now, he wished she would just leave him to lick his wounds in peace.

Gemma stared at him with narrowed eyes. "He has done something while I've been away, hasn't he? He has made his will. He has been breaking in his successor. One of the cousins? Sebastian, tell me what you know."

He could not endure much more of this. He turned away. "I know nothing more than you."

Silence stretched between them. He could not speak, though all the things he wanted to say, all the things he should have said, echoed in his mind.

I love you.

She would never believe him now.

As the slow, steady tick of the mantel clock was about to drive him mad, she turned and strode to the secret door.

"If you will not tell me, I shall have to ask Mama."

GEMMA hurried back to her room, stumbling a little over the trailing brocade of Sebastian's robe. As the secret panel to her bedchamber clicked shut behind her, she slumped against it and let the tears pour down her face. Her lungs had compressed into hard lumps, her throat closing over so tightly, she could barely catch her breath. Harsh, angry sobs tore from her chest.

How could Sebastian do such a thing? How could he play a hand in thwarting the one dream that had sustained her all these years—the one thing she had worked so hard to achieve?

She'd thought he knew her, loved her as a special, dear friend—as she loved him. But everything he had said to her since he'd arrived at Ware had been a lie. He had pretended to support her bid to run the estate, but instead, he'd ridden roughshod over her dream. Coming to him tonight, she'd thought they shared a bond so enduring and special it did not need marriage vows to strengthen it or tie it down, but Sebastian's loyalty to Hugo far surpassed his attachment to her, it seemed. He'd even been prepared to marry her— clearly against his inclinations—since his more fastidious friends had declined to do the job.

She slid down to huddle against the wall, hugging her knees to her chest. She did not want to marry Sebastian, so why, *why* did it hurt so much that he had gone to such ridiculous lengths to avoid marrying her?

Gemma scrubbed at her face with the trailing sleeve of Sebastian's robe, taking perverse satisfaction in the salt water marking the richly patterned silk. She glared up at the moulded ceiling, blinking back more tears.

No, she would not think about Sebastian anymore. She would fix her sights on the future.

In no time at all, she would be back in Sussex, where she belonged, and then she could sort out this ridiculous mess. How *glad,* how truly, utterly ecstatic she was to be going home.

With a low, animal cry, Gemma scrambled up and flung herself on the bed.

❧

GEMMA blinked stinging eyelids against the morning sunlight and raised her head from where it rested on her crossed arms. She supposed she must have slept, but sleep had not refreshed her or made the future appear any rosier, despite the fact she was going home today. She felt wrung out, drained of tears, drained of life.

She still wore Sebastian's dressing gown. Gasping at her recklessness, Gemma stripped it off and hid it in the carved oak blanket box at the foot of her bed. Carefully, she removed the sponge soaked with vinegar she had inserted as a precaution against conception, Sybil's thoughtful gift. Then she washed herself with a wet flannel, scoured her body clean of any trace of Sebastian, and threw the sponge and the flannel into the fire.

Her body ached from the night's pleasure. Her stomach churned and her throat still felt clogged with the aftereffects of her crying bout. Moving like an old woman, she dressed in her demure night rail, her own dressing gown and slippers, and crept along the corridor to tap on Sybil's door.

"Enter."

Sybil was in bed, reading, an almost matronly cap tied over her bright curls. Her face lit when she saw Gemma, but her smile switched immediately to concern.

"Oh, my darling. Come here." She put down her book and held out her hands. Though Gemma edged towards the bed, she did not touch her mother's outstretched hands. After all, she did not know where Sybil's loyalties lay.

"I heard something last night which interested me exceedingly," she said in a brittle voice. "I heard that Hugo made a bargain with Sebastian concerning me."

She detected genuine surprise in Sybil's frown. "You knew nothing of this?"

"No, my dear. What bargain, exactly?"

"Sebastian was to try to find me a husband. And if he failed, he would have to marry me himself." Gemma sat down on the bed. "No wonder this house is full of eligible bachelors. He has gone to the most elaborate lengths to avoid marrying me."

"Well, it takes two to make a marriage," said Sybil. "Would you have accepted him?"

Gemma lifted her chin. "Most certainly not."

Nodding, Sybil flicked a hand. "There you are, then. Two foolish men scheming to do what is best for you. Mutton-headed, but well-intentioned, surely? Is that all that troubles you?"

"All?" Gemma started up. "*All*, Mama? How can you say that? It is the most degrading, humiliating—"

"Mutton-headed," murmured Sybil.

"Yes, all right, mutton-headed thing I've ever heard of. And another thing! I'm convinced Hugo sent me to Laidley to get rid of me while he made changes at Ware. Do you know anything about that?"

"We-ell . . ."

Gemma pounced. "You do! You do and you did not tell me. He is leaving Ware to one of the cousins, isn't he?"

"No, he is not."

"Then . . . you, Mama?" Gemma held her breath. If Ware went to Sybil, she would come home for good and Gemma could go on the way she had before Hugo thought of this mad idea to employ an agent.

"No," Sybil said quietly. "He is leaving it to Charles Bellamy. His grandson." A radiant smile burst over her face. "Your brother, Gemma."

Gemma's surroundings shattered and whirled around her like coloured glass in a kaleidoscope. She clutched at the bedpost as rage overcame her in a red, blinding rush. "*What?* You mean you have a love child? And *he* is going to take over Ware?"

The slap was sharp but it stung Gemma's cheek for only a moment. Sybil's eyes blazed into hers. "*Never* speak to me like that! I have endured unfounded gossip and innuendo for half of my life, but I will not endure it from you, Gemma. Charles Bellamy is your *legitimate* brother. He will inherit Ware. It was not my decision. I had nothing to do with it. If you want to take it up with Hugo, you may, but I can assure you, you are likely to be dealt short shrift. Hugo never intended you to have Ware and you know it."

Stricken at the terrible accusation she had made, bewildered by Sybil's revelation, Gemma put her hand to her hot cheek. "Mama, I am sorry—"

"I am sure you are, my dear." Sybil picked up her book and opened it to read, dismissing her. "I am sure you are."

GEMMA stood by the window and watched the last of the houseguests roll away in their glossy black carriages. She had not bidden any of them good-bye, unsure whether she was in disgrace.

The question of her reputation that had loomed so large last evening hardly mattered now. She could scarcely comprehend all that had happened over the past twenty-four hours. Weakened by sadness and guilt, she submitted to Dorry's ministrations, tormented by thoughts of her mother, and questions about Charles Bellamy. How on earth could he be her brother? But mostly, she thought of Sebastian.

She had been too hard on him last night. She should have realised he would only act out of genuine concern for her future in trying to see her wed. If he had known Hugo was adamant about excluding her from running the estate, Sebastian might well have considered marriage her only choice. He had expended effort and money, remained in a house he despised, to make her future secure. Mutton-headed, but well-intentioned, as her mother had said.

While Dorry braided her hair with swift, practised movements, Gemma closed her eyes on a vision of her mother's face before Sybil slapped her. She dreaded the carriage ride home. What if her mother never forgave her? She would certainly be within her rights never to speak to Gemma again.

Hot shame rushed through her at those unforgivable words she had spoken. She had released her resentment at the wrong person. She hardly knew who was to blame anymore.

Perhaps no one. Perhaps herself?

Heartsick, Gemma bade farewell to Ripton and the other servants, then visited Lady Carleton's sitting room. She found her hostess sitting at her *escritoire* with a ledger of some sort open before her.

Gemma tapped on the door and entered at her hostess's command. "I have come to say good-bye, Lady Carleton, and to thank you for your kindness."

Lady Carleton looked up from her work and smiled. She moved away from her desk and gestured for Gemma to sit beside her on the sofa. "It was a pleasure, my dear. Though if we are to speak of gratitude, I cannot tell you what your being here has meant to me, to our family." She paused. "I can never repay what you have done for Sebastian."

A hot, guilty flush scorched Gemma's cheeks. She hurried into speech. "You saved me from a terrible scold from my aunt on the night of the harvest feast. I never did thank you properly for that."

Lady Carleton chuckled and laid her hand over Gemma's. "You will be glad to know that your mama and I routed the old dear last night as well. Oh, nothing drastic, but you may be sure that we put Matilda firmly in her place for gossiping about you. We smoothed over the stir she caused, but in truth, our efforts were scarcely required. Everyone loves you, my dear. At all events, I don't think Matilda will trouble you again. She took quite a pet last night and announced her intention of removing from Ware to live with her widowed sister in Bath."

Gemma smiled a little at this news. So there was a silver lining to the vast black cloud above her head. "You have done me a great service, ma'am."

She waited for Lady Carleton to mention her gown, but

it seemed that story had not reached her ears. So perhaps Lady Russell had not spread the tale. The relief did not lighten Gemma's heart as it should.

"We will miss you terribly, my dear." Lady Carleton's dark eyes misted and she looked anxious. "What of Sebastian? He is out riding. Will you not wait and say good-bye to him?"

Gemma balked at seeking Sebastian out. She asked instead for Fanny and Romney, but neither could be found. There was nothing to do but wait, she supposed. She did not want to look as if she was sneaking away, and leaving without saying good-bye would be poor return for Fanny's kindness.

Impatient to be gone, Gemma attempted to read Lady Carleton's copy of *Childe Harold's Pilgrimage*, while her hostess wrote letters and attended to household business, but the poet's words blurred before her eyes.

HALF an hour later, Fanny and Romney bounded into the sitting room. Fanny's face lit with a seraphic smile. "We are married!"

Gemma gasped and slammed her book shut.

"What?" Lady Carleton spun around in her chair. "But how? Why?"

"We decided to be sensible, after all," said Fanny, gazing up in adoration at Romney, who was grinning foolishly back. "And we could not wait another week, so we slipped off to the church. Romney is great friends with the vicar now, you know, and he already had the special license, so . . . here we are."

It was the most ridiculous thing Gemma had ever heard. She sprang up to embrace Fanny and kiss Romney's cheek.

"Your mama is very wise," whispered Fanny with a wink.

Lady Carleton viewed them with an expression between

delight and bafflement. Then she began to laugh. "Well, now. This calls for a celebration. A glass of wine to toast the happy couple, I think."

Gemma joined in the toasting and teasing with all the sincerity she could muster, but she could not quite ignore the splinter of envy in her heart. She was not as sorry as she ought to have been to leave the couple's effervescent joy behind.

"You will write to me, won't you, you wicked creature?" Fanny kissed Gemma's cheek. "I wish we could have had more time to talk. About—well, *you know*."

Her bright eyes held a distinct kernel of curiosity, and Gemma remembered she had told Fanny she intended to work her wiles on Sebastian.

Briefly, Gemma shook her head.

A heavy tread approached the door and there he was: Sebastian, come to say good-bye.

He looked pale, but completely master of his emotions. As she stared up at him, their surroundings faded away. She hardly noticed when the others slipped past her and left the room.

"I am sorry, Scovy," she whispered. "I behaved badly last night."

A flicker of hope leaped in his eyes. "You were under a considerable amount of strain. There is no need to apologise. I . . . I deeply regret those things I said."

Gemma looked away. He regretted saying them, perhaps, but it did not make them less true. She swallowed hard against the lump in her throat that threatened to dissolve into raw, betraying sobs. "Well, then."

Awkwardly, she held out her hand. When he hesitated to take it, she realised the insulting coldness of the gesture after the warmth they had shared. On impulse, she reached up to trace his jaw with her fingertips. He closed his eyes briefly, and she smiled, though perilously close to tears.

His eyes flickered open. "I wish I knew what you were

looking for," he breathed. "Whatever it is, I hope to God you find it."

She shut the words out. "Good-bye, Sebastian." And with a wrench so painful, she might have been leaving a part of herself behind, she left.

SEBASTIAN watched the carriage rumble away until it rounded the bend out of sight. After a minute or two, he sensed someone standing beside him. "Mama."

Her eyes looked huge in her delicate face. "Did you tell her, my dear?"

He could have asked the obvious question, but he knew what she meant. "No. I did not tell her I love her. She does not want my love. She is better off without it."

They stood together in the freshening breeze, as storm clouds rolled over the sun.

"How do you know?" she said.

"Pardon?"

"How do you know she is better off? Your love might make all the difference."

His mouth twisted bitterly as a light rain gusted on the wind. "She is so tender-hearted, the knowledge would only be a burden to her. She might even marry me, but out of pity, and I don't want that. As long as she does not know, she will be free."

A few moments trickled by before his mother spoke. Softly, in a voice that had the faraway quality of the storyteller, she said, "There once was a small boy, whose mother loved him more than her own life. To save him from his father's cruelty, she sent him away, confident, or at least hopeful, that she did right. She thought that to cling to him and tell him how much she wished he would stay with her, how much she loved him, would be a kind of burden he should not have to bear. He might not be so happy to go if he knew he left her love behind." She paused. "Was she right to do that, Sebastian? Would it not have been better to have given him the choice?"

He frowned for a long time, digesting her words. The rain pelted down in earnest, blurred the soft green landscape, formed puddles in small potholes on the drive and herded a cluster of deer to huddle under the canopy of an ancient oak. He stood with his mother, warm and dry, sheltered beneath the portico outside his cavernous house, as aching regret and loneliness swept over him like the driving rain.

And when her small hand sought his, he took it. Held it in a strong, tender clasp.

GEMMA and her mother rode home together in Sybil's luxurious turquoise chaise. The rain drummed on the roof, and the noise would have drowned any attempt at conversation, but neither of them spoke for mile upon mile. The countryside swept past in a haze of green and leaden sky.

They stayed in a small inn overnight, and set off again early the next morning. Though comfortable and well-sprung, the carriage rattled over ruts and bumps in the road with cheerful disregard for the taut silence inside it. The postilions shouted. The coachman's whip cracked. Dogs barked as they bounded alongside.

"Gemma . . ." Sybil spoke softly into the gulf of quiet between them. "Your grandfather is dying. Before we left Laidley, I received word that he does not have long."

Gemma's stomach clenched and twisted. A violent wind howled in her ears. "No," she whispered.

"I am sorry, darling. I had to tell you before we got home." Sybil blinked rapidly. "That is why he sent us all away, you know. He did not want anyone to see him like that. Especially not you."

"I don't believe it." Gemma's hands gripped her reticule. It could not be true. Hugo, so full of fire, dying? She could not imagine it, had never contemplated an existence without him.

The last vestige of her anger over her grandfather's bargain with Sebastian evaporated. Sadness engulfed her but she had already wept too many tears. She stared, blank-eyed, out the window at the rain.

After a few moments, she felt her mother's fingers untie the ribbons of her bonnet and lift it away. With a deep sigh, Sybil drew Gemma's head onto her shoulder and gently stroked her hair.

Eighteen

THEY arrived at Ware to see rushes strewn on the drive, muffling the clop of the horses' hooves. The knocker dripped with black crêpe.

Gemma turned a fearful gaze on her mother. Sybil wiped away her own tears with a gloved knuckle. She nodded. "He is gone."

Mrs. Jenkins wrung her hands in her apron as she welcomed them inside, offering words of comfort. "He did not suffer in the end, Miss Gemma. The doctor made sure of that."

Gemma managed to thank the housekeeper, but she could not say more. She fled upstairs, intending to seek the sanctuary of her bedchamber, but on the landing she came face-to-face with Charles Bellamy.

She gasped. His youthful beauty had grown almost haggard. Sadness weighted his broad shoulders and shadowed his fine eyes. He was thinner than she remembered, and his jaw bristled with a new beard, as if he had not shaved for days.

Gemma stared as the implications of his appearance hit her. He had been here all this time? Hugo had let *him* stay?

Seeming not to notice her recoil, Charles took her hand, regarding her with anxious hazel eyes. "Gemma, please allow me to express my condolences. Hugo was a fine man. I . . . I only wish I had known him as you did."

Wave after wave of emotion hit her: anger, hatred, remorse, grief, bewilderment. How was she meant to behave towards this man—the brother she had never known—who had supplanted her at Ware by the mere accident of his sex? She wanted to scream at him like a fishwife, but he did not deserve her abuse. Without a word, she pushed past him and ran to her bedchamber.

HUGO had ordered that the funeral be a simple affair, but mourners came from all over the county. Sebastian was there, tall and unsmiling as they lowered the coffin into the ground. He spoke his condolences to Gemma through stiff lips, his dark eyes burning into hers. He did not come to Ware afterwards for the wake or hear the will read, even though Hugo had left him a handsome legacy. Gemma tried not to take offence or wish for the comfort of her old friend's presence. He had loved Hugo. That was enough.

She wondered if Sebastian resented her. She had been the cause of him breaking his promise to his godfather, after all. She understood now why he had made that promise, and knew she would have done the same. If she had known he was dying, she would have done anything Hugo asked of her, even given up Ware.

If he had asked.

WEEKS later, the pain of losing Hugo was still raw. Gemma wore black even though, with his dislike of fuss,

Hugo had forbidden anyone to mourn him. She grieved for her grandfather, but strangely, the death of her dream scarcely troubled her. Ware had lost its lifeblood when Hugo died.

Or perhaps it was more than that. Perhaps she had changed.

In her heart resided another kind of ache. She missed her life at Laidley with an intensity that shocked her. She missed Fanny and Romney and Lady Carleton. Most of all, she missed Sebastian.

If only he had not spoiled their one night together by making that false marriage proposal, she might remember their passion without regret. Live in the dangerous hope that he loved her, just a little. But that sorry chapter was closed. Bellamy was Squire of Ware now and she must decide what to do with the rest of her life.

As the fog of grief surrounding her slowly lifted, Gemma realised with a kind of horror at her selfishness that she'd never asked her mother how she came to have a long-lost brother—a legitimate one, at that.

Bellamy had taken up his duties as heir with alacrity and a degree of competence that surprised her. It seemed that under Hugo's guidance, Charles had thrived.

Though she relinquished Ware to him without protest, Gemma could not quite bear to see Charles wear his new position like a comfortable old coat. She rode out every day, visiting her familiar haunts, trying to recapture some essence of her place in the world—the place she had lost.

It was no use. She might rail against a distant, ramshackle cousin inheriting the estate, but how could she begrudge her own brother what should always have been his birthright?

She could not warm to Bellamy, for all that. She could not quite bring herself to be gracious in defeat.

Always, he tiptoed around her, as if he walked on the eggshells of her uncertain temper. She knew she had been short with him, but she felt so out of sorts these days, she could not bring herself to be civil.

And then he chose the day her monthly courses arrived to make his proposition.

It wasn't until she saw the telltale specks of blood that Gemma realised she had been nourishing a secret hope. She cringed, sickened at her absurdity. How base and foolish to wish a child into existence when she had nothing to give him, not even legitimacy. But still, she *had* wanted and hoped. And later, when Bellamy stammered and hedged about his proposal, she barely listened, clamped her lip between her teeth to stop herself shrieking at him to go away.

He shifted his stance. "Just, I thought, well . . . Ware has been your life, Gemma and I'm a Johnny-come-lately. I would benefit from your experience and your knowledge of the people and their ways. There is so much to learn. Would you . . . would you consider a partnership of sorts?"

Stunned, Gemma held silent as the implications unfolded in her mind. Bellamy offered her the fulfilment of her life's ambition. Why wasn't she laughing for joy? Why wasn't she shouting her gratitude from the rooftops?

Because now, Ware wasn't enough.

He searched her face, as if trying to gauge her reaction. "After all your hard work here, I owe it to you—"

Quietly, she cut him off. "No. You owe me nothing, Charles." She bit her lip. "But I owe you something. An apology. I have been an unmitigated shrew."

With a wry smile, she looked at him, really looked at him for the first time. Bellamy was a good man, a kind, generous soul. He was young, but he had backbone and intelligence, too.

Softly, she said, "You do not need my blessing, Charles. Perhaps you will think me presumptuous, but I give it, all the same." She put her hand on his shoulder. "You will make an excellent squire, brother."

He took her hand, and gripped it hard, his throat working with emotion. "Thank you, Gemma," he whispered. "Thank you."

⬥

GEMMA sat in front of her looking glass, observing her reflection with a deep, troubled frown.

"Oh, my dear."

Sybil's silk skirts hushed along the carpet as she moved to Gemma's side. She plucked the pins from Gemma's hair one by one and shook out her braids until her gold curls clouded about her face. Then Sybil took up a brush and ran it through Gemma's hair with long, even strokes.

Her mother's gentle touch nearly made her burst into tears. She swallowed hard. "I'm sorry, Mama. I have begged Charles's pardon. I don't know what is wrong with me these days."

For a moment, Sybil remained silent. Then she met Gemma's eyes in the looking glass. "Perhaps it would be best if I tell you the story now. I had hoped to spare you this, but I realise it was unwise of me to keep you in ignorance all these years. You see, as a child you begged me so often for a brother or sister to play with, I did not tell you about Charles because I was afraid I would never find him, terrified I'd disappoint you. When I wrote to Hugo that I had Bellamy with me at last, he wrote back, asking me not to tell you straight away. Oh, but I wanted to, Gemma! I longed to have the two people I loved most in the world united."

So Hugo *had* wanted her out of the way while he trained Bellamy to take over Ware. Gemma blinked, surprised to find the knowledge hurt only a little. She nodded. "I understand."

A lengthy silence followed. Gemma watched those turquoise eyes cloud with dreams. "Mama?"

Sybil gave a slight start, and grimaced. "Your father and I had the tempestuous sort of courtship foolish young women often mistake for grand passion. We were criminally incompatible."

She sighed. "I fancied myself in love and the world well lost. Your father did, too, only his was a possessive kind of passion that thrilled me until I grew more closely acquainted with it."

She frowned over a tangle in Gemma's hair, put down the brush and worked at the knot with her fingers. "I was . . . headstrong. Unused as you are to taking orders from anyone. Hugo let me run wild as a girl. I had no mother to lecture me on the perils of flirtation when one has a jealous husband."

This was something Gemma had not known. No one ever spoke of her papa. She'd always thought it was because tragedy and scandal cloaked his death. Had she considered the matter at all, she would have assumed he was the innocent party. Now, her mother painted a different picture.

Sybil continued, a trifle gruffly. "I never went beyond flirtation, you know. It was the way of our world, the fashion for elegant dalliance. But after you were born, your father became convinced that I was . . . consorting with a certain gentleman of our acquaintance. He became obsessed with catching us together."

"And that man killed my father in a duel over you," said Gemma. It was a statement, not an accusation. She had never felt the lack of a father. She had never known him, and gained ample substitute in Hugo.

Slowly, Sybil nodded. "But that is not the entire story. You see, when I gave birth to Charles barely a year after you were born, your father went a little mad, I think. He decided that the babe was not his."

She drew a painted porcelain oval, framed in silver, from her pocket and handed it to Gemma. "But if you look at this miniature, you will see a striking resemblance."

As she took it, Gemma realised her hands trembled. She had never seen a picture of her father before.

Her eyes widened. The resemblance was striking. Her father's hair was darker than Bellamy's, almost black, but the high cheekbones, the passionate slash of a mouth, and melting hazel eyes were the same. If she had seen this before meeting Bellamy, she would have known instantly whose son he was. If she had doubted her mother's word, she certainly held the proof before her. But she had not doubted. Sybil Maitland did not lie.

Sybil slipped the miniature back into her pocket. "Aunt Matilda visited for my lying-in. She believed your father's nonsensical story—you know how she is, the most credulous being alive—and . . . and she helped him steal my baby."

Sybil stood very straight, dry-eyed, clutching the back of Gemma's chair. "The means by which he discovered a childless couple who studied botany in far-flung destinations are beyond me. I believe they were Devonshire's protégés, so perhaps he met them at Chatsworth. At all events, your father could not have chosen a more effective mode of concealment than to send Charles away with that nomadic pair. I've chased rumours and shadows over the globe for twenty years."

Gemma could hardly believe anyone capable of such a dastardly crime. "But what about Hugo? Why didn't he put a stop to it?"

Eyes bright, Sybil shook her head. "They told him the child was stillborn, that I suffered from a form of melancholia common among women who have lost their babes. It was not until much later that I convinced Hugo of the truth."

Slowly, Gemma said, "And he has been waiting, ever since, to make his will in favour of his grandson."

"Yes. So you see, Gemma, whatever hopes you might have cherished . . ."

Gemma's entire body felt numb and cold. She had tried so hard to show everyone she could run Ware, but she had never stood even the slightest chance. She had hoped, but no one, least of all Hugo, had encouraged her in that hope.

"I understand Charles made you a handsome offer today," said Sybil.

"Yes, it was handsome." Gemma's voice shook. "But I refused." She swallowed. "It is best that the estate has only one master. And there will be Bellamy's heirs to think of, too."

"Are you sure, my dear? I thought Charles' proposal was precisely what you've always wanted."

Sobs rose in her chest. "I don't know what I want anymore. Yes, I do. Oh, Mama! I miss him so."

"Well, there is only one cure for that, my dear."

Feeling immeasurably weary, Gemma dashed a hand across her eyes. "But Sebastian doesn't really want to marry me. He only asked me out of duty to Hugo."

Sybil squeezed Gemma's shoulder. "Sometimes, it is not easy for gentlemen to express their feelings, my dear. Particularly when they are not sure of the recipient returning their affections. You have always been single-minded about Ware."

Gemma remained silent, staring at her pale reflection. She thought back over her time with Sebastian, to the warmth, the laughter, the confidences they had shared. Could it be true? Did Sebastian love her, after all?

She sighed. No, of course he did not. She would be a fool to hope.

A knock on the door preceded a parlour maid, with a knowing grin that split her plump features. "Gentleman to see you, miss."

Joy broke over Gemma like a sunburst. She jumped from her chair and caught her mother's hands.

Sybil returned the pressure of her fingers with a smile. "Now, I wonder who that could be."

"Tell him I shall be down in ten minutes," Gemma instructed the maid. "Send Dorry to me, quickly!"

She trembled too much to do anything but move about like a rag doll while her maid pulled and prodded her, dressed her body and her hair and sent her with a little push out the door.

In the gallery, Gemma took a deep breath and smoothed her hands over the cambric of her bodice, wishing she did not look quite so ghostly in black. What should she say? How would he look? Calling on all the restraint she could muster, she made herself walk, rather than run, down to the drawing room.

Light-headed from nervousness, she paused outside the drawing room to gather her courage. Taking another deep breath, she opened the door and went in.

But the man who spun around at her approach was not Sebastian.

It was Alistair Brooke.

Suffocated with disappointment, Gemma stopped short and stared.

Brooke cleared his throat and bowed, galvanising her. She started forward and managed some sort of curtsey. Remembering her manners, but still unable to command her voice, she gestured wordlessly for him to sit down.

His austere features softened with sympathy. "Permit me to offer my condolences, Miss Maitland. I would not have troubled you at this time if I had known."

Hoarsely, she managed, "That is quite all right, Mr. Brooke." With a monumental effort, she dredged a smile from the black pit of despair. "It . . . it is good to see you."

Something kindled in his eyes. He leaned forward, his hands clasped lightly between his knees. "You must know why I have come."

Sincerely at a loss, Gemma slowly shook her head.

His brows twitched together. "But surely you must guess? I wished to ask your grandfather's permission to court you."

"*Court* me?" Gemma blinked at him. The idea that Mr. Brooke harboured serious intentions had never occurred to her. "You mean with a view to m-marriage?"

Amusement played about his mouth. "That is generally the object of courtship, yes. I understand I must now address myself to your brother instead."

He smiled, and Gemma's stomach lurched. He truly cared for her. She could see it in the softened lines of his face, the warm glow in his usually cold grey eyes. Why had she not noticed when they were together at Laidley? He must have misinterpreted her friendliness as encouragement. What was she to do?

"You must know how ardently I admire you, Miss Maitland. Did not Carleton tell you of my intentions?"

She straightened. "You told Sebastian you wished to court me?"

"Oh, yes. You see, I understood from him that your grandfather had entrusted you to his care. So, naturally I asked Carleton how Sir Hugo might view the match." His shoulders shook. "I must say, I thought he would murder me on the spot. Carleton is very protective of you."

"Is he?" she said vaguely. "Yes, I suppose he is." Gemma's mind whirled. If he had known of Brooke's intentions, why had Sebastian asked her to marry him? Surely his obligation to Hugo was discharged if Brooke paid his addresses. Why not wait until he knew the outcome of Brooke's proposal?

Perhaps he did love her! Excitement blazed through her body. Out of consideration for Brooke, she ruthlessly tamped it down and erased all emotion from her voice. "I am very sorry to cause you pain, Mr. Brooke. You do me a great honour, but I must tell you at once that my heart is given to another."

Brooke held very still. His eyes flared and his thin lips compressed.

Gemma cringed inside. "I am so very sorry if I gave you cause to hope. Indeed, I had no intention . . ."

His mouth spasmed in an effort to smile. Then his fingers gripped the arm of his chair as horrified wonder flooded his face. "It's Carleton, isn't it?"

She hesitated. Compelled by the intensity of his gaze, she nodded.

Brooke surged to his feet. Dashing a hand through his fair hair, he paced away from her. It was the first time she had ever seen him discomposed. He swung back, his face taut with emotion. "That libertine? That worthless, irresponsible rake?"

Gemma gasped. Anger burned her chest at the injustice. She opened her mouth to speak in Sebastian's defence.

But no, Brooke was right. Worthless, irresponsible, promiscuous, that was exactly how Sebastian appeared to the world, an impression he had done everything in his power to cultivate. Only she knew the truth of his integrity, his loyalty and joy and kindness.

Elation spread through her, and with it came a calm, anchoring sense of certainty. A smile burst from deep inside. "Yes, but you see, Mr. Brooke, Lord Carleton is *my* worthless, irresponsible rake."

❧

SEBASTIAN yanked the casement window shut before the gusting wind scattered his papers. He squinted up at the sky, and saw the charcoal storm clouds roil overhead like a devil's brew.

The house seemed to glower at him, sombre as ever, and he wondered that he'd ever thought the old mausoleum transformed by a few rugs and bits of china. Laidley had lit up because Gemma was there. And now that she was gone, it was as if the sunshine would never return.

He'd ached for her when they told him Hugo had left Ware to Bellamy, but when he saw Gemma at the funeral, he had not been able to bring himself to speak of it. His own pain made frankness impossible. He had thought the hurt might dull with time, but even now, it knifed him with a blade as sharp and true as the day she left.

He'd give anything to have her here with him, to share in his small successes, the struggles he faced each day. He had even hoped she was carrying his child, so she would have no choice but to marry him. But he'd squandered his only chance to have her, stumbled over his monumental pride.

His mother's words echoed in his mind. Had he really given Gemma a choice? He had invited her to a loveless marriage, allowing her to believe he asked out of duty, out of obligation to Hugo. No word of love, just need and want, which weren't the same things.

"My lord?"

Sebastian looked up. Jameson, his new steward, hovered at the door, his ruddy face a beacon of excitement.

"Come in. Sit down." He indicated a chair and waited, repressing a resigned sigh. He did not think any news Jameson might bring could cheer him.

"My lord, I have just now received a most handsome offer on your Northumberland property from the current tenant."

Sebastian searched his memory. "The East India merchant? He wants to buy Cheynes?"

Jameson nodded, his stocky frame quivering with anticipation. He passed over the contract, and the sum disclosed made Sebastian purse his lips in a silent whistle.

"I do not see how you can refuse, my lord. I have reviewed the agreement and the terms are reasonable."

Sebastian gave a short laugh and shook his head. "No, I do not believe I can. What is the fellow thinking? This sum would purchase two estates the size of Cheynes. Why, it would—" He stopped.

It would purchase Ware.

Sebastian snatched up his pen, dipped it in the inkwell, and drew the contract towards him. He scrawled his name next to the execution clause and thrust it back at Jameson. "Witness that, agree on an early settlement date. Do whatever you have to do. I want those funds in my hands as soon as possible."

"Yes, my lord!" Jameson added his signature and the date and hurried from the room.

Sebastian rang for his valet. "Pack my bag for a few days' journey. I want to leave within the hour."

He must bring her back. Humble his pride into the dust. Beg her, if necessary. He used to write poetry, for pity's sake, surely there were some words in the English language to express what he felt? And if that did not work, he still had an ace up his sleeve.

He would buy her Ware.

Bellamy could have no particular attachment to the place, after all. He had only just arrived. He could buy another property and play at farming to his heart's content, or he could travel, or set himself up in a house in Mayfair and do the pretty in town.

It was a brilliant plan! Why had he not thought of it before? Sebastian took the stairs three at a time to find his mother and tell her he was leaving.

A half hour later, with the household bustling in preparation for his departure, he sat once more in his library, writing a list of instructions to be carried out in his absence. So many things to think of. He had only begun to realise the full enormity of his responsibilities, but now he knew that with or without Gemma, he was ready to shoulder them.

A light step sounded in the hall. "Abandoning your post already, Scovy? Shame on you! I believe I shall have to take you firmly in hand."

He looked up and saw her standing in the doorway.

"Gemma." He blinked, to make sure she was real.

At the old, teasing glint in her eye, hope flamed inside him. He crossed the floor in three bounds and crushed her in his arms, whirling her into the room.

Sebastian kicked the door shut behind them and framed her face with his hands, scarcely believing she was there. "I was about to come to you. Why aren't you at Ware?"

She bit her lip. "I don't belong there anymore. I don't want to be anywhere without you."

Sincerity underpinned her soft words, but for all that, he could not help wondering. She had lost her dream, the foundation on which she'd built her life. Was he merely the consolation prize? Was that why she had come back? He drew her close, squeezed his eyes shut and breathed in the scent of her hair, fighting the ache in his heart.

Should he tell her of his plan to buy Ware? No. If he told her now, he might always wonder, just a little. He must know if she cared for him. He must tell her how he felt.

He drew back, caressing her cheek with his fingertips.

"Gemma, I love you."

As soon as the words left his mouth, he braced himself for a mortal wound. She felt tiny in his arms, such a fragile being to wield so much power. She could destroy him with a word.

Gemma searched his face, a host of different emotions flitting across hers. Unable to bear the suspense, he attempted a cocksure grin. "Now you say, 'I love you, too, Scovy.'"

She laughed up at him, radiant with love and sunshine, and on a deep, relieved sigh, he consigned the purchase of Ware to the graveyard of plans best forgotten. He wanted her laughter and her warmth here with him always, at Laidley.

Gemma tried to speak, but he stopped her reply with his lips, kissing her so fiercely she could not say anything for a very long time.

GEMMA sat draped across Sebastian's lap with her arms around him, her head resting against his shoulder. His lips dragged against her temple. Sighing, she nestled closer.

She had never dreamed she could be so happy. She had ruthlessly excised the possibility of love and a family of her own from her dreams, believing they could never be hers because of her mother's disgrace. Even when love had stared her in the face she had not been able to recognise it.

"I've been so blind, Scovy. I think I've loved you since you first kissed me that day at Ware. But I didn't know it until . . ." She broke off with a blush, remembering how much she had wanted to have his baby growing in her womb.

He drew back to gaze into her face, looking ridiculously pleased. Eager and boyish, like the Sebastian she had always known. "When? What made you come back?"

Blinking away foolish tears, she shook her head. She stared at his top waistcoat button as if her life depended on memorising its shape. "Oh, nothing. It's just that I wanted . . ."

He tensed. The faintest breath stirred her hair. "You wanted Ware." He stroked the nape of her neck. "I know, Gemma. I know it's not quite the same, but you will have Laidley now, and—"

"No." Gemma swallowed against the lump in her throat. She owed it to him to tell him the truth, no matter how shaming it might be. She sensed his uncertainty, as she always had. Sebastian was not quite as sure of her as he appeared.

With difficulty, she managed the words. "I wanted . . . I wanted there to be a baby. *Our* baby. So much. It was stupid and irresponsible, completely irrational, but . . ." She met his eyes. "I did."

She saw dawning wonder in his face, a special kind of delight that made him so vividly handsome, he took her breath away.

In a husky voice, he said, "Then . . . you're not?"

"No." She smiled and trailed a finger down his chest. "But if we work *very* hard at it, perhaps we might do better next time."

Sebastian gave that lazy, wicked smile that melted her bones, and lowered her onto the chaise longue.

"My darling Gemma," he breathed against her lips. "Your wish is my command."

Enter the rich world of historical romance with Berkley Books.

Lynn Kurland

Patricia Potter

Betina Krahn

Jodi Thomas

Anne Gracie

Love is timeless.

penguin.com